Reflections
of the Distant Fires
A Tale of Old Texas

inspired by a true story

Jose Angel Ramirez

In memory of my mother and father,
who raised five sons in the old traditions,
and taught them to love without end.

Acknowledgments

I would like to express my heartfelt appreciation to Barbara Ardinger, Janet L. Innes, Marilyn Tucker, Barbara Rainess, and Olivia Ramirez for their invaluable help in the editing and proofing of this book. I am eternally grateful for all of their unflagging help, support and encouragement.

The long reflections of the distant fires
Gleam on the walls, and tremble on the spires...

—HOMER, *The Illiad*

Reflections
of the Distant Fires

A Tale of Old Texas

PART ONE

Chapter 1
Juan

Texas, along the Rio Grande
July, 1847
Second year of the U.S.-Mexican War

As NEAR AS JUAN could figure, Timo Martinez had his heart set on sticking the fool American and stealing his mules. Juan rolled off his tattered blanket, stomped a defiant yellow scorpion that scrambled in the dirt, and then strode the few dusty yards toward Timo and his pock-faced brother, Ricardo.

Timo pinched tobacco onto a small piece of dried corn shuck. He rolled it up and folded the end like a miniature tamale, then reached toward the fire for a glowing twig to light it. As Ricardo turned a small goose on a spit, its blackened skin hissing and spitting at the fire, the sweet scent of mesquite smoke washed over all of them. Squatting next to Timo, Juan picked up a handful of dirt and let some of it filter through his fingers.

"Where's that other brother of yours?" he asked. "The one with the broken head."

Timo pushed back his sombrero and looked up, closing one eye against the curling brown smoke from his cigarette. He twisted his mouth into a grin and waved his hand in the general direction of the brush, the hundreds of miles of dusty cacti and mesquite that surrounded them, so thick in the stifling heat that one could hardly move through it.

"Digging peyote," Timo replied. "You shouldn't have broke that mescal bottle on his head last night. He's hurting."

Juan squinted against the white-hot border sun hammering their camp. This time of day, its sting could be painful. Everything around them baked,

1

smelled burnt, and the heat blasted through the meager shelter of scrawny mesquite limbs overhead.

"He was kicking that woman in the ribs," said Juan.

Timo puffed his cigarette. "Who cares about a whore?"

Juan fixed Timo with his gray-green eyes. "What kind of man kicks a helpless woman?"

Timo's grin faded. "You should have let it go."

Juan shrugged. He had run into this bunch at a cantina in Reynosa, all of them hired by James Cornwell, the American, to drive the mules to Point Isabel on the Texas coast. Since he was headed that way, Juan had joined them.

After a long night of drinking, whoring, and fighting in Reynosa, they had taken to the saddle in the morning with no sleep, pushing the mules across the low-running Rio Grande and into the tangled brush. The land along the valley of the Rio Grande was a snarl of ebony, thorny mesquite, *retama*, *huajillo*, and other craggy trees and shrubs like the red-tailed cactus called *tasajillo* and the vicious cat's claw, *uña de gato*. Every living thing, it seemed, protected itself with angry, painful thorns and spikes. The brush was so thick that the mules had little choice but to follow the path, and where there was no path, a traveler had to hack one out with a machete, being careful not to accidentally step on a sleeping rattlesnake or a den of scorpions. Only where the brush eased out into a grassy *sendero* did the mules bolt. But the *vaqueros* were expert horsemen. They dashed through the brush and cacti, whistling and yelling, spinning their lariats, until the mules were back on the path. They had driven the mules until the sun pulled straight overhead. Exhausted and hung over, they cursed their swollen tongues and aching heads. Cornwell insisted they keep moving, but nobody cared what he wanted.

Timo changed the subject. "The American, what does he say? Does he have money?"

"No." Juan shook his head. "Only the mules." They both turned toward Cornwell, who sat in the shade a few yards away, inspecting his blanket for scorpions. The brush literally crawled with them, along with spiders, lizards, ants, and all manner of other stinging, biting creatures. They crawled into boots in the cool nights, slithered under the covers, and dropped into pockets and other warm places from which they could surprise a man the next day. Cornwell pulled up a corner of the dirty green blanket and peeked underneath. In his right hand he held his little black journal. Sitting on the apparently safe blanket, he began to scribble, working his tongue around his mouth as he worked the words onto the page.

To Juan, the man's journal was a pretentious waste of time. Reading was for men with perfumed shirts and shiny boots—men who lived in big cities and should stay there. Out here in the brush, with only the cattle, horses, and scorpions for company, what good was writing? His own father had been highly educated, refined, aristocratic. And now, he was dead, hopefully burning in hell. For all his education, he'd been unable to keep a Mexican bayonet from slicing through his heart at San Jacinto, where he had fought for the damned Tejanos.

Juan looked off toward the river and set his mouth in a thin line. He already knew the answer to his next question. "And now?"

Timo flashed white teeth through his wild beard and made a quick slashing motion with his hand. "Cut him open and steal the mules. But first, we eat."

Juan brought his gaze back, letting a little more dust filter through his fingers. He gave his head another slow shake. "No."

"Who's going to stop me?" Timo asked, his eyes dipping down toward his lap, where the dark point of a pistol barrel peeked through a fold in his serape. "Not you, *hacendado*. You stay out of it."

Juan saw the gun, but it did not bother him much. A lot of guns had been pointed his way, and so far all the men who had pointed them were dead. He rolled his shoulder, trying to rub the sensitive scars along his back against his shirt. The scars, a compliment from his dead, educated father, throbbed at times like this. They captured his anticipation, his sense of danger, and collected it in their tingling ridges. He reached up and wiped away a stream of sweat that had caught on his eyebrow and watched warily as Ricardo circled the fire to stand behind him, clutching his machete.

"This *gringo* is a fool," said Juan, "but you're not going to kill him. He is no threat to you." Juan shot a glance at Cornwell, still laboring over his journal. "The damned Rangers won't care who killed him. They'll start hanging *vaqueros* on the Santa Alicia for it. They'll hang anybody with brown skin." He shook his head again, watching Timo's white teeth slowly disappear and a malevolent look grow in the bandit's eyes.

The eyes told him everything about a man—whether he would fight or quit, if he was brave or cowardly. "You take the mules," Juan threw in. "I don't give a damn."

Timo sucked deeply on his shrinking cigarette, his eyes glowing so brightly that Juan thought the smoke might seep out his ears. "You think you're a big man, don't you, Santos?" Timo said. "Juan Santos—they call you El Gallo, all up and down the border. The Rooster. You think you're a big man with your big ranch?"

Juan looked off toward the river again. Men like Timo liked to talk themselves into killing.

"Just because your mother owns the Santa Alicia," Timo snapped. "Even the *gringos* think she's a grand lady, no? Well, I don't give a *chingada* about her. I don't give a *chingada* about you. This skinny *gringo* is going to die today." He puffed again, pinching the half-inch stub between his fingers. "And Reynosa. You think I'm letting it pass, what you did to Fernando?" He shook his head, smiling again. "No, *hacendado*. *Todo se paga.* All debts must be paid. Now slow, very slow, drop your gun in front of me so the *gringo* doesn't see."

Juan looked up at Timo. His scars were on fire. He felt the blood draining from his face and a growing distance from his senses, as if he were viewing the scene from afar, uninvolved, uncaring. Timo was suddenly transparent. Juan was staring right through him. "I'll be accused of this crime, too," he said, but even his own voice sounded far away.

Timo grinned, and his deep brown cheeks caved in as he sucked again. He puckered his lips and spit the cigarette away. "Maybe you won't have to worry about that."

Behind them, Cornwell jolted to his feet, slapping his arm and shouting, "Ah shit! Ah shit!" A fat tan scorpion flew into the dust, its legs in frantic motion and its black-tipped tail poised over its head.

Timo's gaze broke away for an instant, but that was all Juan needed. He threw his handful of dust into Timo's eyes, then lunged from his squatting position, kicking the heel of his boot into Timo's forehead, sending him sprawling. Without stopping, without thinking, Juan landed and twisted around, drawing and firing his pistol into Ricardo's chest even as the machete slashed the air between them. The ball slammed the bandit backward into the brush in a sudden fog of dust. Timo moaned but did not move as Juan kicked away Timo's gun, then bent over Ricardo, whose glassy stare greeted him from the depths of the brush.

Cornwell came running up beside him, a percussion rifle in his hand and a confused look clouding his face. His Spanish was thick, almost incomprehensible. "Porky? Porky? Uhhh, *porque?*"

Timo moaned again, then rolled onto his knees, cursing and holding his head.

Juan nodded toward Timo. "They were going to kill you."

Cornwell raised the rifle slowly, backing away, pointing it in Juan's general direction. He shifted his eyes over to Timo, then back to Juan, then looked all around him. His eyes darted so much that Juan thought they might jump out of his head.

"How do I know it weren't the other way around?" Cornwell asked, backing another step. "What if they was trying to stop you from killing me?"

Juan suppressed an immense desire to take the rifle from this fool and whack him senseless with it. "You are an idiot, señor. Give me the gun."

Cornwell frowned and lowered the rifle, just as Fernando Martinez stumbled out of the brush, the long barrel of his *escopeta* shotgun pointed at them, his pockets bulging with peyote buttons. The gash from the mescal bottle gleamed raw on his forehead, and black flies feasted on it. The side of his dusty face sported red and blue bruises. He breathed noisily through his mouth, and held the shotgun so tightly his hand shook. "Drop the rifle, *gringo*," he croaked.

Cornwell dropped it, and Fernando leered at Juan. "Did you forget me, *cabrón?*"

Juan was beginning to wish he'd killed these tiresome men back in that Reynosa cantina, when he'd been worked up for it. His scars were itching badly again.

Timo wobbled to his feet and staggered toward them. "Your guns. Kick them over. Fernando, if that bastard moves, shoot him."

A bewildered Cornwell pushed his gun toward Timo. Juan hesitated, then remembered his pistol was empty. He threw it over.

"We shoot him later," said Fernando. "First, I want to cut off his *huevos* and stuff them in his mouth."

"Why not?" replied Timo. "Let's see how big they really are. El Gallo. The Rooster. The big man." He chuckled, then reached up his dark, scarred hands to hold his battered head between them. After a moment he turned to Juan and whacked him on the forehead with his pistol. Juan jerked his hands up to his face too late as blood spurted between his fingers, flowing warm and salty into his eyes and mouth.

"There is no hurry for you, Señor Gallo," said Timo. "We're going to take our time. Slow. That's how I like to pay back my debts."

Cornwell swallowed hard. "What you gonna do to us?"

Juan wiped the blood from his eyes and watched Timo, who ignored Cornwell's question and moved to where Ricardo lay in the brush.

"Our brother is dead," Timo growled. He drew his knife.

The smirk instantly left Fernando's face.

"What you gonna do?" repeated Cornwell, his voice rising an octave in mid-sentence.

Timo walked up to Cornwell and plunged the knife into the American's chest. Cornwell drew in a loud, sucking breath, his mouth wide open, his eyes wild and straining in their sockets. He reached up and grasped Timo's shoulders, choking as blood spurted from his chest and a pink foam spewed from his mouth. Slipping down Timo's body, the American sank to the hot, dusty ground, twitched, and then rolled on his side.

"Cabrón!" roared Juan, holding his hand to his forehead to stem the bleeding. "I told you! My *vaqueros* will be accused of this!"

Timo laughed. "I know. I don't listen too good. Now for you, Señor Santos. Something special. Something slow. Fernando, tie his hands."

Timo held the gun on Juan as Fernando yanked his arms behind his back and tied his wrists tightly with a thin leather strip. Unchecked, the blood from Juan's forehead gushed down his face, obscuring his vision.

He was about to make a blind, desperate lunge into the brush when the tip of Timo's boot slammed into his groin. He sank to his knees beside Cornwell.

"That bird on the spit, *hermano*, turn it so it doesn't burn," he heard Timo say. "I'm working up a big appetite. Smells good, doesn't it, Señor Santos?" He reached down and grabbed Juan by the hair, yanking him to his feet. He poked him in the ribs with the pistol. "Too bad I can't offer you a last meal. I don't think I could enjoy my dinner knowing I still have to kill *you*, El Gallo himself. Better I kill you now. Then I can eat."

Fernando protested. "But I want to—"

"I don't give a *chingada* what you want. If I get tired, I might save a little for you. Now, turn around slow, Señor Santos. Why don't we go down that path to the river?"

Barely able to see, Juan stumbled along, bumping into mesquites and cactus plants that held fire in their thorns. The sound of Timo's nasal, taunting laughter echoed in his ears, until he heard the gurgling waters of the Rio Grande somewhere ahead.

JUAN HELD HIS BREATH until his chest hurt. He thrashed violently in the water, and then slowly stopped struggling. His lungs ached with a desperate desire to exhale, but he waited as long as he could, then squeezed out a steady stream of bubbles. Timo was straddling his back and Juan felt him tighten the grip on his hair and push his head deeper under the water. When all the bubbles were gone, Juan's lungs convulsed with a demand for air and he became dizzy. Just when Juan felt he could hold his breath no longer, Timo yanked his head up and the muddy blue Rio Grande flashed in a blur before him. He sucked in a huge, painful gulp of air.

Timo twisted his head around so they were looking at each other, as if he were professionally inspecting his handiwork. Then he slammed Juan's head back into the river. After a few repetitions, Timo seemed to quickly tire and rolled away. Juan flailed in the water, trying to keep his head up.

"You're not dying too good," Timo complained.

Though his hands were still tied behind his back, Juan regained his equilibrium as his knees found the soft bottom of the river. He sputtered and coughed, then heaved up a great rush of swallowed water.

"Run," said Timo, pulling out his pistols. "Out into the river."

Juan strained to look up at his tormentor. After rolling him in the cacti and mesquite-filled brush along the river, Timo had beaten him with his pistols, kicked him viciously, then tried to drown him. But now the bandit looked a little winded.

"Untie me," Juan sputtered.

"Run, *cabrón*, or I'll shoot you right now."

"Shoot, then. I'm not running."

Timo's eyes came to life. "*Ahora sí*, there's still some fight in the rooster, eh? All right, I'll do this. I'll shoot one ball in your left shoulder, one ball in your right, then I'll reload my pistols." He paused, excitedly shifting his feet. "Then I put a ball in your forehead and at the same time, one in your chest with my other gun. The sign of the cross! And you die with Jesus! What do you think?"

"Go to hell."

Timo laughed and cocked his pistols.

So this is finally it, Juan thought, *the end of my world.* Death held no mystery for him. He had sometimes longed for it. No great fear surged through his bowels or made his knees tremble. His mother's face forced its way into his mind, and he saw her ebony-black hair rolled in great waves on her head, her eyes sad but unyielding, her brow creased with concern. A great gulf existed between them, and nothing could bridge it. As much as he had craved it, she had shown him no love, no warmth until age five. Then she had changed, tried to make it up. But it was too late. A door had closed permanently in his heart, and she could never enter there again. He closed his eyes, her image unwelcome there—her beauty, her sadness, her disappointment in him.

Juan had a single regret—that someone besides himself had killed his father. As far as he could figure, Juan had learned only one thing from Don Alvino Santos—intense pain, once endured, held no power over him. Juan had always guessed he would die violently, but he did not want to die on his knees.

"Wait, you shit-eating pig. Let me stand up."

Timo waved his pistols. "Stand up, then."

Struggling to his feet, Juan tried to stall for time. "I want a last request."

"This is murder, *hacendado*, not an execution. Like I said, *todo se paga*." Timo grinned wider, his white teeth flashing in the shadow of his sombrero. "You want a cigarette? A drink? You going to piss in your pants, big man?"

Juan did not want his bloated body to lie in the brush under the hot sun and rot. He thought instead about floating down the Rio Grande, this ancient troubled river, on past Matamoros and out into the great gulf, where fish could eat his flesh. Whatever he asked for, Timo would probably do the opposite.

"Bury me," he said.

The words were hardly out of his mouth when Timo fired both pistols, the sound of the guns mixing with Timo's laughter. One ball ripped into his upper right arm. The other smashed into his left shoulder, spinning him around as he fell into the river. The water turned a bloody, muddy reddish-brown as he struggled again to right himself.

Timo calmly crouched on the bank and reloaded his pistols, then splashed over to Juan and yanked him up to his feet.

"*Muy bien*," said Timo. "Now, you stand right there. Don't move." He scrambled back a few feet to the bank, turned, and aimed his pistols. "*Adiós, hacendado*. Your horse, I'm going to ride it to your mother's ranch. I hear she's very beautiful—and feisty. I'm going to visit her, *cabrón*. I'm going to tell her I killed her son. Then I'm going to tear off her clothes and spread her thighs." He swiveled his hips and grinned. "Then I'm going to open her up with my knife like that bird on the spit. As you die, a little thought for you." He laughed again, raised both pistols, and fired.

Juan tried jerking his head sideways and falling into the river, but that did not save him. He felt the ball crash into his skull, even as he heard the other one shriek past his ear. In an instant, he felt the blackness flooding through him, and he disappeared into its welcoming depths.

Texas Ranger Captain Tom Starr was watching with interest from the Mexican side of the Rio Grande, crouching behind the thick brush along the riverbank, mindful of the needles, stickers, and other vicious forms of life teeming around him. Hunkered down beside Starr, Ranger Sam Brennan picked his teeth with a mesquite thorn.

"Looks like them bandits ain't getting along too good," said Starr.

Sam grunted, adjusting his leggings so he could put one knee down. "You figure it's just them two?"

"Two or ten, it don't matter much. Do it?"

Sam shrugged. They crept back through the brush to where their horses and seven other Rangers waited. As the youthful Captain Starr approached, the Ranger's horses pricked up their ears and rolled their eyes, shuffling and snorting. The men leaned forward to get the news.

"What's all the shooting, Cap'n?" called Frenchy. He wore a black eye patch, which he flipped up when it suited him, revealing an empty eye socket. The other Rangers had long since tired of Frenchy's tale about the Comanche arrow that plucked out his eye like a hard boiled egg at the battle of Plum Creek, a tale that grew longer and more fantastic with each telling.

"Bandits," replied Starr. "Mount up." When there was action pending, Starr believed in keeping his orders brief and plain. If a man disobeyed orders, Starr was apt to shoot him, and he wanted to be sure he did not shoot a confused man.

After they mounted, each Ranger checked his gear, secured his rifle, and laid a hand on the Bowie knife strapped to his belt. Around his waist each man wore a six shooter, which the Rangers called a "Colts." Most wore two.

Along with the Rangers rode one Mexican, a tall, lanky, chinless man called Don Pepino. He rode with them as a hired servant and occasional guide, though he was usually lost himself. The Rangers, however, would let him lead just to watch him ride. As his horse sauntered along, the Don's head bobbed from side to side, like a duck's, keeping time with the horse while his elbows flapped up and down.

Ranger Uriah Lee, who wore fancy decorated boots from San Antonio, a green vest, and Comanche beads around his neck, winked at

Starr and pulled out his Bowie knife. He stuck Don Pepino in the butt, then chuckled as the Mexican yelped, rose in his saddle, and smashed back down, causing his horse to buck. "I say give the Don the lead," Uriah said, putting his knife away. "A man so brave and able should have the honor." Uriah was a great admirer of "the Don." When anybody suggested to Starr that the Don be replaced, Uriah would not allow it, arguing that although someone else might cook and wash better than the Don, it would be hard to find anyone as entertaining.

"*Oye cabrón pendejo!*" the Don cried, rubbing his butt.

Starr ignored them both. "There's two on the river bank," he said, "but one's dead now. Might be more. Smoke from a campfire back beyond the brush. Be alert."

On Starr's command they hurried out single file, spurring their horses down the narrow game path to the river. As they dashed into the water, each man drew a Colt.

ACROSS THE RIVER, Timo spotted the Rangers emerging from the brush and abandoned his sport with Juan. He raced up the path through the brush, burst across the campsite and jumped on Juan's horse, bareback. Seeing this, Fernando scrambled to his feet and shouted, "*Que pasa?*"

"*Rinches!*" Timo yelled over his shoulder. Rangers! He grabbed the white horse's mane and groped for the bridle. The animal snorted and reared. Yanking the bridle, Timo rammed his large Mexican spurs into the mare's flanks, and the powerful horse scattered the terrified mules and crashed into the brush.

Fernando blinked and stared after his brother for a heartbeat, then ran for his own horse, but the Rangers were upon him as he tried to mount. He turned and threw his hands up. "Don't shoot," he cried. "*No me maten!*"

Sam Brennan rode past, firing two balls into Fernando's chest, then charging into the brush after Timo. The shots burned holes in Fernando's shirt and then exited his back. Blood and bits of flesh exploded into the brush as he spun around, dead before he fell.

Starr reined in his horse at the dusty campsite and assessed the situation. There were crazed mules running everywhere. Three bodies lay in the camp and one floated in the river. Rangers came crashing through the brush looking for bandits, but the shooting had stopped after Sam killed the lone bandit left in camp.

Dismounting, Starr walked over to Fernando's body and flipped it over with his boot. He took the man's pistol and stuck it in his own gun belt. One look at Ricardo's body in the brush was enough to satisfy him. He strode over to Cornwell just as Frenchy broke out of the brush and slid to a halt.

"Here's an American," Starr said as Floyd Johnson rode into the camp, dragging Juan by a rope looped around his heels. Floyd had caught a Mexican ball in the leg at Salado Creek, which nearly ruined it. The Don brought up the rear, pistol cocked and ready, bobbing his head menacingly at the brush.

Floyd jerked his chin at Juan. "This one's from the river. He's still breathin', Cap'n."

"Why didn't you give him the *tiro de gracia?*"

Floyd sat his horse and flicked his rope clear, then started pulling it in. "Almost did, then I thought you might want to look him over. Looks like one of them *rancheros* to me."

Starr nudged his hat up. "Not a bad idea. Might know who this fella is." He pointed his boot toe at Cornwell, then glanced up at the Don. "Get out there in the brush."

Floyd spurred his horse forward into a small break in the brush, and the Don hurried after him. Frenchy dismounted and bent down over Juan. "Shot three times, Cap'n. Head wound creased his skull. Blew a patch of scalp off. Bleeding bad from the shoulder. Want me to patch him up?"

"See if you can bring him around first. I don't plan to waste much time on him."

As Frenchy bent to work on Juan, Starr noticed something lying in the dirt near Cornwell. Frowning, he kicked at it, then bent down to pick it up. "A diary," he said, flipping through it to the last entry.

After a few minutes, he said, "Better try to patch him up good, Frenchy. That there's Juan Santos. You heard tell about a Mexican they call El Gallo? That's him."

"The Rooster?" Frenchy moved back a little, looking Juan over with a critical eye. "Don't look like much to me," he mumbled.

"Well, hell, Frenchy, you wouldn't look like much your own self if you were beat up, shot up, and drowned to boot."

Frenchy rose and moved to his saddlebags. "Don't think he'll last too long, anyways, way he's bleeding. Guess he weren't so tough after all."

Starr was still flipping through the diary. "This here fella's name is James Cornwell, from Kentucky," he said. "He was driving mules to sell to the army. Hired these bandits to help him. Not too bright, was he?"

"You suppose El Gallo here killed him?"

"Don't matter much if he dies. If he makes it, I reckon we might hang him for it."

"Hell, Cap'n, he sure was in on it. Why don't we just shoot him now and be done with it? *Tiro de gracia*. Right in the forehead."

Starr walked over to the campfire, squatted, and turned the goose, which was just about ready. "Ever hear of a Mexican named Alvino Santos?"

"Can't say that I have."

"He was well known in Matamoros. Austin, too. Big landowner, *ranchero*. Politico. Fought alongside Houston in Juan Sequin's Texas-Mexican squad at San Jacinto. Got himself killed." He poked at the fire with a stick. "His widow is Doña Ophelia Santos. Runs the Santa Alicia ranch up near Fort Brown. That's their boy right there."

"I've heard tell about Doña Ophelia."

"Yep, I reckon you have. Cattle, mines, big ranch here in Texas, and more land than you could ride across in a day in Mexico. I heard Sam Houston once had the notion to call on her, courting like. If he could ever sober up long enough. Never seen her myself. Hear she's awful pretty."

"I hear she's meaner than a hellcat," Frenchy replied. "But it don't change nothing. If he's riding with bandits, don't much matter who his ma is."

"Maybe, maybe not. She's got connections, might work in our favor to patch him up."

Frenchy shrugged. Starr knew that Frenchy did not bother to think too far ahead. That was why they had Starr to do their figuring, though he was not yet thirty. He was not the tallest man in the Ranger troop. Others were taller, bigger, meaner—but he was better on a horse, with a gun, and with his fists than any man who had ever tested him. They all knew he was by far the smartest, too. Educated back in Virginia, he possessed a keen mind and a knack for keeping things clear and simple. He spoke their language. When it came to fighting, he had enormous confidence in himself, and men gravitated toward him in that mysterious way that leaders emerge. The Rangers usually elected their captains. Only men who commanded respect would do, for each Ranger was fiercely independent, a tough frontiersman, not given to taking orders. It took the right combination of steel-willed discipline, sheer toughness, and cool judgment under pressure to make a good captain. Men who served with Starr knew that his orders were to be obeyed without question and without delay.

Sam Brennan rode back into camp, followed by Jeremiah Wood and Ambrose Bradshaw. The other Rangers and the Don joined them a minute later.

"Get him?" Starr called as they dismounted and approached the campfire.

"Lost him," Sam replied. "Too damn many mules scattered through the brush. Wiped out his trail."

The Don let out a huge sigh and removed his sombrero, wiping his forehead with his bandanna as he eyed the roasting bird. "He ran like there was a firecracker up his butt," he said, sneering. "He must have known we were Rangers."

At this bit of puffery, Uriah smirked and slipped his hand toward his Bowie knife, causing the Don to edge away.

"You ain't no Ranger, you paper-collared ass."

Starr said, "I reckon he'll run out a bit, then double back and cross into Mexico. I doubt we'll catch him—but, Sam, take Ambrose and Jeremiah upriver and try to cut his trail. Jim, rest of you boys, head downriver a few miles, then turn back on the Mexican side."

"What's on the spit here, *Capitán?*" the Don asked hopefully, lifting his nose and sniffing the mesquite smoke.

Starr did not answer. His order had been given. Repeating orders was not his practice, and they all knew it. The men fell silent, then turned, mounted, and rode out, taking with them the reluctant Don, who threw a wistful look back at the roasted goose.

Frenchy stood up, wiping his hands on what remained of Juan's shirt. "Plugged up the hole in the shoulder, Cap'n. Tore up his shirt and stuffed it in. Won't hold long, though. He's bleedin' like a stuck pig. I don't reckon he's going to live much past sundown."

"Tie him to a mule," said Starr. "The de Leon ranch is upriver a bit, as I recall. I think old man de Leon has some medical training. Might be a good idea to let one of El Gallo's own take him in." Starr stuffed Cornwell's journal in his vest pocket. "I'll ride him on up. You bury Cornwell here, and throw those Mexicans in the brush. When the boys come in, round up the mules and come on up to the de Leon ranch. We'll leave them there for the army to collect."

"Right, Cap'n."

A few minutes later, Starr kicked his horse forward and followed a scant trace in the brush, leading a mule with the bleeding Juan Santos strapped across it.

SITTING AT HER DRESSER, Lidia de Leon yanked at her hair with a brush. Delicate nostrils flaring, she glowered at her reflection in the mirror. Her lips, usually so lush and full, were pulled taut and thin. She tugged the brush harder, then flinched when it caught, jerking her head down.

"Mother, this is impossible! I won't do it, and I hate him for trying to make me!"

"Don't ever let your father hear you say that," her mother warned from the chair nearby. "He'll slap you."

"But why must I marry this man from Bejar? I haven't seen him since I was a child. I don't know him. It's ridiculous. This isn't ancient Spain."

"*Hija*, he is from one of the best families in Bejar. The Jaramillos have vast lands and other holdings. I'm told that Alfredo Jaramillo is very handsome. Your father has agreed to the marriage. It's settled."

Lidia whirled in her chair, her dark hair flying over her shoulder. "It is not settled," she cried. "I want to decide who I marry. Why can't I decide?"

"Because, *hija*, you are almost eighteen. Every suitor that you've had, you've rejected. You should have been married two years ago."

"None of my suitors suited me."

Doña Martina de Leon ignored her daughter's sarcasm. "You chased them away with your temper. Listen to me," she pleaded, her eyes growing moist. "Please, my daughter, listen to me. Your father is at the end of his patience. I'm at the end of my wits. Your father has indulged your stubbornness too long. You must now do as he says. I cannot stand it when you fight with him. It breaks my heart to hear the things you say to each other." Her eyes brimmed with tears as she bent forward, putting her face into her hands.

Lidia sat up straight, squaring her shoulders as she looked at her mother. In times of stress, Doña Martina de Leon either cried or chattered endlessly. Family matters were guaranteed to generate tears.

As long as Lidia could remember, her mother had been unhappy. Often when she had come to kiss little Lidia goodnight, her red, puffy eyes betrayed secret tears. If Lidia asked why, Doña Martina merely forced a smile and shook her head. "How could I be sad with a lovely little *princesa* like you?" Then she tickled Lidia into a fit of giggling to take her mind off her sadness. After the giggling, Doña Martina held Lidia's hand in hers and sang, over and over, in a lovely soft soprano, the same melancholy verses—"*Oh, María, madre mía, oh consuelo, immortal...*" until sleep overcame the child.

Now, looking down upon her gray-haired and still-sad mother, Lidia softened and placed a hand on her head. "Mother," she said, "don't."

A commotion in the courtyard swirled in through the open window. Doña Martina pushed herself up and shuffled over for a look. The white lace curtains moved gently in the thin afternoon breeze as she peered out.

"What's the matter?" Lidia asked.

"*Dios*, there is a *gringo* on a horse, and he's got—" She gasped.

"Got what? What's wrong?"

"Run downstairs and find your father, *hija*. One of the *vaqueros* is hurt!"

Lidia raced down the stairway and spotted Ramona, the house servant. "Ramona, where is Don de Leon?"

"He's in his study, señorita. What's the matter?"

"Prepare a bed in the spare room, quickly, and bring water." Lidia turned without waiting for a response and ran toward her father's study off the main hall. He was already rushing toward her, white hair disheveled, buttoning his coat.

"What's all the shouting?" he demanded.

"Someone's hurt, Father. In the courtyard. Mother said to bring you."

STARR LEANED FORWARD in his saddle and stared as Lidia emerged from the house, her green dress billowing softly around her and outlining her small body. Her hair flew freely around her face and framed her large, clear brown eyes. The girl was exquisite. Her face transfixed him, a face so exotically beautiful that he found himself holding his breath as he gaped at her. He had never expected to see such beauty out here in this wild country, amid the cacti, thorns, and dust.

The señorita seemed worried, but she walked with a purposeful gait, full of poise and grace. When their eyes met, she looked away, as if dismissing him with no further thought. His horse stamped at the smooth graveled yard, and Starr slouched in the saddle, following her with his eyes as she walked behind Don de Leon.

"What happened?" barked de Leon as the ranch hands cut Juan down. He directed them toward the house.

"Santos boy," said Starr. "Found him shot bad a few miles back. Thought you might be able to patch him up."

Don de Leon arched his thick eyebrows. "Santos? Which one, Blas or..."

"It's Juan."

Hearing a stifled gasp escape from Lidia, Starr turned to face her. Her brow creased with concern, her eyes registered shock. Did she know Juan? Was he her lover?

Slowly, she drew Starr into focus, and a hard look came upon her.

"Did you shoot him?" she demanded, crossing her arms.

"No, ma'am. Sure didn't. 'Twas bandits. Saw it myself."

"And you didn't try to stop it?" she shot back.

"Well, now, we..." Starr halted. He did not like being interrogated by anybody, especially not by a Mexican—and surely not by a woman, no matter how lovely. Although, as he watched the angry lines on her forehead, the pout on her lips, the head thrown back, and the hands now on her hips, he found himself staring again.

He turned to her father. "Name's Tom Starr, Captain, Texas Rangers. You might remember me. Passed through last year, bought some mounts from you."

Don de Leon frowned. "Yes, *Capitán* Starr," he said. "I do remember you. Please excuse our manners. I must tend to young Juan, but my daughter here will see to your needs." He switched to Spanish. "Lidia, refreshments for *Capitán* Starr." Then he turned and hurried into the house.

"Señorita de Leon," Starr nodded, lifting his hat.

Lidia crossed her arms again and pushed her nose high in the air, but her eyes avoided his. Without a word, she whirled and stormed toward the house.

Starr dismounted, handed the reins to a Mexican boy, and followed her. Inside, he found Lidia explaining the situation to her mother.

"Oh, not Juan!" Doña Martina moaned. "Oh, poor Ophelia. We must send a rider to the Santa Alicia immediately. Let me write a note, *hija*, and you have Ramona bring up a *vaquero* to carry it." When she saw Starr standing at the door, she stiffened.

"Mother, this is *Capitán* Starr of the Texas Rangers," Lidia said, and Starr noticed that she watched her mother's face intently. "He found Juan and brought him to us."

Doña Martina hesitated, then nodded her head slightly. "We are in your debt, *Capitán*. On behalf of our dear friend, Doña Ophelia, we thank you. May we offer you some coffee?"

Starr snatched off his hat and replied in perfect Spanish. "That would be very kind of you, ma'am."

Lidia turned to her mother. "I'll see to *Capitán* Starr, Mother. Go write your note. I'll take care of everything, then I must go see about Juan."

Doña de Leon wrung her hands. "Oh, do not bother your father. You know he won't let you in." She hurried off, leaving Lidia and Starr in the parlor.

Starr considered commenting on the extraordinary amount of tension he was apparently generating in the house, but decided to let it pass.

Lidia seemed to divine his thoughts. "My father extended you hospitality, *Capitán* Starr," she said, "but Rangers are not exactly welcome here right now. My mother's brother and two of my cousins were killed by Rangers three weeks ago near Mier. They were simply traveling along the trail, and were murdered."

"Miss Lidia, I understand. But that was none of my doing. I ain't been near Mier in months."

"Perhaps," she said, "but it was Rangers, nonetheless. They dragged the bodies into town and dumped them in the town square as if they were common bandits."

"Well, there is a war on, ma'am."

"Against civilians? I find your way of war to be dishonorable."

"Ain't much honor in killing, ma'am, one way or the other. Best way to end a war is to fight it all-out. Better to end it quick."

She glared at him.

"Anyway," he continued, fiddling with his hat, but staring right back at her, "that's the way it is."

Her voice was solid ice. "They were unarmed. Like so many Mexicans on both sides of the river who have been found dead. Your army forbids Mexicans to carry arms. I suppose killing unarmed men is also part of the Ranger philosophy of war?"

"We generally shoot first and investigate later. But that don't only apply to Mexicans. Applies to Comanche, thieves, troublemakers of all kinds."

"I see. Well, I call it murder, *Capitán* Starr."

Starr shrugged. "Call it what you wish, ma'am. It generally gets results. And what we do, we do out in the open. We don't go sneaking around at night, like some Mexicans, sticking knives in people in the dark. That *todo se paga* bullcrap, if you'll pardon my language, ma'am. Now, if I ain't welcome, maybe I should just wait outside till my men come in."

Lidia tossed her hair back and ran her eyes up and down the length of his body. Starr could almost read her mind. His blond hair was dirty, his boots were muddy, and he stank. She was probably thinking that he ought to be waiting in the barn, where his odor would be more compatible with his surroundings. But Don de Leon had invited him in, and it was Lidia's duty to entertain him.

"Please be seated, *Capitán* Starr," she snapped. "I'll get your coffee."

Still standing in the middle of the parlor, he watched her storm off toward the back of the house. He saw the long brown hair bouncing from side to side, the thin shoulders, the straight back, and the angry clenched fists held stiffly at her sides. Despite the layers of her green dress and petticoats, he could also see the swaying of her hips. It seemed to him that she was surely the most desirable woman in creation, and the sight of her filled him with a strange feeling of pleasure he had never felt before. He even found her anger adorable. Starr watched her until she left the room, then reached up, scratched his whiskers, and smiled.

Chapter 2
Ophelia

Before dawn, the next day
Santa Alicia Ranch

FROM THE GLOOM that enveloped Doña Ophelia, a hulking shadow emerged to stand at the foot of her bed. Ophelia sensed him from the edge of sleep, that peaceful place where clarity and haziness drifted through her mind like opposing mists. She lay on her stomach and squinted, straining to focus on the intruder. At first he seemed only a figment of her imagination, an unpleasant dream. Then she thought she saw movement—the turn of an arm perhaps, or a hand placed on the bedpost. She was not sure. Real or not, he did not advance. He just stood there looking at her.

A moment passed, and little beads of sweat formed on her scalp and rolled down her cheek. She struggled to make no movement or sound that might let him know she was awake. Trying to keep her breathing even, she became conscious of each of her limbs, willing them not to move. *Who could it be?*

Then the brutish, rancid odors of stale sweat, greasy leather, and mescal swept across the room. Whatever tricks her eyes might be playing with her, she was not imagining that stench. It turned her stomach. A wild panic rose up within her, but she pushed it down, down and tried to think about her options.

She kept a loaded pistol in the drawer next to her bed, but the intruder was close enough to disarm her if she reached for it. She could scream. Conchita, her personal servant, slept in a small room down the hall, but what could that helpless creature do except scream as well? There were no men in the house. Her older son, Juan, was in Reynosa on business, though he had been due back days ago. Blas, her younger son, had gone to Matamoros to ask about him. Her *vaqueros* were asleep in their *jacales* across the yard, likely too far away for her screams to awaken them.

The shadow's vague shape merged and then materialized out of the blackness of the room, his stench preceding him, until he reached the left side of the bed. Ophelia's head rested on the edge of her pillow, facing right, one leg hanging slightly over the edge. Without moving her head or turning over, she could no longer follow his movements.

Her eyes wide open now, her hands gripping the sheets, a bitter taste formed in her dry mouth. Her breathing came in short pants that barely sustained her. As long as she could see him she had managed to stay reasonably calm, but now black fear spiraled feverishly beyond her control, engulfing her.

She lunged for her pistol, but a massive hand caught her arm and slammed it against her body. She opened her mouth to scream, but to her horror nothing came out. *I'm dreaming*, she thought, *I'm dreaming*— but fingers dug at her flesh, a hot stinking mouth ravaged her neck, and a tremendous bulging weight straddled her, grinding on her back. She fought back, struggling to turn over, to push him off, but she seemed suddenly frozen. Her arms and legs felt as if they weighed hundreds of pounds. Unable to fight back, unable to scream, but unwilling to give up, Ophelia's chest heaved with fear and anger as her chemise was ripped off her body.

She concentrated all her strength, and finally forced out a cry. "No!" She closed her eyes and moaned as an elbow dug hard into the small of her back. His knee forced her naked legs apart.

"No!" she managed to cry out again. He grabbed her shoulder and flipped her over. She tried to push him away, but her limbs were intolerably heavy. She felt him fumbling with his pants, and she whimpered, tears of rage and frustration springing from her eyes, rolling down her cheeks into her pillow.

He spoke then, a guttural croak. "Tell me how you like this, you fancy whore."

Then she felt pain, sudden piercing pain that paralyzed her whole body and took her breath away. He placed a heavy hand on her face, pushing her deep into the pillow as he mounted her, and all the time she could feel his reeking breath on her skin, mixing with his stench, numbing her mind.

Panicking, suffocating, she clawed at the sheets and flailed helplessly as he used her, the bed creaking rhythmically in a vile accompaniment to his grunts. Faster, faster, faster, until her eyes seemed to bounce in her head and her teeth cracked against each other. She felt herself being crushed farther and farther into the mattress.

The gorge came up from her stomach and stuck in her throat, but she choked it back down and finally managed to turn her face and suck in a huge gulp of air. Her tongue salty wet with tears and entwined with strands of her own hair, she clenched her fists and screamed with all the pent-up fear and pain and anger within her. Louder and louder, over and over and over.

"Doña Ophelia, Doña Ophelia, what is it? *Dios mío,* what is it?" Conchita stood at the door in her nightgown, a candle in her hand. Ophelia caught herself in mid-scream and rolled up in bed, blinking at the flickering candlelight.

"Where is he?" she cried. But the shadowy intruder had vanished, leaving her alone in a tangle of sheets wet with tears and sweat. "Where is he?" she cried again.

"Who, señora, who? There is no one! Was it the dream?"

"He was here!" Ophelia moaned, and she rubbed her arms where his grip had hurt her, except that the pain, so intense only seconds before, was gone. She no longer felt the elbow digging in her back, or the torn flesh between her thighs. The veil that clouds the sleeping mind drifted away, the room came into sharp focus, and Ophelia wiped the tears from her face.

Though her heart still pounded, she knew that Conchita was right. It was the dream again. She forced herself to stem her tears, choking them back so Conchita would not see. A servant should not see those things— but the humiliation, the pain, the horror of the dream swirled around her still. Even now, the intruder's stench lingered in her nostrils. She put her pale, shaking hands to her face, and a flood of tears spread through her fingers.

Conchita rushed to her side and placed the candle on the bed table. She reached her arms out to her mistress and pulled her in. Ophelia resisted, but Conchita enveloped her anyway. "Shhh, shhh," The elderly servant stroked Ophelia's hair, holding her, calming her. "Was it the old dream, señora?"

Ophelia drew a shuddering breath and nodded. She felt Conchita pulling the wet strands of hair from her face, brushing them back with her plump fingers, slowly rocking her until the sobbing began to subside.

She kept telling herself she should not let a servant be so familiar, but those big arms held her tight and safe. They felt so ample and comforting, so calming, that she felt like climbing into the old woman's lap. "Shhh, shhh," Conchita repeated and rocked, repeated and rocked, until Ophelia's crying died away. With a heavy sigh, Ophelia took a deep breath of the warm night air.

"Señora," Conchita ventured, "I do not understand this dream, but I know it makes you afraid. If you would let me, I can get Vicenta to help you."

Ophelia pulled back, rubbing the remnants of tears from her eyes. She took another deep breath to clear her head, then squared her shoulders and gave Conchita a hard look. "You must never tell anyone about my dreams, Conchita. Especially not that superstitious old *curandera*, Doña Vicenta. I think she kills more people than she cures."

Conchita smiled, and her small brown eyes lit up with mischief. She had developed a simple routine to deal with Ophelia's nightmares. Let her cry, then make her angry.

"When they die, Vicenta cuts off a piece of hair and saves it for spells." She could have told other stories about Doña Vicenta, too. She was full of opinions about everyone, including Ophelia and her sons, and she was apt to blurt them out at the most inappropriate times. She had absolutely no sense of propriety. Ophelia liked to keep a distance between herself and her servants, but Conchita did not seem to understand she was a servant, and so Ophelia had given up trying to keep her in place. She had often been tempted to replace her, but infuriating as she could be, Conchita was a comfort, a familiar and dependable companion who knew her mistress' fears and rages. She had practically raised Juan for five years, during Ophelia's "illness"—a shameful time that she did not like to think about.

"Dreams have meaning," Conchita insisted. "What if this means trouble is coming?"

Ophelia shook her head and looked at the flickering candle by the bed. She knew what it meant, this curse of a dream, this black yoke that she bore all alone. But upon her life, upon her soul, she vowed again to keep it secret—a secret so full of pain that she would take it to her grave. With only one grudging exception, no one must ever know—especially not Juan, her bold, beautiful, troubled son. "It doesn't mean anything," she finally replied.

"But the same dream, señora, it has to mean something. What if we sacrifice a goat for you? Tomas can do it in secret. Nobody will know."

Ophelia's first instinct was to lash out. She hated *brujerías*—the heathen superstitions and rituals left over from the native Indian culture. Doña Vicenta specialized in these useless practices. Spells, dances, sacrifices, murmurings by the light of the moon, strange supernatural creatures—they were all the fantasies of ignorant minds. But the rage softened as she let go of the dream, and an image of Tomas crowded in. It was ludicrous —the ranch's first and most respected *vaquero* slaughtering a goat in the brush for her. She could imagine his quiet voice complaining about having enough real work to do without having to contend with reluctant, smelly goats and witches' spells.

"Tomas is our top *vaquero*, Conchita. Cows and horses, that's all he does. That's enough now. Let it go."

"Señora, for you, Tomas will do anything. Everybody knows that."

That was true. He was the first *vaquero* her husband Alvino had hired when they built the ranch house and moved here in 1823. Tomas had always been a faithful friend, especially since Alvino was killed.

She rubbed her eyes and folded her hands in her lap. Tomas. He was the one who had come to her when it happened. Alvino had been away fighting with the Tejanos at San Jacinto. She was alone, sitting in the parlor drinking sweet chocolate, looking out the window at the gray morning. It had been raining, and a cold wind blew from the north. She could hear it howl around the corners of the house. When Tomas came riding up, Ophelia knew right away that something was wrong. His horse was lathered from riding all night. He jumped off, ran up the steps, and then stopped. She waited, but he never knocked. She got up and went to open the door. He was standing there, his sombrero in his hand. His eyes were red, tears streaked the dust on his cheeks, and he just stared at her.

Her husband was dead, and though Tomas obviously grieved, Ophelia did not know how she felt about it. Their marriage had long ago ceased to be intimate. When Alvino marched off to war, she lit no candles for him, said no prayers, cried no tears. She admitted to herself then that she wished he would never come back. She and Alvino had fought for years over Juan, over those terrible beatings. It had been the beatings that had finally roused her, made her take pity on the boy, made her feel *something* for him. Before that, she had been incapable of feeling. She had ignored the boy and left his care up to Conchita, who called those years the period of Ophelia's "illness."

After Alvino's death, she had been left with Juan and Blas to look after, and Tomas helped her in his own way. He guided her, protected her. He made her feel safe.

Pausing in her reverie, Ophelia recalled what Conchita had just said—Tomas would do anything for her. Ophelia did not want Conchita getting the wrong idea or starting any rumors about her and Tomas. He was just a hired hand—a servant. Just like Conchita. "Tomas has his work to do," she said frostily. "Let him do it and leave him out of this business about my dreams."

Conchita frowned. *Something else troubles her,* thought Ophelia. Conchita saved up for months, waiting for these intimate moments to ask these very personal questions that were actually none of her business. At times like these Ophelia felt a need to talk, to be comforted, and Conchita, like the sly, clever busybody that she was, took complete advantage of the opportunity.

"What is it?" Ophelia asked.

"I was thinking about Blas," Conchita replied. "Growing up without a father. He needs somebody to show him what to do, señora. You know he tries so hard, but he can't seem to do things right. He never complains. He never says anything. I worry about what will happen to him…"

Ophelia could see Conchita searching her face, looking for a signal that their personal chat was over. But it was not over. Wondering where the old woman was going with this concern about Blas, she nodded to encourage her.

"…and he wants so much to be like Juan," Conchita concluded purposefully.

Ophelia shook her head. "Blas doesn't need to be like Juan! Juan is rebellious and does nothing but drink and fight. Here I am, trying to save the ranch for him from these American squatters, and he doesn't even care. He forgets his station, his birthright. He spends all his time with the *vaqueros*. Look at him now. I sent him to Reynosa to see about selling some cattle, and he disappears for three weeks! Why would Blas want to be like Juan?"

"Ah, because Juan is loved, señora. The people adore him."

Ophelia stared at Conchita, vacantly at first, and then her eyes focused, her jaw tightened, and she brushed her hair back with her hand, the candlelight flickering from her movements. "Bring me my robe, Conchita. It's almost morning, isn't it?"

The chat was over. "Yes, señora." Conchita reached for the green robe on the bedpost. "Why don't you wash yourself? I'll start the stove and make you some hot tea. You can come into the kitchen with me. Would you like that?"

Ophelia nodded, staring down at her bare feet on the rough mesquite floor. Then she hesitated. She didn't want to be alone just yet, but it was time to get hold of herself, to set things back in place.

"No." She looked up slowly. "I'll have the tea on the porch."

Her mistress was herself again. Conchita smiled. She had done her job, and done it well.

"Si, señora."

TOMAS SANCHEZ uncocked his rifle and lowered the dark brown stock to the ground. Barefoot and shirtless, he stood beneath the bedroom window of the ranch house. He stared at the flickering light of Conchita's candle as it threw dim shadows on the curtains. Inside, the hushed voices faded. He could not make out the words, but he had heard enough to satisfy himself there was no real danger. Ophelia's screams had carried across the hundred yards to his *jacal*, to his ears especially tuned to her voice—as his eyes were tuned to her face, his heart to her soul. Tomas had heard the screams when no one else would have, so faintly did they float on the warm night breeze. He had known immediately that it was Ophelia. He'd been out the door with his gun before he was even fully awake, his legs churning and bare feet pounding across the warm hard earth and gravel of the courtyard.

He slung the rifle over his shoulder and returned gingerly across the yard, peering ahead through the gloom. The threat of snakes, scorpions, and the sharp little rocks and twigs which now jabbed his feet—he had been oblivious to them all when he had dashed for the house. Overhead, the stars spilled in a vast, brilliant cloud, and a faint hint of gold rimmed the eastern horizon. He reached his *jacal* and entered its single door, leaning his rifle inside.

Like all the others, his *jacal* was a one-room collection of sticks, branches, and limbs tied together and topped with a thatched roof. There were no windows, for it was said that evil spirits could enter most easily through windows. The dusty floor was made of hard beaten earth, and in one corner Tomas kept a straw mattress and blankets. Nailed to one wall was the rough crucifix Ophelia had given him, and hanging on the opposite wall were a sombrero, leggings, bullwhip, horse-hair rope, and a gun belt with pistol.

As Tomas stood in the doorway, the dim light behind him cast his shadow against the far wall and caught on a canvas sack hung above his pillow. He walked over and took it down, then carried it to the table and laid it there, seating himself on the stool. One loop at a time, he opened its tight leather strings and slid his hand inside. He sat there for a long time, his hand resting inside the bag, and then he pulled out a book and laid it on the table. He ran his fingers up and down its edges and then opened it, though in the dark he could not see the writing. But that did not matter, for Tomas could not read.

Outside, he heard his neighbors stirring. The women would soon be building fires to boil the daily supply of corn for tortillas. Tomas sat still, touching the pages of the illustrated Bible, turning them one at a time.

The sweet young girl had brought it with her on that night when he waited outside her gate, expectant, excited, more nervous than his horse. Camelia had come to him, defying her disapproving father, filling Tomas' life with light and beauty, with a joy so intense he could scarcely contain it. He worshipped her, closing his eyes each night reluctantly, afraid she'd be gone when he awakened. He lay awake on moonlit nights, marveling at her face, her hair, the perfection of her skin—but Camelia had been his wife for only a few months, and then she was gone.

She had died of yellow fever shortly after Tomas brought her to the Santa Alicia from Camargo when he came to help Alvino Santos build the ranch. Camelia was buried right out there, beneath a large, gnarled mesquite tree. Alvino had to dig the grave himself because Tomas could not do it. He had gotten so drunk that he thought he would die from it, and Alvino carried him to the graveside for the funeral. Two weeks later, he had stopped drinking and gone back to work, and he never said a word about it again, not even to Ophelia.

Tomas had spent years raging against God for taking Camelia, raging against himself for bringing her out here, raging against the world for going on without her, a day at a time, like the pages he was turning. Though he could not read the words, he stared at them, watching the letters grow more visible with the dawn.

A horse neighed in the corral, a woman's voice drifted in on the moist morning air, a rooster crowed. Tomas sat and listened to the growing sounds of the ranch until the smell of mesquite smoke and bacon told him breakfast was ready. He returned the book to the bag, closed it up, and hung it back on the wall.

After dressing, he walked out into the yard and headed for Mingo and Vicenta's *jacal*, where he usually took his breakfast. Mingo's wife was a good cook and knew how to cure people when they were sick. She kept a garden of flowers, weeds and herbs for healing. She used roses to treat bleeding sores and made hot teas from various herbs, treating all manner of common ailments, from nerves to coughs. For serious illnesses or for spells or evil spirits, she had more powerful remedies. As he approached her fire, Tomas could see she was cooking *nopal* cactus with eggs.

"*Buenos días*, Doña Vicenta," he called. "Smells good."

Vicenta glanced up from her cooking, tightening a colorful *rebozo* around her shoulders against the morning dampness. "Good morning, Don Tomas. You say the same thing every morning for ten years. Do you even like my cooking?"

"Hell of a time to ask, after ten years," he replied, tucking in his shirt. "I like everything you cook. Except those soups for healing the bewitched. They smell bad."

"They have to smell bad," she curtly replied, "or they won't work." Today Vicenta was covered with ribbons of all colors—tied to her hair, her *rebozo*, the hem of her dress—no doubt to ward off some pending evil. Her shoes made a wet sucking sound as she walked, but he did not bring it up. He was fairly certain she had put tomatoes in her shoes again, a cure she often prescribed for aching joints. She put her hands on her hips. "Besides," she continued, "do you think demons and witches smell good?"

Though he had started it, Tomas did not like the direction of this conversation. At any moment, Doña Vicenta was likely to declare him ill, whip up one of her concoctions, and demand to heal him. He changed course. "Did Mingo eat?"

Doña Vicenta took her hands off her hips and bent back down to her task. "He went with Blas to Matamoros to look for Juan. They didn't come back last night. I think Mingo got drunk, and probably got Blas drunk, too. It's not right," she said, flipping a corn tortilla for emphasis. "It's only six miles to Matamoros. They could have made it if they were sober."

Tomas looked off toward the horizon, now brilliant red as the sun edged up from behind the dark rim of the earth. "Well," he said, "they'll be along soon. They won't be anxious to miss a day of work. Me, I'd rather sweat all day in the sun with a hangover, my head bursting, than face Doña Ophelia."

Doña Vicenta handed Tomas his breakfast in a clay bowl, which he carried to the wooden table outside Mingo's *jacal.* "I have a cure for hangovers," Vicenta said. "For Mingo's hangovers. I wrap his balls in cactus spines and squeeze." Tomas flinched and felt his testicles contract.

As Vicenta brought him fresh corn tortillas and black coffee, Blas and Mingo cantered their horses into the yard and tied them at the corral fence. They walked through their own dust toward Mingo's *jacal* and sat stone-faced at the table with Tomas. He searched their eyes. They looked tired, but he saw no redness in the eyes, nor did he smell the stench of mescal seeping from their pores.

"Look at him!" Vicenta snarled. "Drunk all night and doesn't even say anything! *Buenos días*, Vicenta. Good morning, husband. Did you sleep well, dear wife? Yes, good husband, better than in weeks. Would you like some—"

"Shut up, woman," Mingo roared, "and bring us some breakfast."

Vicenta stood with her mouth open for a second, then snapped it shut and moved to obey.

Tomas sipped at his coffee. He was surprised by Mingo's mood. Mingo usually bubbled with playfulness and high spirits, especially in the morning when the day was fresh. Tomas lifted his chin, questioning his friend with his eyes.

Mingo shook his head. "Nothing. *Nada.* Nobody knows anything about Juan. I hope he's still in Reynosa." He bent forward. "We heard there's Texas Rangers all up and down the river, looking for bandits. That's why we didn't come in last night. If they had caught us out there at night, they'd have shot us down like dogs. Left us lying by the side of the road."

Tomas looked at Blas. His youthful face was puffy, and his eyes had a cautious look to them. "What else?"

Blas frowned. "There's new shacks going up around Fort Brown. More squatters. Mama will be furious."

Tomas grunted and pushed his plate away. "*Chingado.* You may be right. Juan could still be in Reynosa, or maybe he's gone up to Camargo. But with those Rangers out, he might be hanging from a tree, too. Damn that boy! Why does he ride out alone?"

"I wanted to go with him," said Blas, looking down at his boots. "Mama told him to take five *vaqueros*, and I wanted to go, too. But he snuck out at night, while everybody was asleep."

Tomas glanced over at the eighteen-year-old boy's smooth, hairless face. Normally, a boy his age could grow a mustache, but underneath this boy's nose there was only a faint shadow of hair.

"Well," Tomas said, "Ophelia always wants bad news *pronto*." He stood up. "Come on."

They pushed back from the table and marched toward the ranch house just as Vicenta reappeared with their breakfast. She stood near the table, pointing a crooked finger at them, alternately opening her mouth to speak, then shutting it. She rocked sideways in her shoes, making wet sucking noises as she squashed the tomato mush with her toes. Finally, when they were across the yard, too far to yell at, she shook her head and whirled about to put away the dishes, her brightly colored ribbons flapping gaily in the early morning light.

Fort Brown, Texas
North Bank of the Rio Grande

OPHELIA LIFTED THE HEM of her ruffled blue gown and stepped onto the muddy gray loam surrounding Fort Brown. Slamming the carriage door behind her, she adjusted her hat and glared at the abomination despoiling her land. The fort's nine-foot earthen walls, naked and dirt-raw, towered above her, as if they had been pushed rotting and stinking from hell in the dead of night. She heard the American flag snapping in the warm breeze. Beside it flew the bold flag of Texas, the Lone Star.

In the morning light, this place did not look much like a fort. It looked more like a crude six-sided dam surrounded by a ditch twenty feet wide and ten feet deep, the source of soil for the walls. She knew this because she had spent weeks in a rage when the American soldiers were digging it. The fort was simple, but it had shielded the Americans from the furious cannon fire lobbed from the Mexican city of Matamoros, just across the river.

War had broken out between the United States and Mexico on the morning of May 3, 1846, the two nations at odds over ownership of the Nueces strip. This land, south of the Nueces River and north of the Rio Grande, formed the huge southern tip of Texas. After winning its independence from Mexico in 1836, the bold new Republic of Texas had declared that its borders extended west to include most of New Mexico and south all the way to the Rio Grande. But Mexico refused to acknowledge the claim, correctly claiming that the northern border of the Mexican state of Tamaulipas had always been the Nueces River. When General Zachary Taylor moved into the area, Mexico sent its troops charging across the Rio Grande to confront him. Now the war was in full bloom, although the fighting was farther south in Mexico City.

Ophelia dropped her gaze and looked east toward the banks of the Rio Grande snaking through the valley. Down the river she saw the road to Point Isabel and the Brazos de Santiago harbor break out of the brush at the ferry crossing. A horse-drawn coach from the Neal stage line was unloading passengers—probably more Americans rushing to set up business in booming Matamoros across the river. She watched the rope-drawn ferry being pulled across the river by mules to the busy Mexican town. Twenty miles farther down the river toward the gulf was Boca del Rio, the official Mexican point of entry from the sea.

White-winged doves cooed their mesmerizing mating songs from the mesquite and ebony trees along the banks, and smoke from cooking fires wove a white mist through the brush. Dozens of shacks ringed the fort, others were scattered along the river. Ophelia frowned at the sight of the dirty, hairy men busily constructing new ones. Children scrambled along the dusty paths between the shacks and the fort, as dogs loped beside them, yapping, growling, and chasing horned toads through the brush.

Drawing a deep breath, she squared her shoulders and marched toward the gate, signaling her men to remain with the carriage. She crossed the rough *encina* planks over the ditch and walked up to the taller of the two guards slouching at the walls.

She set her chin. "I am here to see Major Roberts."

The tall American stared down at her for a minute, then frowned and shook his head.

"*El no habla* no Meskin," the other guard drawled, in atrocious Spanish, "and the major's busy anyhow."

Ophelia turned to stare at the second guard, who seemed almost a midget. The two made a ridiculous looking pair. "You will advise him," she said in her sternest voice, "that Doña Ophelia Santos demands a meeting."

Authority, Ophelia understood, was recognizable in any language. At the sound of her name, the midget's eyes widened and he slowly straightened up.

"Is he expectin' you, ma'am?"

"If he isn't, he certainly should be."

He frowned and shot a look at his tall companion, but Ophelia knew that fool had no idea what was being said. The midget finally shrugged and nodded toward the gate. "I'll take you to the major."

As Ophelia entered the fort, a chaotic mix of sound and action engulfed her. Wagons were being loaded, others were being unloaded. Horses were being shod, a squad of soldiers drilled in the center of the yard, men were riding out through the gate. A constant pounding of hammers and the shouts of men at work assaulted her ears, and her eyes itched from the smoke and dust fouling the air. All around, the cacophony of English accosted her, a language harsh and foreign to ears so long comforted by the soft melodic sounds of Spanish.

She followed the guard to a series of rooms built against the wall of the fort and waited where he left her to be announced. Within a minute, Major Roberts emerged. He was tall and thin, with a balding head and a large dark mustache. He seemed to quickstep toward her.

"Señora Santos," he said, then gaped, owl-eyed, as if that was the extent of his Spanish. She waited, taking his measure. "I'm honored," he finally managed. "Doña Ophelia Santos, I've heard so much about you. We all have. You're even lovelier than—than—would you like you some coffee, señora?"

Watching him blush, Ophelia nodded and followed him into his office. The room was sparsely furnished, with only a table, two chairs, and in the corner a brass spittoon. On the table were his papers and a lamp. Hanging from the wall behind him were his saber and rifle. In the opposite corner stood the colors of the 7th U.S. Infantry Regiment.

"Please be seated, señora," he said, pouring coffee from the small steaming black pot at the end of his desk. "I regret we have no sugar. We've run out, and don't expect another shipment for a month."

Ophelia took the tin cup, lifted it to her lips, and sipped the black, bitter liquid. "Where did you learn Spanish, Major?"

He glanced up, a smile forming. "Is it that bad?"

"Not at all. I'm impressed that you've learned our language."

He nodded and tugged on his mustache. "My father came to Texas from Mississippi twenty years ago. I followed and lived in Gonzales for a while. If you come to live in Texas, you find out quick you need to learn Spanish. So I did."

She tilted her head. "I'm afraid I haven't compelled myself to perfect my English yet, but I get by. By the way, have you tried *piloncillo?*"

"I'm afraid I don't know what you mean."

She smiled. "*Piloncillo.* They are cones of sugar made from boiling sugar cane. For your coffee. If you like, I will send you some, but you can buy them from the ranchers up and down the valley."

His face lit up, his grin revealing large, tobacco-stained teeth. "That's very kind of you. Very thoughtful, indeed. I'm glad you've come here friendly-like. Frankly, not all the *rancheros* are friendly."

Ophelia paused, for she wanted no misunderstandings. Dealing with Americans was a tricky business. Their directness and single-minded approach to solving complex problems could lead to misunderstandings. Here they were, sitting across from one another, smiling. The difference was, as the Mexicans along the border knew too well, Mexicans smiled because they were polite, whereas these damned Americans smiled because they had probably just dispossessed you of something.

"This is not a social call, Major Roberts. I am not here to make friends—though I don't want to be unfriendly."

His face fell in an instant. Sitting up a little straighter, he shrugged once, then again. "Why did you come, then?"

"I want you to dismantle this fort and remove it from my land. I want you to move all settlers and squatters off my property. I want you to burn those filthy shacks outside your gates."

"Dismantle the—did I hear you right?"

"Shall I repeat myself?"

He shook his head, then fixed her with a regretful stare and rubbed his hand over his balding head. "Señora Santos, we're in the middle of a war here. We don't have time to squabble over whose land we happen to be on. Besides, those people have claims."

"Claims?" she snapped. "What claims?"

He drummed his fingers on the desk, then poured himself another cup of coffee. "There's been enough fights over this land, señora, that I checked to make sure. Most of these settlers along the river have deeds. Headrights from the Republic of Texas granting them land as a reward for being veterans in the service of Texas. Others claim they bought their land from the city of Matamoros, which bought it from your family back when Matamoros was founded. Some of this land has been sold more than once."

Ophelia wanted to jump out of her chair. "Impossible! I alone have legal right to my land, and I'm passing it to my sons. The other *rancheros* along the river own their land legally as well." She paused, inhaled deeply, and tried to explain. "My great grandfather received a grant from the King of Spain and settled here when there were only a few pathetic, starving Indians for company. He fed them. He brought cattle onto the land." She clenched her hands into fists and slid them into her lap beneath the table so he would not see. "The towns and ranches up and down the Rio Grande—our families built them. We've lived and died here for generations. The city of Matamoros *never* owned this land because they never *paid* my family for it. We have legal rights to this land! No one else!"

Roberts blinked and fingered his coffee cup.

She knew this man was not the total dunderhead he appeared. He was, after all, a major in the United States Army. Certainly, political appointments were not uncommon, but she sensed that this man was competent. Somewhere during her outburst, she had perceived a change come over him. He had stiffened, set his jaw, his eyes had taken on a flat, determined slant. Ophelia was beginning to realize that below the outer layers of crudity and ignorance, the slow words and the mangled language, a core of solid brass anchored most of these Americans. But that was all right. The breed of men and women who settled this unforgiving country was tough, too, and she was made of the same stuff.

"Well," he finally said, "that may be so under Mexican law. But this is now part of the United States."

This again. "And so, I am a citizen of Texas," she said. "The same Texas government that is issuing headrights to my land has also issued a proclamation honoring my husband for fighting and dying at San Jacinto. Are Americans so craven that they cheat those they honor, from one day to the next?"

She watched him swallow. The conflicts in title claims along the river valley were common knowledge, but Ophelia could see that the major wanted no part in resolving them.

"Señora, most Americans coming here consider this land public by right of conquest. I'm afraid there are more coming every week. I can't tell them to leave. And I certainly can't tear down the fort."

"Are you not charged with defending the rights of United States citizens here?"

"Yes, but—"

"Is not Texas now part of the United States?"

"It is, señora, but—"

"I am an American citizen. My rights are being violated. You must protect my rights."

"But, really, Señora Santos, dismantling the fort is ridiculous. How can I protect you without a fort?"

"You have a fort now, and you're not protecting me."

His face and neck grew red. "This is insane! I'm afraid there's nothing I can do for you."

Ophelia scanned the major's face, watching his exasperation build. She saw the twitch in his cheek, his obvious anger, and decided to take a different tack. "I disagree," she said. "There is something you can do." She paused, took a deep breath, and eased further back into her chair. "I recognize that your hands are tied in this matter…."

A look of relief flooded his face. "You know I would help you if I could, Señora Santos. You're a woman of stature, and your husband surely was a Texas patriot. His family deserves respect."

She nodded her acknowledgment. "I intend to take this issue up in the courts, Major Roberts, once I determine what courts have jurisdiction here. I don't trust the local government, but I understand there is a federal judge in New Orleans. If I don't win there, I will pursue other means until I do win. Since you won't enforce my property rights, then I ask you to keep an open mind and be evenhanded in managing these disputes until this is settled. But you must at least forbid more construction! You are the law here, for now."

He rose, paced to the window, and turned toward her with a dramatic pose, his chin in the air. "There is no need to even ask, madam. Fairness is a natural part of every officer's character."

She smiled thinly.

"But there is one concern I must raise with you, señora."

"Yes?"

"We must have order. Any sort of lawlessness will be dealt with harshly. You must keep your men under control."

"My men are *vaqueros*. They herd cattle. I have heard some Americans use a strange term for them—cow boys. But I have no army, nor do the other *rancheros*."

"Yes, yes, I know that. But since March, when the Army imposed the Walker Tariff on goods entering Mexico, smuggling has increased tremendously. There are bandits and smugglers all up and down the river."

Ophelia leaned forward. "And they steal from me as much as from the American squatters. We aren't outlaws, Major, nor do we deal with outlaws. But since you bring the subject up, may I remind you that the Rangers are roaming up and down the valley? Killing every Mexican they find? Most of the people they're killing are innocent and unarmed. You know the Army won't let Mexicans carry guns. Isn't there something you can do?"

He shrugged. "I've given up trying to control the Rangers. They are an entity unto themselves. They're completely wild, and they absolutely despise Mexicans." He stopped and lit his pipe, pacing toward the desk, then back to the window, looking out at the beehive of activity within the small fort.

Ophelia could see the morning light beyond his shoulder. It had already turned white, and the heat was radiating through the windowpanes into the room.

"In a fight," he continued, "the Rangers are magnificent. They've provided us with cavalry to counter the Mexican cavalry. Our mounted dragoons are simply unsuited to this type of warfare. The Rangers provide reconnaissance. They scout, they form the vanguard in any action, and they're the deadliest, meanest, most courageous men I've ever seen. But on the whole, they're impossible to get along with. They obey only their accursed captains and would just as soon fight American troops as Mexicans, or anybody else who stands in their way."

"If you can't control them, who can?"

He paced back to his desk, hands clasped behind his back, his heavy boots thumping on the wooden floor. "That's an excellent question. Technically, they're volunteers, serving under the direction of the U.S. Army."

"But that's you, Major Roberts."

He grunted, looking down at his boots, his balding head reflecting the light from the window. "Oh, they say 'yes, sir' and 'no, sir,' and they absolutely accomplish whatever task you give them, Señora Santos. But when I order them to stop killing unarmed Mexicans, they claim they're either acting in self-defense or that the killings are the work of bandits stirring up trouble along the border. And what can I do? We need them."

Ophelia stood, pushing back her coffee cup and smoothing her dress. "Major Roberts. You said you'd be fair in these matters. My family and many others on this side of the river chose to fight with Texas against Santa Anna. He is a dictator and deserves to be overthrown. We became Texas citizens. And now we're American citizens. There are bands of Rangers and bandits alike, roaming up and down the border, murdering us at their leisure. The Army, which you represent, is here on my land, claiming to protect United States interests, citizens, and property." She paused, drew herself up, and thundered, "We are Americans. Protect us!"

JUAN OPENED HIS EYES to darkness. He had no idea where he was or where he was supposed to be. He felt searing, crippling pain shooting from his head, his shoulders, his arm, his feet, his legs. Then, slowly, fragments of what happened came back to him—the mules, Cornwell, the cactus, the river, the shooting. He heard Timo's slow laugh and gruff, nasal voice taunting him. *"Todo se paga, todo se paga."*

Juan felt cheated. He had always believed that death brought oblivion. Apparently, he was doomed to suffer the pains of his mortal wounds for eternity.

And then from the darkness, a pinpoint of light appeared and slowly grew brighter. He watched in fascination, thinking that perhaps an angel approached, glowing bright in the eternal blackness, coming to claim him and end his pain.

This surprised him, for he had not thought of angels since he was a little boy, running from the harsh, secret beatings in the barn and out in the brush, skulking to his room to cry. He could still see the look of pleasure on his father's face as he stood over him, usually with a strap, sometimes with a thorny mesquite switch. When Juan lay in bed on dark nights, bruised and crying, he had closed his eyes and imagined an angel holding him, wrapping him safely in its wings, taking away the pain.

The light grew brighter, though not closer. It stayed out there, seemingly within reach, but growing bigger, sharper, until objects around it began to take shape. There was a table, a chair—someone was sitting in the chair. Staring, straining, he could see that it was indeed an angel whose sweet face was bathed in the glowing light of eternity.

"So," the angel said, "you're finally awake. I've sat in this uncomfortable chair for two days and two nights, waiting for you to wake up. I'm sore from sitting here."

The angel sounded rather harsh. She came closer, holding a candle, and as the light flickered he could see a familiar face. As he recognized her, a tingling wave coursed through his body, warming it even as he fought off the pain.

"Can you speak?" she demanded, but her voice broke and betrayed her.

"Am I dead?" he asked.

"You should be, but no. You're at our ranch. The *Rinches* found you shot and brought you in. Father treated you." She paused. "Do you recognize me, Juan?"

"Lidia?"

She slipped onto the side of the bed and placed the candle on the nightstand. "Yes," she replied, her eyes misting over. "Oh Juan, I've been so worried about you. How do you feel?"

"Pain."

"It's a miracle you're alive," she whispered. "You lost so much blood. Your head looks terribly bad. We spent all day yesterday pulling cactus thorns out of the rest of you and wrapping you in bandages. Some of the wounds have festered."

"I'm thirsty."

She picked up a cup, lifted his head gently, and let him sip some water. Then she inhaled deeply and composed herself. "We sent a message to your mother. She's coming tonight. She was at Fort Brown when our rider got to the Santa Alicia. He said she became very angry and issued orders that you not be moved until she arrives. There's twenty of her *vaqueros* camped right outside the gate. They just arrived, armed to the teeth and very angry." She chuckled. "They're right across the road from the *Rinches*, all eight of them."

He did not respond. Lifting the candle, she saw that he had fallen asleep again, so she laid his head back on the pillow and allowed herself a tiny smile.

In all the years she'd known him, she had never seen him this vulnerable, this dependent, except that one time, when she was six and he was twelve. Ophelia had brought him to the de Leon ranch for one of their frequent visits, and Lidia had followed the boy out to the corral, where he threw rocks at the horses, getting them to buck and kick. Then he had run among them to watch them scatter. She had stood at the fence, laughing at his antics, but then she suddenly fell silent and backed away as a huge diamondback rattlesnake slithered along the fence toward her. She stumbled and fell in the dust.

"Lidia," Juan had called above the noise of the thrashing horses behind him. "Lidia, look out."

She turned toward him with her mouth open, her hands flailing, but she made no sound. Her eyes bulged, wild with fear, as Juan raced to the fence, then reached across, and grabbed the snake by the tail. He hurled it over his head into the corral, away from her. The horses, already in a panic, went insane. One of them bit Juan in the shoulder and another kicked him in the back of the legs, sending him sprawling. A sleepy looking *vaquero* came out of the barn to investigate the racket, put a boot on the snake's neck, and neatly sliced off its head with a knife.

Before anyone could see his wound, Juan jumped to his feet and bolted from the corral, then limped toward the river. It had all happened so quickly, and even now as Lidia remembered that day, it was all still a blur.

She had pulled herself together and followed him. She found him sitting in the weeds on the sunny bank, struggling to remove his bloody shirt, choking back his pain. She approached him quietly and sat down a few feet away. When he took off his shirt and washed it in the brown water, she gasped at the sight of the scabs and scars on his back. They looked even more grisly as blood trickled down from the horse's bite. He turned toward her, his chin set firmly, as if to show her the pain was nothing.

"You just grabbed that snake," she said, her voice trembling. "I was so scared. I thought it would bite me. I think you are braver than anybody."

He looked away, wringing out his shirt and using it to dab at his wound. She heard him suck in his breath.

"Does it hurt bad?" she asked in a soft voice.

He grunted, but she could see tears welling, his face a mask.

"Let me help you. Should I go get your mother, or—"

"No!" he growled, his eyes swimming with pain. "I don't need help!"

She shrank back and was silent for a moment, then pointed. "Why is your back like that? What are all those red marks?"

He whirled on her. "Why are you such a nosy little *malcriada?* Why can't you just leave me alone?"

His fury startled her. She buried her face in her tiny, delicate hands and burst into spontaneous tears. She struggled to stop but only managed to switch to huge gasping sobs, until she felt him slowly prying her fingers away from her tear-stained face.

"Don't cry," he said gruffly.

She quieted at his gentle touch, then looked up and saw him sitting there, still holding her hand. The blood was oozing down his shoulder, but he still held her hand.

"I won't let snakes bite you," he murmured.

"I hate them."

"Do you promise not to tell anyone about what happened?"

"I promise," she replied solemnly.

He squeezed her hand, and sat holding it until her tears subsided. Then he let her go and picked up his shirt again, saying nothing more. She wiped her tears away and watched him, her heart bursting with warmth and admiration for him.

"You should marry me," she blurted.

Juan froze, then turned his head slowly toward her. "You're just a baby," he said. "You're what, maybe only six right now? Maybe when we get older. But you probably won't want to marry me then." He studied her radiant face. No one had ever looked at him like that.

"Oh, yes, I will!" she replied, nodding vigorously, and she had loved him from that moment on. That day, she had seen the caring, sensitive boy who lived underneath the tough outer shell he showed others. No matter how hard he seemed now, the Juan she knew was that tender boy by the river.

Their courtship sprang to life when she was fifteen, though it was never really official. One day, they were childhood friends, then, suddenly, they were truly in love. Juan certainly had prospects, but her father scorned his lack of education and his distinctly non-aristocratic lifestyle. As a suitor for Lidia, Juan was not acceptable. Despite this, Juan and Lidia were irresistibly drawn to each other. They were young, beautiful, passionate, and unyielding, but it did not matter. Don de Leon informed Lidia that Juan would never be acceptable and ordered her to break it off or he would send her to Mexico City to live with relatives. As young as she was, she had no choice but to obey.

Lidia knew that her mother and Ophelia had both been devastated by the breakup. They had seen in the courtship, in the joining of the two families, the best chance for either of their children to have a normal life—normal, at least, for them. The two mothers had reasoned that Lidia would civilize Juan, soften him, lead him to the cultured lifestyle that was his birthright. And Juan could tame Lidia's fury, stand in the face of it and laugh, and bend her passion to more sensible pursuits, such as making babies.

But it was never to be. Lidia sometimes sighed, restless in her bed on hot summer nights, the soft breeze billowing the curtains, as she thought about what could have been. Juan perplexed her. The rare times when he let himself, he could be as sweet and charming as that little boy she remembered. She had reveled in his strong arms, the secret stolen kisses that made her lose her mind, his innocence about a woman's heart. He was an exotic fruit with a thick hard shell and a sweet, hidden center. She knew his rough reputation, but when he held her close, looking deep into her eyes, she saw what no one else could see. It melted her resolve. As she watched him sleep now, it was so hard to remember that he was a dangerous man, a killer and a gambler known in cantinas all along the border.

Eventually, though, her father had convinced her that danger was not what she wanted in a man. Juan had been a childhood love, yes, but in a husband she wanted a polished *caballero*, a gentleman. Her father had been right. Juan just would not do.

It did not matter that he was achingly handsome, lying there now, helpless, nearly naked under the sheets. She studied the shape of his jaw, the rough month-long beard that framed his sunburned cheeks, the broad shoulders and bandaged chest. Now that she reflected on it, she thought that he had come after her like an invading army, catching her unawares, kissing her for his own pleasure, not hers. Yes, her father had been wise to reject him. He had been right.

Hadn't he?

She placed the candle back on the nightstand and tiptoed to the door. Looking back over her shoulder one more time, she smiled happily and went to inform Don de Leon that his patient had regained consciousness.

STARR SPRAWLED on the thin grass beside the campfire, watching Sam Brennan slice off a chunk of beef with his Bowie knife. The Señorita Lidia de Leon had provided them with large portions of the ranch's beef for roasting, and the men lounged in the flickering firelight, eating until they were gorged. The light threw dim, moving shadows on the brush surrounding the small clearing, and above them the bright full moon slipped in and out of the high, thin clouds. A slight breeze came in soft bursts, like sighs of contentment in the summer evening.

Guitar music from the *vaquero* camp floated across the road, the melancholy voices of the musicians joining in, singing about a love lost long ago. Jim Carson passed the coffee pot around, then sat back and lit his pipe. The Don had slipped across the road to the *vaquero* camp where, he claimed, he would "scout the enemy."

"By God," said Sam in his twangy Texas drawl, "that was good meat. Sure beats *pínole* all to hell. I'll need to sleep standing up, I'm so damn full." *Pínole* was a mixture of cornmeal and brown sugar. Rangers seldom stopped to cook during the day when they were moving through enemy territory. Instead, they mixed *pínole* with water in their tin cups to keep off hunger until evening.

"Don't think we'll sleep much tonight," Starr replied. "Storm coming."

As the men sniffed the air, Sam stood up in the middle of the clearing and scanned the horizon. "Might be right, Cap'n. I see flashes to the west, but it's a long way off."

Frenchy stretched his arms, bent them back behind his head, and inhaled the sweet South Texas air. "I ain't sleepy, anyway. What say we have a little fun with them *vaqueros* over yonder?"

Uriah perked up. Starr knew he liked pestering Mexicans almost as much as scalping Comanche. "I could drop cartridges in their campfire," Uriah offered. "That oughta get them crappin' in their *pantalones*."

"Wouldn't be right," Starr replied. "'Cause a ruckus. De Leon's doing us a favor and all, feeding us and holding them mules. Best we leave them boys be."

The men grumbled a little, and then Frenchy had another idea. "How about just a friendly game of monte? And we won't start nothing, Cap'n. That's a promise."

Starr considered this. There was no way his Rangers could jaunt across that road and not start some sort of trouble. He knew it, they knew it, and the Mexicans knew it. Starr also knew his men had been riding hard for weeks now and had seen little action except the chance encounter with Timo's bandits. After Timo had escaped, his men were restless, itching for some form of entertainment, and the prospect of twenty armed *vaqueros* provided endless opportunities for deviltry. But there would be complications.

Starr could not help thinking that just a few yards away, in a warm, soft bed likely spread with white, ruffled sheets, slept the most beautiful woman he had ever seen in his life. Lidia's face had popped into his mind all afternoon, unbidden but not unwelcome. She had taken root there, bringing unexpected smiles to his face. What would Miss de Leon think if the morning brought more dead Mexicans lined up along the road outside her gate? Shaking his head, he scolded himself. He was letting that woman disorient him. It was best to keep things simple and clear. Best forget about her.

A voice floated out of the darkness, from the direction of the Mexican camp. "*Hola, Rinches!* Where is *Capitán* Starr?"

The Rangers drew their Colts and scrambled away from the campfire with practiced efficiency. Starr put out a hand, cautioning them to hold their fire, and squinted at the solitary figure standing in the road, barely outlined by the dim moonlight. The moon slipped from behind a cloud, and the road gleamed in silvery light, then dimmed again.

He replied in Spanish, "Who are you? What do you want?"

"My name is Tomas Sanchez. I work for Doña Ophelia. I'm coming in."

Starr looked to his men, motioning them to watch the brush around them. Frenchy crouched low and disappeared into the cacti behind the camp, where the horses were tied.

"Come on ahead," Starr replied. "Real slow."

He watched the figure move toward the camp, sidestepping the cactus and Spanish Dagger plants. Thorns and branches scratched against his leggings. Starr could see the shadow of a sombrero outlining his head, and then something in his hands caught the moonlight and gleamed.

"He's holding a gun," Sam whispered, lifting his Colt to shoot.

"Hold your fire," Starr snapped. Sam shot Starr a look, but he lowered his gun.

"Hold up!" Starr called. "What's that in your hand?"

Tomas stopped. He stood motionless for a second, then surprised Starr by resuming his approach. Starr cursed and cocked his gun, squinting at the shadows as the moonlight faded again. The Rangers nurtured a tradition of unquestioned supremacy—a Ranger never issued the same order twice. To ignore a Ranger order was to invite a swift death.

"Don't shoot, *Rinches*," Tomas called. "I'm not holding a gun."

Starr did not fire. Instead, he watched Frenchy bolt out of the tangled brush behind Tomas, his Colt drawn and pointed at the *vaquero's* back. Tomas strode into the inner circle of firelight, then stopped.

"You stupid greaser," Sam spat. "You were told to hold."

Frenchy dug his gun barrel into Tomas' back and pushed him forward, so that Tomas stumbled a bit.

"I'm Starr." He watched Tomas turn and was impressed to see the man completely at ease, as if the Rangers were no concern to him.

Tomas fixed him with a steady gaze and handed him a bottle of mescal. "From the men," he said. "To thank you for helping Juan."

Starr stepped forward and accepted the bottle. He nodded, holding the bottle up to the firelight. "*De nada,*" he said.

Adjusting his sombrero, Tomas gave a slight nod in reply, threw a hard look at Sam, then sauntered back out into the brush. The Rangers stood in a knot watching Starr, the firelight flickering on their faces.

"That miserable little rooster," growled Carson. "Why didn't you shoot him, Cap'n?"

Frenchy agreed. "Won't do to have them disobey an order. We oughta go over and fix him, boys."

Starr looked at the bottle, then tucked it into his saddlebags. "Don't nobody mess with them *vaqueros* tonight, boys," he said. The Rangers looked at each other and shrugged, mumbling as they spread their blankets around the campfire, setting their pallets in a circle. "Jim," said Starr, "you take the first watch. Best check the horses again, case the storm blows this way."

Half an hour later, wrapped in their blankets and lying on clumps of coarse grass, their minds drifting in the prelude to sleep, the Rangers heard the thunder of pounding hooves.

"Carriage coming," Jim called from the darkness. "Headed toward the ranch house."

Starr rolled over on one shoulder and watched the carriage roll by. That, he figured, would be the lady Ophelia.

OPHELIA STEPPED OUT of the carriage and swept toward the house, Conchita stumbling to keep up with her. Blas rode up behind the carriage and brought his horse to a halt in the graveled yard, then five *vaqueros* pulled up behind him. Dust flew everywhere. The sultry night air was suddenly alive with the snorting of tired horses and the musky smell of equine sweat.

Meeting the visitors at the door, Doña Martina de Leon threw her arms around her dear friend. "Ophelia, thank heavens you've come. What a terrible thing! He's so young, and shot so badly. I don't know how it happened, I—"

Ophelia put her index finger to Martina's lips. "Hush, hush. Tell me quickly, how is he? Tell me he's still alive." Martina nodded, and an immense wave of relief came over Ophelia. She closed her eyes and felt the room spin around her. When she opened them again, Lidia had come up behind Martina. Ophelia was startled by the girl's haggard look—the wrinkled, sweat-stained dress, the unruly hair, the shadows under her red, tired eyes.

Lidia spoke, her voice cracking, "Ophelia," and they rushed to embrace. Lidia's body felt limp, her arms light as they wrapped around Ophelia's shoulders. Her hair smelled stale.

"Lidia, Lidia," she whispered. "What have you been doing, my foolish angel?"

"She's exhausted," Martina said, her eyes misting at the sight of the embrace. "She refuses to leave his side. I can't make her sleep or eat."

Ophelia yanked off her hat and handed it to Conchita. "Where is my son?"

Martina grabbed Ophelia's arm. "Oh, good news. Wonderful news! He woke up just an hour ago. Tell her, *mi hija.*" She turned to Lidia and nodded energetically.

Lidia smiled. "He did wake up. He spoke to me."

"Luis is examining him now," Martina continued. Her gaze drifted to the door, where Blas stood like a stone pillar, his sombrero in his hands, his eyes glued to the floor. "Blas, young Blas. Come in, boy. Don't just stand at the door. Lidia, where are our manners? Conchita, come in, come in! Ramona, bring coffee and sweet breads!"

At the mention of Lidia's name, Blas' cheeks flared crimson. He shoved his sombrero back on his head and stomped out the door. Over his shoulder, he called back, "Have to find Tomas."

The women stared after him. "He's a little shy," Ophelia said, and they all smiled.

Martina cupped Ophelia's face in her hands. "We just finished praying a rosary for Juan," she whispered. "You must be worn out from your ride. Would you like some refreshments while we wait for Luis to finish? We have some supper saved for you."

"I couldn't eat, Martina. I just need to see Juan."

Martina's eyes fluttered about the room. "Well, I'm not sure. Luis threw us all out so he could examine him. He becomes cross when we interrupt him—Lidia?"

Lidia stepped forward and took Ophelia's arm. "Oh, Mother, of course she can see him. Father's had more than enough time. Come on, Ophelia. Come see your son."

They walked arm in arm down the hall to Juan's room. Lidia tapped on the door, then lowered her head to listen for a reply through the thick, dark, wooden door.

"I'm not finished yet," Don de Leon called.

As Lidia opened the door anyway and stepped into the dim room, the antiseptic smell of ointments and medicines rushed out to greet them.

"Father, Ophelia is here."

Ophelia saw the look Luis de Leon flashed his daughter—instant disapproval, irritation, a stinging rebuke formed and ready to unleash. When Ophelia stepped into the room, and Luis swung his gaze toward her, she watched a cloud of displeasure cross his face. It was a look she had come to expect from him. This man had been a close friend of her husband, a confidant, a peer who was privy to the history of those early years when Alvino had brought his new bride to this wild land north of the river—the hardships, the tragedies, the despair. He knew the secrets Ophelia guarded with a vicious obsession. He knew, but Luis de Leon had been sworn to secrecy decades ago, with a blood oath upon his immortal soul.

Ophelia was tired, distraught about Juan, and no longer interested in formalities. She nodded a curt greeting, but made no attempt to soften her tone. "How is my son?"

Luis stiffened. "I don't know yet. He's lost so much blood, it's a miracle that he's alive. He came around briefly and spoke to Lidia. That's encouraging."

She turned to Lidia. "Was he coherent?"

Lidia nodded and gave a weak smile. "He wanted to know if he was dead. Then he recognized me and asked for water."

"He needs to rest," Luis grumbled. "Rest and more rest, and we need to watch him all the time. We need to feed him broths to keep up his strength. If he wakes up, we should do nothing to excite him." He shot a sidewise look at Lidia. "No excitement whatsoever. He's done well so far, but it could turn at any moment."

Ophelia stepped forward to the bedside and looked down at her son. Shocked at the sight of his bloody, bandaged head, she put her hand to her mouth and sucked in her breath. Blood was seeping through the fresh linen, dripping down his cheeks. "Luis," she cried, lifting her eyes to meet his. "Luis! Can you save him for me?"

His look softened a little and he shrugged, reaching up to unroll one sleeve. "I don't know. I will try. Now, we should all keep very quiet. No noise."

"Yes," she replied, looking back down at Juan, "but I need a few minutes with him. Alone, please."

Luis unrolled his other sleeve, letting it dangle unbuttoned, then turned to Lidia and nodded toward the door. "Just for a few minutes, then he must rest quietly. Lidia, out."

They left, their passing causing the candles to flicker, and Luis gently closed the door behind them. Ophelia slipped into a chair beside the bed. She looked at every line on Juan's face and saw that he had been carefully washed and shaven. Reaching under the blanket, she found his hand and held it gently, rubbing her fingers against his. She saw the bandages on his arm and shoulder, then lifted the blanket to find hundreds of angry red eruptions from the cactus thorns all over his body. Some had blistered and oozed green pus, but she saw with satisfaction that these had been cleaned and treated with ointment, and were now only wet with fresh seepage.

Next, she slid her hand under his armpit, checking for fever. Placing two fingers on his throat, she found his pulse, and sat quietly, feeling the tenacious life barely moving there. His face looked so peaceful in sleep. She bent to kiss his cheek, her eyes suddenly filled with tears, and her nostrils flared a little, for she knew if he was awake she could never kiss him. He would not let her.

"This is all your fault," she whispered. "You think nothing can hurt you? Now maybe you'll listen to me, now..." She stopped, blinked the tears away, and slowly straightened up. Now, or ever, nothing would change. Juan's rebellious nature, his rejection of her world had been forged a long time ago.

It was a nightmare that haunted her dreams and hung like a massive weight upon her shoulders. When it entered her mind unawares, for she never thought about it purposefully, her stomach twisted in knots of fear, guilt, and revulsion. The memory blackened everything around it. Newly married, Ophelia had been raped in her ranch house by the leader of a passing band of renegades. The man had vanished, leaving behind a shattered, defiled young bride, crumpled on the floor, a pistol in her hand, wishing she had the courage to take her own life. Alvino had come home and found her naked in a tub of cold and bloody water, incoherent, babbling about needing new clothes, and his friend Luis de Leon had tended her, vowing to keep her secret, even after it became evident that she was pregnant. But whose child was it? Her husband's or that stinking deserter who had taken her, a fifteen-year-old bride? And so began her terrible nightmares of a secret so dark, so horrible that she trembled when the memory returned, unwelcome, unavoidable. No one must ever know, especially not Juan. She would rather die than have him doubt his parentage and know her shame. Even worse, it was not only the rape that gave her nightmares, it was also the unspeakable sin she committed afterward by abandoning him, so damning in a mother that she shut it out of her mind. Even if he was not Alvino's son, and as he grew older she thought maybe he was, the child had been innocent and deserved his mother's love. This is what haunted her.

"Nothing will change," she whispered. Alvino had rejected the boy, and, driven by his father's contempt and his mother's apathy, Juan had set his own path even as a child and lived by his own rules, whether or not they made sense. As he grew older, he became more rebellious. If she ordered him to stay sober, he drank for days until the *vaqueros* brought him home in the back of a wagon, wet and stinking from liquor, whores, and sweat. If she asked him to stay, he left for months and did not look back. He ignored everything she and her family had spent over a hundred years building, a life she wanted so desperately for him to be a part of. He had broken her heart every day of her life since he had come into the world, and she knew—in the depths of her soul she had no doubt—that he would break it every day until she died.

AFTER A FEW SILENT MINUTES, Ophelia traced the sign of the cross on Juan's face, kissed his forehead, and then slipped out of the room. In the hallway, she found Lidia leaning against the stucco wall, her eyes hollow from lack of sleep.

"No," Ophelia declared. "I will not permit you to do this, Lidia. You are to go to your room and sleep. Come along. I'll take you."

Lidia tried to protest, but the older woman would hear none of it. "I'll send Conchita in to watch him for a while," she said, "and then I'll sit with him myself tonight. And you'll sleep tonight, too—even if I have to come and watch you instead. Now what do you prefer? That I sit with you, or that I watch my son?"

She grasped Lidia's elbow and steered her down the hall to her bedroom.

"Ophelia, I can't sleep. I can't bear to think he might die."

They walked into Lidia's room, and Ophelia set about preparing the bed and putting out Lidia's nightgown. "He's not going to die, *gracias a Dios*. Your father has seen to that. But you surprised me, Lidia. I know you were fond of him once, but why this irrational devotion now? Is there something I should know?"

Lidia sank onto the bed, fingering the lacy nightgown. Ophelia waited a moment, then began to undo the stays of Lidia's dress. Helping Lidia into her nightgown, she then led her to the dresser, sat her down, and began brushing her hair. "It seems the older you children get, the more childish," she said, trying to smile. "In the morning, I will personally supervise your bath."

Lidia reached up and grabbed Ophelia's hand, clutching it and the hairbrush in a tight grip. The two women looked at each other in the mirror.

"When I saw him shot like that," Lidia began, "so bloody I could scarcely recognize him, I thought he was dead. My stomach went hollow. My knees went weak." She turned to face Ophelia. "I thought it was over between us long ago. I was convinced he was wrong for me, that I didn't love him, that I never had loved him. But when I saw him, I—what I was thinking and what I was feeling were completely different. Ophelia, what's happening? I cannot love him. My father won't permit it, and Juan does not love me anymore."

Ophelia reached up with her other hand, removed the hairbrush from Lidia's grip, and stroked the girl's hair back with her hand. "I don't think it means anything, child. You're a sensitive young woman, and even though Juan is not your betrothed, you're still fond of him. Our families have always been close. Perhaps you even think of him as a brother. Isn't that so?"

"I don't feel toward him like a brother."

"Then what do you feel?"

"I don't know," she turned in her chair and faced the mirror again. "I don't know. But not like a brother."

A flicker of hope warmed Ophelia, bringing a smile to her lips. Perhaps some good would come out of this after all. "Let's concentrate on getting him well," she said, "and then we can try to sort this out. All right? You need sleep."

She helped the girl into bed, covered her with a light cotton sheet, then walked to the window and opened the shutters. The warm evening breeze washed in, blowing the curtains around Ophelia and cooling the thin film of perspiration on her face and scalp. The candle flickered, throwing shadows on the walls. Returning to the bed, she sat on the edge and looked down at Lidia, noting her furrowed brow.

"Sleep will make everything clearer, my angel." She reached down and rubbed her fingers on the girl's forehead, then slipped her hand down and closed the eyes that looked up with such confusion. She left her hand there, gently resting it so that the warmth of her palm would soothe Lidia's tired face.

"Sleep now," she whispered.

After a few minutes, Lidia's deep breathing told Ophelia that she had at last succumbed. The older woman pulled herself up, blew out the candle, and walked to the door with only the moonlight from the window to guide her.

Outside the door, she found Conchita. "Go and sit with Juan," she ordered quietly. "I need to speak with the de Leons."

Conchita placed a rough, brown hand on Ophelia's elbow. "Oh, señora, is Juan going to die?" Her voice wavered. "I love him like a son."

Ophelia looked into her servant's weathered face and saw dread in her misty eyes. Juan *had* been a son to her—for five long years, Conchita had been the only mother he had known.

Placing her hands on Conchita's broad, round shoulders, Ophelia gave her a tiny shake. "He's not going to die, for heaven's sake. Now come on, I need you to sit with him for a few minutes. I must speak with our hosts. Then I'll come in, too."

Ophelia had always thought that Conchita's eyes did not quite fit the rest of her. She had thick, large hands and arms, a dark Indian face, and a heavy body. But her eyes were small, bright, alert, and unusually pretty.

She settled Conchita on a chair in Juan's room, then walked to the main part of the house, where she found Luis and Martina de Leon in the parlor. Martina was drinking sweet, hot chocolate with cinnamon, and Luis was pouring himself a brandy.

"Ah, Ophelia," he called as she approached. "Would you like some brandy?"

"Actually, yes," she replied. "Just a little, to soothe my nerves. It's been a difficult day."

Martina fidgeted in her seat. Ophelia knew she was bubbling over with things to say, but her husband must speak first.

"He's very seriously wounded," he said. "It's very bad. There's nothing much we can do now except wait, keep his bandages clean, and watch him. It's in God's hands now." He handed her a small glass of brandy.

Ophelia crossed herself. "It's always in God's hands." She sipped the brandy, and shot Luis an even look. "What happened?"

Luis grimaced. "All we know is that *Rinches* brought him to us, shot up. They claimed that bandits did it, but I'm not sure I believe them."

"*Rinches?* Why would they bother?" she asked. "Thank God they did, but why? And if they shot him themselves, why would they try to save him? Why bring him here?"

Luis paced over to his gun rack and stared up at the rifles, shotguns, pistols, and muskets that covered almost the entire wall. "The Ranger captain is named Starr. He's camped just outside our gates, across the road from your *vaqueros*. The bandits they apprehended killed an American and stole his mules, and they asked that we hold the animals here for the Army. Ordinarily, these days I'd want nothing to do with Rangers. But on your behalf and in thanks for bringing Juan to us, I agreed."

Ophelia sighed, feeling a sudden wave of weariness. She had traveled from the Santa Alicia Ranch to the de Leon ranch in just over seven hours using the military highway and borrowing fresh horses from ranches along the way.

"Of course, Luis," she replied. "You did the right thing. I want to meet this Ranger captain." The brandy was making her cheeks hot.

"He's leaving in the morning, but I'm sure you'll meet him. You see, he says he wants to question Juan. Impossible! I'm fighting to keep him alive, and this fool wants to question him. You can help me persuade him to just leave. Take his stinking Rangers with him and just go."

"Question Juan about what?"

Luis shrugged. "*No sé. Esta loco.*"

Ophelia sipped at her brandy, noticing Martina's increased fidgeting, now bordering on apoplexy. Martina was a large, horsy-looking woman, the complete opposite of Lidia's petite loveliness. Luis was short, with a receding hairline and a round, pale face. From the hips up, he had the torso of a large man, but his legs were short. He had the appearance of someone who had been constructed from two different men—one large, the other small. Ophelia had often wondered how these two oddly shaped people had produced such an exquisite jewel. Perhaps Lidia took after one of her grandparents.

"Lidia seems to be taking it hard, isn't she?" Ophelia asked.

"*Ahí Dios, sí,*" Martina finally burst out. "I don't know what's come over her. I've never seen her so concerned about anyone, not even when Luis had that fever last year. You would think she still had feelings for Juan."

Luis grunted. "It wouldn't matter if she did. She's betrothed now to Alfredo Jaramillo of San Antonio de Bejar."

Ophelia froze. After a moment, she set her empty glass down and stared at Don de Leon. "Lidia is betrothed?"

"Yes!" Martina wailed, her hands fluttering, "but she's so unhappy about it—"

Don de Leon interrupted. "It doesn't matter she's unhappy."

"Oh Luis, how can you say that? Our only daughter…how can you say it doesn't matter? Don't you want her to be happy?"

He stomped around the couch, poured himself another brandy, and threw his head back, swallowing it in one gulp. "*Basta!* We've talked about it until I'm sick of it. She must marry. I've made the arrangements. It's settled."

"I don't mean to meddle," said Ophelia, "but I'd like to ask a question."

He grunted, squared his shoulders, and turned to face her. "Ophelia, we've known each other too long to mince words. We are all very tired. Whatever you have to say, just say it."

Ophelia nodded. It was true—she had never required permission to speak her mind. "What if Lidia still loves Juan?"

The room grew silent. The women looked at Luis, and he looked down at his empty brandy glass.

"It's too late," he finally replied. "I know that you two want them to marry, but it's too late. I've made the arrangements. Besides, I've never believed that Juan and Lidia are suited for each other."

Martina started to protest, to draw again the rosy, imaginary picture that she and Ophelia had painted in their heads together—how their children would calm each other, grow together, and somehow overcome their differences.

Luis cut her short. "Stop dreaming, Martina. Ophelia, it's much too late. Besides, I know my daughter. I'm not convinced that all this sudden concern for Juan isn't just her way of trying to get out of the betrothal. If it is, it won't work. It's quite a show—staying up all night, crying, no doubt telling you she loves him. She's even got you tricked into believing her."

As Ophelia blinked, Martina gasped. *"No es possible!"*

Her husband continued. "Think about your daughter, Martina, and then tell me it isn't possible. How many times has she ruined our plans for her? I'm sure she's in there right now, watching him, trying to convince us that that fairy tale is true."

"Luis," Ophelia replied, "I think Lidia's concern is very real. I think she's confused by it. And, no, she isn't with Juan right now. I put her to bed. Conchita is watching him."

Martina wrung her hands. *"Oh, gracias a Dios!* I couldn't even get her to go to her room. Now she can rest."

Ophelia continued to stare at Luis, but he avoided her eyes, gazing instead at his empty glass. Finally he looked up, and their eyes locked. Her face formed a question, a question about the deep and ancient secret they shared concerning Juan, but Luis would not answer her. Something passed between them then—an accusation, a denial, a lament, a retreat. Ophelia closed her eyes. She understood. The rape. It did not matter about the betrothal. In Luis' eyes, Juan would never be good enough for Lidia.

"Well, it's irrelevant anyway," he finally said, turning away. "I'm taking her to San Antonio in four weeks to meet her betrothed. She will marry him. It's disgraceful that she hasn't married yet, with her beauty and her dowry. Completely disgraceful, and I won't have it! She had every chance to select a husband herself. Now, she will marry Alfredo Jaramillo, and that is the last I will say on this subject!"

The women fell silent. Luis poured himself more brandy. He offered Ophelia another glass, but she ignored him.

"I must return to Juan," she snapped, her words so icy cold they might have smashed into a thousand pieces as they struck his ears. "Is there anything I should do for him?"

"No," he replied, blinking in the face of her fury, then downing his brandy. "If his breathing changes or his fever gets worse, awaken me. Otherwise, I'll check him early in the morning."

They rose, said their polite goodnights, and then Ophelia walked back down the hall. When she entered Juan's room, she found Conchita kneeling on the hard, smooth-tiled floor beside the bed, a rosary with ruby red beads strung through her fingers, her lips moving silently in prayer. On the bed, Juan had turned his face turned toward the door. His eyes were closed, his hand lay on Conchita's shoulder.

Chapter 3
Starr

TOM STARR pulled his horse through a break in the brush, edging past the clumps of prickly nopal cacti onto the de Leon ranch road. He mounted, then pushed his head back to breathe deep the moist, sweet scent of the blooming wildflowers. The morning had dawned crisp and clear in a vast wash of orange sky, damp from the violent thunderstorm that had swept through the valley before sunrise.

All over the bushy landscape, field mice and chipmunks hustled in and out of their burrows, turning over loose brown leaves and branches as they looked for nuts and mesquite beans. White doves and speckled quail also ran among the thorny bushes, cooing and flapping their wings, and hawks soared overhead, riding high on the early morning drafts. Occasionally one would swoop down, scream, and help itself to one of the small furry creatures scurrying below. Starr could see heavy smoke from the *vaquero's* camp across the wet road, where the Mexicans were burning green, wet mesquite for their morning fires. He also heard mourning doves cooing melancholy notes from the trees along the river, which was half a mile away.

The Rangers were excited. A rider had come into camp at dawn with orders from Major Roberts to report to Fort Brown immediately for redeployment. This could mean a chance to take part in some real fighting before the war ended. The men led their horses out of the camp single file, except for the Don, who rode his. The Don was unable to walk because he had lost his boots playing monte with the *vaqueros* the night before.

The Rangers had sat around the fire this morning at breakfast and listened to his heated explanations. "They cheat," he had cried. "They try to confuse me, then they bet up real high, more money than I got."

Uriah had grinned as he sipped his tin cup of scalding black coffee. "Now, Don," he'd said, "why didn't you quit when you ran out of money? Why'd you bet your boots? What the hell kind of a scout are you? You gonna go barefoot?"

Ambrose had jumped in, too. "I'll be damned if I'm going to have a barefoot Meskin scouting for us."

The Don had shot a pleading look at Starr. "I find some boots. I be all right. I can still scout, *Capitán*. Really, I can. You see! And I still fight real good, just like I been doing."

The Rangers had laughed. "Yeah, Don," said Jeremiah, "you been fightin' real good."

"Let's go," Starr cut in, throwing his coffee into the fire. Starr figured the boots were the Don's own concern. He felt sure the old thief would be well provisioned before they got too far down the road.

THE INTENSE SMOKE from the *vaquero* camp drifted across the road like a fog, carrying the smells of fresh corn tortillas, coffee, and beans. Mounting their horses, the Rangers rode a few yards, then turned into the ranch courtyard and rode up to the door, where they sat their horses and watched Don de Leon emerge from the big house.

Starr tipped his hat. "*Buenos días.*" His Spanish was smooth, rich, and only slightly anglicized.

"*Buenos Días, Capitán* Starr. Are you leaving us now?"

"We are. Thank you for the food and for handling the mules for us. Now we'll talk to the Santos boy and be on our way."

Don de Leon stiffened. "Why do you insist on talking to him, *Capitán?* He is much too weak. He only stays conscious for a few minutes. I'm trying very hard to save his life. I cannot allow you to question him, perhaps aggravate him. He needs rest and quiet."

"Yessir, I know all that. Now if you'll lead me to him, I'll ask him two, maybe three questions."

"It is impossible, *Capitán* Starr."

Starr felt his blood rise as he listened to this back-talking Mexican. "Señor de Leon," he said, "we can do this easy or we can do it another way. But it's going to be done."

Don de Leon bristled. "This is my home. This is my ranch. I have extended you my hospitality. Surely you wouldn't attack us after we've treated you as a guest. That would be the height of barbarity, *Capitán* Starr!"

The Rangers shifted in their saddles.

"We aren't much for Mexican social niceties," Starr said. "Now I'm coming inside."

Before he could dismount, however, Ophelia and Martina stepped out of the house and walked up behind Don de Leon.

"You're the Ranger who saved my son's life?" Ophelia asked.

Starr cocked his head and pulled off his hat, looking her over. This could only be Doña Ophelia Santos, the blue-blooded Mexican *patrona*. He saw the fair skin, the oval hazel eyes that coolly returned his gaze. Her face was calm and elegant, with a hint of a smile. He guessed she was somewhere in her early forties, and she was indeed beautiful. Looking at her face, he could not deny that the woman's reputation was well deserved. She carried herself with authority, and her presence had immediately transfixed everyone in the yard. She still wore a widow's black—he bent his head down a little at the thought.

"My name is Tom Starr, ma'am. Texas Rangers. We found your son along the river, saw him shot by bandits." He plopped his hat back on his head. He could see her face soften a little at the sound of his Spanish. "We chased them, killed one, lost one. They killed an American named James Cornwell. I aim to talk to your son, Señora Santos, to see what he knows about it."

Starr could see Ophelia watching his face as he spoke. He felt the penetration of her eyes almost physically, as if she were reading his mind by the set of his jaw and the tone of his voice.

"You think he killed this American?" she asked.

Martina de Leon gasped.

"Not saying he did or didn't," Starr replied. "But if he's awake, I need to find out."

"He is awake, *Capitán* Starr, but he is very weak. Don de Leon believes he could die if he is in any way agitated. And although I owe you a tremendous debt for saving his life, I cannot agree to you taking it back."

Starr felt his men making small preparations behind him. Ambrose leaned forward in his saddle as Uriah casually pointed the barrel of his rifle at Don de Leon. Jim, Floyd, Sam, Frenchy, Jeremiah, Uriah, Ambrose— how many times had Starr seen action with these men? Together they had battled Comanche, Kiowa, Mexicans, and rogue Texans. They had learned to think as one. There was no need to exchange words or even glances. Even though the old man and two women facing them were no real threat, they reacted instinctively, efficiently.

Just then, they heard men riding through the front gate. It was Tomas with his *vaqueros*, the hooves of their snorting horses thudding on the wet gravel. They slowly circled the yard, their huge sombreros shading their brown faces from the morning sun, until they had positioned themselves on the Rangers' flank. Tomas signaled his men to hold their positions, then dismounted and strode to Ophelia's side, his large Mexican spurs clattering out a ringing chime as he walked.

Mingo pushed to the head of the line where Tomas had been. The Rangers, faced with twenty armed and mounted *vaqueros*, seemed unaffected, but Starr knew that they were watching him. He made a simple gesture, and they spread out in a thin line, drew their Colts, and waited, though the barefooted Don stuck close to Starr. Starr knew that his eight Rangers, armed with Colts, could fire at least forty-eight times without reloading, and they were all deadly shots. Most of the Rangers carried two Colts, adding to their firepower. The *vaqueros*, on the other hand, were cowmen, experts with ropes, horses, and knives. They did not lack for courage, but their guns were a motley collection of pistols, ancient smoothbore muskets, and shotguns they called *escopetas*, none especially accurate and all good for only one shot before reloading. The eight Rangers possessed more firepower than the twenty *vaqueros*. But Starr was used to these odds. The Mexicans he fought were always incredulous that so few Rangers would challenge their far greater numbers, but the fact that the Rangers nearly always won any encounter reinforced the carefully cultivated reputation they had earned among the Mexicans—that these bearded, grim-faced, superbly armed Texans knew no fear. They were cruelly efficient killing demons. Their nickname, *Diablo Tejanos*, was well deserved.

The two groups of men glared at each other across the twelve yards that separated them.

Starr looked at Ophelia, his eyes two thin slits under the shadow of his hat, his jaw set like stone. "Ma'am, do I get to talk to El Gallo?"

"No," she shot back. Then she stepped forward between the two lines. Tomas seemed aghast, scrambling after her, but she threw him a look and gestured for him to wait.

"Ophelia," Tomas protested, "they kill women."

"Then let them kill me if they want." She whirled and faced Starr, her fists on her hips and her eyes blazing. "The great Texas Rangers, fierce men, one and all. One man can kill a dozen of his enemy, especially an unarmed woman!"

Starr turned his face toward her, but her presence did not matter anymore. Before him were twenty men he might need to kill, and he could feel the anticipation of his fellow Rangers. Their horses felt it, too, for they shifted and snorted, their heads bobbing, their ears pricked up. Starr saw the fear in the eyes of the young Mexicans. Among them were a few old Dons, gray-bearded men shielding their dark weathered faces with their sombreros, their eyes heavy-lidded and shifting. It would be too easy to kill them. It always was.

A sudden blur of yellow moved from the house toward Ophelia and hovered there. Starr pried his eyes away from the *vaqueros* and forced himself to look, to focus on the movement. Another woman now stood beside Ophelia in an exquisite yellow gown. Olive-skinned, she stood with her thin arms crossed, chin in the air, hair falling back and then blowing over her face in the morning breeze. It was Lidia.

Starr felt a wave of electricity jolt his chest awake and flow through his body, growing in intensity as it went. He took a deep breath and stared at her angelic face, her long hair, the haughty look she fixed him with. She was like a vision, a hallucination. He had to remind himself to breathe again, to remember there was a fight to be won. Martina de Leon screamed something at Lidia in Spanish, and Don de Leon shouted something else, but he blocked them out. He hesitated, transfixed by the young girl standing beside Ophelia in the yard, her feet set, her beautiful eyes defiant. It was a sight to behold.

For a moment, no one moved or spoke. The warm morning breeze whipped at their clothes, and the women's skirts flapped. The sun's rays were already stinging the Rangers' faces. Then, Starr thought of a good enough reason not to shoot.

"Well," Starr said finally, "I reckon I don't want to get the two prettiest women in Texas killed, boys." The Rangers cursed in unison, holstered their Colts, and stood down. Starr knew they were humiliated. He knew it because he felt a touch of confused humiliation himself.

To the Rangers, defeat was inconceivable, and they rarely backed down from a fight. Starr's words could drive his men to elect a new captain, but he could not take the chance that Lidia, this beautiful creature, might get hurt. He dismounted, to his surprise, somewhat unsteadily, and approached Ophelia. Out of the corner of one eye, he could see Tomas hasten to draw near.

"Tomas," he said without looking directly at him or even breaking his stride, "you come one step closer and I'll kill you where you stand."

Ophelia threw up her hand, and Tomas halted, his face clouded with obvious indignation. He stood ten feet from them, swaying on his bowed legs, his hand opening and closing near his pistol.

Starr was now steps away from Ophelia. "Now I know why Sam Houston wanted to marry you, ma'am," he said.

"Sam Houston is a drunken fool," Ophelia replied, "but my husband died by his side. We are friends."

"I know that, ma'am. It occurred to me that he'd take exception if you got hurt in this fight." He glanced at Tomas. "And regardless of what some may think, we Rangers are not in the habit of killing women."

At last he turned to Lidia, who resembled an exotic cat, wound tight and ready to pounce on her prey. "You two must be kin," he said to her.

Lidia looked at him with such contempt that he turned back to Ophelia. "What about your son?"

"He should be strong enough in a week or so."

Starr scratched his whiskers. "I got orders this morning to report back to Fort Brown. We'll pick this up later."

"Perhaps."

"Good day, ma'am." He tipped his hat, then turned to Lidia and smiled. "Much obliged for that beef last night, Miss Lidia. I look forward to returning the favor some day."

"For the beef, you are welcome, *Capitán* Starr. But I need nothing from you. Goodbye." Lidia whirled and marched back toward the house, her parents fussing after her.

Her departure caused Starr an immediate pang of despair. He furrowed his brow and told himself to get his mind straight. This was insane. Nevertheless, he stared after her, watching her every movement all the way to the door. When she was gone, he turned to Ophelia. "She always like that?"

Ophelia lifted her eyebrows, tilted her head back slightly, and replied, "Good day, *Capitán* Starr."

T OMAS SAT HIS HORSE on a small rise and watched a thin plume of smoke rise from the thicket along the river. Earlier in the day, he had tracked the Rangers from the de Leon ranch until they stopped for the night and set up camp. He observed them as Starr sent the Ranger who walked with a limp and that ridiculous Don Pepino, not surprisingly now fitted with stolen boots, scouting eastward along the river.

Tomas put his horse forward, cutting slowly through the thick brush, finding the game paths, and circling around, until the hot breeze that barely stirred the listless wilted grasses carried smoke into his face. He could hear the noise of the camp, but he also knew they could not hear him as easily. Soon he spotted their sentry, Ranger Carson, and saw that he had circled in the opposite direction and was busy urinating on a huge clump of cacti.

Stone-faced, Tomas spurred his horse and drifted into the camp, watching as the Rangers turned toward him and froze where they stood. He stopped his horse, pulled tobacco out of his leather vest's pocket, and said, very casually, "*Buenas tardes,* señores Rangers."

Starr cursed. "How'd he get in here? Carson!"

Carson came crashing through the brush. "I never saw him, Cap'n, I swear!"

Tomas watched them, noting with satisfaction the surprise and rage that showed on their faces. He dropped the reins and squeezed his knees against the nervous horse's flanks to calm him. Rolling a corn shuck cigarette, he twisted both ends and stuck it in his mouth, all the while keeping the Rangers in his peripheral vision. He knew one of them would move toward his gun, perhaps all of them.

Frenchy stepped forward. "It's that Tomas fella from the de Leon ranch." Without further comment, he slid his Colt out of its holster and fired. But he missed because Tomas had anticipated the move, uncoiled his bullwhip from the saddle horn, and knocked the gun out of the Ranger's hand with a thunderous snap so loud it sent quail flapping and squawking out of the brush.

"That was not friendly," Tomas said in English, rolling his whip back up.

Starr kicked Frenchy's Colt back over to him.

Holding his hand and staring at it, Frenchy seemed to be trying to figure out how his gun got on the ground.

Starr glanced up sideways at Tomas, as the final, fading yellow rays of sun slanted in over the mesquite trees and onto the Ranger's face. "You want to get down off that horse? Or you want to die in the saddle?"

Tomas shrugged. "I do everything from this saddle except piss, shit, and fuck. It would suit me to die from it, too." He smiled. Yes, it would be all right to die, if it came to it. Besides his bullwhip, he had two pistols in his belt. He had his rifle, a knife in his boot, and his machete. He thought he might be able to get one or two Rangers, at least, starting with this *hijo de la chingada*, Tom Starr. He saw Starr's face redden. Tomas listened to the distant doves cooing in the gathering dusk, conscious that this might be the last time in this life he heard their soothing song.

"You trailed us. Why?" Starr demanded.

Lighting his cigarette, Tomas took a deep drag and watched them from the shadow of his sombrero. "There are no beautiful women between us now, *Capitán* Starr," he said. "This morning you ordered me to stop where I was or you'd kill me. You didn't even look at me. You insulted me, and I did nothing because of Doña Ophelia. But now I'm here. Alone."

"Jesus," Uriah muttered from across the campfire. "He's calling you out, Cap'n. This greaser's got balls. Ain't too bright, but he's got spunk. Want me to plug him?"

Starr waved him off, keeping his gaze on Tomas. Tomas could see that Starr's expression had changed a little. There seemed to be a spark of interest in his eyes. The other Rangers also seemed to be moving differently now. They started holstering their guns and standing around, like boys waiting for a cock fight.

"That right, Tomas?" Starr asked. "You followed us to call me out?"

Tomas nodded. He was trying to stay calm, but the morning's episode had stung his pride, and it was all he could do now to keep from separating Starr's head and neck with his machete. But the challenge had been issued, and the other Rangers had not shot him yet, so he was pleased. So far.

"Well, now," Starr said. "Much obliged there, Tomas. Most Mexicans would get even by sneaking around and trying to stick me when it's pitch black and I'm flat drunk."

"I don't give a *chingada* about any of that. I just want you." He could see all the other Rangers grinning. He knew they thought he was as good as dead, and he also knew they relished the entertainment they would get in watching Starr dispatch him. He did not care. He would deal with them as best he could after he finished with their captain.

"All right," Starr replied, smiling. "What you got in mind?"

Tomas shrugged. "I said the challenge. You choose a weapon."

"I got my weapon right here," he said, sliding his hand down and caressing his Colt. "And all you got to do is get down off that damn horse."

Tomas nodded. "Use it, and I will use mine. But I won't get off my horse. You get on yours."

As Starr smiled again, Tomas could sense his building interest. It was like play to him. "Brush is too dense along here," Starr said. "Let's do it here in camp. Just climb on down and pick yourself a spot."

Tomas flicked his cigarette at the Ranger campfire. "There is a little valley half a mile from here, on the other side of the river. Wide open. We can go there. Or we can fight here, in the brush, in the river, in camp. But I'm staying on my horse."

He was annoyed that Starr did not seem to understand. It was well known that *vaqueros* considered most tasks that required one to dismount as unworthy. Certainly, fighting and dying were things worthy of being done on horseback. But Starr seemed wary, and Tomas thought he might be concerned an ambush could await them if they rode out to that valley. They stared at each other, apparently at an impasse.

Sam stood up and looked at the opponents. "You boys want to eat something first?" he asked.

The fight was taking a while to develop, and Tomas could see what remained of the de Leon beef roasting in the fire, sending off a delicious smell. A black pot of pinto beans with a slab of salt pork simmered next to it, and the coffee was boiling.

"Starting to get dark," Starr said, looking up at Tomas. Tomas knew that Rangers did not like to look up at a man. "What say we eat some grub, bunk down, and take this up again at dawn?"

"Señor, again you slap my face. You dismiss my challenge until the morning?" Tomas watched Starr scratch his whiskers. Mexican pride was apparently beyond his comprehension.

"No," the Ranger said after a minute, "I ain't dismissing nothing. We can shoot it out right here. On foot. Ain't enough room for two horses to manoeuver. But I ain't going to no valley in the dark. You hungry, you can eat with us, sort of as a last meal to honor your challenge. Seems more decent than making you pitch camp out by yourself to wait for morning."

Tomas considered this. He heard at least some measure of respect building in Starr's voice. The edge was off Tomas' anger, just in the simple act of talking it out, in showing them he did not fear them. The Ranger captain seemed to be in earnest, and the smell of coffee and beef from the fire was making his empty stomach growl.

"I will eat," he said as he dismounted.

Tomas and the Rangers gathered around the campfire, devoured the food, then sat back and sipped the scalding black coffee as the sky turned blackish blue.

The full moon, a huge mud-orange ball, struggled to free itself from the horizon.

"Comanche moon," muttered Ambrose Bradshaw.

"Also bandito moon," said Tomas. "On nights like this, bandits raid Doña Ophelia's cattle."

The Rangers kept silent for a while, perhaps feeling as odd about his presence among them as he felt, then Uriah Lee leaned forward. "What do you do if you catch them?"

"We hang them."

Uriah laughed. "Where in this God-forsaken *brasada* you gonna find a tree high enough to hang them, unless you ride all the way down to the river?"

"We use the Mexican way. Put four ropes around the man's neck, then ride our horses in four different directions."

The Rangers seemed sobered by this news. "Seems to me," Frenchy commented, "that might yank the man's head clean off. Don't it get messy?"

Tomas sipped his coffee and leaned back against his saddle. Before speaking, he pulled out his tobacco and rolled himself another cigarette. "The horses are trained. Stop after they feel the first tug. Doesn't take much to break a man's neck. But I have seen worse. The Apache will skin a man, burn his balls, gouge out his eyes—all while he is still alive—to steal his power, his medicine. They won't do this to a woman. A woman they will rape and then kill."

"You ever fight Comanche?" Sam asked. "You think Apaches 're bad, you should fight Comanche. Comanche take you, you'll wish you'd shot yourself first. We never leave our wounded on the ground when we fight Comanche. It's better to shoot them your own self if you can't carry them off."

Tomas nodded. "*Tiro de gracia*. The Comanche sometimes come all the way down here to steal horses. Leave nothing alive behind them, but at least they do not eat you. I hear of a tribe up along the *Tejas* coast that will eat you alive if they get you."

Starr sipped his coffee and nodded. "Karankawa. Up along the fever coast. Sorriest men in creation. I can't see no reason the Lord ever made them."

Uriah grunted, leaned an arm back on his saddle, and spit into the fire. "They took a chunk out of me, once. Had me trussed up good, and they was sort of crying around the campfire. I mean they was bawling real tears. Then one of them came over and sliced a chunk of my butt off and took it back to the fire. I watched them cook it." He shook his head, almost contemplatively. "Strange people."

Tomas was stunned, and when he looked around at the faces of the Rangers, he could tell they were, too. This was something they evidently did not know about their comrade.

"*Dios mío,*" he said. "So it is true? Such men exist?"

"Well, them particular men don't exist no more. While they was chewing on my butt, I chewed my way through their rawhide rope, made a jump for my gear, and sent them all to hell."

The men were silent. Tomas stared in awe at Uriah, pondering what it must be like to watch part of yourself being cooked and eaten. He shuddered. "I do not understand," he said. "Why they were crying before they ate you?"

Uriah spat into the fire again. "You know, I've wondered about that my own self. Near as I can figure, they was too happy. Never in their entire man-eating lives had they caught a man who looked so juicy, and their mouths was watering at the thought that soon they'd taste me. Then their eyes started watering, too."

The Rangers burst out laughing, and Tomas smiled, nodding slowly. "They were too happy. But, still, I do not understand. With all the meat they could choose, why did they cut off a piece of your butt?"

"Well, it's real simple there, Tomas," Uriah replied, rolling himself a cigarette. He ran his tongue along the edge of the paper, then reached into the fire, looking for an ember to light it with. He found one, then slowly moved it up and lit his cigarette. The twig made a flaming arc as he flung it away. He puffed twice and looked around the fire at the expectant faces. Tomas knew he was stalling to build up the suspense. Finally Uriah blew a puff of smoke into the air and said, "The Karankawa think us Rangers are fierce and tough, and that our strength is in our butts."

There was a general groan around the campfire.

"It's true," Uriah continued. "Way they figure it, how else could we ride so good and shoot so good if we didn't have good butts?"

"What's your butt got to do with it?" Jeremiah protested.

Uriah looked offended. "Well, you got to steady yourself while you're shootin', don't you? You got to have a good steady butt to do that."

Now there was even more groaning, and Tomas shook his head. "I have only one more question," he said. "Will you show us your butt to prove your story?"

Uriah shot him a look of indignation. "I reckon you don't believe me, señor. Why, I should call you out."

Tomas nodded, spilling out the coffee that had grown cold in his tin cup. "I see."

"And besides, I ain't in the habit of dropping my trousers in the company of men."

The Rangers winked and grinned at each other. "Thank God and Sam Houston for that," quipped Frenchy, then threw his head back and brayed, as did the others, drowning out Uriah's shouts of indignation.

TOMAS ROSE BEFORE DAWN, when the eastern sky was just beginning to glow a pale yellow-orange. The cool morning breeze carried the sweet scent of mesquite and the dewy earth. He turned his boots over, checking for scorpions, then pulled them on, then stumbled past the sleeping Rangers toward a small stand of mesquite trees at the edge of camp to relieve himself. There he found Starr, pissing on a clump of cacti. Tomas paused, then moved forward a few more feet so they were side by side. For a minute they pissed together.

Neither man looked at the other, neither spoke. It did not seem appropriate to greet a man you were intent on killing, at least it didn't in the soft darkness before the dawn. Tomas could see a bit of steam rising as their urine soaked into the parched earth. The morning was quiet, so quiet that they could hear the gentle movement of the water along the banks and the flapping of a hawk's wings across the river.

They buttoned up and headed back toward camp, but Starr paused just past the mesquites. He pulled his hat down on his forehead a bit and turned to face Tomas.

"You still calling me out?" he asked in a low voice. It seemed to fit the quietness of the morning.

Tomas whispered back, "I still intend to kill you." He watched Starr scratch his stubby whiskers and ponder it, surprised perhaps at his stubbornness. Tomas did not believe in letting things go, or easily forgiving wrongs. This was the same stubborn, mule-headed, obstinate streak that most people who came to Texas seemed to share, but it was most prevalent among the white settlers. Tomas had issued the challenge, and now it had to stand, but the sting of his embarrassment had worn off during the night because he had eaten and slept in the Ranger camp.

"I'll kill you sure, Tomas," Starr said. "You seem like a good hand, a regular sort. Doña Ophelia's gonna need you bad, you know, with all this war and such. And Miss Lidia wouldn't much like it if I killed you. Why don't you just ride on out?"

Tomas was surprised by Starr's mention of Lidia. "Why don't you ride?"

"Hell, it's my camp!"

Tomas shook his head. So that was the problem. Captain Starr had accidentally let it slip. Now it made sense—the backing down at the de Leon ranch, the hesitation to fight him in the camp. The Ranger captain had feelings for Lidia. Tomas looked sideways at him. May the blessed Virgin bless him and have pity on him. He was going to need it.

The sun was beginning to paint the clouds on the horizon a faint yellow. As they walked back to camp, the other Rangers stumbled past them toward the mesquite stand to pee.

Sam Brennan had a pot of coffee boiling, and soon Frenchy was mashing some beans and mixing in fried salt pork. Frenchy kept sneaking glances at Tomas, always keeping him in view, but Tomas ignored him. Each man in camp walked out into the brush and fired his pistols into the dirt until they were empty, then reloaded them with fresh, dry powder.

"Why don't you shoot this stinking greaser and let's move on, Cap'n?" Frenchy growled, kicking a rock at Tomas.

Leaning back against his saddle, Tomas reflected on how men with generally mean dispositions seemed even meaner in the morning, when they were stiff from sleeping on the ground, sore from a full bladder, and hungry. "Maybe you want to fight in your *capitán*'s place?" he shot back.

"Hell, I don't believe in duels. A man needs killing, I kill him right off. No need to play-act at it—" He stopped talking because just in the instant he had looked away, Tomas had drawn his knife and brought the tip to a point just above his Adams apple. One second Tomas was sitting against his saddle on the ground, the next he was standing and looking up at him, his black eyes gleaming in the slanting yellow rays of sun.

"I can kill that way, too," Tomas said.

"By God! By God, Cap'n," Jim protested, "that's enough. We can't allow it. You going to shoot this little rooster before he sticks us all with that blade?"

Starr was smiling. "Frenchy, you can pretty much see it won't do to insult this fellow. Eat up, then go unhobble the horses." He turned to the other Rangers. "Let's all eat up. Then we can ride over to that valley with Tomas and get this over with. We need to get down the river to Fort Brown directly."

The Rangers grumbled, but they moved. Tomas was still holding the knife to Frenchy's throat, staring into the Ranger's eyes, when the sound of hoofbeats came rolling across the river.

Jeremiah called from the perimeter of the camp, "Riders coming, Cap'n, sounds like two, other side of the river."

"Tomas," Starr commanded, "put your knife away before one of these boys shoots you." He looked around. "Two riders. Might be Floyd and the Don."

Tomas listened. "It is your men," he said, lowering his knife and slipping it back in his boot. "I recognize the gait of Pepino's horse. He favors his right foreleg, probably a loose shoe. That idiot Pepino would never notice."

Starr poured Tomas another cup of coffee and handed it to him. "What? You don't think much of our guide?"

"He is a traitor. He would have been hanged long ago, but everybody thinks he will get you all killed sooner or later, so they leave him alone."

Starr grunted, and the Rangers sat back down on their pallets, waiting for the riders to cross the river. Moments later, Floyd and the Don rode into camp, their horses lathered and snorting from a hard ride. Dismounting, the Don headed directly for the food. Floyd limped over to Starr.

"Saw bandits, Cap'n. About ten miles down-river, just crossing over to the other side. Must be about twenty, heading into Mexico. Got about eighty head of wild Santa Alicia cattle."

Starr turned to Tomas, the shadow of a hawk racing briefly across the Ranger's face. "We're going to have to put this off, Tomas."

Pushing his sombrero back from his forehead, Tomas nodded and approached the Ranger captain. His bowed legs scratched against a cacti clump topped by a prickly red pear. "*Capitán* Starr," he said, "I will ride with you."

SURROUNDED by the dry thorny tangle that Mexicans called *la brasada*, Timo Martinez slumped in his saddle in the morning sun, his chin resting on his chest. His sombrero protected his face from the sting of the early morning sun, and its shade cooled his head. His hands lay crossed on the saddle horn, the reins looped casually around his fingers. He had one leg pulled up and hooked over the horn of his saddle. He breathed deeply, inhaling the dry mesquite-scented morning air. Except for the occasional chirp of a distant bird, all was silent.

His scarred and battered mare also seemed to be asleep. Head lowered, she rested one hoof. The biting black flies ignored the halfhearted swishes of her tail.

Both man and horse were covered with the scratches, bruises, and cuts common to those who worked *la brasada*. Along the horse's knees were swollen lumps where mesquite thorns festered, and dried blood streaked her flanks and legs. Timo was in no better shape. His shirtsleeves were torn to shreds, and large pieces of his red bandanna had been lost to the fierce entanglements of brush choking most of Doña Ophelia's Santa Alicia ranch. Like all the *vaqueros* who worked wild cattle in the brush, he was used to this. Today he rode Nublada, a strong horse accustomed to brush work. He often used up two or three horses a day when engaged in serious brush work, and after the long night's roundup, it would take several days for them to recover. Some horses never recovered.

When popping noises echoed across the brush, man and horse raised their heads simultaneously and looked toward the river. The popping rapidly grew louder, and soon Timo identified it as *vaqueros* crashing their horses through the brush, driving the stubborn longhorns before them. Above the shouts and whistles, he heard the constant pop and scratch of the brush grudgingly giving way. The rolling wave of noise came closer. It sounded like the land itself was creaking and groaning under its burden.

As Timo unhooked his leg from the saddle horn and shoved his boot into the covered stirrup, Nublada lowered her resting hoof to the dusty ground. Timo jammed his spurs into the horse's sides, and the powerful animal launched herself into the mass of thorns and branches, adding her own popping and scratching sounds to the din. Timo leaned sideways in the saddle, avoiding the larger branches, then straightened as Nublada's forelegs landed hard in the brush. Shifting his body, he leaned forward in the saddle as Nublada leapt again, this time clearing the brush. They landed in a small clearing, then crashed into the next thicket. Thorns tore the flesh of man and horse, and Timo dared not close his eyes, lest a branch separate his head from his shoulders.

The instant they cleared the brush, Timo and Nublada both spotted five gaunt, outlaw longhorns and the *vaqueros* pursuing them. In the course of a hundred years of ranching along the river, men like Timo had learned to handle wild longhorns, but in the brush they were especially stubborn. Even in open country, they were capricious and willful, refusing capture and herding unless tricked or forced. When Timo and his *vaqueros* had crossed the Rio Grande this morning, the cattle had bolted for the brush on the Mexican side. Of the eighty head they had brought across, fifty were now out crashing through the brush, while a small group of tamer cows was being driven farther south, following a narrow javelin *sendero*.

Once Nublada got into the pursuit, she became almost frenzied. The mare crashed into brush after brush, seemingly oblivious to the thorns and cuts, until she was upon the longhorns. Timo ignored the stragglers and went straight for the leader, a wizened old bull who had been nothing but trouble all night. Timo had seen his kind before. They were generally useless, serving only to stir up the other cattle. They fought when roped, and even when thrown to the ground, they often remained defiant, sulking and refusing to get up. Nothing—not branding, kicking, twisting their tails until they broke, rubbing dirt in their eyes—nothing could make one of these stubborn animals get up. Timo decided not to waste time on this one. He would do the one thing that might humble the beast—he would tail it.

He rode up behind the animal and reached out as both of them crashed through another low bush. Grabbing the bull's long, skinny tail, Timo twisted it around the horn of his saddle, then spurred Nublada slightly forward and to the side of the longhorn. The rangy old bull flipped head over heels and fell to the ground in a thunderous, dusty crash. Nublada pulled up, snorting and stamping and turning back toward the bull as Timo pulled out his lasso. The bull struggled to regain his feet, so dazed and winded that he merely pawed the ground and looked stupidly at the surrounding brush.

Timo rode up to him, casually dropped the lasso around his horns, and yanked him up. As the bull stumbled meekly behind Nublada, the cows fell in behind him. Timo threw the rope to one of the young *vaqueros* and they all turned toward the main herd, yawning at the sunny day.

Trailing along behind the other *vaqueros*, Timo heard faint hoofbeats behind him from the direction of the river. He twisted in the saddle, but waves of brush and a huge pale green clump of cacti blocked his view. Holding the reins in his hand, he climbed on top of his saddle and stood there, raising his head just above the cacti. Off in the distance, he saw two riders galloping west along the river. Timo spit on the ground. "Ranger spies."

The Rangers, it seemed, were everywhere. After they'd robbed him of Cornwell's mules, Timo had eluded their pursuit and met his *vaqueros*, as had been arranged weeks before, under the full moon on Doña Ophelia's ranch. Now his brothers were dead, and the meddlesome Rangers were threatening to relieve him of even these few stolen Santa Alicia cows.

Rejoining the main herd, Timo learned that his *vaqueros* had retrieved about forty of the fifty head that had bolted for the brush. This did not surprise him. He had started out with one hundred and twenty head, pried out of the Santa Alicia brush the previous day, then driven across the Rio Grande just before dawn. Now he had only seventy of the stubborn wild longhorns.

Driving his five head into the herd, Timo saw three more break away on the opposite side. One of the *vaqueros*, Julian, spurred his horse in pursuit, trying to catch them before they vanished into the thick brush. Timo watched as young Julian twirled his lasso twice over his head and let it sail toward the lead animal. The lasso formed a figure eight in midair and caught the forelegs of the steer, one in each loop. The animal stumbled, then brayed in outrage as Julian jerked the rope tight. The noise and dust coaxed the other runaways into turning back toward the herd.

Francisco Ybarra, whose grizzled face was burnt almost black from years of chasing cattle through the brush, rode up to Timo. He looked weary from twenty-four hours of backbreaking saddle work, but they had at least another six to go before they reached the corral they had constructed deep in the brush on the Mexican side of the river.

"We lost fifty head," Francisco said. "Could have been worse. Let's kill one and eat. I'm starving."

Timo shook his head. "No. The river, we're too close." He hesitated. No one had seen the Rangers but him, and he knew they would be coming. He was not sure yet what to do about it. For now, he decided to keep the information to himself. "Keep the cattle moving as fast as you can. If any run, let them go."

Francisco frowned. "Why not chase them?" He looked around. "Is somebody following us?"

"Nobody is following us, but the sooner we get to the corral, the sooner we can eat and rest. These Santa Alicia cows, I'm tired of them. They're as stubborn as their owner."

Francisco smiled. "Not as pretty."

Timo grinned. "That Doña Ophelia. I'm going back to that ranch soon and pay her a visit, like I promised El Gallo. Maybe she thinks she's too good for a dirty *vaquero* like me, but she'll spread her thighs for me, one way or another."

Francisco looked at the early morning sun, already white hot on the horizon. He flicked his quirt at a fly on his face. "The men are damned hungry, Timo. Let's take a rest, or they won't be worth a *chingada*. The horses are already spent."

Timo stood in his stirrups and surveyed the *vaqueros* driving the herd. Yes, they looked exhausted. It would be useless to try and outrun the Rangers. These men were as good as dead, but they could still serve a purpose. "The herd," he said. "Take it up another couple of miles, then set up a brush pen and camp. Eat, rest. I'm going to scout the trail ahead."

Francisco smiled again. "I'll tell the men."

As he watched Francisco ride off, Timo muttered, "*Adiós*," then turned toward the river, where the *remuda* of fresh horses trailed the herd. As he approached the horses, Timo motioned to Tenorio, the *vaquero* in charge of the *remuda*, then held up three fingers. Tenorio nodded. As Timo dismounted and removed Nublada's saddle, Tenorio approached, leading Juan's horse.

"Where did you get this horse?" Tenorio grinned. "He's too good to work in the brush."

"I need to scout ahead," Timo replied. "I don't need a brush horse for that. This horse used to belong to El Gallo, but where I sent him, he won't need it anymore. We got a good herd, *no hombre?*" Timo nodded toward the scrawny bunch of longhorns. "Francisco is going to butcher one in a while."

"You're not going to eat?"

"Later," Timo grunted as he transferred the saddle to the new horse. After he finished, he reached into his saddlebags and pulled out a half-empty bottle of mescal. "Here." He handed the bottle to Tenorio. "For the men. It was a good night's work."

Then he mounted and headed south, trotting forward to the front of the herd and then pushing on ahead of it. The horse was fresh and full of himself, and he seemed impatient for a good run, but the trail was narrow and wound around the perennial clumps of brush and cacti. The going was slow.

Timo heard the lumbering longhorns behind him, heard the shouts of the rejuvenated *vaqueros* eager to pen the herd so they could rest and eat. He knew they would spend the rest of the day drinking, cooking, eating, and sleeping. They were tired, and they thought they were safe, but Timo knew the Rangers would come. It was only a matter of time, time he would use to escape. A grin spread over his face as he rode, glad to be free on his own. He pushed south for a while to make sure that his tracks corresponded to the plan he had given Francisco, then, he veered east toward Matamoros so he could let this fine fresh horse have his way.

STARR TIGHTENED the cinch on his saddle and cocked his ears on the argument behind him.

"I am," Tomas repeated. "I am coming with you."

"Cap'n, I don't believe you're listening to this," growled Frenchy, his gray-streaked hair sticking out sideways from under his hat. "Let's shoot him and get after them bandits. Hell, he's probably in with 'em, sent to throw us off the track. Here, I'll do it!" He started to draw his Colt.

Starr turned on Frenchy and fixed him with a cold stare. Frenchy froze, then shoved his Colt back in the holster, cursing and using his whole body for emphasis. Then he turned and kicked a clump of cacti, sending it flying off into the brush. "Jesus and Mary! If we ain't gonna shoot Mexicans, what the hell we doin' here?"

Starr watched him stomp around a while, then looked on as he slammed a saddle on his horse's back. The horse spooked, spun around, and knocked Frenchy into a nearby cacti patch.

At this, the Don laughed, but stifled it as soon as he saw the murderous look on Frenchy's face as he climbed out of the cactus. Frenchy's neck and cheeks were deep red. They all watched him as he reared back and slammed his fist into his horse's face, setting the horse off on another bout of kicking and snorting.

Shaking his head, Starr turned back to Tomas. "What about our fight?"

"If you let me come, I won't fight you. Those men stole Doña Ophelia's cattle. If you attack them, you are helping me serve my *patrona*. I will be satisfied."

"That's good enough for me, Tomas." He offered his hand, and Tomas took it. They shook solemnly. Then Starr ordered, "Mount up!"

The Rangers, plus Tomas and the Don, mounted their horses and waded across the river, with Floyd leading the way. They rode hard for about eight miles, then Floyd held up a hand for them to slow down. Up ahead, they saw a thin plume of white smoke rising from the brush into the bright blue sky. Starr could smell the burning mesquite wood and the unmistakable aroma of roasting beef. They slowed their horses to a walk, crouching low in their saddles as they drew near the bandit camp. As Starr moved into the lead, then inched up his hand, the men stopped and dismounted, their hushed movements slow and deliberate. Each man took a rifle from the scabbard on his saddle, checked it, and the Rangers also examined their Colts for loose powder in the cylinders, which could cause a gun to explode when fired.

Moving closer to the camp, Starr crouched among the clumps of mesquite and cacti. The others followed. About a hundred yards out, he signaled for the men to split up, sending three Rangers to either side of the camp, keeping Tomas with him. They approached to within thirty yards of the campfire. Now Starr removed his hat to crawl forward until he had a clear view. He counted fifteen bandits sitting around the fire in small groups. The *vaqueros* were passing a bottle of mescal around, staring impatiently at huge chunks of beef trussed on poles over the mesquite fire. The beef sizzled, sending up a wonderful steam and smell. Behind the men, the cattle milled around in a crude brush pen.

Starr lifted his rifle, picked out the bandit who seemed to be guarding the horses, and shouted, "Fire!" The brush exploded in a thunderstorm of gunfire. Half of the *vaqueros* slumped to the ground.

"Rinches!" the bandits cried, trying to rise, some reaching for their guns, others running toward the horses. But the unrelenting thunder of fire from the Rangers continued, cutting the bandits down in twos and threes, until they were all hit. The Rangers ran into the camp, dispatching those who were still struggling to rise and fight.

Frenchy loped across the camp howling like a wolf and jumped on Julian's back as the boy, shot in the abdomen, crawled on the ground. He let out a grunt as Frenchy's weight fell on him, then he lay helplessly in the dirt. Frenchy drew his Bowie knife, grabbed Julian by the hair, and cut the boy's throat from ear to ear. At the same time, Uriah rushed past him and disappeared into the brush after Francisco, who had managed to roll away from the clearing. Two shots rang out, and a minute later Uriah walked proudly back into the camp carrying Francisco's scalp.

Frenchy grinned and dropped Julian's limp head into the dust. "What's that for?"

"For nothing," Uriah replied, and he flung the scalp out into the brush. He walked up to a *vaquero* who was groaning and writhing on the ground, drew his Colt, and shot the man in the forehead.

Over near the campfire, Tomas rolled one of the wounded *vaqueros* over. The man stared up at Tomas and coughed up blood.

"You going to give him the *tiro de gracia?*" Starr inquired casually as he kicked one of the dead *vaqueros* nearby.

Tomas knelt beside the wounded *vaquero*. "I know this man," he said. "Tenorio. Tenorio Valenzuela." He bent closer to speak to him. "Why are you stealing from Doña Ophelia?"

Tenorio coughed again. "Tell my *chula* goodbye from me, will you? Will you, Tomas?"

Tomas nodded. "Next time I'm in Camargo, Tenorio, I'll go see your *chula*."

Tenorio looked up at him, clutching his bloody chest and shuddering. "But why this, Tenorio? Why are you stealing from Doña Ophelia?"

Tenorio groaned. "Timo. Timo said we wouldn't get caught. He said the *rinches* wouldn't catch us if we crossed at night." He coughed up more blood, then he sighed. His face froze into a permanent frown.

Tomas lowered Tenorio's head back to the ground.

"Who's that fellow he mentioned?" asked Starr. Two more sharp pistol shots rang out as Rangers dispatched other wounded *vaqueros*.

"Could be Timo Martinez," said Tomas. "I heard he's back on the river again. I knew him many years ago, when he used to work a small ranch near Mier. Tejanos killed his family during the war against Santa Anna." He shook his head. "He used to be a good hand. Fallen *muy* low."

Tomas stood up and walked around the ravaged camp, turning over every one of the dead *vaqueros*, even the ones who had crawled off into the brush to die. "I don't see Timo here," he told Starr. "He must have gotten away. We should try to catch him. He's a bad one."

Starr took Cornwell's diary from his vest pocket and flipped the pages toward the end, reading the final entry. "Timo," he muttered. "I've run into him before. He's the fella that shot your man, Santos." He turned and barked out orders to Sam, Uriah, and Jim. "You boys, circle around the camp and see if you can cut trail on this Timo bandit. He may be on foot or mounted. Try east and south. We came in from the west, and he wouldn't have crossed back into Texas." Then he remembered that the last time he had encountered Timo, the bandit had doubled back and thrown them off his trail. "Don, Floyd, cross back into Texas and see if you can cut his trail over there. Rest of you boys, strip anything of value off these corpses and pitch them in the brush. Then get this herd back across the river."

"You're not going to bury them?" Tomas asked, frowning.

"Don't have time."

"They may be bandits, but they were men. Not dogs. We should bury them," Tomas insisted.

"They were nothing but low-down, stinking greasers," Frenchy snarled as he wiped the blade of his Bowie knife on Tenorio's pants. "Just like you."

Tomas turned and faced Frenchy, whose big face was flushed red from the exertions of battle.

"*Mira hombre*," Tomas said, "I saw you cut that helpless boy's throat. You butchered him like a hog. Is anything lower than that, *rinche?*"

Frenchy slid his Bowie knife into its sheath and moved to obey Starr's command, starting with Tenorio.

"What about burying them, *Capitán* Starr?" Tomas persisted.

"No." Starr replied as he moved off to inspect the *remuda*. He doubted that the horses would be worth anything. *Vaqueros* were very hard on horses. A constant supply of new horses was required to keep a cattle ranch going in *la brasada*. These horses were usually supplied by *mestengeros* who captured some of the thousands of wild mustangs roaming south Texas, broke them, and sold them to the ranches. Starr took a good look at the horses and shook his head. They were all used up. They looked pitiful. He ordered Ambrose to shoot them.

As Ambrose led the *remuda* out into the brush a little so he could tie the horses up while he shot them, Starr noticed that Tomas was dragging bodies out of the camp and a few yards into the brush. He shook his head and wandered over there. "Now what are you doing?"

"I'm going to drop them into that little pit over there," Tomas said, "then cover them with rocks and branches."

Starr let out a long sigh and called on the other Rangers to help him. Frenchy, in protest, pulled the bodies by the feet so the dead men's faces dragged in the dirt, mixing it with their blood to form black clots of mud around their mouths and noses.

Minutes later, Sam and Jim rode into camp. "Cap'n," Jim called, we cut trail just south of here. One rider, riding hard. But we can catch him up, all right. Uriah stayed on the trail, followed it south.

Starr fired his Colt into the air three times. "Couple a you boys stay with the herd. When Floyd and the Don get back, get the herd across the river a few miles and turn it loose. Then head east on Zachary's military highway to Fort Brown. If this bandit tries to cross back to Texas, you get him." He turned to Tomas. "Tomas, you coming?"

Tomas shook his head. "You Rangers will never drive this herd. You don't know how. And Timo, you won't catch him, *Capitán*. Juan's horse isn't here. Timo must have taken him. That's more horse than you got."

Starr grunted. "We can't just let him go."

"He's already gone, *Capitán*."

Chapter 4
Lidia

LIDIA LIFTED THE SPOON carefully, guiding it from the soup bowl to Juan's lips. He was lying back on three pillows. She sat on the edge of his bed, balancing the bowl on her lap. The merciless heat poured in from the windows, despite the broad covered patio that surrounded the house, and she could feel a stream of perspiration running down her neck. No breeze stirred the listless day, nor had one stirred the day before. Summer along the Rio Grande valley was a deadly serious affair. The land was seared dry and brown, and few living things moved in the heat of the day.

"Why are you giving me soup? It's too hot for soup."

"Because your mother said for you to eat this, Juan. She even taught Ramona how to make it. It's made with special herbs your mother sent over." Lidia brought the spoon to her own lips and sipped at it. "It tastes good. And it's not hot. I let it cool before I came in."

Juan glared at her.

"You're too old to pout," she said.

"I'm going to get up and get some steak. And *frijoles, chiles,* and *tortillas.*"

Lidia set the bowl and spoon on the bedside table and slid to her feet. "All right, Señor Gallo, I see you need your red meat to keep up your ferocious growl. Go ahead. I'd like to see you stand up."

Juan threw off the thin sheet and swung his legs out of bed. "Don't look at me!" he barked.

"Oh, as if I haven't seen you nearly naked for two weeks now? Who do you think changed your bandages every day? Do you think it was only Father who tended you night and day?"

"I'm sick of being in this bed. I want to go outside." He put his feet down on the cool tile floor and sat up, but then he slowly lifted his hands to his head.

She rushed to his side. "You feel dizzy, don't you? Let me see your scalp." She unwrapped the bandage and checked his wound carefully. "It's healing nicely," she said. "Soon your hair will start growing back. But don't be surprised if you end up with a big bald scar down the side of your head."

Smiling brightly, trying to cheer and tease him out of his foul mood, she stepped away and sat in the chair beside the bed. "They can change your nickname to *El Gallo Pelón*." She stifled a giggle. Juan seemed unhappy about her christening him The Bald Rooster. She watched him as he tried to work the knots out of his unused muscles. He looked thin, haggard, and angry.

His shoulders were still as wide and firm as she remembered them. She could see the muscles rippling down his beautiful bare chest and stomach, which made her feel a twinge of desire to touch them. But Lidia knew his moods, and he was in no mood for touching. She was sure he felt sick, disoriented, and she knew he hated feeling powerless. He had refused to let her shave him this morning, refused to let her wash him, and now he refused to eat.

"You know," she said in a mild voice, "if you open up that shoulder wound, Father will sew it back up and make you lie still for another two weeks."

He made fists, then loosened his hands and did it again. "I want to go back to the Santa Alicia. Where are my *vaqueros?*"

"Most of them went back with your mother. There are five of them outside. We let them bunk in the barn. And you know Blas stayed here in the house." She smiled as a wicked thought raced through her mind. "Blas is sweet on me, Juan. Are you jealous?"

He turned a dark face toward her. "You stay away from him, Lidia. I'm warning you."

"But he's so darling. Once he turns those big calf eyes on me, I can't resist smiling at him. And then you should see him blush—"

Suddenly he lashed out with one hand, catching the soup bowl and sending it crashing against the wall. "I said leave him alone, god damn you!"

Lidia gasped, then whirled on him. "I was only teasing," she snapped. "How dare you talk to me like that! You know Blas is like a brother to me. *Dios!* You and your moods and temper!"

Juan sat back silently, breathing heavily, then turned to look at her and scowled. "Oh, hell, Lidia, I'm sorry. I'm going crazy in this room, I'm sick of being in bed. I have to get out of here."

Despite the crude language, it was a rare apology, and Lidia softened. She wiped her eyes and sat beside him on the bed, and they both stared at the floor, watching the soup form little pools as it dripped down the walls. "If I go and get another bowl of soup—" she started to say, but Juan angrily shook his head.

"Let me finish, you big baby. If you eat some soup, then tonight, when everyone is asleep, and it's cooler outside, I'll get Blas to help me take you out to the garden. We can sit in the moonlight and listen to the owls. I'll have the *vaqueros* cook up some *carnitas*. And I'll bring *tortillas* from the kitchen."

He turned to face her. "You would do that for me?"

She searched his face, to see if the question hinted of passions beyond those for food. But the gray-green eyes looking back at her looked merely hungry. "If you promise to be careful," she replied. "We can't risk opening that wound. If Father finds out, he'll take the bullwhip to me."

Juan nodded. "Tell Blas to get me some mescal."

"No mescal."

"What do you mean, no mescal?"

"Just what I said. I did not nurse you back to health to watch you get drunk."

"I'll drink mescal if I want to."

"Fine. Then you can just figure out how to get it in here, because I won't take you outside."

She could feel his dark stare. "You already said you would," he spat.

She spun to face him again. "I *changed* my mind."

As he glared back, fuming, she reveled in the intensity of his wrath, in the black fury from which she felt quite immune. But she knew he was weakened, subdued. She could see his anger waning. Finally, she watched him let out a long sigh.

"I'll do anything to get out of here. To get some real food."

"Good," she said, jumping up and smoothing her skirt. "Now, let me help you lie back down, and I'll go get the soup."

After she got him back in a horizontal position, with the pillows fluffed and the sheet up to his waist, she leaned over and touched her hand to his forehead. She could feel his heavy breath on her face, and her breast just barely touched his arm. When he reached up and put a hand on her cheek, she looked down at him with mild surprise.

"What is it, Juan?"

He rubbed her face with his coarse fingers, but they felt warm and gentle in their caress. "When I knocked the soup away and cursed at you, you almost cried," he said. "It's been a long, long time since I've seen you cry." He paused, looking at her face inches from his, remembering that day when they were children and they had sat on the riverbank nursing his wound. She had broken through to him that time. But that was long ago. "Things seem different. I don't know why, you just seem different. And...."

She smiled, looking down at him as he struggled with his words. She wanted to say it for him and save them both the effort. He was seeing a side of her they had never taken the time to find before. Their love had been so fast, so unrelenting, that they had never really gotten much beyond the surface. They had always spent most of their time fighting because she was unwilling to cede to him what he demanded, total submission to his powerful will.

But now she had him here, under her care. Vulnerable. And they had all the time in the world.

"And what, you foolish man?" She laughed, bending closer and smiling as brightly as she could. A fraction of an inch closer and their lips might touch. She looked into his eyes, her own eyes feeling moist and full of hope. Did he care, after all?

But he only gave his head a small, bewildered shake. "And nothing," he said. "Get the soup."

Lidia and Blas had moved a table from the patio to the garden, where they sat watching Juan gorge himself on the promised feast. He made little grunting sounds of pleasure as he ate. They sat under mesquite trees in the bright moonlight, and Juan relished the musky scent of the river carried on the warm breeze. The night tingled with an electricity that hinted of cooling rain somewhere out in the *brasada*. They looked to the west for some hope of lightning flashing against the distant black horizon, but it was a clear night.

"Juan, you're going to make yourself sick," Lidia warned. "Slow down."

He grunted that he did not care and continued gorging. Out of the corner of his eye, he saw Lidia turn to look at Blas, who had been staring at her like a lovelorn puppy. When Blas locked eyes with her, he suddenly looked like he needed a place to hide.

"Blas," she said, "did you bring the surprise?"

When Blas nodded, Juan perked up. "What surprise?" he tried to say with his mouth full.

Blas grinned, reached under the table, and brought up a glistening bottle of mescal. He held it out to Juan, but Lidia intercepted it.

"Just three drinks is all you get. I don't want you drunk and howling at the moon."

Juan choked down his food, wiped his hands on his shirt, and reached for the bottle. She pulled it back.

"I said three drinks."

"*Madre de Dios*, give me the god damned bottle!"

"You watch your language. And not until you agree. Three drinks." She looked at Blas, raised her eyebrows, and smiled.

Blas nodded. "Juan, you better promise," he said. "I think that's the only way you're going to get even one drink."

"Anything!"

She handed him the bottle, and he cradled it against his breast, caressing it, looking down at it as if it were an object of passion. "A drink," he whispered. "You have no idea how I've needed a drink. And now, now—"

"Stop making love to it and drink it," Lidia snapped. "We need to get you back inside."

He uncorked the bottle and touched it to his lips, lifting it almost straight up, taking several large swallows.

"*Espera!*" She reached for the bottle. "I said *three drinks.*"

He pulled his head away, denying her the bottle, and forced down one last swallow. "Right," he said. "Well, that was one drink." He grinned.

"That was not one drink! It was more like six."

"Those were swallows, not drinks."

She looked over at Blas. "I knew it. I knew I couldn't trust him."

"Lidia," Blas said, "I think Juan can handle more than three drinks."

"Damned right." Juan raised the bottle again. "What does a woman know about drinking?"

Lidia jumped up, her fists on her hips. "You foul-mouthed, deceitful, lying ingrate! What was all that talk today about how things are different now? What's different? I'll tell you what's different! I changed my mind. I brought you a drink because I knew it would make you happy." She looked around and stopped shouting. "I shouldn't even be out here with you, with no chaperone. If Father catches us, he'll bullwhip you and lock me in my room for the rest of my life. What isn't different is that you're still a selfish, uncaring liar."

Juan shrugged. "Blas is here."

Blas nodded. "*Sí.* It's not like you're out here alone."

"And you!" She whirled on Blas, whose face disappeared under the shadow of his hat. Juan marveled at Lidia's power to make his little brother cringe like this. But the sight of two men sitting there dumbfounded at her anger seemed to dismay her.

"I'm out here alone with *two* men. That's worse. But El Gallo doesn't care about my reputation. He doesn't even think about me. All he cares about is breaking promises." Her voice cracked as she sat down again and turned her back on them.

Blas stared down at the table while Juan guzzled another drink. They were silent as they listened to her sniffling.

Finally, Juan glanced over at Blas. "Take a walk."

Tipping his hat at Lidia, Blas rose and wandered toward the back of the garden. Juan corked the mescal bottle and set it on the table beside Lidia. She rolled her eyes toward it, wiped her tears, and turned to face him.

"Lidia," he said, "you're crying again. Why?"

"Are tears what it takes to make you stop? Make you care what I feel?"

"I don't know what you feel. I can't predict you."

She let out a huge sigh. "Well, everyone can predict you, especially me."

He looked at her, her face bathed in soft moonlight, and murmured, "You're as beautiful as ever. I've never known a more beautiful woman. It's just—"

"Just what?"

"We fight like cats in the barn."

"Oh, Juan, don't you see that I'm changing? Would I have brought you a bottle before?"

"No," he admitted. "You hate to give in, even when you're wrong." He wrapped one hand around the bottle, rubbed it up and down. He felt wary, unsure of what she wanted from him, uncertain he wanted to give it. But she looked so lovely, so fragile, so irresistible. Looking at her made him want to pull her to his chest, wrap her in his powerful arms, and steal kisses from her. "Maybe if you can change," he offered tentatively, "I can change a little, too."

An owl hooted from a mesquite tree down by the river. A coyote yipped from across the river in Mexico. The scent of roses filled the garden. Then the breeze shifted slightly, and the musky smell of horses in the barn washed over them.

Lidia placed her hand on his as he caressed the bottle. "We thought you were going to die," she said. "It made me realize how I feel about you. I—I have done nothing but be kind to you, and you treat me as if I don't mean anything to you."

Juan sat quietly, taking in her words. "How could I let you mean anything to me, after what happened last time?" he asked her. "What about your father? He won't let me court you anymore."

"Since when do other men tell you what to do?"

"You're the one who wants to respect all the customs. I don't give a damn about Spanish custom, all that courting. You're the one who wants to be a lady."

She pulled his hand to her and laid it between her breasts. When she sighed again, he felt her breath on his hand, and through her dress he could feel her softness, the gentle heaving of her chest.

"I don't know if I want that any more," she whispered. "Juan, all I know is that when I saw you shot and almost dead, something changed. As long as I knew you were out there somewhere, I guess I always believed you'd come back someday, and we would try again. I think that's the real reason I never married."

She lifted her chin, and in the moonlight he could see her majestic face as she spoke. Perhaps it was the mescal, perhaps it was his wounds, but he felt strange. He kept phasing in and out. One moment he was here, and the next he felt detached, like he was watching this happen to someone else.

"But when I saw you dying," she continued, "I felt like I was dying, too. I thought if you died, I couldn't stand it." She paused and looked at the bottle on the table. "I told your mother that I thought I still loved you."

Suddenly, all of his senses snapped back to her. He let out a long, silent breath. "Do you?"

She gripped his hand harder and raised it to her cheek. "Yes," she whispered. "I love you, Juan."

Now he felt more confused and overwhelmed than ever. In all the time he had courted Lidia, she had never shown such vulnerability, had never made him feel she really needed him. He was suddenly suspicious, cautious that it might not be true. How could he trust her? How could he trust anyone? But her whispered words echoed in his head, and he could feel the crust of armor around his heart begin to melt. That armor had protected his deepest feelings for so many years, since the first time his father's belt lashed his back, and the first time Ophelia pushed him away. From behind the armor came a sudden rush of love for her, stronger than anything he had ever felt before.

"Lidia, I—" he tried to reach out to her, wanting to embrace her, but his wounded shoulder sent sharp fiery pains through his body, and he winced. She pushed him away gently.

"No. None of that. You're in no shape for that." But she laid both of her hands on his shoulders and moved her face close to his so that they could look into each other's eyes. She gently touched her lips to his, then pulled away, wrinkling her nose. "You smell like mescal."

"I'll never take another drink again," he declared rashly. He was so full of love he would have promised her anything.

She smiled wistfully. "Let's not start by making promises you know you can't keep." She gave him a peck on the cheek. "But it's sweet of you to say that. Have one more drink, then we need to get you inside."

"No. I want to stay out here longer. It's nice here." He put his arm around her waist and drew her near.

She smiled and nodded. "It is nice. But it's not polite to keep Blas waiting in the back of the garden, is it?"

"I'm not a polite person. Let's send him away."

"I need his help to get you back upstairs. Come on. Let's not overdo it this first time."

"I want to come out here again tomorrow."

She tilted her head sideways. "Maybe not tomorrow. I'm afraid you'll open up your wound. But soon, maybe the next night."

Despite the pain, he pulled her face up to his and kissed her. He felt the moist softness of her lips, tasted the sweetness of her. He wanted to smother her, to kiss her all over, to carry her in his arms down to the river and make love to her in the moonlight. He knew that she wanted him too when he heard her moan softly as he bent her back a little, when he felt her hot breath on his cheeks. As he slowly pulled away, she blushed and lowered her eyes.

"Lidia," he whispered, pulling her back to him, delighting in the feel of her heaving chest. "Lidia."

"WHEN CAN I GO HOME?" Juan asked again, though now he really did not want to leave. He sat on the edge of the bed, bare-chested, his feet on the cool tiles, while Don de Leon inspected his wounds and checked his temperature, making little clucking sounds as he worked. Lidia sat on a chair by the window, gazing out at the searing afternoon.

"This is impressive," said Don de Leon. "Three weeks, and you've healed so quickly."

"You're a good doctor."

Don de Leon waved the compliment away. "It's your young body, Juan. And your strong blood."

Juan's eyes drifted toward Lidia.

Don de Leon seemed to follow his gaze. "Why don't you walk around a little, maybe in the evening when it's cooler? Get out of this room. It would do you good."

Lidia continued to stare out the window, but Juan grinned. "Good idea. Maybe Lidia could walk with me?"

The old man smiled back. "Certainly. Chaperoned, of course."

"Of course."

"Only the walk, young man. Don't get any ideas."

"I know your feelings, Señor de Leon."

Don de Leon seemed to be searching Juan's face. His small brown eyes were firm and steady. Juan returned Don de Leon's stare. He knew it would be difficult to get this old man to understand, but whether he understood or not, he would have to accept it. The heat of the room was making him lightheaded, dizzy, but he did not look away.

AS THE EARLY MORNING light bathed her room in pastel yellow, Lidia smiled at her reflection in the mirror. She sat in the chair at her dresser, brushing her hair and humming a soft tune as her mother looked on.

"*Mi hija*," said Martina de Leon, "I'm so glad to see you happy again. I hate it so much when you and your father fight. Are you reconciled now? Will you go to Bejar?"

Lidia turned, put down the silver-handled brush, and put her arms around her mother. "Oh, Mother, we'll see." She closed her eyes and thought again about Juan's insistent kisses, remembered the feel of his arms around her waist as they sat night after night in the garden. At first Blas had been there to help her move Juan. But then Juan had ordered his little brother to stay in his room, and Lidia and Juan had been blessedly, wickedly alone. She knew that if her father found out, there would be hell to pay, but she did not care. Those kisses, those sweet, strong, demanding, gentle kisses. They made her dreamy and light, slowly stoking the building fire within her. She opened her eyes, took her mother's face into her hands, smiling softly, and repeated, "We'll see."

Martina moved out her daughter's caress and frowned. "But it's only next week. You have to go next week. You are going, yes?"

Lidia tilted her head and laughed, sweet music to her own ears. She realized her mother had no idea what was going on, and hoped her father did not, either.

"Juan seems much better," Martina said, changing the subject. "Your father says he can go home today. Blas is getting a carriage ready, because Luis refuses to let him ride a horse. Are you sorry he's leaving? You've nursed him every day. You'll be bored now. Of course, you have to start getting ready for your trip, so it's better if he's gone, so you can—"

"Mother, please, stop rattling on so. Are you nervous about something?"

Martina swallowed, took a deep breath and closed her eyes. "Yes. Yes, I am nervous, *mi hija*," she replied. "I'm afraid of what's going to happen with you and Luis over your trip. I don't know what is in your head, and you won't tell me. Why don't you talk to me like you used to? You never kept secrets from me. Why don't you tell your mother—"

Lidia smiled at the mirror. "Mother, I said we'll see. Help me with my dress."

Martina helped Lidia put on her dress, a beautiful blue gown trimmed with white lace. It was an arduous task, with all the layers and hooks. It fit her snugly, showing off her breasts and hips.

"You should have worn something a little more modest to say goodbye to Juan," she said. "I don't think your father is going to approve of this dress."

"No," Lidia said, "probably not." She picked up her fan. "Let's go see Father now," she said. Fanning herself, she opened the door and walked out into the hall. Martina followed quickly, clucking like a hen and shaking her head.

When they reached the drawing room, Luis de Leon and Juan were already there. Juan was dressed very nicely—not in the filthy *vaquero* garb he was wearing when he arrived draped over a Ranger horse. Ophelia had sent clean clothes for him, though at first he had refused to wear them.

They were things a *caballero* like Don de Leon would wear. Juan made Lidia retrieve his own clothes from the trash, wash them, and mend all the tears and holes. Even then, they barely held together. She had finally persuaded him to throw them out again and wear the clothes Ophelia had sent.

Juan rose as the ladies entered.

"Please," Martina protested, "sit down, Juan. How are you feeling?"

He nodded. "Good. But then I've had good care." He smiled at Lidia, and she beamed back at him.

"I have something to say," he continued. "Don de Leon, first I want to say thank you for saving my life. I'm told I was near death when they brought me here, that no one expected me to live. But you saved me. Thank you." He took a deep breath, then plowed on. "Now, I have something else to say."

Don de Leon smiled, nodded his head, and motioned for Juan to be seated. "Come now, Juan, there's no need to thank me. Don't be so formal. Sit down and let us talk for a bit while your carriage is prepared."

Martina and Lidia sat down, but Juan remained standing. Fixing his gaze on Lidia, he squared his shoulders and made his speech—the one he and Lidia had rehearsed for several nights as they plotted their strategy.

"Don de Leon," he began, "I know that I have been a guest in your house, and that it has been a worry and a trial for you. I know that you have saved my life. I know that you and I have not been of like mind over many things in the past, and that I have caused your family grief and hardship. For all this, I am truly sorry."

Don de Leon nodded, still smiling.

Juan continued, speaking the strange words from memory, knowing that they were coming out stiff and stilted. "And I know that in the past, you have denied me..." he paused, shifting his gaze from Lidia to look directly into Don de Leon's eyes, "...as an acceptable suitor for Lidia."

Martina de Leon sucked in her breath. Juan saw a look of concern come over Don de Leon. He rushed on.

"But now, Don de Leon, I would like to ask that you reconsider. I have come close to death. Day and night, Lidia has nursed me back to health. We have reconciled our differences. I can truly say that whatever problems existed in the past will not recur." Though he felt completely, utterly exposed and foolish, his speech continued. He squared his shoulders and stood even straighter, still looking directly at Don de Leon. "So...I would like to formally ask, respectfully ask, for your permission to court your daughter."

Juan turned back toward Lidia, speaking now from his heart. "I love Lidia, Don de Leon. I love your daughter, and she loves me. Please say yes."

Martina de Leon's face broke into a tremendous smile, and she quickly hugged Lidia, who laughed softly, nodding her head, and hugged her mother back. They looked in each other's eyes, and a thousand questions and delightful exclamations flowed between them. But they were silent, because Don de Leon had not yet spoken. Mother and daughter joined Juan in waiting for him. He appeared to be lost in thought.

"Let me see if I understand this," the older man finally said as he rose to pace the room. "All the time you have been recuperating under my roof, you have been pursuing my daughter?"

Juan looked down for the first time. "Not exactly, sir. I know how it must seem—yes, it may look bad, but I can assure you nothing has happened."

Don de Leon chuckled a little. "I see," he said. "I see. There's only one problem—something Lidia perhaps forgot to tell you." He turned to look at his daughter, and Juan saw a strange pleading look cloud her face as she stared up at her father.

"Lidia," said Don de Leon, "is already betrothed. She is leaving next week for San Antonio de Bejar to be married. Didn't she tell you?"

Juan felt like someone had punched him in the stomach. He turned and shot a stricken look at Lidia, who had a look of horror on her face.

Don de Leon chuckled again. "My dear Lidia, how could you have led poor Juan on, when you know I have already given your hand to another? I don't think it was fair to Juan. It seems you have been dishonest with him."

"No!" she shot back, her voice quivering. "I haven't been dishonest with him. Father, I love him!" She turned to Juan, her eyes filled with tears. "Juan, I'm sorry. I couldn't tell you. I was terrified it would drive you away. And there was nothing to tell. I told Father before, and I will tell him now,

I'm not going to marry this man he has chosen. I'm not going to marry anyone but you."

Juan probed deep into Lidia's eyes. Was she telling the truth? Had he foolishly let her break through? Should he have known better?

"It doesn't matter!" thundered Don de Leon.

"What doesn't matter?" Lidia asked, her voice trembling.

"It doesn't matter what little trick you've planned to get out of this, Lidia. It won't work."

"Father, I love Juan, and that *does* matter. Nothing can keep me away from him. Not even you!"

Her mother gasped. "Oh, Lidia. Please, please don't talk like that to your father."

Don de Leon was not finished. "So, you used a sick man to try to wrangle your way out of a bethroal? Not only used him, but lied to him. Even got him to dress up like a *caballero*. Maybe you feel sorry for him? But you'll get over it. Once he gets back to his ranch and to his friends—once he goes out with his *vaqueros* to the cantinas, the fighting, the whoring—will you still want him then?"

Without a word, Lidia stood up and walked over to Juan. She took his hand and stood beside him. "He's given all that up, Father. He promised me last night in the garden—"

"Last night in the garden?" Martina repeated incredulously. "You were in the garden, alone? Unchaperoned? Lidia, how could you?"

"We've been alone in the garden every night, sometimes all night!" Lidia announced.

Juan blinked. He could see Lidia holding her head straight, bracing herself for what surely would be a terrible, explosive reaction from her father. Why was she confessing this?

"Alone," said Don de Leon. "All night. Unchaperoned. You think you are ruined. You think I know that, don't you? No one will want you now, especially not Alfredo Jaramillo of San Antonio de Bejar? Except for one thing, Lidia," he said calmly. "I knew about your little game."

Juan was stunned. He could see Martina's shoulders fall. He could feel Lidia's reaction.

"You—you knew?" she stammered.

"Of course, my dear. I knew you would try something to get out of your betrothal, so I kept an eye on you. Every night, from the very first night when Blas helped you get Juan down to the garden, I've watched from the little room over the chapel. Oh, yes, my tricky little dear. I watched. I saw every embrace, every kiss, and heard every word. Thankfully, Juan was in no condition to press his advantage, or maybe he was enough of a gentleman to remember that he was and is still a guest in my house. Given your disgracefully aggressive behavior, I must say that he acted with restraint. So you see, my dear, you *were* chaperoned. By me. You are not ruined. You are still quite marriageable. Your little plan to use poor, unsuspecting Juan failed."

Juan backed away from Lidia, his head reeling. A trick? She was betrothed? *Betrothed?* He looked down at his fine clothes and felt suddenly, completely foolish. Those black, ancient memories of his father's rejection and his mother's betrayal came flooding over him, washing away every loving word and gentle kiss he and Lidia had shared. He'd been a fool to let her reach him, to let *anybody* reach him. A thick wall crashed down around his mauled feelings, protecting him, pushing him far away.

He stared at Lidia. Behind the defeated look on her face, he saw something else. Anger? Whatever she was feeling, he did not think it was about him. Was she angry that her selfish plot had been discovered?

At this moment Blas entered the room and immediately halted when he saw everyone standing silent and motionless. Without a word, he spun on his heel and went right back out. Juan whirled and stomped out the door right behind him.

Blas stopped and turned. "What's wrong?" he asked.

Juan was so full of anger he could barely speak. "Get me out of here," he growled.

Ignoring the sudden jab of pain in his shoulder, he flung the carriage door open and climbed inside, then slammed the door shut behind him so hard that it cracked and hung limp on the hinges. He pounded on the carriage roof.

Before anyone else could move, Lidia was standing beside the carriage, looking in through the window. Then she opened the mangled door and leaned inside. She seemed to Juan like an apparition, a horror visiting him in a nightmare. He was struck dumb. What could he possibly say to her? She had used him, and he had let her use him. Stupid! Stupid! He should have known better. All he wanted was to get as far away from her as possible. Seeing her only reminded him of how foolish he was, how completely naive he had been.

"Juan," she was pleading, "Juan, it isn't true. Whatever you're thinking, it isn't true! I do love you. Everything I said, I meant. Please don't leave me. You said that if Father did not approve, you would steal me away. You promised! Don't leave me here. Please? I never...."

He saw her mouth moving, her lips parting, her tongue working up and down. He felt her words hitting his ears. But the words meant nothing to him. He could not comprehend them. She might have been speaking some language neither of them had ever heard before. Nothing Lidia said ever again would have meaning for him. He was so humiliated that he physically recoiled from her. Reaching out, he laid the palm of his right hand on her forehead and gently pushed her back. He carefully closed the door and pounded again on the carriage roof, causing the whole carriage to heave and roll.

He heard Blas yell "*Vámonos,*" and then felt the carriage lurch out of the courtyard and onto the road.

THE ROAD UP AHEAD forked, north to the Santa Alicia ranch house, south to Fort Brown, then to the mule-drawn ferry across to Matamoros. Blas turned the carriage north, but when he heard Juan pounding on the roof, he pulled on the reins and stopped. The *vaqueros* ahead also pulled up and turned in their saddles to look back, curious about the unscheduled stop. Those behind the carriage clattered to a halt, too, kicking up vast clouds of fine, dry dust. They were surrounded by endless clumps of pale green, prickly cacti.

"*Que pasa, patrón?*" one of them called to Blas.

Blas shrugged as he jumped off the carriage seat and walked around to the door. He opened it and looked in, fearful that Juan might be in pain from the jostling of the rough trail.

"What do you—"

"I need a horse," Juan spat.

Blas stared. "A horse? For what?"

"Just get one."

Blas looked down at his boots and shook his head. "No, no, Juan," he murmured, "I don't think—"

"Don't think. Don't do a god damned thing. Just get me a horse. Get me a god damned horse. *Now!*"

Juan had never used that tone of voice with him. Blas felt his cheeks burn, almost as if Juan had slapped him. As he backed away, shaking his head, Juan followed him out of the carriage, except to Blas it seemed Juan was not really looking at him. He was looking right through him, focusing on some far-away object. His eyes were dull, his face showing little of the emotion behind the words. It was rigid, like a mask, the colors pale and the skin like leather.

Juan motioned to one of the trailing *vaqueros*.

"*Sí, patrón?*" the man responded.

"Give me your horse."

The man instantly dismounted and handed Juan the reins.

Finally jolted into action, Blas stepped up. "What are you doing? Where are you going? Juan, Mama will kill me if I let you ride a horse."

Ignoring him, Juan mounted slowly, groaning as he did so.

"I'm coming with you," Blas declared.

"I don't give a *chingada* what you do."

And Juan was gone, back down the trail toward Fort Brown and Matamoros, whipping the horse with his quirt, sending up great clods of dirt and sand. Blas immediately motioned for another horse, and gave orders for half the *vaqueros* to drive the carriage to the ranch, the other half to come with him.

They found Juan at the Vieja Loca cantina in Matamoros, standing at the bar, the bottle of mescal before him already a third empty. Blas motioned for the *vaqueros* to wait outside, and he slowly sidled up to his brother.

"Leave me alone," Juan growled.

"Not until you tell me what's wrong."

"Wrong?" he snorted. "What's wrong is I'm a fool, Blas. And any man who believes what a woman says is a fool, too. She lied to me. She lied to me, and I followed her around like a stupid puppy. She played with me like I was a god damned doll. Look, she even dressed me up. And I let her!" He smashed his fist down on the bar. "Drink with me," he ordered, "but don't talk to me. I'll shoot the next *hijo de la chingada* who talks to me." He poured Blas a drink. Blas took it, sipped at it, and watched Juan drain his in one swallow.

Juan drank another one, and another, and another, once in a while pouring one for Blas, who sipped slowly and stared down at the bar. There were only a few other men in the cantina, rough-looking men playing monte or just drinking. They all knew Juan, and they left him alone. After a while, Juan grabbed his bottle and stumbled to one of the rough-hewn tables in the farthest corner, away from the weak light of the lanterns. He slammed the bottle down and dropped heavily into the chair, wincing as he did. Blas stayed at the bar, turning around to lean his elbows on it so he could watch his brother.

Juan poured another shot and downed it. He stared at the bottle, then shut his eyes tight. Lidia! He could picture her beautiful face, feel her soft lips, smell her sweet breath. But she had used him all along. She never really cared for him. She had only been pretending. He felt a pang of grief in his chest. It spread to his abdomen. He was in pain, and she was tearing him apart. She did not love him. It was all a trick. She had used him to trick her father, and he had believed her. Knots twisted in his stomach.

He gritted his teeth and reached for another drink. Then another, nodding his head, thinking how he had let himself love her so much, how she had used him, how much he hurt. What had she been trying to tell him as he rode away? Whatever it was, it was lies. All lies. He would never believe her again. He would never again open himself to a woman like he had to Lidia.

Lidia. Lidia. Her name echoed in his head, try as he might to drive it out. He whispered it slowly, lingering on the three syllables. He downed another shot, and then another. He would never love her again, that much he knew. He would never love anyone. His heart was already hardening, becoming even harder than before. He closed his eyes and nodded again.

A man with a guitar began playing and singing over by the bar. There was always a man with a guitar in these cantinas, and they all played sad songs about *vaqueros* who loved women who did not love them, or about women they loved who died, or about *vaqueros* living alone because the girls they'd loved in their youth married other men. They were sweet, slow, mournful, haunting love songs, and the men listening in the cantinas drank slowly, brooding over their mescal, nodding their heads in the dim light, staring with heavy-lidded eyes at their bottles. These dark, silent, hard, and scruffy men listened to the love songs, remembering their women. They listened and drank. So Juan drank, and he listened. When the bottle was empty, he demanded another.

In the morning, Blas had the *vaqueros* come in and help carry Juan to a boarding house across the road. He knew he could not take Juan home to Doña Ophelia in this condition, so they picked him up gently, careful not to reopen his wound, and they carried him out the door into the harsh morning light.

And there, outside the cantina, stood Doña Ophelia Santos, her eyes ablaze and her mouth set in a thin, grim line.

Chapter 5
There's Something

Matamoros, Mexico
July, 1847

"LOOK AT HER." Charles Pownall lit a cigar and shook the match at the window, the smoke curling its way among the thin curtain folds. "She rides in here like she owns this town, like she owns the by-God river."

"Señor Pownall, she owns everything."

Pownall turned away from the window and scowled at Timo Martinez, who was sprawled in the corner chair of Pownall's office, his muddy boots scratching the floor. The bandit studied his unlit shuck cigarette, apparently waiting for a light, but Pownall did not offer one. Instead, he turned back to the window. Across the street, Ophelia Santos' confrontation with her drunken, wayward son had drawn a small crowd. As he watched, she raised her hand. The *vaqueros* stopped and laid Juan on the ground. She bent down to inspect his shoulder. A bright crimson stain streaked Juan's white ruffled shirt.

"That Santos boy looks out of uniform," Pownall said, puffing on his cigar. "Doesn't usually dress that fancy. Who shot him?"

Behind him, Timo did not answer right away. Eventually he replied, "Maybe the Rangers."

"Too bad they didn't finish the job," Pownall said. "That whole Santos clan is nothing but trouble. Think because they have old land titles they can change the outcome of the war. Well, they can't. Mexico is losing. That means Ophelia Santos is losing." He watched the *vaqueros* lift Juan into the black carriage. Then Ophelia boarded, and the whole procession clattered out of town.

He turned from the window and seated himself behind his desk, feeling hot and sticky in his coat and tie. "You didn't get my cattle this time," he said in precise Spanish. "I paid you an advance, and you didn't bring me a single head of Santos beef. I want my money back or I want the cattle. Which is it going to be?"

Timo shrugged. "Money," he said. "I need *more* money. The *cabrónes* Rangers, they killed my brothers. And all my men. I need more. And after this job, I go away. Too many Rangers here."

Pownall shook his head. "That's *your* problem. I already paid you. It's up to you to get more men, or you don't get the rest of your money. That's it." He leaned back and casually steepled his fingers. The big black cigar stuck out of his mouth and blue smoke curled into the air between the men.

Timo pulled his sombrero on and scraped his chair back, banging it against the wall as he rose. *"Mira*, Señor Pownall, you give me more money, now." He stomped to the desk, reached over and grabbed Pownall by the lapel, pulling him out of his chair.

Pownall felt a sudden hollowness in his bowels. The cigar drooped in his mouth. Timo touched the tip of his cigarette to Pownall's cigar, puffed twice, then let him go.

Pownall fell back into his chair and blinked. He took a few breaths, then pulled the cigar from his mouth and laid it in a marble ashtray on his desk. Clenching his fists, he looked up at Timo. "Don't you ever touch me again," he said in a voice so low he was almost speaking to himself. "Nobody touches me, especially not a dirty greaser like you!"

Timo grinned, took a long drag, and blew acrid smoke in Pownall's face. "You are dirty, too, Señor Pownall. Maybe more dirty than me, no? You want me to go? I go." He flicked his cigarette in the general direction of the ashtray and started for the door.

"Espera, hombre," Pownall called, asking him to wait, suppressing a most urgent desire to see this dirty, stubborn, and despicable bandit hanging from the nearest rafter. Despicable, but damned good at stealing cattle. He fumbled in his coat pocket for a small purse, shook a few coins from it, and

tossed them across the desk. Timo caught them in mid-air with one swipe. He jingled them, opened his palm to look at them, and grinned.

"I will get you some nice Santa Alicia cattle, Señor Pownall. In a few days, when the moon is out, so we can work the brush at night."

"If you get caught, I don't know you."

"No." Timo paused and looked at the door. "What about the great lady?"

"You would hurt a woman?"

Timo shrugged. "Why not?"

"I only want her land. Leave her alone—she doesn't deserve to have the likes of you pawing her, at least not until I say so."

Timo jerked his chin up. "You? She deserves you instead?" He started laughing.

Picking up his cigar, Pownall puffed twice and turned his chair toward the window. Behind him, he heard the door creak open. Timo's boots and spurs scraped the floor, then the door closed. Beyond the door he heard Timo's nasal laughter fading away. *Despicable.* Pownall took a handkerchief from his coat pocket, wiped his brow, then rose and walked to a side door. He pushed through this door and entered another office, where four men sat around a large wooden table, inspecting a map of the river area.

"Charles, Charles, look at this," called Franklin Dresser, pointing with his coffee cup. "I think this spot has possibilities." He put the cup down and stabbed a finger at a location on the map.

Pownall walked closer and watched Dresser's finger as it traced the curve of the river. "This is Stryker's Banco de Santa Rita here," said Dresser. "It floods damned awful."

Rufus Hightower laughed. "Stryker didn't get a bargain there, did he?" The other men also laughed. "I don't know what he expected. When the river shifted course and exposed that little strip of land, the Mexicans were glad to give him title to it. Why not? It's only dry half the month."

"Right," Dresser said. "Right. But that's not where I mean. I mean, look here." He pointed at a spot down-river from Stryker's strip. "Here, he said, "right next to Fort Brown. It'll be perfect. The fort can protect our new town. There are already plenty of shacks there. Hell, it's like the town is already started."

Pownall leaned over the map, edging Benjamin Winkle aside. He looked more closely at the spot Dresser was pointing at and shook his head. "Look at this, gentlemen," he said. "Down-river on the Mexican side is Boca del Rio. It's a bad port. The sandbars are hard to navigate, you have to wait for high tide, and the Mexican customs are there, waiting for you when you land. Now, all you men are like me. You came here to make money. To do that, we have to bring in goods. But we have to do it on the Texas side. So we need a town on the Texas side." He moved his finger along the Gulf coastline, across the mouth of the Rio Grande, and toward the Texas coastline. "Ships landed here when the war broke out," he said, pointing to Port Isabel. "Now that the Walker Tariff has re-imposed duties on goods coming into Mexico, it's more expensive to bring them into Boca del Rio. So let's bring our goods into Port Isabel."

"And then?" asked Harold Frost.

"And then we sneak them across the river when the Mexicans and the U.S. Army aren't watching."

The men nodded, all of them smiling.

"But we still need a town," said Pownall, "and we need one that won't flood. Fort Brown is on this *resaca*. The river used to flow right through there. Just like Stryker's, it floods. We need something higher."

The men were still nodding, but now with frowns of concentration as they leaned forward to stare more closely at the map.

"And I think I know where," continued Pownall. "I was speaking to Major Roberts from Fort Brown the other night at dinner. I often invite the poor man to dinner since he appears to have few friends. I gave him all the brandy he could drink, and do you know what he told me?"

"That he's been faking stupidity all this time?" quipped Dresser.

"No, no, I believe that is quite genuine." Pownall shook his head. "No, he told me that Fort Brown is to be moved next year. To higher ground." He put his finger on a spot on the Texas side just opposite Matamoros. "Here," he said. "Look at all that empty land around this spot."

Dresser shook his head. "Charles, that land belongs to Ophelia Santos. That whole section, including where Fort Brown is now, is in fact hers."

Pownall smiled and stepped back from the table. He picked up his cigar and sucked at it, but it had gone out, so he relit it and worked it up again, then blew the smoke over the map and turned to pace toward the window. "You're wrong, Dresser. Your legal training has failed you this time, I'm afraid. She used to have title to it, but I happen to know from the *alcalde* of Matamoros that her family ceded that piece of land to the city of Matamoros when it was founded." Another puff. "To allow for city expansion. Since then, the title has transferred to others. So we can buy it. If we do it quietly."

Franklin Dresser held up his hand, palm outward. "I'm a better lawyer than that, Charles. Your *alcalde* friend forgot to tell you that nobody ever paid the Santos family for the land. The transaction was never consummated. She still owns it, legally. Or at the very least, title is uncertain."

Frost spoke up. "Remember what they say about land, gentlemen. Possession! Possession!" He sipped his coffee, waiting until they all nodded to continue. "I agree with Charles. If we move quietly and quickly, we can buy that land, set up our town, and there won't be a damned thing she can do about it."

Winkle pushed his chair back from the table. "I'm not sure I like this. She does own the land, doesn't she? Why don't we just offer to buy it from her?"

"Technically," Pownall grunted. "She may own it *technically*. *If* she can undo the tangle of conflicting claims that have already accumulated. *If* she can prove it in a court of law. But why should she? It isn't that much land, really. That's probably why she hasn't bothered to clear this up before. And what about us if we buy from her? Then we might face litigation from the present owners."

He returned to the table. "Think about it, Winkle. We can petition the state to form a town company. We can lay out plots and get rich selling them to the hordes of settlers and businessmen who will head here after the war is over. And we can set up shop and move all that material through Port Isabel into a rebuilding Mexico. Think, man, think!"

The five men puffed their cigars, sipped their coffee, and stared thoughtfully at the map. They occasionally looked out the window at the hot July morning blazing white and dusty, but their attention always returned to the spot, the potential town, that Pownall had shown them on the map.

"Well," said Dresser, "I don't guess it's such a bad idea. Seems like a simple plan, and those work best. Build the town and then fight her off in court if she sues. Seems easy enough. Hell, except for Pownall here, we're all lawyers."

"And Charles is bright enough to be one," put in Hightower.

"I doubt if intelligence," Pownall interjected dryly, "is the key ingredient for lawyering." No one seemed eager to inquire what the key ingredient might be.

Winkle frowned. "You think she'll fight?"

"You can count on it," Dresser replied. "She's a feisty one."

They puffed their cigars and considered the map.

"Don't worry too much about her," Pownall finally said. "We'll find a way to keep her distracted."

"What about that boy of hers, El Gallo? He could be trouble."

Pownall snorted. "Hell, all he cares about are whores, horses, and mescal. Looks like he's hell-bent on getting himself killed, too. Don't worry about him. He won't be any trouble." He walked back into his adjoining office, then returned with a bottle of brandy and five small glasses. He opened the bottle and filled a glass for each of them, took a puff of his cigar, then raised his glass.

"Gentlemen," he said, "to the Brownsville Town Company."

They raised their glasses. "To the Brownsville Town Company." They drank. Pownall beamed as he refilled their glasses, and they drank again.

TOM STARR LOOKED BACK at his Ranger troop as he led them northward from Fort Brown, toward the Nueces River. He had orders to sweep out the Comanche, who had been attacking river settlements from havens within the thick brush. With him were his seven Rangers and an orphan boy who had joined them at Fort Brown—a strong lad of about sixteen years named Billy. They had brought him along to wash and fetch, but as they rode along through the thick brush and cacti, Starr regretted including him in the troop. The boy talked too much. They also had a new guide. Don Pepe, their self-professed fierce guide and fighter, had, to Uriah's great disappointment, been found in a Matamoros alley with his throat cut. Their new man was Ramiro, a grim-faced man who had none of the comical eccentricities that had endeared the Don to the Rangers. Ramiro was quiet, disciplined, and effective, which suited Starr.

Billy was currently riding beside Uriah, explaining in great detail how he had been bitten in the leg by a rattlesnake south of San Antonio.

"You gonna talk all day long?" Uriah barked.

"I'm just telling you what happened to me."

"Hell, boy, my ears are starting to hurt. Go talk to the Cap'n."

Starr pulled his horse in and waited for Billy to ride up, then waved him aside.

"Cap'n, sir, I was just telling Mr. Lee about—"

Starr cut him off. "You keep your mouth shut on a scout, boy."

Billy fell silent, his face disappearing into the shadow of his hat. "Yessir."

Starr looked back at the two mules bearing their packs, wrapped in water-tight leather *cayaques*, then nodded at the boy. "Take those two mules and ride back behind us a bit. If there's action, don't let them get loose."

Billy said "Yessir" again, then reined his horse over to the mules and took their lead from Ambrose Bradshaw. After he had dropped back a few yards, the Rangers began to again appreciate the magnificent silence of the open brush country. Except for the sound of their horses' hooves, muffled in the soft reddish sandy soil, they heard little else but the distant scream of a hawk or the coo of a dove. The morning sun was already beating down, and they adjusted their hats to shade their faces.

They moved in silence throughout the day, searching for Indian sign. Starr threw out two men as an advance, and set another man on each side as outriders. There was no actual trail to follow, so the men wound their way through the brush and *nopal*, using game traces and often finding themselves boxed in by huge clumps of the prickly green cacti that was taller than a man standing on his horse and twenty yards long. Eventually, they crossed a stream meandering through the brush, a pitiful trickle, but enough to water their horses.

Ahead, the brush opened toward a tiny, muddy pond, where a flock of large white geese had gathered. Ramiro broke off and rode among the big birds, scattering them, spinning his bullwhip over his head and sending it smashing into the flock. A loud crack split the air, and a goose fluttered to the water amid a snowfall of tiny feathers. Another crack, and a second goose fell into the pond. Ramiro spun his horse about and scooped up the two kills, leaning over in his saddle at a full gallop.

"For dinner," he called, grinning, and then hurried back toward the Rangers.

"That was magnificent!" cried Billy.

Starr shrugged. Any real *vaquero* could do that.

Ramiro plucked and dressed one of the geese as they rode along. They traveled all day in the dusty, blistering heat, pushing the snorting horses hard, dragging the mules, and navigating the brush as best they could. In the late afternoon of the second day, they stopped under a stand of *retamas* to rest, herding the horses into a bushy corral with abundant grass. Soon a smoky mesquite fire blazed and a goose dangled on a spit. Starr took some coffee from his saddlebags, and Ramiro produced a banged up pot to boil it in.

"After today," Starr ordered, "cold camp."

Uriah nodded. "I can smell 'em, too, Cap'n. Them savages are out there."

Toward evening of the third day, they reached a wider trace in the brush, part of an ancient system of roads blazed by the Spanish to link Mexico with their eastern Texas colonies. They swung right toward San Patricio.

"Cap'n," Frenchy reported, "there's tracks here. Carriage and horsemen, maybe ten riders."

Starr rode up to where Frenchy had dismounted. "Where they headed?"

"Same way we are, San Patricio. Reckon they don't know about the Comanche."

Billy rode up, still leading the mules. "Cap'n, sir, Cap'n, are those Comanche tracks there?"

Uriah grinned, turning the cylinder on his Colt. "Now, boy, what the hell would Comanche want with a carriage?"

"Well, if it ain't Comanche, who is it?"

Starr shrugged. "Some *ranchero* with his *vaqueros* heading to Corpus Christi, I'd say. Carriage means he must have his señora with him." He looked around, found an open area near the road, and pointed to it. "Let's make camp right there, boys. No fire tonight. Graze the horses now. We'll sleep in a circle, horses in the middle. Every man sleeps with his Colts under his blanket."

As the men moved to obey, Starr rode a few yards further up the road and looked at the tracks in the gathering dusk. He stopped just out of sight of his men and stared down the road ahead of him, then looked around at the huge cacti clumps around him. He sensed something. He could not put his finger on it, but he felt uneasy. It was more than just the general presence of Comanche. It was something about this carriage, those people up ahead.

That night they slept in a circle, their pallets arranged around their horses and mules to keep the Comanche from stealing them. As darkness fell, they noticed a glow on the horizon.

Frenchy rolled up on his elbow. "Campfire," he said. "About five, six miles, I'd say."

"Is it Comanche?" Billy asked, sitting bright-eyed on his pallet.

"Doubt it," replied Floyd. "More likely that bunch with the carriage."

Starr got up and walked toward the road, unbuttoned his pants and urinated. Overhead, thousands of stars glittered, sending down just enough light to outline the brush around him. It was so quiet he could hear his urine bubble and snake away down the road, falling into one of the cracks in the dry earth. A soft warm breeze blew the clean smells of mesquite and cacti across the land. As Starr looked toward the horizon, at the distant campfire glow, his disquiet grew. *Something*, he said to himself. *There's something*. But he did not know what, so he returned to his pallet and wrapped himself in his blanket, his Colt loaded and ready in his hand.

REFUSING THE PLATE of beans and *carnitas* offered by her mother, Lidia turned her nose up and twisted her head away from the campfire.

"*Mi hija*, you have to eat. Luis, tell her to eat." Martina de Leon turned to her husband, who sat across the campfire with several *vaqueros* scooping their food up with tortillas.

"She doesn't want to eat, let her not eat," he sputtered. "She'll be hungry soon enough."

Martina placed the food on the flat rock beside her daughter, then stood up, her hands on her hips. "Well, I'm not going to let you starve. What will you look like when you meet your betrothed?"

"I don't care what I look like for him," Lidia snapped. "It doesn't matter. It's all settled, remember? It's even been established that I'm not damaged goods. I wonder if he'll check my teeth and make me stick out my tongue. He'll probably ask me to trot around the room a few times to make sure I'm spry enough for him—"

"Enough!" Don de Leon roared, throwing his plate to the ground. "We are going to continue to San Patricio. There we will meet my brothers. They've sailed all the way from Vera Cruz for your wedding. We will all travel together to San Antonio de Bejar." He stood up and pointed his finger at her. "You will not embarrass me. You will be a model of charm and hospitality. You will not humiliate our family!"

Martina de Leon twisted her hands together and looked at Lidia with an expression that pled for her to stop. Lidia glanced at her mother, raised her nose again, and fell silent. Then she rose and moved away from the fire. Stepping into her tent, she slapped the flap closed.

She slept poorly that night. She thought about her forced marriage, which filled her with humiliation and renewed anger, and finally shifted her thoughts to Juan. As she lay staring at the tent ceiling, she replayed the scene at the de Leon ranch over and over—Juan sitting in the carriage as she tried to explain, the look of total disgust on his face.

She shut her eyes tight and turned on her side, a quick movement on the cot that threw off the thin sheet. The quiet of the night seemed to wane. She heard the snoring of her parents in the next tent, the shuffling of the hobbled horses, the cry of a night hawk, and the mumbling of the *vaqueros* on night watch. She rose, wrapped the sheet around her, and stepped out into the night. The moon had risen. It washed the edges of swiftly passing clouds with iridescent light, peeking out occasionally at the earth below, perhaps to see if anybody was looking. Lidia looked around the camp, and in the intermittent light of the moon she saw thousands of lumps of cacti.

After a few minutes, she wandered over to the fire and sat on the rock, wrapping herself tightly, not against the cool of the evening because it was in fact quite warm, but for comfort. She hugged herself, but even that small comfort was inadequate. She felt betrayed by everyone who had ever claimed to love her, and from the dark inner folds of her mind where she put things she never wanted to see or think about again, a disobedient thought slipped out. Perhaps this was all her fault. Perhaps she should have told Juan about the betrothal. But she knew him, knew his dark and powerful pride. If she had told him, he would have shut himself off from her at the onset, never given her a chance. She crammed the thought back into its dark corner. Looking up at the moon, she wrapped herself even more tightly.

If God was punishing her for some transgression, He was no better than her father. She wanted nothing more to do with Him. The moonlight washed down on her upturned face. *No*, she thought, *I don't mean that. But let Him do his worst to me now and get it over with, as long as I can get Juan back!* She lowered her face, brought her hands to her eyes. Her shoulders shook, her long hair fell free across her face. Her salty tears flowed into her hands, seeped between her slender fingers and fell to the parched soil, soaking in immediately, leaving only dark stains to mark their passing.

She sat there for hours, and when she had no more tears left, she returned to her tent, where she lay awake until dawn, staring at the ceiling. She knew the workings of Juan's mind, and she knew that once a thought took root in that brain, it was immovable. Juan believed that Lidia had used him, had tricked him, had in fact betrayed him and played him for a fool. She would never be able to change his mind. And in a few days, she would become another man's wife. So it was over. As the first light of dawn crept through the sleeping camp, she began to wonder if this was the way women like her mother began their lifetimes of sadness.

Not long after dawn, they breakfasted and resumed their journey. The morning found her tense, irritable, oppressed by a strange, heavy air. She still rode in the carriage with her parents but she would not look at either of them. Her face felt swollen and her eyes grainy as she peered out at the brush and cacti. She saw a rattlesnake slither out of the way, and two others coiled by the side of the road in the shade of the mesquite brush.

"Are you not speaking to us today, Lidia?" Don de Leon inquired.

"I have nothing to say."

"You didn't eat supper last night. And nothing for breakfast." He frowned. "You will eat today. I won't have you falling ill."

"No. It would spoil the wedding, wouldn't it?" She flashed him a venomous look, then returned her gaze to the scenery.

"Someday you're going to regret the way you talk to me," he said in a somewhat softer voice. "You think I'm an old fool. Doing this for my own prestige. But it's for *you*. You think you love Juan, but he cannot make you happy. I know things. You must trust me."

Lidia sat for a moment and let his words soak in. They were rare words, coming from him. But she refused to look at him, and the moment passed, though she felt a vague reluctance to let it go. Something changed in that moment. She sensed it, but it floated past before she could look at it, before she could grasp it. She could almost feel it. Finally, she turned to look at her father, to see if he felt it, too. The land outside her carriage window was still drenched with sunshine, but something was wrong. She felt as if the sky had suddenly conjured up a black day growling with thunder. She felt her senses sharpening, breathed in and expelled the smell of cactus blooms, horses, rawhide, and dry mesquite shrugging off the morning dew. She heard the creaking and jingling of their gear, the rumbling of the wheels, the whistles of the *vaqueros*. The blood coursing through her veins made noises in her ears, sounding like an army of soldiers marching through her brain.

Something had happened in that moment, she knew, and she looked at her father mostly in wonder, for her anger seemed to have floated away with the moment. Don de Leon briefly returned her stare, then turned away.

Arrows came singing through the air, and one of them slammed through the open carriage window and embedded itself in Martina de Leon's chest. A cry arose from the *vaqueros*, and the carriage lurched forward as the driver cracked his whip over the horses. Pistol shots, shotgun and rifle fire rang out. Lidia heard herself screaming. She looked in horror at her mother's dead eyes and frozen face.

Lidia fluttered her hands over the arrow shaft, not knowing where to grasp it, then she grabbed it with both hands and tried to pull it out. "Mother!" she cried, but the arrow had passed through Martina and stuck deep in the wooden frame of the carriage seat. She could not budge it.

At the same time, Don de Leon shrank away, his eyes bulging and his whiskered jaw hanging open.

"Help me," she cried, but he only blinked, as if he could blink away the arrow, perhaps blink away the day and the horror it visited. "Father! Help me!"

"*Dios mío*," he muttered finally, drawing a pistol. He stuck his head out the carriage window and fired once, then leaned back into the carriage, still blinking. He reached over and tried to pull Lidia's hands away from the arrow, but she would not let go.

"No!" she cried. "Mother!" The speeding carriage lurched violently, and in the next instant flew through the air and landed upside down. The last thing Lidia saw was a huge clump of pale green, prickly, *nopal* cactus rushing toward her.

DON DE LEON writhed beneath the carriage, his legs pinned under it. He tried to turn onto his back and lift the carriage off his legs, but excruciating pain slammed him back down. His head swam as he reached for his pistol, which had landed beneath a cacti clump. But it was too far away. The *vaqueros'* guns roared, and the ground shook with the constant pounding of running, screaming horses. The smoke and dust of battle swirled over him in the crisp morning air. Falling back on the carriage, the *vaqueros* encircled it, firing their pistols and *escopetas*. The Comanche, perhaps fifteen of them, rode in a circle, hiding from the *vaqueros'* guns by leaning over the side of their ponies and firing arrows from underneath their horses' necks. The *vaqueros* fell one by one on the sandy ground. When only two remained, they crashed their horses into the brush, as if they were driving longhorns. The Comanche riddled them with arrows.

As Don de Leon made one last lunge for the pistol, he felt something give in his lower spine. A sudden shifting of bone, sinew, nerve. A tremendous wave of pain wracked his body. He cried out and then fainted. When he came to, someone had grabbed his hair was jerking his head up. Through closed eyelids he could see shadows moving between him and the sun. The soft voice of a young man speaking foreign words rolled over him. He struggled to understand. Then a tingling sensation stung his forehead. It traveled around the side of his head to the back, to the other side, then to the front again. He heard a strange rolling sound as the knife sliced through his scalp, and when the young Comanche brave tore the scalp from his head, Don de Leon heard a thunderous ripping sound. His face dropped back into the dirt.

AS LIDIA REGAINED CONSCIOUSNESS, she felt the *nopal* needles pricking her hands. Dirt clogged her nostrils and stung her eyes, but she could see and hear her feet scraping behind her as someone dragged her by the arms from beneath the cacti. The Comanche brave pulled her several feet through the red dirt and then stopped and brought his face down close to hers. He ran his eyes over her, tugged at her hair, and grunted. Lidia pushed herself along the ground, trying to get away from him, but her efforts only seemed to amuse him. Behind him, she saw other Comanche walking around the carriage and through the surrounding mesquite brush, leaning over corpses and cutting away their scalps. Several of them had broken open her mother's trunks and were scattering her clothes all over the cacti. Red dust flew everywhere. She followed the busy Comanche with her eyes. The braves seemed to be ignoring her, even as she sat in their midst. *Perhaps I'm dead*, she thought, *and I'm just a spirit.* She decided that was wrong, however, for her bruised arms and legs hurt too much. She had a sensation of floating, like her head was full of cotton, and these people were from a dream. Perhaps she was still in her tent. Dozing. Having a nightmare.

Then someone yanked her to her feet, and the sudden motion made her dizzy. When she opened her eyes, a dark man with feathers in his hair stood before her. He was smeared with pungent grease. The smell of him penetrated into the inner corners of her foggy head and pushed away the dreaminess. He stood there, leering at her, tugging at the folds of her dress, poking at her boned corset. As her mind slowly cleared, her eyes grew large and her heart pounded. She inched away from him, but he grabbed her arm and shoved her toward his horse. There he tried to rip her skirt off, but it was so tightly buttoned and hooked that he dragged her down instead, and she rolled across the prickly cacti screaming, trying to find her feet. He laughed, then spoke to her in a soft, strange tongue as he pulled her back up. He spun her around and tied her hands behind her. Lidia cried out again, and the pain cleared her head completely. She realized that everyone was dead. Her mother, her father—all of them, dead.

"Nooooo!" she screamed.

The brave turned her around and frowned, barking something she did not understand. As his pungent breath blasted her face, she worked to push down her fear. If she was going to die anyway, what good was fear? She would not give these heathens the satisfaction of watching her cower.

She said the first thing that came into her mind. "Give me that scarf," she demanded, jutting out her chin. The defiant look in her eyes would be unmistakable, even to this savage. She nodded at the blue garment lying on a nearby cactus. It was one of Martina's favorites.

The brave followed her gaze and went to retrieve the scarf, which he looped around her waist. He then jumped on his pony, pulled her up sidesaddle in front of him, and pulled the ends of the scarf around his own waist and tied them in a knot. This done, he threw his head back and unleashed a high pitched cry, and soon all of the Comanche were riding in a circle around him, answering with their own cries. They raised their bows into the air in their victory salute and then thundered off toward the north and the Nueces River.

Lashed sideways against her captor, Lidia strained hard to stay on the horse. She gasped at the pain in her legs, and when she opened her eyes again, she saw the thin, muscular chest of the man who was abducting her. She smelled the bear grease rubbed in his hair, and saw the knots of dirt and debris among the feathers and leather bands. They rode fast, and they rode all day, crossing the Nueces in the mid-afternoon and then swinging west. When evening came, they slowed down but kept going, stopping only to switch to the spare horses they had taken from the *vaqueros.* They left their own mounts strung out along their trail, spent and useless, standing trembling in the dark with their hooves set wide apart, staring dully at the riders moving away.

Hours later, when even their new mounts began stumbling, the war party finally stopped. They were near a stream. Lidia felt the scarf rope loosen, then she slid gratefully off the horse and landed in a dusty heap on the ground. She heard the braves laugh, and she knew they were laughing at her. She lay still for a while and watched the strange men prepare their camp, ignoring her. She must have dozed, for sometime later she came awake with a start as she felt herself being dragged again, by the legs this time. She could see a small fire, and when the dragging stopped she looked up to see the Comanche braves standing in a circle around her. The one who had abducted her stepped forward and flipped her skirt up.

"*Ay Dios,*" she cried. "*Ay Dios, No!*"

"*Mira, Capitán!*"

Starr and the other Rangers sat their horses and looked off toward the east where Ramiro was pointing. Beneath the rising sun, a wide red cloud of dust hugged the horizon. Billy pulled his mules up and looked, too, putting his hand up to shade his eyes.

"Reckon it's that Mexican bunch all right," said Starr. "Could be the Comanche are after them."

"Nice o' them greasers to find the red bastards for us, ain't it boys?" Frenchy grinned.

"Billy, hang on to those mules," Starr barked. "Let's ride." The Ranger troop moved out at a full gallop up the road, directly toward the dust cloud. When they came upon the overturned carriage and human wreckage scattered through the brush, Starr dismounted quickly. Inside the carriage, he found Martina de Leon's body. A frigid claw of fear suddenly gripped his chest and sent him reeling.

"De Leones," he muttered. They could not have been so stupid as to bring Lidia with them, could they? He urgently scanned the bodies strewn around the carriage. Don de Leon lay pinned underneath, scalped, but Starr noticed a slight movement. "Help me here, boys."

They pushed the carriage back on its wheels and pulled Don de Leon out, and Starr called out to his men, "Look for the girl!"

But the scout walked up, shaking his head. "They no leave no girl," Ramiro said. "They take." He pointed toward the north.

Don de Leon moaned.

"Frenchy," Starr said, "take a look at de Leon here. Will he make it?"

Frenchy dismounted and examined the scalped man's head, then ripped open the man's pants and examined the legs. "Many a man's lived through a scalping," he finally said, "but this here leg will need to come off."

Don de Leon moaned again.

Billy rode up in a dead run and slid to a halt, leading an extra horse. "Cap'n, Cap'n, looky! I found me a horse them Comanche never caught!"

Starr knew that without spare horses, it would be almost impossible to catch the Comanche, but they had Lidia, and he would follow them plumb to hell if need be. He turned to Billy. "Hook the mules up to this carriage. San Patricio ain't but a couple days' ride up this road, boy. Take Don de Leon on in."

"Oh, hell, Cap'n, you don't mean I got to coddle a dying Meskin? We got Comanche to chase! They ain't but an hour gone—"

Billy stopped talking because the look on Starr's face told him to stop. Uriah Lee grinned and winked at Frenchy, who flipped his eye patch up so he could scratch around his empty eye socket. The men stood in silence. Finally Billy dismounted and began to harness the mules to the carriage.

The Rangers placed Don de Leon in the carriage, then wrapped a soiled sheet around the body of Martina de Leon, whose eyes still stared in horror at the last moment of her life. They buried her quickly, scooping out a shallow depression in the soil, rolling a few rocks over the grave. They stacked the dead *vaqueros* in the brush.

Then Starr mounted and rode up to Billy. "This carriage better get into that town, boy. If it don't, I aim to shoot you."

Billy nodded sullenly, and then watched as the Rangers tore off single file toward the Nueces River.

The Rangers rode all day, seldom stopping. Starr put Ramiro out in front and threw out one man on each side as spies. Toward evening, they crossed the Nueces and watered their horses briefly, refilling their water gourds, mixing up some pinole, then riding on. The Mexican scout pointed them westward, and they turned in the gathering gloom toward the brighter of the two horizons. Along the way, they found discarded trail horses, left by the Comanche, still shivering in exhaustion. They rode long into the night, picking their way by the thin light of the moon as it peeked through the clouds. About midnight, Starr called a halt.

"They ain't but two hours ahead," he said, "but they switched horses. They took horses off the dead *vaqueros* back there, except for this one here. We can't catch them this way." He gripped his saddle horn, twisting it as he spoke, knowing Lidia was only safe as long as the Comanche kept moving.

The Mexican scout nodded his head.

Starr continued, "We're better mounted, but we been riding hard and only got one spare. Ramiro?"

"They will stop soon, *Capitán*."

Bradshaw scratched his head. "Don't figure, Cap'n. Why would they stop?"

"I can think of one good reason." Uriah grinned. "That de Leon girl would stop me. Shame, pretty one she was, too. Ruined, now."

Starr greeted this comment with bitter silence.

Uriah added, "If they'd attacked a settlement, they'd still be riding. Out here, they likely figured nobody would know to chase them."

"We're pushing on," Starr growled. "Ramiro, you ride on ahead, take the extra horse. If the Comanche do make camp, ride on back and lead us to it. If they don't, wait up the trail a ways till we catch you up. We'll short-rest our mounts here and then follow."

"*Capitán*." Ramiro nodded and reached out for the reins to the spare horse, then jammed his spurs hard. He disappeared in a swirl of dust.

The Rangers dismounted and hobbled their horses, then ate jerked beef and drank warm water from their gourds. They sat in silence and listened to the horses chewing on whatever weeds and stray grasses they could find that didn't have thorns. A short while later—too short to actually rest the horses—Starr ordered them back in pursuit. They walked as much as they rode, picking their way in the thin light.

The moon hung low on the horizon when Ramiro came riding back, his horse lathered and shivering and barely moving. The Rangers gathered around him.

"They make camp," Ramiro said.

Starr ran his hand through his dust-encrusted hair, swallowing hard, trying not to fix his thoughts on Lidia and what might be happening to her. "All right," he said hoarsely, "keep moving. We can hit them first light."

Two hours later, they crouched among the cacti, their horses muffled, and looked at the glow of the Comanche campfire beside a glistening creek. The eastern horizon began to throw a faintly bluish light on the world.

FROM THE FRINGES of oblivion she came back, against her will, back to the cold dusty ground and the mesquite and the cacti. She opened her eyes and instantly began to cry again. The cool pre-dawn air hurt her lungs, sharpened the pain screaming from her loins, her hips, her arms. She curled up and watched the blue light of dawn spreading upward.

There had been five of them. Dirty, grunting, hurting, stinking. She had vomited in horror, humiliation, and pain, but they'd just dragged her to another place and kept at her. Five had used her, but the other six were too exhausted from the long ride. They had gotten tired of waiting and fallen asleep. As she lay now in the dim, gray dawn, the horrible realization grew that the other six would want her now. She shut her eyes as waves of pain racked her blood-streaked body. Writhing, she sought comfort that was not there, would never be there again. She lay thinking of her slain parents, wondering who would bury them. The thought that they lay exposed to the hot Texas sun convulsed her with grief, and she cried all the more because there was nothing she could do about it.

And then she thought about Juan. She thought of him dressed in his fine clothes, riding tall on his horse. The stallion would step and dance down the street, and Juan would remove his sombrero and smile down handsomely at her when he came to ask for her hand. It had almost happened, it was almost true. But that was the old dream, before he abandoned her, before the Comanche, before this nightmare. If he had only believed her, none of this would have happened.

She saw one of the Comanche braves stretch and then flip over near the fire. She thought perhaps if she begged hard enough they would kill her when they were done with her. Everything she cared about was gone. She was raped and despoiled. Her life was over. She looked up at the fading stars and closed her eyes. She tried to talk to God, but her thoughts became fragmented, incoherent. When she could not think of what to say, she sobbed and let the tears flow down her cheeks and turn the dust beneath her into mud.

"Pass THE WORD," Starr whispered. "Look out for the de Leon girl." The word was passed down the line as the Rangers crouched in the mesquite brush as it swayed in the cool morning breeze. They had spread out into a line about thirty yards wide, their backs to the morning light so that the Comanche would have to squint and strain to see them. Starr looked to his left, then to his right. They were ready. He saw a lone brave flip over near the campfire about fifty yards away, and toward the left he could see the horses grazing in the weak morning light. The Comanche, he figured, would be in no hurry this morning. The horses would be allowed to graze, for they had been ridden hard the day before and would be doubtless ridden hard today. On the right, just beyond the circle of the campfire, he spotted Lidia. She was lying, moving on the cold hard ground, and he felt a pang of despair. Her body shook so much that he knew she was crying. He also knew he was too late. As he kept his gaze on her for a long minute, his anger grew until at last he turned his face toward the enemy and smoothly mounted his horse. The Rangers all down the line did the same. They drew their Colts and turned to look at their captain. He put his horse forward, and the entire line of Rangers lurched out of the brush, kicking up dust and turf and smashing through the cacti so hard that it went flying everywhere.

Hearing the charge, the Comanche jumped for their weapons as the first Ranger gun fired. They ran for their horses, and the five that were closest to them leaped on the fear-crazed animals. The others unleashed a volley of arrows even as the Ranger guns began blazing. Starr drew a bead on one brave and shot him in the head, then fired at the brave next to him but missed. Out of the corner of his eye he saw one of his Rangers fall off his horse as they galloped into the camp.

The Ranger firing was thunderous, but the arrows whistled past their heads, riddling the field with deadly effect. Another Ranger fell, and his horse careened sideways and crashed into Starr's horse, sending them both sprawling among the thorns. Starr rolled over and came up firing. He saw two braves go down, but now the ones on horseback were pressing, firing arrows at the Rangers from the flank, screaming and hooting.

"Frenchy, Sam!" he called. He pointed at the riders, and the three of them pulled out their rifles and fired, but the Comanche slid over the sides of their horses and let the volley pass. "Shoot the goddamn horses!" Starr cried as he remounted. He looked toward the camp again, where half a dozen Comanche were still trying to get to their ponies. But the Rangers were now riding through them, scattering the screaming animals in a dust-choked melee, then turning to fire at the braves. Confusion reigned, men whooped and yelled, blood splattered everywhere, screams of pain rang out across the brush. The mounted Comanche attacked, the dismounted ones fought from the campfire, and the Rangers scrambled in ten different directions, cursing and shooting constantly at the elusive braves. Starr drew down on one brave by the campfire and shot him in the chest. As the last one fell, the mounted Comanche crashed into the creek. The Rangers fired after them with rifles, and two Indian ponies thrashed in the water. The rest were soon lost in the thick brush of the opposite bank. In a minute, the firing stopped, the air full of smoke, hoof beats fading away. All around them, the wounded moaned. The battleground writhed with fallen horses, Rangers, and Comanche.

"Damn red bastards sure can fight," Frenchy muttered with a curse as he and Starr bent to examine Jeremiah Wood, who lay gasping on the ground with an arrow sticking into his abdomen and out his back.

"I'm kilt, ain't I?"

"That you are, Jeremiah," replied Frenchy, "and your horse, too." He nodded over at Wood's horse, which was thrashing around in the cacti with an arrow in its windpipe.

"You do him for me, Frenchy."

Frenchy rose and pulled his Colt, then walked over to the choking animal and fired twice into its head. The thrashing stopped.

Over beyond the horse, Starr saw Floyd Johnson lying with an arrow in his throat, already dead. "Damn, there's Floyd," was all he said.

"Damn filthy Comanche!" Frenchy cursed again. He walked over to the body and snapped off the arrow. He pulled Floyd up over his shoulder and walked to the campfire with him. Uriah Lee and Sam Brennan busied themselves shooting the Comanche wounded in the head as Frenchy laid Floyd down by the fire.

There were dead and dying men to attend to, but Starr hurried over to Lidia and kneeled down beside her, cutting her hands free. She immediately scuttled away from him.

"It's all right, Miss Lidia. It's me, Tom Starr, remember?" He reached out to touch her shoulder.

She screamed, clawing out against him, her eyes wildly searching for an escape. Starr backed away, watching her push back from him until she curled up against a rock, sobbing deeply into her slender hands. She would not look at him. Starr just stood back and let her cry. He walked over to his horse, untied his bedroll, and pulled out a blanket. He gently put the blanket around her shoulders, watching her jump each time a gun fired to end the life of a wounded Comanche.

Jim Carson walked up. "Cap'n, what we aim to do about Jeremiah?" Starr rose to tend to his men.

Uriah Lee rode to the creek, dragged the Comanche bodies out of the water and scalped one. The second Comanche was alive, and he spoke softly to the Rangers, moving his hands weakly, pointing at his back where a Ranger bullet had broken his spine.

"Filthy injun," spat Uriah. He dragged the wounded man into the brush, and with his Bowie knife sliced his throat open, then continued cutting around the side and back of the neck to the other side, cutting through the neck bone, then held the severed head at arm's length so the blood could drain out.

"You don't let the girl see that," Starr ordered.

"Cap'n, she won't much care. She won't care about nothin'. Best thing we can do for her is shoot her." The Rangers all looked at each other and nodded.

"Cap'n," Sam Brennan added, "she's no good no more. The Comanche done used her. Them Meskins think they go to hell if they kill themselves. Don't seem right not to help her."

Starr gave them an icy stare. "Anybody goes near that girl, I'll kill him myself."

They quietly went about the business of setting up camp. The horses had to be rested and fed, and the Rangers themselves were exhausted and hungry. As they sat around the fire that night, Starr looked across the flames at Lidia, still huddled in her blanket, refusing all contact with them. The men were right, he thought, but he could still see that helpless, crying face he had looked upon this morning as the first yellow rays of sun touched her filthy cheeks. Dirty and despoiled as she was, to him she was still Lidia. He could imagine her head pressed against his chest, could see her hair tangled wild over them, and he knew that he would still cherish her. Any man who thought less of her now would have to answer to him.

He feared that Ramiro might look with pity upon her and kill her, but then he reflected on this a further minute and relaxed. The Mexicans were much more pragmatic. Ramiro would more likely see Lidia's rescue as having some mystic meaning, beyond him to question. If she had survived, then let her survive. Far be it from him to question God's will. The greater danger came from his own men.

They hobbled the horses again and turned them out to graze, then cooked up some beans with the creek water and made coffee. On the northern horizon they saw flashes of lightning in the evening sky, and they heard distant booming thunder as they laid down their pallets for sleep. An hour later, a sudden cool wind picked up, bringing the smell of wet earth, blowing away the sweltering, clinging, July heat. Later still, a storm awakened them. They huddled under their blankets and felt the cool rain slant over them in windblown sheets, putting out the fire and washing the blood-stained cacti clean. Starr pulled his blanket over his head, and stretched it to cover Lidia as she slept on the ground.

They rose before dawn the next morning. By the time the sun sent its first exploratory finger of flame over the horizon, Ramiro had scoured the hills for almost-dry mesquite, and worked his muddy way through the cacti back to the Comanche camp. Soon, coffee was boiling and beans were sizzling over a smoky fire.

Jeremiah Wood was dead.

"He die in the rain," said Ramiro.

Lidia sat by the fire, still wrapped in the rain-soaked blanket. She did not look up or acknowledge any of them.

Starr bent over Wood and closed his eyes, then covered his head with the blanket. The man had no chance of surviving, he thought, wounded like that out here in the brush. He had simply bled to death.

Then he went over to Lidia and knelt gingerly beside her. "Miss de Leon," he said, "how are you feeling?"

She did not respond, did not even seem to hear him. She just stared at the fire.

"We killed them, Miss Lidia, all but one or two who got away. You don't need to fear them coming back."

She kept her gaze fixed on the fire, and Starr felt his spirits sink. He longed to hold her, to comfort her, but she was absolutely unapproachable. "You're going to be fine, Miss de Leon," he concluded.

They had already buried Floyd, but Jeremiah Wood was freshly dead, so Sam and Jim worked at the soft, moist soil with their Bowie knives until they had dug deep enough to cover his body. Starr took hold of Jeremiah's legs while Frenchy and Jim took hold of his arms, and together they dragged him into the hole, then covered him up with packed dirt and rocks. Frenchy fashioned two crude crosses from mesquite branches and drove them into the earth at the heads of the graves. Then they pulled off their hats and stared down at the two mounds.

"These were two good men," Starr said, and the others nodded. A long silence followed. Starr was not big on speeches, but it was up to him to send these men on their way to eternity. "These men rode with me all over Texas," he finally went on. "We fought Apache, Comanche, Meskins, and outlaws. They did their duty and fought like men." He paused, then added. "We'll miss them." He cleared his throat. "That's all."

When the Rangers returned to the campfire, they found Lidia staring at the graves, gripping her blanket so tightly that her knuckles turned white. She rose weakly to her feet, crying so hard that her whole body shook.

Starr went to her side. "Señorita, what's wrong?"

Lidia wiped tears away with the back of her hand and finally turned to look at him. "I wish it were me buried here," she cried. "In this empty place."

"You'll feel better when we get you back to your ranch."

She did not answer. She turned her face skyward, shut her eyes tight, and let the tears wash down her cheeks. Starr put one arm around her waist to hold her up, but she felt stiff and cold to his touch.

"Ohhh," she cried, "who's going to bury my mother and my father?"

He pulled her closer and with his other hand turned her face toward him. He realized that she did not know. For some inexplicable reason, they had not told her. He undid his bandanna and used it to wipe her tears away. "Look at me, Miss Lidia. Your father was still alive when we found him. I sent him on to San Patricio. Your mother is dead. We buried her." He watched her red and swollen eyes grow wide, heard her catch her breath. "I swear," he said. "I will take you to your mother's grave. Then I'll take you to your father."

She collapsed into his arms, and he pulled her tight against his warm, strong body and sat her down by the fire. She turned her face to his chest and buried it there. He held her at last, her body light as air, frail and delicate as a garden bloom, until she fell asleep.

Two Months Later
Along the San Patricio-San Antonio Road

DOÑA JESUSA CANTU FLORES refused to get out of the carriage again. Lidia begged her, but her aunt continued to claim that evil insects waited out there to enter her private parts. Dressed in black mourning clothes, they sat side by side in the carriage while outside the men prepared the camp for evening.

"*Tía* Jesusa, there are no evil insects. Just the normal kind."

"In Mexico City," the plump older woman replied, "they say that *Tejas* is crawling with them, cursed by the *gringo* Tejanos."

Lidia threw up her hands. "Well, then, you can sleep in here, *Tía*. But look, we have a tent already set up. And there is a cot for you to lie on. You don't have to sleep on the ground."

Doña Jesusa shook her head. "When I volunteered to accompany you to San Antonio, I had no idea we would be sleeping in the woods."

"Did you think we have roadside inns in *Tejas*?"

"I don't know what I thought. I don't even know why I came. For that matter, I don't really understand why you're going to San Antonio."

Lidia gave her *tía* a hard look, then reached into an inner pocket in her skirt. She pulled out a folded letter, the seal already broken. "You know why I am going to San Antonio," she snapped. "Listen to this.

> *To Señor Luis Cantu de Leon,*
>> *Due to the unfortunate experience of my betrothed, the Señorita Lidia de Leon, I regret to inform you that she is no longer suitable to become my bride. Therefore, the betrothal is hereby annulled. The wedding is cancelled.*

"It is signed simply, 'Jaramillo'," she said.

She crumbled the letter in her fist and stuffed it back into her pocket. "Before this letter, I only wanted to die. But when my poor father, scalped and both his legs cut off, read me this letter, he wept in humiliation. And then, I only wanted one thing—to find this pompous *cobarde* and throw his letter in his face!" She doubled both fists and clenched her jaw.

Doña Jesusa only twittered in the face of Lidia's fury. "Understandable, of course, my child, though actually going there is…well… somewhat unreasonable. A bit eccentric, you know. But since you are going, and I've never been to San Antonio—I've never been anywhere, I want to go see. Maybe your Ranger captain will shoot him for you?" she added.

Lidia softened. "No, it is my business. Now, *Tía*, if you want to stay in the carriage, stay. I'm going to the tent."

"Lidia, Lidia. You won't leave me here by myself?"

Lidia was already opening the carriage door. One of her men helped her down.

Doña Jesusa scrambled after her, squawking like a hen, her movements composed of thousands of tiny jerks. "Do you guarantee that there are no crawly insects?"

Lidia turned. "The only thing I guarantee is that you will itch in places you didn't know you had, *Tía*. But come down anyway. They'll get you in the carriage, too."

"Oh, *Tejas* is a horrible place."

Lidia took her aunt's hand and led her into the tent, then emerged to look around the camp. Five *vaqueros* accompanied them, as well as Captain Tom Starr. He had never left her side since the Comanche camp. Lidia had come to depend on his presence, on his strength. She stood beside the tent in the gathering gloom and watched the men drink coffee by the fire. Starr rose and walked toward her, offering her a cup.

"Coffee, Miss de Leon?"

"Are we still so formal, *Capitán* Starr?"

He looked down at her and smiled. "I don't aim to be disrespectful, ma'am."

She took the coffee and sipped. "Come walk with me, *Capitán*. To that pond I saw when we stopped."

They turned and walked into the post oaks and willows and followed a deer path to a small pond with clear, still water. It mirrored perfectly the orange and yellow wash on the western horizon.

She said, "I want you to call me Lidia from now on." She reached out to touch his hand. "And I want to thank you for everything. I owe you an enormous debt, *Capitán*. I wanted to tell you this."

"Miss Lidia, you don't owe me a thing. Well, maybe you could call me Tom, instead of Captain?"

She smiled. "Tom."

"Miss Lidia. One thing I don't understand."

She looked at him and saw it again—that yearning. She knew what he felt for her, it burned in his eyes. Turning her head, she faced the brilliant water. "I don't understand anything either, Tom. I'm confused. I'm hurt. I don't know who I am anymore or what I feel. Except anger. Deep, burning anger. Don't you see?"

He nodded, and after a moment said, "I just have a question."

"What is it?"

"Why are you going to San Antonio if the wedding is off? Why don't you just go home? I'll take you there, you know. I'll take you anywhere."

She looked up at a flock of birds swirling over the pond, chasing flying bugs in wild confusion. *Home.* How empty that sounded now. "No."

"That doesn't answer my question," he persisted. "Do you love this man, Jaramillo?"

She turned to him and placed her hand on his arm. "Oh no, no. I've never loved him. Don't think that."

"Then why—"

"Because he rejected me. He—" she stopped and looked away.

Starr shook his head. He reached down and took her small hand and held it in his. She let him hold it for a minute and then withdrew it.

"The man's a fool," he whispered.

"No," she replied curtly. "He's a coward. I'm going to San Antonio to tell him so."

"My God," he whispered, and he stepped back a bit, as if to comprehend her he needed to view her entirely. "My God, but you are a remarkable woman."

She felt his gaze upon her, felt the warmth of his presence, and it comforted her. A soft breeze swept over the water and washed their faces. He placed a hand on her arm, and she let him keep it there.

"You are missing the war, escorting me around, aren't you?"

"I'm a volunteer. The war can wait." He turned her toward him, but she twisted away gently and walked a few feet along the bank.

"Tom, please. I'm not well. I—I can't."

He stood there, as if rooted to the spot. "I'm an idiot," he said. "I should have known."

"Known what?"

"It's Juan, isn't it?"

The image of Juan flooded her mind and washed through the rest of her, filling her heart to overflowing and then surging back out, leaving her as before, empty and soiled. Juan! She burst into tears and put her hands to her face. "No," she lied.

He watched her silhouetted against the reflective water, like a lost, wayward spirit, beyond his reach. She did not want him. He did not know what she wanted, but he knew she did not want him. He walked up to her and took her in his arms, grateful and surprised when she slipped into his embrace. He held her close, her tears seeping into his shirt, wetting his chest, and he closed his eyes and gloried in their warmth. *So close*, he thought. *I'm holding her so close, and yet it's as if she's not really here. It's like I'm dreaming this.* He stroked her hair and wiped her tears away. This was all she wanted from him. He knew that now. *But in time*, he vowed, *in time she will want more.*

PART TWO

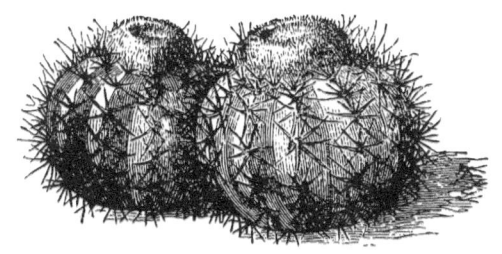

Chapter 6
Twelve Sad Years

De Leon Ranch
September, 1859

LIDIA STOOD BY THE WINDOW in a light blue dress, her hair braided and rolled on top of her head, her small hands just touching the edge of the bed. "Father," she said, "Ophelia sent word last week that she would visit us on her way home from Laredo. Do you remember?"

"I don't want to see her."

She slumped into a chair. "But she's your oldest friend!"

Ignoring her, Don de Leon spooned more food into his mouth and chewed deliberately, savoring the *arroz con pollo* that she had brought him.

She turned away and looked out the window. Outside, the day was cloudy but still sticky hot. August was only a few days gone, and there would be no relief from the heat until late September, maybe not until October. Lidia sent a bitter look at her father, a shriveled hull of his former proud self, and tried to feel pity for him. He had lost his legs, his scalp, his wife, and his self-respect all on one horrible morning twelve sad years ago. His daughter had been despoiled, her wedding abruptly canceled. The relatives had sailed back to Mexico. That which he had wanted to avoid most, the humiliation and embarrassment of the family, had happened in stupendous fashion. Twelve lonely, desolate, painful years. Now, unwilling to spend any but the briefest minutes outside his room, he lived his days shuttered away and being tended by his still unwed daughter. But it had been his fault, the whole thing. It was his pride, his scheming, his arrogance that had ruined them all. She swallowed hard and blinked back angry tears.

He shoved his empty bowl at her elbow. "Take it away," he growled. "Give me my coffee."

"You are *not* to have coffee," she said without turning. "It makes you wet your bed."

"Bring me coffee or I'll have Ramona bring it. I'm still the *patrón* here."

"Why are you being difficult today, Father? Is it because Ophelia is coming?" She turned and watched his face. "Why should that bother you? We haven't seen her in almost a year. Besides, you only have to say a few words to her. She'll want to see you. She cares about you. She's the *only* one out there who cares about you, and that includes our relatives."

He looked at her through eyes filled with misery, but he would not talk to her about things that mattered. He repeated, "I want my coffee."

Her eyes clouded, but she refused to cry. "All right," she snapped. "I'll get it. And later, when you are swimming in your pants, don't call me."

He fell silent for a moment, then turned his face away. "I will talk to Ophelia alone. I don't want you in the room."

Lidia took a deep breath. "She'll like that." There was more he wanted to say, she thought. She felt it boiling just beneath the surface of his stubbornness—hurtful, angry words. Watching him swallow those words, she remembered how he had railed at her during the first terrible years following the disaster. He had called her whore, ingrate, stupid. It was all her fault, he had cried, throwing plates of food at her and then thrashing on the bed. But late at night, his sobs often echoed through the quiet house, jolting her from her own haunted dreams. She had spent long nights listening, his laments cutting through her, praying for the first gray light of dawn to come and silence him.

She rose and placed the bowl on a tray, then balanced them on one hand as she left the room, closing the heavy door behind her. Standing in the tiled hallway, she drew another deep breath, closed her eyes, and slowly released it. Ramona came scrambling to take the tray.

"Bring him some coffee," Lidia ordered. When Ramona gave her a questioning look, she rolled her eyes. "I know," she said. "I know. But let's humor him today. Ophelia will want to see him, and I don't want him shutting himself away in his room like the last time."

As a clatter of hooves sounded in the courtyard, Ramona cried, "They're here!" Lidia's hands flew to her hair, then fluttered down to straighten her dress. A moment later, her arms hung tightly around Ophelia's neck. Finally, the two women pulled away and stepped back to look at each other through tear-filled eyes.

"My God," cried Ophelia. "A year! And look at you! You have a more mature look about you, _querida_. But why are you wasting such beauty on all this cactus?"

"Me? Look at you! You could be my sister." They hugged again, laughing brightly, reveling in each others' presence. "Or perhaps," Lidia added, "we've spent too much time looking at horses, and so any woman looks good." She turned to Tomas, who stood at the door clutching his sombrero.

"Tomas," she said. "Ever constant Tomas. How are you?"

He nodded stiffly and looked away. His strained look told her he wanted to be elsewhere, perhaps out with his horses and cows, anywhere but in this room of women and polite talk. "_Muy bien_," he said, and nodded again. She waited in vain for him to elaborate.

Ophelia smiled. "He's a man of very few words. He won't tell you how he's really been, which is fine, except a horse threw him in February and he was in bed for two months until his back straightened out. He's still in pain when he rides too long."

As Tomas shuffled his feet, Lidia offered, "Would you like to say hello to my father, Tomas?" He nodded, and she led him to Don de Leon's room and closed the door behind him. As Ramona returned with the old man's coffee, Lidia instructed her to bring some for Tomas and then come to the parlor and serve Ophelia.

When Lidia and Ophelia settled in, sipping sweet coffee with cream, Lidia knew that they would talk for hours, long into the night, and they would talk again the following morning. They had a year of life to share with each other, and many topics to explore, many people to catch up on.

"Tomas is always with you," Lidia mused. "You're never without him near." She paused a second, choosing her words. "After all this time, it seems a devotion has grown between you."

Ophelia appeared flustered. "No, no," she countered, but then she fell silent for a few seconds, looking up at Lidia with those lovely hazel eyes—a look that seemed strange, her face taut and grave. "I do love him," she finally whispered, "but only like a brother. I think he loves me in another way, but I don't encourage him. It would be awkward…after all these years."

Although Lidia nodded, she was not sure that Ophelia was being honest with herself. "Only like a brother," she sighed. "Perhaps." She looked at the floor, a brief lament rising up inside her. Their days came and faded away, it seemed, their lives were slowly spent, waiting, wishing, the nights full of misery. And here was another love denied—such a pity, such a shame. But it was strange, she thought. Ophelia had always encouraged her to be honest with her own feelings, to confront herself and then live accordingly. Ophelia had tried to teach Juan the same thing, but Lidia doubted that he ever gave the matter much thought. Now it seemed to her that Ophelia needed a gentle reminder of her own advice.

"Don't sit there smugly thinking I'm hiding something," Ophelia snapped. "Tomas is my oldest friend. I helped him live through the death of his young wife, and he gave me strength when my Alvino was killed. But, Lidia, I'm never going to marry again. And, besides, he's a *vaquero*. I don't intend to live my life in a *jacal*. And he's not likely to transform into a *hacendado*."

"So," Lidia replied, "basically, he's not suitable."

Ophelia wrinkled her nose and waved the words away. "Stop twisting it around and trying to make me sound like I don't know my own mind. I don't want to talk about it anymore. There is nothing to talk about."

Picking up a small tray of *pan dulce*, Lidia pushed it across the small table toward her friend. Ophelia shook her head at it, but then reached for a cookie shaped like a pig. Lidia sipped her coffee.

"And your land?"

Ophelia nodded. "Yes. Well, you know I finally decided to file a lawsuit. Those *gringos* just moved right in and built that little scratch of a town, they call it Brownsville, on my land. They didn't even ask. I might have let them, you know, though I would have made them name it after my husband. But no. They are so arrogant! They just take what they want."

Lidia nodded, watching Ophelia grow agitated. All these years, and still no resolution.

Ophelia continued, "So I filed a lawsuit to get clear title to the Brownsville strip. The Treaty of Guadalupe Hidalgo clearly states that all Spanish and Mexican land titles were to be honored after the war. But I've seen so many of the *rancheros* simply leave their land. The *gringos* come and tell them to leave. They harass the *ranchero's* family. Steal the stock. In some cases, they put a gun to the *patrón's* head and force him to sign over his title. That happened to my Uncle Antonio."

"Have any of them tried that with you?"

She laughed. "I would love to see them try. Back when they started building that little town of Brownsville, it was all I could do to keep Tomas and Juan from riding down to the river and burning it. I didn't think it was necessary, however. I should get what I want in court. The treaty is clear, and nobody is going to intimidate me into giving up my land."

Lidia sat pensively, her hands folded in her lap, and gazed out the window. On the table beside her, a vase overflowed with freshly cut roses picked from her garden. The room was heavy with their sweet scent. A long silence lingered between the two women, both of them lost in thought. They both knew the common subject of their musings.

Ophelia finally spoke. "He's fine," she said.

"Is he?"

"Oh, yes, Juan's fine. But he's driving me and everybody else insane. I don't see him for weeks, sometimes months. Do you know that there are three warrants out for his arrest in Brownsville alone?" She laughed. "But Juan rides in there any time he chooses, sits in the cantina, goes to the barbershop, gets a haircut. Nobody dares try to arrest him. I don't blame them. He has the shortest temper now. Much worse than mine."

"He's always been that way."

"Well, it's worse now, Lidia. It has been since you two broke up. Do you know what I found out the other day?"

"What?"

Ophelia turned toward Lidia and hesitated a moment, then looked into her eyes. "I never knew this," she said in a gentle voice, "not until recently. When Juan heard about what happened to you with the

Comanche, he disappeared for two months. I never knew where he had gone, I just assumed he was roaming along the border, getting drunk and generally doing what he does. But do you know where he was?"

"I have no idea."

"He was up in the Comanche territory. By himself. Hunting them. Nobody knows how many he killed, or if he ever tracked down those who escaped Starr that day he rescued you. When he came back, he had a string of Comanche ponies, but he didn't say a word about it. Tomas figured it out, and Juan finally admitted it to him. Eventually, Tomas he told me. He took his sweet time, but he told me."

Ophelia put her cup down, and Lidia looked up to meet her eyes, a look of pain on her face.

"What's wrong, Lidia?"

"Wrong? Nothing..."

Ophelia held her gaze for a moment, then realized Lidia was reliving the breakup with Juan. She closed her eyes and let it go. Nothing good could come from stirring up those dead ashes again. Then she took a different tack. "Well, yes, there is something wrong. You sit out here at this ranch with your crippled father. You see nobody except me, and that's only once a year. You're quiet, withdrawn. Even your spirit seems drained."

Lidia was barely listening. Ophelia's revelation about Juan had electrified her, but she felt more mystified than ever about him. Had he really done that, and for her?

Ophelia was still speaking. "All your youth and beauty are just wasting away out here. You ask about me and Tomas, but I think perhaps it is yourself you are thinking about." Ophelia pointed a slender finger at her. "You seem to be waiting for something."

"I'm not waiting for anything. Father needs my care."

"Your father could get the finest care in Matamoros or even Monterrey. That's not why you stay here. Many women wait their entire lives for something to happen, and it never does. What are you hiding from, *querida?*"

It was Lidia's turn to grow impatient. "The Comanche ruined me. I am an embarrassment to polite society. My betrothed rejected me. Even your son rejected me. Ophelia, where do you want me to go?" She took a breath and held her hands up to cool her hot cheeks. "The only man who seems interested in me is that Ranger. Tom Starr."

Ophelia raised an eyebrow. "I thought he might have given up by now."

"He writes to me often. He's operating a newspaper in Austin now, and he seems interested in politics. I think he intends to run for governor of Texas some day."

"Really?" Ophelia paused. "And do you write back?"

Lidia reached over to smell a pink rose. "Yes." She looked away, trying to hide her frown from Ophelia. She knew it made no sense, her relationship with Tom Starr. Even she herself could hardly comprehend it.

Ophelia looked wary, as if she disapproved.

"Tom's a strong man," Lidia explained, "and highly disciplined. Believe it or not, Ophelia, he has a good heart. I know he's killed so many *Mexicanos*, but that was war. And he saved my life. After that, I just felt so close to him. He took me to San Antonio." She turned her head, gazing out the window at the glowing day for a silent minute. "He never left my side. It was all I could do to keep him from shooting the coward who had jilted me. I could hardly hold him back. So you see, I feel a very strong bond to him. It's just that I don't *love* him."

Ophelia took Lidia's hand. "Are you sure, *querida?*"

"I wish I loved him, but I don't. At least, I don't think so. When he writes he says he wants to visit me, but I keep telling him not to come. I tell him Father has refused to welcome him. That isn't true. Father stopped caring about my virtue twelve years ago. I don't know. Maybe I'm afraid that if he comes, he won't want to go."

Ophelia nodded. "*Sí, sí.* Like I said, you are hiding here." She thought for a moment, then squeezed Lidia's hand. "There is one thing I have learned about love. It is completely irrational, and you cannot help who you love. The heart makes up its own mind, it doesn't care what you think is right, wrong, good or bad. You can try to ignore it, to suppress it, even to fool it, but in the end, you love who you love, and there is nothing you can do about it."

Lidia leaned back in her chair and let out a long breath. "So you are saying I still love Juan? What good is it, Ophelia? He doesn't love me!"

Ophelia smiled. "In two weeks, there is a wedding in Matamoros. Do you remember that little Garcia girl, Leticia? She's marrying a *ranchero* from Mier, Francisco Montoya. It will be a big wedding and everybody will be there. I want you to come with me, Lidia. No, no, I won't take any excuses. I'll send Tomas over to bring you, and you will dress in your finest clothes and you will come. It's time for you to remember just what effect you have on people when you walk into a room and they see how beautiful you are. I'm ashamed of myself for not forcing you to do this sooner." Ophelia locked eyes with her friend. "It's time for you to stop hiding, to come back into the world. It's time for you to stop waiting."

A rose petal fell from the vase and landed on the table. Lidia reached over and took it up, held it between her trembling fingers briefly, then crushed it. She felt its inner moisture on her fingertips. The soft scent, released from its hiding place, drifted up.

"I don't know," she replied, her throat suddenly dry.

Ophelia reached over and took her hand, steadying it. The rose petal fluttered to Lidia's lap. "Promise me."

Lidia looked into those reassuring eyes, her pulse racing, and nodded.

IN THE COOL GRAY HOUR before dawn, the men wrinkled their noses at the alien fish smell lacing the persistent Gulf breeze. Dust and sand kicked up by the wind blew in their faces, making their teeth gritty. The *vaqueros* were more accustomed to the aromas of sweaty horses and dusty longhorns, of fragrant mesquite and blooming cacti, than to this ripe, salty smell.

Twenty of them hunched in the dry, wide arroyo with their horses, waiting. Juan and Tomas had crept forward in the predawn gloom to inspect the sleeping Karankawa Indian camp a few hundred yards ahead, ordering silence until they returned. This particular band had been raiding ranches along the river, attacking travelers, stealing cattle—a surprising development, for everyone thought the Karankawa extinct.

Sensing the tension, one of the horses whinnied, and Mingo turned to Juan's little brother crouched beside him. "Blas," he whispered."

Blas nodded and walked down the line in the dim light, cautioning the men, their upturned faces mere shadows beneath their sombreros. They needed to look up at him because he had grown so tall, even taller than Juan. He'd grown into a strapping young man of twenty-eight with deep black hair and a sharply chiseled face. His look was quick and direct, his manner, brisk. But the *vaqueros* recognized a sharp distinction between Blas and Juan. Now that they were grown men, they looked much alike, except that Blas had developed into an aristocrat like his mother. No one ever confused Juan with an aristocrat.

Blas returned to his place in line, nodding that the job was done. Ordinarily, he did not take orders from anyone, but Mingo was different. Blas had always treated Mingo more like an uncle than a ranch hand. There was a time when he had idolized Juan and followed him around, trying to be like him. But Juan had no time for little brothers, and so it had been Mingo who filled the void.

Handing Blas his reins, Mingo turned to search the pale horizon. They saw the weak glow of the Karankawa fire and heard the surf roaring against the Texas beaches a mile away. A few minutes later, the rustling, popping brush told them someone was approaching. Mingo signaled the men to be ready.

A minute later, Juan and Tomas slid down the slope of the arroyo. Both men were trim and wiry, their movements sure, clean, confident—but a fire flashed in Juan's eyes. He thrust his chin out and gave them a curt wave to gather near.

"They're asleep," he growled, reaching up to pull some painful cactus spines out of his neck. "They had a guard, Tomas *lo mato.*" He made a cutting motion across his throat. "Our cousins are lying on the ground." He paused. "I think they're alive."

The men gave no reaction, but Juan knew they understood what he meant. The Karankawa kept their enemies alive as long as possible, ritually slicing off parts of their bodies over several days, roasting the flesh and eating it as the victims watched, until they bled to death. Such men were beneath contempt, worth less than even the wild dogs and the carrion eaters of the brush, worthy of only one thing: extermination. And now, they had Juan's cousins.

"They are not many," added Tomas. "They have their women."

"If the women fight, kill them, too," snapped Juan. "But be careful, don't hurt our cousins." He threw a look across the knot of horses and men, turned his head toward the sky, and judged the light sufficient to begin the attack. *"Vámonos!"*

They led the horses up the arroyo walls, walking single file and in silence through the brush. Soothing the nervous animals, they moved forward until only a few yards separated them from the heathens' camp. Juan halted. Everyone spread out, and he gave the signal to mount, then looked down the line as the faint sounds of stretching leather, tinkling spurs, and snorting horses rolled through the cacti. The men's faces disappeared into the shadows of the brush, their heads barely silhouetted by the dim morning sky.

Then all eyes turned toward Juan, and he raised his hand, a thick, black surge of pure rage coursing through him. He did not want to think what these despicable creatures might have done to his helpless cousins. Just be alive, he thought, just hang on a little longer.

"Adelante!" he cried.

Twenty horses leaped out of the brush and pounded the sandy soil. They quickly closed the few yards, then crashed into the camp, where the Karankawa rose sleepily to receive the charge. They were huge men, heavily tattooed and painted, and their shell ornaments clacked as they rose. They stank from the shark liver oil they smeared on their bodies. The horses trampled those too slow to rise, and hurled others into the brush. Explosions cracked sharply as a few *vaqueros* fired their muskets and *escopetas*, their flashes lighting the camp, briefly illuminating the shocked faces of the dying Indians. The *vaqueros* drew their machetes, long knives with razor sharp edges that could cut a man's head off in one swipe. They hacked the terrified cannibals to death in a wild and bloody carnage that became strangely quiet. The *vaqueros* gave no battle cries. The Karankawa were swiftly annihilated.

When it was over, Juan and Blas dismounted and found their cousins lying on the ground, naked, their arms and legs bound behind their backs. Even in the still gray light, Juan saw that they were both alive. Their dark brown eyes looked up, but they did not speak.

"*Primos*," Juan whispered softly. Cousins. He bent down to inspect them, then recoiled in horror, stumbled backward, and turned to vomit in the surrounding brush.

Tomas came forward, nudging a rigid Blas out of the way, and bent down to untie the boys. The rest of the *vaqueros* backed away, milling around the campfire. Juan wiped his mouth on his sleeve, ashamed of his weakness, but he continued to hang back, letting Tomas handle the boys. He heard Tomas' low voice and then the gasping, higher pitched replies of the captives.

"Bring some water," Tomas barked, and Mingo stepped forward with a gourd. After a few moments, Tomas pulled Juan, Blas and Mingo away from the rest of the men and spoke to them in a somber, resigned voice.

"They won't live."

Juan hung his head and cursed the now definitely extinct Karankawa. "Nobody's going to shoot them," he ordered.

They fell silent for a moment, as the sun burst over the horizon and bathed the giant morning clouds with brilliant, reddish light.

"You saw them," said Blas. "They're all cut up. They're crawling with worms."

"You heard me," Juan exploded. "Nobody touches those boys."

Blas snapped his head up at the rebuke, then a venomous look slowly spread across his face.

Overhead a hawk shrieked a warning, then floated away toward the sea. The men stared at their boots a moment longer until one of the captive cousins broke down, his deep sobs painful to Juan's ears.

"Juan," Tomas whispered, drawing close, "Frederico told me he can feel the worms inside his belly. He begged me to kill him, and so did Timoteo. They are suffering very much—they won't live. They are little more than piles of worms already. You saw them."

Juan drew a ragged breath, a horrible fury spinning within him, but he nodded stiffly. To find them alive, and then to shoot them—he could hardly contain himself. He wanted to destroy something, anything. Kill something, burn something, hurt something.

"We should clean them up first," said Blas. "Put clothes on them."

Tomas shook his head. "You move them, they will be in even more pain. Be merciful, Juan. They want to die quickly."

Juan clamped his eyes shut, letting the salty wind blow sand on his cheeks. "Give me your *pistola*," he finally growled. He stomped to the campfire and ordered everyone back to the arroyo. As the *vaqueros* collected their horses and rode away from the camp, Juan watched them leave, then approached the two boys lying on the ground. Their eyes turned up to meet his, and what he read in them was pain, misery, and fear. They were so young.

He bent down and spoke softly to them. "*Muchachos*, do you have anything you want to say to me?"

One of them sobbed louder and shook his head. The other simply jutted his chin forward and sputtered, "Tell our mother good-bye. Now do it quick."

Juan nodded, then rose and walked behind them, a pistol in each hand. He stopped, his pulse racing, cocked each pistol, and pointed at their heads. He tried blotting what he was about to do out of his mind, to just do it without thinking, but he could not. Each second seemed to last an eternity. He saw the bright colors of the morning, smelled the fresh dampness of the brush, felt the grit against his skin. One of the cousins clinched his eyes shut, and the other lifted his head, as if for one last look at the bright morning sun.

A second later, two staccato shots skipped and echoed across the empty morning landscape out to where Tomas and the rest of the glum *vaqueros* waited by the arroyo.

CONCHITA WAS A HEAVY WOMAN, much too heavy to be gathering speed as she moved around inside the house. She barreled into the bedroom as Ophelia was preparing for siesta, the old woman's big arms extended to her sides to provide balance. "They're back!" she cried to her mistress.

Ophelia stopped unbuttoning her dress and hurried to the window, throwing the thin lacy curtains aside. Juan and the *vaqueros* clattered into the dusty courtyard, their lathered horses snorting and neighing. As she watched, they stopped by the corral, dismounted, and removed their saddles and gear. Eager to drink from the troughs, the horses danced and whinnied, kicking up even more dust. Out on the horizon, a dark cloud rumbled, but otherwise the day seemed flooded with flat, white light that generated immense heat and encouraged no breeze. Conchita joined Ophelia at the window.

"Finally," Ophelia sighed. She had heard about the abduction of her nephews after Juan had already left with the rescue party, but that did not stem her anger. He had not consulted her. Certainly she would not have objected, but she had become more and more concerned by his violent nature. In this case she would have agreed with him, but what about other situations that came up frequently? She wanted him to at least consider other options, to limit the exposure of the family to potential risk. But Juan never thought about things like that. He was too impetuous, and he did not care about the implications. Defying anyone who blocked his path, he always took immediate and direct action.

Both his violent nature and his tendency to spurn the social elite had always endeared him to the Mexican underclass. Now his popularity was soaring even higher, and when the elections came around, he easily gathered a horde of voters, entertained them all night with a drunken *paranda*, then took them to cram the ballot box the following morning for whichever candidate Juan wanted to win—or, more accurately, against whichever candidate he happened to dislike most.

Ophelia strained to look out the window. "I don't see my nephews," she whispered to Conchita, who was looking over her shoulder. "I see Juan and Tomas. Mingo. Everybody seems all right." She pursed her lips and stepped back from the window.

A few minutes later, Juan stomped into the room, trailing dirt on the floor and smelling of horse, sweat, and Texas. "I went to get my cousins," he stated, removing his hat and staring directly into her eyes.

Conchita flew from the room. The directness between Ophelia and her son always unnerved her. That, and the strained, awful distance between them.

"They're dead," Ophelia concluded from the look on his face.

"Yes. I shot them."

Ophelia gasped, then sank into a chair, grasping the armrest, her body rigid. She knew what Karankawa did to their enemies, and she understood instantly why Juan had shot the boys. She wondered what deep, dark emotions were coursing through his heart after such a terrible duty, and she wanted to reach out to him, to comfort him. But that was impossible. He would never let her.

She merely nodded. "We will have a rosary for them tonight." She paused, wiped the back of her hand across her face, and then looked up at him. "You buried them?"

"Out in the *brasada*, near the coastline." He paused, and his gaze drifted out the window. "They said to tell their mother good-bye."

Ophelia did not respond. She was having trouble grasping this. Both of them dead. She nodded again. "I will go and see her. You've sent her word?"

He shook his head.

"I should go," she said, rising to call Conchita, but Juan still blocked her path.

"After siesta," he counseled. "I'll get a coach ready for you. Conchita and some of the men can go with you." He stopped. His eyes went unfocused and his gaze drifted past her. "I should go, too."

There was a brief silence, then Ophelia understood. Despite the calm outer shell, she knew her son was in turmoil. The last thing he wanted was to see the family of the boys he had killed, but he felt a duty to go.

"What you did," she said quietly, "was an act of mercy. Their loved ones will thank you. I understand why you want to face them. But don't. It will be best if I go alone."

"I should face them."

She felt her cheeks burning, and she yanked on his hand until he looked into her eyes. "It would be best if you don't go with me," she snapped, trying to break through to him. He was so stubborn, so immovable. But she knew he did not want to go, so she gave him an easy reason not to. "I don't want you to go. My side of the family doesn't like you very much."

Juan huffed, a half sneer forming on his face. He pulled his hand away. "None of our family likes me very much."

The heat blasted in through the window on a rare gust of wind, and she rose to escape it, walking to the edge of the bed. She leaned against the heavy, dark, wooden bedpost.

"It's not just you," she said. "Yes, they are angry with you. You never think about what your actions do to them, politically. The family is having many problems, but we're not alone. All the leading families are being constantly harassed by those damned petty bureaucrats and merchants in Brownsville. They annex our land, they pass laws, they hold up our goods when we transport them across the river. They're angry because their little town is going broke, and they seem to blame us."

Juan shrugged. "I don't care what happens to them."

"Did you hear that Fort Brown has closed?" she asked

He nodded.

"After all these years," she said. "Finally. The army is gone, but it's making the town feel insecure."

He turned to go.

She knew her son's opinion of that little wart of a town. Had it been up to him, it would have burned down years ago and the *gringos* herded into the river to drown like rats.

"Wait!" she called.

He stopped at the door and turned to face her again. She considered quickly how best to address the subject of the wedding. It was a terrible time to bring it up, with what he had to do out there for his cousins. But the issue was pressing, and she had to broach it somehow. Directly, she decided. That was the only way with him.

"There is a wedding in Matamoros next week," she began. "I know you don't like social affairs, but I need you to accompany me. You remember Leticia, don't you? You always liked her."

"She slapped my face last time I saw her."

Ophelia smiled. "Will you come with me? You don't have to do anything, just come with me."

"You'll be in mourning. How can you go?"

"I have to go. I'm in the wedding."

He turned and walked out, closing the door behind him. He did not say no, she thought. That did not mean yes with Juan, but she knew if he had ruled out going with her, he would have said so. So it meant maybe. She sat on the edge of the bed and thought about her dead nephews, sons of her sister Angelica who lived on the Mexican side of the river. Angelica was a strong woman, but Ophelia doubted any woman had the strength to endure the death of two sons on the same day. She felt an urge to leave immediately, to go to her sister's side with the sad news. But Juan was right. Nothing much moved between two and four in the afternoon in the blistering border heat. Nothing except perhaps those strange *gringos*, who wore shirts buttoned up to their necks, and even ties and coats on the hottest summer day.

She removed her heavy dress, and lay down, resting her head on the pillow and stretching out her legs. Beads of perspiration rolled down her sides. The one breeze she had felt earlier had died away, and no others stirred. Inside, the room baked. It was all she could do to breathe. She put her hand to her forehead, sweaty hand to sweaty head, and covered her eyes against the blinding light of the afternoon.

Both of them dead. Finally, the tears came and flowed down the sides of her face. Angelica. How would she live through this? She remembered the little boys, sitting politely on the porch eating *pan dulce*, years ago. Somebody's birthday. She cried for a few minutes, then wiped her eyes, leaving her hands across her eyes to ward against the light. She suddenly felt incredibly drowsy. *An hour*, she thought sleepily. *Just an hour, and then I must go to her.*

She closed her eyes, then opened them again to stare at the brilliant white room, and she followed a fly as it crawled and flew in quick hops across the ceiling. She closed her eyes again. An hour, she repeated to herself. An hour won't hurt. Juan is right, it's too hot. Too hot. Too hot.

Suddenly, her eyes flew open. Someone was there, someone was standing at the foot of the bed, moving in the darkness. She could smell him, his greasy liquored smell, and it almost choked her. Why was it dark? Where was the day? She must have overslept. She sensed him moving to the side of the bed, where she could not see him, and panic overwhelmed her. She breathed in short gasps, the fear bitter in her mouth. Outside, she heard screaming, crying, shooting, dismay. She threw off the covers and tried to run to the window, but her legs were heavy, and behind her she heard a sinister, nasal laugh. *Faster*, she thought, *move faster*. But her legs moved with great reluctance, one painful step at a time, until finally she stood at the window and parted the thin curtains to look out at the moon-washed courtyard of her ranch. There she saw her *vaqueros*, lined up on the ground, stripped to the waist, their hands tied behind their backs. Around them walked twenty or so men with rifles, savagely kicking them. A huge bonfire burned in the middle of the courtyard, and she saw the intruders throwing pieces of ranch furniture on it to keep it going. Beneath a huge mesquite huddled the *vaqueros'* wives and children, looking on in horror, screaming each time one of the men got kicked. Behind her, the laughter stopped, then she felt someone's breath on her bare shoulder, someone fingering her hair. She could smell his rancid breath and hear him breathing with his mouth open.

"The gold," he whispered. "Where does your traitor husband keep the gold?"

She opened her mouth, but nothing came out. She felt his hands scrape against her body, running down her hips and then up slowly, across her firm torso, up to her breasts. He cupped them roughly, a gasp escaping him as they overflowed his hands. He pushed himself close and slowly rubbed against her. He raised his hand and dipped it under her chemise, fumbling in growing haste for her nipples. His other arm fell to her waist, and she felt him pull her hips back, back to where his own hips pushed forward. His stench was overpowering.

"The gold," he insisted as he pushed against her.

Outside, the intruders stopped, looking at the window where she stood. The man behind her let go of her nipples and made a hand signal. Two of the intruders picked up one of the *vaqueros* and dragged him toward the window. There they stopped and waited.

"The gold," the intruder repeated.

Ophelia could not answer. She tried. She opened her mouth, tried to push air out of her lungs, pushed with her abdomen as hard as she could until it hurt. She did not even know what she was trying to say. She did not know about any gold, and her husband was long dead.

He growled. "Where is it?"

She shook her head, her tears falling to the window sill. Then the two intruders outside yanked back the vaquero's head. A thin cry forced its way out of her lungs, hurting her throat. The man between them was Tomas. "Noooo," she cried weakly, but she was still unable to move.

The intruders kicked Tomas, beat him with their pistols until he fell to the ground. She watched him curl himself up in a ball to protect himself, but the intruders took their time, looking for openings and delivering savage kicks. "Nooooo," she moaned even louder, trying to get away from her tormentor.

"The gold," he said. "The gold, the gold?"

She felt his hands reach down and pull her chemise up over her hips, exposing her bare skin to the warm moist night air. She felt his hands running over her bare thighs, felt his fingertips touching her, felt her goose bumps rising up to ward off his rough hands. Outside, the beating continued. She felt her chemise ripping away.

"The gold," he repeated, but he sounded distracted now.

She tried to twist away, but he held her firmly, her legs pinned against the sill and her face shoved out the window. She cried out, and everyone outside stood transfixed, some staring at the two intruders beating Tomas, others at the *patrona* standing like an apparition in the window. She felt a sudden pain, a rough, dry entry, and then he leaned her out the window and used her, faster and faster. She heard him grunting, felt his powerful fingers on her shoulders, digging into her delicate skin. Faster, faster, and she heard his breath coming faster, too, until she felt his body stiffen, his breath become a strange moan, and just at the moment of his climax she saw him gesture with one hand to the intruders outside. One of them yanked Tomas' head back and the other produced a machete and slashed his throat. As Tomas' blood spurted high into the night air, her tormentor convulsed in his release.

"Tomas! Tomas!" Finally she screamed, the fear, loathing and pain combining into one long and terrible cry. She screamed and rolled on the bed frantically until she fell off. When she opened her eyes it was daylight again, and in a moment Juan was there, lifting her up. He set her gently on the bed. He had seen this before.

"*Madre*," he said, "*calmate, calmate. Fue un sueño.*" He repeated the words, reassuring her it had been a dream.

Ophelia looked about the room with wild eyes, searching for her tormentor. But he was gone. She spun to look out the window, but the curtains hung limp "Tomas!" she cried, the fear refusing to leave her even as her senses told her that the horrible scene, so fresh in her memory, was not real.

"Tomas is asleep in his *jacal*," Juan replied. He was a little groggy himself. He rubbed his head as Conchita came pounding into the room, Blas a half-step behind her in the hallway. "Go back to sleep," he told them. "Mother has had a bad dream."

Conchita stood at the door and crossed herself, then walked away, but Blas stepped up and leaned in. Ophelia glanced up and saw that he, too, looked worried. The brothers exchanged looks, and when Juan shook his head, Blas turned quietly and closed the bedroom door, his footsteps fading away as he returned to his bedroom.

Alone with his mother, Juan looked down at her and was struck by how small she seemed. *Such a strong woman*, he thought, *in such a frail body.* He felt her tears sprinkling on his arm. How rare it was to see her this way, vulnerable and weak, almost clinging for protection and comfort. This made him uncomfortable. How many times had he come to her as a child, bruised and weeping, wanting just a gentle touch, a kind word? But she had always sent him away, never wanted anything to do with him, and so he had scurried to Conchita, crying even harder. Why? He had never understood it. Then, as he grew older, she had changed and tried to make it up to him, but it was too late. The branch had been bent, and Juan never forgot, never forgave, even when he wanted to.

A light rap on the door sounded, and Conchita swept into the room with a cup of tea. She set it on the table near the bed and then stood looking down at Ophelia.

"Let me tend her," she whispered.

"Take her," he growled.

As he walked out the door, he heard Conchita cooing words of comfort to her mistress, who cried even harder. He stood in the hallway, breathing heavily, then scratched his arm where her salty tears had seeped through his sleeve and made his skin itch. He walked back to his room and sat on the edge of his bed, yawning. But sleep had left him. In a few minutes, Conchita would be in the kitchen, stoking up the fire to make coffee and to bake bread. He pulled on his boots, grabbed his sombrero, and leaned out the window. Tomas was walking away from the house, barefoot and shirtless, a rifle in hand. Mingo's wife, Vicenta, hurried across the hot gravel to the water well. Overhead, the sun had complete ownership of the sky, for not a single cloud could work up enough moisture to drift up and try to throw some shade on the parched land below. He walked out of the house and across the burning courtyard toward the *jacales*. Under the sparse shade of the mesquite trees, old men were lying on tattered blankets, waiting for a rare passing breeze. A thin layer of mesquite smoke spread through the camp, and he knew it would get thicker as the afternoon fires increased.

He walked up to Vicenta and found her laying a beef head wrapped in canvas in a pit lined with live coals. She would place a layer of earth above the beef head and then leave it to cook all afternoon and all night. In the morning, the delectable *barbacoa* would be served with fresh corn tortillas and the hottest sauce of chiles she could make. He asked if she had coffee.

"You don't need coffee," she said in her sing-song voice. "You need this." She bent down toward a box lying beside the fire, opened the lid, and produced a pint-sized blue bottle sealed with wax.

Juan shook his head. "I'm not in the mood for witchcraft today, Vicenta. All I want is coffee."

She shot up, a look of supreme indignation written on her face. "I'm *not* a *bruja!*" she cried. "I'm a *curandera*. A healer. And you need healing. You have a look about you, like something deep is broken. I can fix it."

"All I want is coffee," he insisted. Then, "Where is Mingo?"

"Sleeping. You kept him out all night against those Karankawa."

They both fell silent, and Juan's thoughts riveted back to those two boys looking up at him from the gloom of the coastal brush, wanting to live but begging to die. He could still see their eyes—a sight he knew he would never forget. Those intense brown eyes looking up at him, burning with pain and despair.

"That is why," Vicenta whispered. "You are broken because of those boys. You need this."

"What is it?"

"Medicine."

"What's in it?"

"You don't need to know what is in it. Eat some. It will take your troubles away."

Mingo appeared at the door to his *jacal*, buttoning his pants. "More likely kill you," he grumbled. He walked up to them and looked at the bottle, then changed his mind. "Ahh, the blue bottle." He winked at Juan and handed it to him. "It's all right," he said. "I took this. When that bull gored me and Vicenta had me in bed for two weeks. I was in a foul mood until she gave me this." He made a sign with his hand, like it was floating in air. "It made me feel better."

Juan opened the bottle and dug out a bit of the stuff with his finger. It looked like mashed up root of some kind. Vicenta nodded vigorously and urged him to eat it, which he did. He took three fingers full and sat waiting, but he noticed no immediate effect.

"Can I have some coffee now?"

Vicenta took the blue bottle away from him and rushed back to the fire, where a big black pot of coffee was boiling. Ignoring it, she set the bottle back in the box and took out a small rattle. Chanting something incomprehensible, she proceeded to shake the rattle over Juan as she danced slowly around him.

"Woman," Mingo muttered with growing impatience, "the *patrón* has asked for coffee. That's enough *brujerías*."

Vicenta continued shaking the rattle, but stopped long enough to repeat, within the rhythm of her chant, that she was *not* a *bruja*.

Juan and Mingo shook their heads, then poured themselves some coffee and carried their cups through the growing mesquite smoke to Tomas' *jacal*. Tomas sat in the shade, skinning a *liebre* for his dinner. The two men squatted across from him and sipped their coffee.

"Hot," said Mingo.

The others nodded. They sat a while without speaking, watching Tomas skin the hare. When he was done, Tomas rose and stuck the carcass on a spit over his smoking mesquite fire. He returned with his own coffee pot and refilled their cups.

"*La patrona?*" he asked.

So he heard the scream, Juan thought. He remembered seeing Tomas walking away from the house, half naked in the blistering afternoon heat, after Ophelia's nightmare. "She's all right," he replied. "She'll leave tonight to tell Angelica about my cousins. She will want you with her, Tomas."

Tomas nodded. "And you?"

Juan shook his head, sipped his coffee. "She does not want me to go." He was beginning to feel a little strange. "I might take a ride into Matamoros. *Vamos*, Mingo?"

MINGO AGREED, and in a few minutes they were saddled and riding down the dusty road toward the river. They rode side by side when they could, but often the brush was so thick it crowded the trail, and they were obliged to ride single file. They trotted down the main street of the little town of Brownsville, where the townspeople stopped to stare at Juan. Men stood peering out of shop windows, arms crossed, eyes squinting as the sun dropped low on the horizon. Turning the corner toward the ferry, Juan spotted Marshal Garrison standing outside the dry goods store, lighting a cigar. They rode past him without a second glance. Technically, the marshal should have arrested Juan right then and there, but he had passed up too many opportunities already.

A warrant stood open for Juan, over a decade old, for the murder of James Cornwell. Another warrant stood open for shooting a gambler in the Brownsville cantina, although most witnesses admitted the gambler had been cheating, and Juan had merely beat the two other locals at the table in dispatching him. The Brownsville merchants looked for every opportunity to oppose Juan, and several had enthusiastically accused him of cold-blooded murder. But no one wanted to go after El Gallo. He was violent, unpredictable, and foul-tempered. No one knew what might set him off, so they mostly left him alone.

Juan and Mingo crossed the Rio Grande on the mule-drawn ferry, then rode into the heart of old Matamoros, where they tied up at the Las Flores cantina. No sign marked the place, but the music, laughter, and shouting announced itself a block away. When Juan stood at the door, the general din of the cantina dropped to a few hurried whispers, then picked back up again as he and Mingo moved to the bar and ordered mescal.

Juan turned to look over the clientele. Three Americans stood at the far end of the bar, hugging one of the local whores and chugging whiskey straight from the bottle. At least, that's what he thought he saw. Vicenta's root medicine seemed to be playing tricks with his eyesight, because when he blinked he thought he could see four Americans. All the way down from the ranch, he had been feeling the root take effect, making him feel lighter, carefree. Several times he had fought the urge to laugh for no reason. Now he drank the mescal eagerly to prolong the effect of the root, maybe even increase it. He could feel his head floating, just like Mingo had said.

Except—something bothered him. Through the general noise of the cantina, the talk and laughter of the patrons, the sweet music of the guitars, he heard sounds that grated on his nerves, accosted his ears. Turning to seek them out, he found them readily, for the sounds came from the throats of the Americans. They were speaking English.

"Looky here," said the one who was wearing buckskin clothing and a hat with feathers stuck in the band. He was holding up a scalp, waving it in the face of the whore, who wrinkled her nose and pushed it away.

"It's an Apache scalp," he boomed. "We caught them red sons-a-bitches nappin'. Braves was all gone 'cept for a few old men. Scalped the whole bunch. See?" He shook his body, and around his belt several other scalps flapped as he danced. The other five Americans Juan was seeing did the same, and the room broke out in laughter at the sight.

"Apache!" the Americans yelled, and the room cheered.

Except for Juan. He turned to the bar and ordered more mescal, and Mingo eyed him cautiously.

"*Vámonos, patrón*," he said, but Juan was not ready to go, saw no reason to. He shook his head.

The American with the feathers in his hat kept dancing, shaking his butt and causing the scalps on his belt to flop up and down. The musicians caught the spirit and launched into a lively *corrida*, which further excited the Americans. They stepped up their dance, howling with pleasure. The crowd laughed and clapped and cheered, but Juan turned his back to them, brooding over his mescal. His thoughts spiraled, leading him back to the morning out in the brush and the look on those boys' faces. When the song ended, the crowd cheered, and the Americans bowed and hooted, yelling "Apache!" again.

The musicians resumed playing, a ballad this time. The Americans turned back to their whiskey and their whore, shouting in each other's faces.

"Jim," said the youngest one, the one with the scalps, "I think this here gal's got a sister named Juanita over in Laredo."

"Damn, kid, she's got sisters all over Texas!"

"Naw," the kid replied, stumbling, with one hand around the whiskey bottle and the other on Jim's shoulder. "I mean, truly. Looks just like her, Jim."

Jim took a huge slug of his whiskey and handed the bottle to Hale, the tallest of the three Americans, who drank it down and then slammed the empty on the bar. The bartender quickly brought another one. Jim said, "They all look the same when you lay them down, kid."

The kid put his hands on the bar to steady himself, then slid his head down between his hands. "Not like Juanita," he muttered. "Juanita was so beautiful."

Hale picked up the whiskey bottle and took another huge gulp. "He's gonna start talkin' 'bout that whore again. Why don't he shut the hell up?"

Jim stuck a finger in the whore's ear, howling as he watched her squeal and squirm away. *"Habla inglés?"* he asked.

She shook her head no, and then squealed again as Jim moved his finger from her ear down her neck to her cleavage. *"No habla inglés?* I got something I'll bet you *habla.*"

She squeaked, and the three men laughed and passed the bottle. A few feet away at the bar, Juan slowly turned to face them.

Mingo whispered desperately, *"Vámonos, patrón!"*

But Juan ignored him. *"Gringos,"* he growled.

The noise stopped, and all eyes turned toward the bar. The Americans looked up at the sudden quiet, but they had not heard Juan.

"Gringos," Juan repeated.

The Americans turned toward Juan, and Jim said, "You talkin' to us?"

Juan did not understand—he shook his head. "I don't like your English," he said, but the Americans did not understand, either. They shook their heads. Juan pointed at them and held his hands to his ears. *"No hablen inglés,"* he said.

Hale snorted. "What the hell's he jabberin' about?"

"I don't think he wants to hear English," said Jim.

The kid lifted his head from the bar. "Why's it so quiet in here all of a sudden?"

"Fellow at the bar there is tellin' us to shut up."

"No hablen inglés!" Juan roared, and then it really got quiet.

Mingo stepped away from the bar and moved forward a few feet so that he and Juan were both facing the Americans. "He wants you to go," Mingo said, and he motioned toward the door.

The whore squirmed out of Jim's grasp and disappeared into the crowd, which was edging away from the men, shuffling boots, tables, and chairs on the hard packed dirt floor.

Jim stepped away from the bar and approached Juan, his hands spread open. "You tellin' us to shut up, Meskin?"

Hale stepped close to Jim. The Americans had pistols in their belts and huge Bowie knives strapped to their hips. They were filthy and smelly, their hands and faces full of scars. Hanging from their belts were all those Apache scalps. The kid slid to the floor and then struggled to get up. He looked up at the four men facing off and fumbled for his pistol.

For Juan, everything came suddenly into focus. He saw the kid pull the pistol, and in a heartbeat his own pistol fired. The ball crashed into the boy's skull and blew away one side of it. He sensed the tall American, Mingo, and the American called Jim all going for their guns. In two swift motions Juan swung his now empty pistol and caught the side of Hale's face with it, then struck out with his boot, jabbing the tip deep between Jim's legs.

Jim doubled over. Hale stumbled back from the blow to the head, and Juan saw Mingo pursue him. Juan slammed Jim headlong against the bar, then drew his knife as Jim bounced off.

"Filthy Meskin," Jim roared, turning, firing wildly. A *vaquero* in the crowd clutched his shoulder and moaned. Juan's knife plunged deep just below Jim's ribcage, angled up to pierce the heart. The man crumpled to the dirt floor in a huge gush of dark blood.

"*Sube las manos!*" Mingo yelled at Hale, pointing a pistol at his chest. The American dropped his gun, but ignored the order to put up his hands.

This infuriated Juan even further. He reached down and pulled Jim's Bowie knife from its sheath, intent on stabbing Hale with it, but Mingo stepped between the unarmed American and his *patrón*. Putting his hand on Juan's chest, he gently pushed him back, shaking his head. "*Se acabó*," he said. It was over.

But for Juan it was never over. He looked at the floor and saw two dead Americans, their blood and brains and stinking Apache scalps scrambled in a sticky mess on the floor. It was not enough. He backed out of the cantina, the crowd still quiet, watching him.

In an instant, he returned, riding Prieto, the bold and spirited new horse Ophelia had bought him. He rode into the cantina, a horsehair lariat forming a loop in his hands. He flung the loop toward the American. It fell over Hale's head and slid down to his chest. Juan pulled back on the rope and backed Prieto out through the cantina's door into the night. The American stumbled along, his hands gripping the rope. As he passed, Mingo relieved Hale of the knife strapped to his hip.

"*Adiós*," Mingo grinned. *Juan will not kill him now*, he thought. He would have done it in the cantina. The fight was over, and Juan did not kill helpless people.

The crowd recovered from their shock and stared at each other. It had happened so fast—Juan's movements a series of blurs, easily missed if one blinked. Except for the carnage on the floor, it seemed they might have imagined it. They saw Mingo laugh, and they laughed, too. An amazing thing to see, this fight, and now it seemed comical. They piled out of the cantina to see what other entertainment Juan might provide, and spotted a faint dust cloud far down the street near the river. Hurrying, they caught up with Juan just as he dragged Hale into the dark silvery water of the Rio Grande. They lined up along the river in the moonlight and watched the American sputter and cough as he splashed in Prieto's wake. The river ran relatively shallow at the time, so Prieto quickly pulled up the bank on the Texas side. They saw a faint dark object follow him out of the river. Buoyed by the water, the American tried to stand, but he soon fell as Juan spurred Prieto forward.

"Help! Somebody help me!" he cried.

As Juan dragged Hale through the streets of Brownsville, the man's cries echoed off the plain wooden buildings. He coughed up more river water. Lights came on in some of the houses, and several men from the cantina stepped out into the night to observe in silence. Juan saw Garrison peering out the window of the marshal's office, his silhouette outlined dimly. But no one stepped forward. No one helped as Juan dragged the man down the main street, out the other end of town, and a mile into the cacti and brush.

There he stopped, dismounted, removed the horsehair rope, then sat his horse again and sighed. The blind rage was dissipating. He gazed down at the bloodied and moaning American, who turned on his back and looked up at him.

Juan pointed north. "Go that way," he said, suddenly feeling very tired. "Back to where you came from. I don't want to hear your English again."

Hale gave him a blank look. Juan spurred Prieto forward hard, and the animal leaped over the American, spraying him with dust. Hale threw his arms up and rolled his face into the Texas dirt.

After Juan had thundered away, Hale sat up slowly, his body aching with every movement. He rubbed his thighs and chest, recoiling as he touched spots where cactus spines had stuck. He spit dirt out of his mouth, then bent over to vomit the river water he had swallowed. He stood up and looked where Juan had pointed, but saw nothing on the horizon except dark lumps of cacti and brush. To the south, he saw the faint lights of Brownsville.

"That was one mean, crazy sum-bitch Meskin," he muttered to

himself, as he limped his way back south to Brownsville. "Wonder what set him off?"

THE MORNING AFTER THE FIRE, Charles Pownall stood on the sidewalk outside the Villarreal Bank gazing at the charred remains of the Taylor warehouse. The explosion had rocked many of the 2,300 inhabitants of Brownsville out of their beds in the middle of the night. When they recovered from the shock, they raced out to find the new warehouse completely gone and the surrounding buildings engulfed in flames. Six people were dead. Bucket brigades were quickly set up, forming long lines from the river to the burning wooden buildings. Over a hundred Mexicans had come over from Matamoros to help. The buildings had burned down, anyway, but at least the fire had not spread.

Pownall lit his cigar, took a few quick puffs, and smiled. Robert Taylor was one of Brownsville's small merchants. He had no business having a warehouse. Only the larger merchants, such as himself, could afford warehouses. Warehouses were important because the Mexican trade required that a large variety of goods be available whenever shortages arose. Pownall firmly believed that it was important to keep the small merchants in their place, lest they band together and start competing with the large merchants like himself for the Mexican trade. Yes, he and his friends had to be ever vigilant. With the new Benito Juarez administration in Mexico, trade along the Rio Grande had been liberalized with a free trade zone that stretched from the mouth of the Rio Grande through Matamoros to a spot near Laredo. Goods could enter Mexico from the U.S. duty free as long as they did not move farther south than a twelve-mile strip along the border.

For Pownall, the free trade zone was both good and bad. Good, in that he enjoyed connections and businesses on both sides of the river. Like most of the other large merchants, he had simply shut down operations here in Brownsville and moved them to Matamoros. Bad, because now most U.S. and foreign goods entered Mexico though the Mexican port of Bagdad, not through Port Isabel, thence to Brownsville. That meant his ferry and steamship businesses were suffering. He pulled on his cigar and let the smoke drift out through his nose. Well, at least he would not have to worry about Robert Taylor anymore.

Pownall watched as Marshal Garrison pulled Taylor toward the jail house. Taylor had apparently been storing gunpowder in his new warehouse, which explained how he had been able to afford to build it in the first place. It now seemed clear that the ambitious Taylor had been engaged in smuggling arms and ammunition to the conservatives in Mexico fighting against Juarez and his liberal policies. The wealthy and the military were literally up in arms against the Juarez government. At any rate, storing gunpowder in Brownsville was illegal. The town might blow up.

Pownall chuckled. Well, he said to himself, it *had* blown up. So Taylor was going to jail. Which suited Pownall, since Taylor had not used Pownall's ferry to smuggle the guns across. This whole episode had given him an idea. A shortage of guns and ammunition had just been created.

He crossed the street and walked over to the Frost & Hightower law offices, where he saw Rufus and Harold standing at their window, arms crossed, also watching Robert Taylor going to jail. A broad grin on his fact, Frost opened the door.

"That was some firecracker went up last night, eh, Charles?"

Pownall smiled and nodded. "Got any coffee, Rufus?"

Hightower walked over to the stove and brought the steaming coffee pot to the front of the law office. He picked up a tin cup from one of the shelves and poured Pownall a cup, then refilled his own and Frost's.

"So Taylor was running guns," Pownall said. "Explains how he got so prosperous so soon, don't it?"

They drank their coffee as they watched what was happening on the street. Marshal Garrison was in his office, sitting at his desk now. The town seemed unusually quiet. The dusty streets were emptier than usual, the air was clear, and it was already hot. A heavy stink of burnt wood and wet charcoal from the fire clung to their nostrils.

"This town is going nowhere, Charles," Frost said after a minute. "It did quite well there for a while, we sold those lots so fast. Now...." He let his voice trail off as they still stood at the window and peered out.

Finally, Hightower moved back from the window and sat down at his desk, the other two men following. "And now the army's gone," said

Hightower. "So far this year, Yellow fever killed 130 people, this damn fool Taylor just killed six more. You large merchants have picked up and moved to Matamoros. I'm telling you, Charles, the locals are getting in an ugly mood."

Pownall smiled at Hightower. "What the hell you want me to do about it, Rufus? It's not my fault the small merchants are having problems. We sold them the town lots, then we dissolved the damned town company. We're done with it. It's up to them to make the town prosper. And, by the way, when they lose money, I lose money on the ferry business."

Frost spoke up. "Some of them think you large merchants are actively working against them. They think Villarreal is refusing them credit at the bank to squeeze them out of business."

Pownall snorted. "Villarreal is a good banker. Makes his own decisions about what *is* a good risk and what *isn't*. I've got nothing to do with it."

They were quiet for another minute, staring at their cups. Frost reached over and poured them all a little more. "Well," he said, "we just thought you ought to know that they're getting worked up. They blame you and the Mexican families for all their troubles. Green and Miller were just in here. They're especially riled up. They think Taylor was set up."

"Taylor is an idiot," said Pownall. "He thought he could sneak guns into Mexico without anybody finding him out. He forgets these Mexican families have connections and interests all over Mexico. You can't fart in the brush without Ophelia Santos or Emiliano Ugarte or any one of the rest hearing about it the next morning. And, in general, they're all supporters of Benito Juarez. Anything that weakens the army is popular up here because it keeps the military out of local politics."

Hightower scratched his head. "Let me get this straight," he said. "Juarez is at war with the wealthy conservatives because his policies favor the middle class over the military and the wealthy. Despite this, the wealthy, landowning Mexican families along the border favor Juarez because it keeps the military out of their business. Meanwhile, the small merchants are mad at the Mexican families because they give you big merchants the advantages of their connections but would not give that connection to them. And the small merchants are losing their shirts, and that makes you mad because they aren't using your ferry." He shook his head. "What a hash."

"Don't feel bad," replied Pownall. "Nobody else can untangle the mess, either. Which brings me to the point of my visit. Doña Ophelia Santos' legal action against the town of Brownsville. If she's successful, we all stand to lose our shirts. I don't want the townspeople to come after us for compensation if she wins."

"You shouldn't worry so much, Charles. We know how you like your anonymity. Everything you own is set up with front companies and distant, phantom owners. It would take years to untangle it. As for Ophelia Santos, she doesn't even know that the lawyers representing her are our dear friends, Franklin Dresser and Benjamin Winkle."

Pownall nodded impatiently. "But I don't trust her," he said. "I wouldn't be surprised if she isn't just playing along with them and working some back angle. She's well connected in Austin, you know."

Frost laughed. "Charles, you're making my brain hurt with all these plots and counterplots of yours. Look, it's real simple. As long as Dresser and Winkle keep telling us everything they're doing, well in advance, we can block all of their motions, stall, delay, drag it out. She'll lose patience eventually and drop the suit. Or we'll manage to get her to lose."

They sipped their coffee and stared at the floor for a while. Outside, a horse trotted past the law office, kicking up a small trail of dust. The sun angled in through their front window.

"Charles, I don't get it," said Hightower. "What *do* you want from all this? Seems to me you've got conflicting interests with the small merchants, the large merchants, the Mexicans—"

Pownall stood up, put down his coffee cup, and picked up his hat. "What do I really want, gentlemen?" He smiled. "I want to always keep everybody else guessing about what I really want."

He bid the lawyers a good day and walked out into the bright, sunny morning.

POWNALL CROSSED the dusty street, headed toward the jail house. The old wooden door creaked loudly as he stepped in to find Marshal Garrison throwing the cell key ring on his desk.

"Got a full house today, Garrison?"

"You betcha. Besides Taylor, I got what's left of that Tennessean El Gallo chewed up and spit out last night."

"He in here?"

"Sleeping in the back cell."

Pownall peered toward the back of the gloomy jail, but all he could see was a dark shape lying on a cot. "How bad?"

Garrison scratched his beard and his ass at the same time. "Beat up is all, some lumps. Cactus spines."

"He fared much better than his companions."

Garrison stopped scratching and looked up at Pownall, suddenly wary. "That didn't happen here," he said defensively. "That was across the border."

"But they were Americans."

"So what if they was?"

"You could arrest Santos for murder."

As Taylor sat up in his cell and cocked an ear toward the conversation, Garrison lowered his voice and brought his face closer to Pownall's.

"Look," he whispered, "even *you* can't change the law. If the Meskins want to arrest him, let them have at it. I can't. Besides, way I hear it, them bounty hunters drew first."

Pownall moved to block the view from the cells with his body, then reached in his coat pocket and pulled out a small bag. He jingled it a little, then laid it on the table before the marshal. "Maybe you can find a way," he whispered. He opened the bag and pulled out a few coins, looked up, then took out two more. "Could it be that Santos set that fire?"

Garrison scooped the coins off the table and slipped them into his vest pocket. He grinned. "What you up to, Pownall? You know nobody can touch Juan Santos, way these Mexican families are connected."

Pownall lifted his chin. "Is it his connections that worry you? Or is it El Gallo?"

"You calling me yellow?"

Picking up his little coin purse, Pownall shook his head, then looked pensively at it. "No," he said, "I wouldn't say you're yellow. *I* wouldn't. But I will say that if you happen to figure out a way to put him in jail, it would be worth double what I just gave you."

"Why?"

"Let's just say I want to help bring him down a notch."

Garrison grinned. "That'd play real good with these townsfolk. They hate all the families. But El Gallo's special. They wouldn't mind it if somebody hung 'im."

"Maybe you could do it...."

When Garrison's head snapped up, Pownall saw a knowing look spreading across the marshal's face, as if the vision of Ophelia Santos roaring into town to get her boy, with the town waiting for her, had become enticingly clear.

"It's *her*. You're after her, ain't you. You don't give a shit about him."

Pownall stepped back, impressed by the marshal's intuition. Whatever else he might be, the man apparently wasn't stupid. "That's my business," he said. "You just keep in mind what I said. Find a way, Garrison."

"You want me to face down El Gallo?"

"You don't have to do it alone, for Christ's sake. Get some Rangers down here. They shoot Mexicans for the fun of it."

Garrison leaned back in his chair and looked up at Pownall, a gleam suddenly in his eye. "Rangers, eh? Where you from, Pownall?"

"Up north," he replied with an edge to his voice. He was beginning to lose patience with this cagey marshal. "What's that got to do with anything?"

"Up north, huh? Now, that don't figure. You been around here a long time—I'll bet you got a lot of investments down here, is all. And those fellows you keep company with, seems to me they're mostly Southerners. I heard some talk. You boys trying to stir up a war with the Meskins again? Maybe get a little more territory off o' Mexico? Add another slave state or two?"

Pownall put his purse back in his vest pocket and shook his head at the marshal. "Garrison," he said, "you think too much." He turned and walked out the door to the street, then crossed to the livery stable to retrieve his horse.

Riding west out of town, he found the marks where Juan had dragged the tall American out into the brush. Next, he followed the road until he came to a spot dotted with hundreds of longhorn skeletons, all piled up, one on top of another. He stopped his horse, then turned off the road and rode around skeletons. There were other spots like this, he had heard, all over Texas. Huge piles of bones, created when a sudden norther came blowing in and put a deep freeze on the land south of the Nueces River. It didn't happen very often, but when it did, the cattle had no defense against it and very little tolerance to survive it. They came out of the brush, banded together tightly for whatever warmth they could generate, and if it wasn't enough, they simply froze to death. Hundreds of them, in hundreds of little clumps like this one.

He rode a few yards into the brush, then stopped and waited. Nothing but mesquite and cacti, and he knew he was hidden from view of the road. In a minute, Timo Martinez stepped out of the brush and approached him.

"*Buenos días*, Señor Pownall."

"Nice job on the warehouse."

Timo shrugged. "It was easy. All that gunpowder."

Pownall was glad Timo had returned to the border, fleeing a hangman elsewhere, no doubt. He was good. Pownall pulled the coin purse from his coat pocket and threw it to Timo, who hefted it then stuck it inside his shirt. The two men looked at each other for a brief moment under the hot morning sun. The only shade available was provided by their hats, but they were used to it. The air smelled clean, of mesquite and dry earth. Pownall noted that Timo had black gunpowder stains all over his clothes.

"You better wash those clothes."

"*Sí.*"

"You get caught—"

"You don't know me."

"Right. You'd better get lost for a while."

Timo grinned his crooked grin. "Santos beef, you sure you don't want any more? Why not?"

"That's my business."

Pownall watched as Timo turned and disappeared back into the thick brush. He waited and listened for a few more minutes, sitting in the hot sun surrounded by buzzing flies and all that cactus. But he did not hear or see Timo ride away. The man was good. Damn good.

Chapter 7
A Wedding

Matamoros
Two Weeks Later

B<small>LAS</small> <small>STEPPED</small> <small>OUT</small> of the scorching sunlight and into the dark and noisy *Vieja Loca* cantina. The afternoon light was so bright, it took a minute for his eyes to adjust to the gloomy interior, and as he stood there the stench of liquor and sweat and dirt washed over him. He heard laughter, guitar music, singing, shouting—and somebody crying over in the corner. He had ridden up and down the streets of Matamoros until he found Prieto tied up in the corral behind this particular place. That meant Juan was probably here. Probably already drunk.

His vision restored, Blas scanned the bar patrons and, sure enough, found his brother standing at the far end, talking with great animation to Tomas. Blas squared his shoulders and walked toward them. As he went by, *vaqueros* tipped their sombreros at the young *hacendado*, but he ignored them. He trailed his hand on the bar as he walked, then pulled it back in disgust. Something wet and sticky had touched his fingers, and he pulled a kerchief from his vest pocket to wipe them clean.

As he approached Juan's blind side, he saw Juan go suddenly tense and whirl about, a hand resting on his knife.

"Little brother, don't ever sneak up on me like that."

"Why? Don't you like surprises?"

Juan pushed his sombrero back and grinned. "We'll both be surprised. I'll be surprised it's you, and you'll be surprised to lose an ear."

Blas did not smile. He stared at Juan with the same face he'd made when he'd touched the wet and sticky bar a moment before.

"You're drunk," he said finally.

"Not that drunk. Not yet. Want a drink?"

Blas shook his head before Juan even finished the question.

Juan turned to Tomas, who was sipping a shot of mescal. "Damn smart little brother, don't you think, Tomas? I taught him everything— riding, shooting, fighting. But he won't drink with me. I don't think he likes me."

Tomas shrugged. "*Que pasa*, Blas?"

"Mother sent me to find my brother. She's angry because he was supposed to accompany her to the wedding this afternoon. The ceremony came and went, and my brother is still in the cantina."

Juan tossed back his shot of mescal and turned to pour another. "I'm here," he said. "I'm in Matamoros. Look, I even dressed up."

"The wedding wasn't in this stinking cantina. It was in the church. The reception and dance are being held in the plaza. Mother wants me to bring you."

Juan kept his back to Blas for a moment, then slammed the bottle down on the bar. He turned and stared at his brother with a look that caused Tomas to step between them.

Juan pushed him aside. "Be careful, little brother."

"Why do I have to be careful?"

"Your tone of voice. I don't let any man talk to me in that tone of voice."

Blas sneered. "Don't try to scare me, Juan. It won't work anymore. I used to think you were so special. But now I know better. I'm not afraid of you now."

"Maybe you should be."

"Why, are you going to kill me, too? Add me to your long list of murders?"

"Maybe I'll just snip off your ears."

Blas snorted and shook his head. "I think if you weren't my brother I would call you out."

"I don't play at fighting, little brother."

"No. You don't like rituals. You don't like tradition. You don't care about family. In fact, I haven't found anything yet that you care about except mescal and whores."

"Don't forget horses," Juan offered.

"Horses, cows, goats, anything but people."

Juan frowned. "Not goats."

"You're a disgrace to the family. I don't know why mother even bothers with you."

Juan turned toward the bar, his back toward Blas, and shrugged. "I already know all that, little brother. I'm not going to fight you for telling the truth."

Blas stood staring at Juan's back, then turned toward Tomas, who still looked poised to intervene. Tomas shook his head, motioning toward the door.

"You already know all that," Blas said to his brother's back, "and it seems all of Mexico and *Tejas* knows that, too, but I guess it took me a while to find it out for myself. And I don't like it."

Juan did not respond, did not turn around. After a moment, the music started again, and the murmur of conversation grew. Glasses clinked. A man in the back laughed. Tomas finally grabbed Blas by the arm and led him out to the street.

"What the hell are you doing, Tomas?"

"Saving your mother another heartbreak, and getting you out of there while you can still walk. Go and tell Ophelia I'll bring him along."

"I don't take orders from you, Tomas. And I don't care if you bring him or not." Blas stood in the bright sunshine again, squinting.

"No. But Ophelia does."

Blas looked back at the gloomy interior of the cantina, but from the street it looked so dark that he could see nothing. "Why doesn't he just leave? Everybody in the family hates him."

"Your mother doesn't."

"You don't have to keep saying that!" Blas kicked at a pile of dirt on the black, lumpy street, then kicked it again. Without another word, he walked over to his horse, mounted, and rode away.

AN HOUR LATER Juan and Tomas stood at the entrance to the plaza, sombreros in hand, both looking very uncomfortable and very unhappy to be there. When Ophelia spotted them, she could not help covering up a small laugh, despite her annoyance. She walked up to them and gave them both the sternest look she could muster.

"Are you sober?" she asked.

They both grunted in the affirmative, but she took a step back to see for herself if they were standing up straight or leaning on each other. "Juan," she said, "Blas came back and said you were drunk already. Are you?"

"Blas gets drunk on holy water. How would he know?"

Tomas stifled a laugh, but not very effectively, as Ophelia reached out and took Juan's dusty sombrero and handed it to Tomas, then took Juan by the arm and walked him into the crowded, gaily decorated plaza.

"I want you to be polite and sociable," she murmured as they walked.

They passed a group of elderly *hacendados* dressed up in their finest clothes. The men greeted Ophelia with great deference, then nodded at Juan. Ophelia nudged Juan in the ribs with her elbow and whispered, "Smile." He managed to curl a lip at them.

"It won't kill you to smile," she said when they were past.

"Why? Those men don't like me and I don't like them."

"Because it's a wedding. And those men may not like you, but they respect you. You should respect them."

"All they respect is the number of votes I can deliver for the county elections across the river."

"No. That's not all. They knew your father. You are his son. You live on his land, passed down to you. You are a *hacendado*."

Juan stopped and pushed Ophelia's hand from his arm. He took a step back. "Is this why you brought me here? I don't belong here, you know that. I belong with Tomas outside with the horses, or out in the *brasada*. As for the land, I don't want anything from my father. Give it to Blas, or let the *gringos* have it—"

She cut him off. "Nobody is getting our land. That land is for you and Blas. And don't tell me you don't want it. You don't know what you want."

Juan laughed. "I know I want a drink."

Ophelia left it at that. This was no place for an argument, and she did not want him turning moody, which would make her next move impossible. She walked him over to a table laden with food and drink, and they poured themselves some wine from a huge barrel. Then, grasping his arm firmly, she led him to an area occupied by a tight bundle of men, all talking at once.

Ophelia said, "*Señores, por favor*," and the bundle of men peeled open. And there, at the center of the circle, stood Lidia, wearing a breathtakingly beautiful pale green gown, her hair piled in swirls atop her head, emeralds glittering on her neck and ears.

The sight of her took Juan's breath away. He stared at her like a cat dragged out of the river, crouching in fear on the riverbank, wondering which way to run. But he couldn't run. His mother held him firmly. The other men took one look at Juan, looked back at Lidia, and then slowly melted away.

"Don Juan Santos," said Ophelia, "may I present to you the Señorita Lidia de Leon of the Rancho de Leon. Perhaps you already know each other?"

Juan scowled at his mother and set his mouth in a thin line. She had tricked him, and now she tightened her hold on his arm. He turned back to Lidia and grunted. She ignored his glare and smiled, and suddenly, upon looking at that face again, he felt his anger fading. After years of whores, cattle, horses and rangy *vaqueros*, the only beautiful face he could truly admit to have seen in his whole life was Ophelia's. And now, here stood Lidia, lovelier than he ever remembered.

Lidia laughed, the sound delighted his ears.

"I assume that grunt is what passes for hello out in the *brasada?*"

In the recesses of his mind, something shifted. That voice of hers found a familiar track somewhere in his memory, and it fell into place smoothly, comfortably. Her laughter, full of life and hope and beauty found another groove, and it snapped into place as well. It felt as if Lidia were coming together in his consciousness as little pieces of a puzzle, pieces long ago scattered and long thought lost. He felt mesmerized by this, and pleased, too. He relaxed and smiled.

He was vaguely aware that Ophelia looked up at him. He might have heard her sigh. He felt her release his arm and give him a slight push forward.

"Juan," she said, "why don't you talk to Lidia? I'm going over to talk to the bride's parents. I'll be back later." She reached over for Lidia's hand, placed it on Juan's arm where her own hand had been, looked at Lidia with twinkling eyes and walked quietly away.

Lidia flashed a radiant smile, and Juan felt another piece of the puzzle snap into place.

"Why are you here?" he said.

"Are you sorry I'm here?"

"I didn't say that."

She laughed again, giving his arm a tiny squeeze. "You are a complete surprise to me, too. A wedding party is the last place I thought I'd ever see you."

"Mother set this up." He stepped back and looked at her lovely face, her elegant neck, her tiny waistline and delicate hands. "Lidia," he finally said. "I had forgotten."

"Forgotten what?"

"How beautiful you are."

She blushed, and her eyes turned soft and dreamy. Over on the bandstand, three men with guitars, a violinist, and two trumpets started to play.

"Would you please dance with me?" she asked.

Before he even thought to protest, she led him to the center of the plaza, where a large tiled area had been reserved for dancing. His hand slid to the small of her back without hesitation, finding in the feel of her body another long lost puzzle piece snap into place. He felt the movement of her body as it rubbed against the inside of her silk dress—soft fabric and even softer skin. He looked into her eyes. They were large, clear, and full of merriment. Her scent wafted up to him as he drew her nearer, a delicate sweetness that made him close his eyes, almost overpowering his senses. They began to move to the music, and in her gracefulness he felt another piece of the puzzle slide into place.

She lifted her eyes to his as they danced. "You haven't changed much, either," she said.

Juan's dancing left much to be desired. Mostly, he danced with whores at drunken *parandas*. He stepped on her foot, then did it again. "I have changed," he said quietly. "I'm not a nice person anymore. Ask those peacocks you had flocked around you just now."

"They just don't understand you."

"And you do?"

"Don't I? I have known you since you were a little boy."

He shook his head. "Lidia, it's been too long. I don't think you do."

She made a face, mocking him playfully, then cried, "Ouch!" as his boot clipped the side of her foot again. "Juan, dancing should not be painful."

He grunted and they took another step or two.

"Tell me what you've become that I wouldn't understand."

"I have a very bad temper. Sometimes people die."

"As I recall, twelve years ago you already had that reputation."

"Well, it's the same now, only worse. Those mice over in Brownsville have been trying to arrest me for years. The mice in this room roll over and piss on themselves whenever a *gringo* waves a gun at them. I like to piss on the *gringos*."

Lidia moved her arm on his shoulder and passed her hand along its length. "I think the *gringos* need to be pissed on once in a while," she said. "They need to remember whose land this is. Who built this country."

Juan grinned. "When I piss on them, they tend to leak a lot themselves. Only they leak blood."

"Now you're getting too crass."

"I told you I wasn't nice anymore."

"You were crass before, though. So it's no different." They took a few more steps in silence.

"So," he said, "I never was very nice?"

She tilted her head and smiled even more brightly. "Ohhh, no, no Juan. *You were nice.* I remember...I remember a garden in the moonlight...."

Juan felt his face slowly drop all expression, for in his mind a puzzle piece with dark and ragged edges was trying to force its way into a place it did not belong. He felt as if cold, bony fingers had suddenly gripped his heart. From deep, hidden crevices of his mind the shadows emerged, bringing images of a young boy clinging to a father for love, but instead having his head slammed against the cold hard ground. Images of a boy crying at the foot of his mother's bed, wanting comfort, watching her turn away. And images of the garden in the moonlight. He shuddered and forced himself to focus back on Lidia. He remembered the garden, too, and he remembered the next day standing before her father and fumbling for the right words to ask for her hand. And how Don de Leon had told him about her betrothal, shown her for what she was, a cool seductress who had used him for her own purposes. She had lied to him, betrayed his trust. He stopped dancing, put his hands on her shoulders and pushed her to arms' length.

"What is it?" she asked, for the look on his face frightened her.

"You betrayed me," he said.

She heard the words coming out of his mouth, words she expected he would say eventually, no matter how much Ophelia wanted them to be together. It was just as Lidia had predicted. He never forgot, and he never forgave. Except that it was not true!

"Is it always that I must understand you?" she snapped. "Do you understand me? *I* was the one who was tricked and cheated, but you refused to listen or believe me!"

She looked at him now, standing there, judging her, as if he were the one aggrieved, the one to lose it all. And it had all been his fault. Everything was his fault!

"You were a coward!" she cried. "You didn't stand up to my father. And what happened to stealing me if he did not consent? You are the one who betrayed me! I thought that—that no matter what happened," she was stumbling over the words, "that we would be together. Oh Juan! You should have had the faith in me I've always had in you."

"Faith? You were already betrothed! When were you going to tell me? I stood there like a fool and asked for your hand."

She hissed. "Betrothed? To a man I did not want or love. And you left me to him. You ran away! What happened to me with the Commanches was your fault! You and your stupid macho pride! El Gallo, the big bad El Gallo. Nobody better make him mad! Well, you ruined my life, Señor Gallo! You *did!*"

She burst into angry tears and then swept her hand to his face, but Juan caught her arm in mid-air. He gripped so hard that it sent pain shooting down her whole shoulder. The music wavered. The people nearby were already staring at them.

Suddenly Blas stepped between them, pulling Lidia away. He let her cry on his shoulder and gave Juan a withering look.

"Another surprise, Juan?" he said. "It doesn't seem to matter whether it's a cantina or a ball, a drunken *vaquero* or a lovely señorita. The outcome is always the same, isn't it? Isn't it!"

"Mind your own business, little brother."

Blas disengaged himself from Lidia and pushed her behind him. "I'm making this my business now," he said. "You insulted our hosts, you insulted Lidia, you've embarrassed the family yet again."

Juan tried to shove his brother away, but Blas shoved back. In an instant, they were moving toward each other. Then they heard Ophelia's voice.

"What do you two think you are doing?" she said, and they both froze. The boys stood with heaving chests, and then Juan took a few steps backward. He turned and headed for the street. Ophelia turned to Blas, but he stomped away as well. That left Lidia, holding her hands up to the sides of her head, standing in the middle of the plaza in her beautiful dress, tears flowing down her cheeks.

Ophelia put her arm around her and led her away to a secluded corner, where she tried to soothe her. "Lidia, *querida*, what happened?"

Lidia sobbed. "He remembered what happened with father, and he became very angry. He said I betrayed him. And then I—" She burst into another round of sobs, her tears flooding down her cheeks and dropping into the folds of her dress. "—and then I became angry with him. For abandoning me."

"Oh, no," Ophelia said, "oh, no. This is my fault. I shouldn't have surprised him like this. He's so unpredictable."

"No," replied Lidia, drying her tears a little. "He is completely predictable, Ophelia. He won't forget what happened. He thinks I betrayed him. He will never change his mind about that. I know him. You know him, too."

"He could change his mind," Ophelia said. But she did not go on, she did not say how, or what Lidia could say or do that would cause him to change it. "I know he could change his mind," she said after a minute. "He wants to, you saw it tonight. Remember what I taught you, Lidia. Love is irrational, it doesn't care what we think is possible, it will find a way."

"No," Lidia replied. "It's over, Ophelia. It was over twelve years ago. I knew it then, but somewhere in the back of my mind I've always had a little hope, a tiny dream." She looked up and took Ophelia's hand. "And I know you had the same dream. But we were both wrong. Even you must now see that there is no hope. He will always judge me and feel betrayed. It's over, Ophelia, it's over. He'll never let me back into his heart, never again."

Ophelia hugged her, holding her close until the tears subsided. "Let me take you to the hotel, to your room," she finally said.

They walked across the plaza to Lidia's hotel room, where Ophelia sat her in a chair by the window and poured her a glass of water. The music from the plaza, the clattering noises of horses and carriages swirled through the open window. In the distance they heard a steamboat tooting.

"I'm all right now, Ophelia."

"I'm afraid to leave you alone."

"Please, I want to be alone for a while. I'll be all right, I promise. I'm going to lie down. My head is splitting."

Ophelia rose from the edge of the bed and came forward to kiss her cheek. "I'm so sorry, Lidia. You didn't need this. It was my fault. I had forgotten how tempers could flare between you two. But I thought maybe—"

Lidia shook her head. "I wanted it to be true, too, Ophelia."

They looked at each other for a moment, and then Ophelia turned and left the room, closing the door behind her. Lidia sat for a long time in that chair, reviewing the events of the day, how the dance had started so wonderfully, how it ended so horribly. The look on Juan's face as he pushed her away, haunted her. It had been so totally devoid of feeling. She could imagine if she were a man and saw that face, she would fear for her life. She had been a fool to even hope he would forgive her, and it made her so unbelievably angry because it was all so unjust.

She lifted her tearful eyes to the ceiling, asking herself again, *Why can't I let him go? Oh, why? He makes me miserable, and yet I long for him.*

When they were together she felt whole, in harmony with him, as if he were part of her soul and she part of his. Without him, she felt so lost. Why could she not just let him go from her dreams, from her heart? Maybe she wanted him because she could not have him, this wild, dark, and dangerous spirit.

Every day for the past twelve years she had missed him, dreaming of his warm touch and hungry lips, his handsome face, his husky voice—the way she felt in his arms. She remembered the childhood incident when she first saw the real Juan—that first glimpse when he let her into his private world, when he cracked the shell he lived under to let her come inside. He had been hurt, crying, vulnerable, sitting by the riverbank, and she had comforted him, gained his trust. She knew he never let anyone else in. Just her, just at that rare and tender moment, and he had let her stay in his heart until that day at the ranch when he asked for her hand. On that day, he had pushed her out forever. Now, it was clear that El Gallo did not need anybody.

A rap on the door disturbed her thoughts. It was a strong, masculine rap. Her heart fluttered, she held her breath. *Please, let it be Juan.* She rose slowly and walked toward the door. *It isn't him,* she told herself. *That's over. It's over. It isn't him.*

She opened the door a crack, and there stood Blas, his hat in his hand, looking down at her. "Señorita de Leon," he said. "Lidia. I came to apologize for causing a scene downstairs. It was unseemly."

She let out a long breath and looked down, then she lifted her face and tried to smile for him. She noted that Blas had Juan's hazel green eyes. She shook her head. "You did nothing wrong, Blas. I'm grateful for your help."

"My brother," he said. "He...he behaved badly. I intend to defend your honor."

She flung the door open and grabbed his hand, yanking him inside the room. "Listen to me, Blas! I've had enough of Santos machismo for one day! I forbid you to fight your own brother over this, do you hear me?"

His eyes opened wide. "But—"

"But nothing! I will be very offended if you do anything. Blas, I want your word that you will not!"

His face betrayed his confusion. "But he insulted you."

"And *you* will embarrass me. To have two brothers fighting over me. Everyone will think I'm an evil woman."

"Oh." He seemed to ponder this, a new concept. He finally said, "All right. But I insist on escorting you home in the morning, or even now if you want."

She felt tempted by this offer. First, it would get Blas out of town and away from Juan. Second, she was tired of this place and wanted to go back to the de Leon ranch.

"Thank you, Blas. That's sweet of you. But I don't want to cause any more trouble between you and Juan."

"Why should he care? Juan has no claim on you."

"No. That is very clear."

"Then why should there be trouble?"

A thought struck Lidia that Juan's family, including Ophelia, did not seem to know Juan as well as she did.

"Because I know Juan," she replied. "And if you take me home, he will feel insulted. Believe it or not, he will look past that shoving match in the plaza. He will forgive you because he wants to forgive you. You are his little brother, his blood. Don't let his tough act fool you. He might slap you around, but he would never really hurt you. He'll kill anybody that tries to hurt you, because he loves you."

She let go of his arm. "But if I let you take me home—I can't explain it. There is something dark that lives inside him. I've seen it—like a hurt, brooding, overgrown child. You're right, he doesn't want me. But if his brother moves in, or even appears to, then he will feel betrayed. That he would not forgive. So, no. Thank you, but no."

Blas scratched his head, the confused look still clouding his youthful face. "I don't know what you just said," he told her. "I think you're making things too complicated. I would like to drive you home, but if you would prefer that I don't, well, then, I won't." He turned to go, but she called him back.

Leaning forward, she kissed his cheek, whispered, "Thank you," then smiled and closed the door. She put her back against the door and listened to his footsteps as he walked away. She leaned there for a long time, feeling her heart pound, looking at the hot light streaming in through the window, listening to the noise of the city below. *This*, she thought, *is the loneliest I have ever felt in my life.*

CHARLES GREEN stepped out from the alley behind the Villarreal Bank and confronted the Mexican rancher, who seemed startled to see the red-faced merchant staring down at him.

"Gomez," said Green. "I'll have a word with you." He slurred his Spanish, but he knew Gomez understood enough to catch his meaning. Gomez was a small rancher from further upriver, one of many who owned only a few hundred acres, purchased or inherited from the original Spanish grants. The lawyers Frost & Hightower had been out to see Gomez several times, bringing pitifully small offers for his land on behalf of some mysterious client.

But Gomez knew who the client was. It was Green himself. Green and the other small merchants from Brownsville had a strong need to reduce the influence of the ranchers who, with the help of Juan Santos, could determine the outcome of politics and elections in the county. Green's approach to the problem was to get rid of them and gain the land in the process.

"Señor," said Gomez, "I know what you want. I have guessed who the lawyers speak for. I will not sell my land."

Green's eyes bulged, his face turned red. "You dirty, stinking greaser," he snarled. "You saying no to *me?*"

Gomez backed away, spreading his hands and shrugging his shoulders. "It was my father's land. I do not want to sell."

Green reached out and grabbed Gomez by the collar, dragging him off his feet and sending him stumbling into the alley. There, Daniel Miller waited. Miller tore Gomez's sombrero off and flung it down the alley, then smashed him against the wall of the bank.

"Check for a knife," growled Green. "These greasers always carry a knife."

Miller found the knife tucked inside the rancher's boot. He pushed Gomez hard against the bank wall, then did it again, then slammed his knee into the small of his back. Gomez groaned and slid to the ground, where Green and Miller kicked him repeatedly for several minutes. When they stopped, they realized a small knot of townspeople had gathered at the corner.

"Hey, Charles," one of the men called, "need any help there?"

Green shook his head, then delivered a savage kick to Gomez's ribs. The satisfying cracking sound carried all the way to the street. He turned to the onlookers and said, "Maybe you *can* help, Brown. Lend me a rope from your store."

An hour later, Green and Miller squatted on the ground and smoked as Gomez dangled by the neck from a thick mesquite tree on a secluded spot along the river. Onlookers slowly drifted away.

Marshal Garrison trotted his horse to the edge of the water and dismounted, throwing a quick glance up at Gomez as he joined the merchants. "You boys had a busy mornin', I see."

Green looked up at their handiwork. "Greaser wouldn't sell out."

Miller nodded.

"What you boys want a ranch for? You wouldn't know the business end of a longhorn steer if the other end crapped on you."

"Garrison, we don't pay you to make jokes."

"You don't pay me at all."

"I'm the mayor of this goddamn town," Miller replied, "and you're the marshal."

Garrison flicked a mesquite bean at the water. "If I relied on what this pissant town pays me, I couldn't buy enough beans to make a fart."

Green leaned back on his elbows. "If you were doing your job, we wouldn't have to be at this ourselves." He nodded up at Gomez, who was quite blue now. The man's pant leg showed a dark stain where his bladder had drained. "And when are you bringing in El Gallo?"

"Bastard killed two Americans just the other day—" Miller began.

Garrison cut him off. "That was in Matamoros. I got no jurisdiction there."

"Hell! What difference does it make, Tom?" said Miller. "You know you can ride over there anytime you want and take whichever sumbitch you want. Them Mexes won't do nothin' about it."

"Coulda done it while the army was here," said Garrison, "but they're long gone now. And Cantu still has the Meskin army garrison right there in Matamoros."

The merchants laughed, then Green stood up and pushed Gomez's boot so he could watch the dead rancher's body swing back and forth. "That there is the most pitiful excuse for an army I ever seen, Tom," he said. "They start anything, we get us a few Rangers down here. Be no trouble at all. 'Sides, you don't need to go over there to get him. Hell, El Gallo rides in here almost every morning. Has coffee right over there in the Mendoza coffee house with his friends."

Garrison shook his head. "Ain't got nothin' on 'im."

"You got warrants for his arrest for cattle rustling, one, and for that Cornwell murder ten, twelve years ago."

Garrison stood up and pulled a knife from his vest pocket. He walked over to the tree and began cutting at the rope.

"Wait," said Green. "I borrowed that rope. Let's just lift him up and you can undo the knot."

But Garrison kept on cutting until Gomez dropped to the ground in a puff of dust. "Too late," he said. "You boys know that cattle rustling warrant is a joke. Old Ben Floyd got caught stealing some of James Harrison's cattle. He was just starting them across the river when old Harrison and about thirty *vaqueros* rides up and gets ready to string Ben up, right there, just like you done this ol' boy here."

He folded up the pocket knife and dropped it back into his vest. "Well, Floyd up and claims he bought the cattle from El Gallo that very morning, and Harrison came in here and swore out a complaint the next day. Only trouble was, El Gallo was over to Reynosa the whole week it happened. 'Course, he coulda been lying about that. But I didn't push it. To tell the truth, boys, there's a heap of cattle movin' across that river ever night, both directions. And that Cornwell warrant, who's gonna help me serve it? You?"

Green and Miller looked at each other, and Miller said, "That ain't our job, Tom. That's why we got you."

Garrison kicked his boot toe at the body of the rancher. "Looks to me like you did a pretty good job right here. Help me put him in the water. I don't want to have to bury this fellow."

They dragged him over to the edge of the water and threw him into the river, where the current would carry him to the gulf within the hour. They stood for a while watching him float away. After a few minutes, they lost him in the thousands of tiny brilliant reflections of sun upon the water.

Miller said, "Well, we got one. There's more to get."

Green nodded. "And you got to get Juan Santos, Tom."

"You tell me how."

The exertions of the day had Green breathing through his mouth. "I hear tell he sets a lot of store in his people. We could put Tomas in jail, say, or maybe Blas."

"You tryin' to get me killed?" the marshal asked.

"Now, wait, just hold on," replied Green. "We could back you up on this now. We could be hiding, waiting for him when he comes in to get them out of jail."

Garrison shook his head. "You boys don't know what you're talking about. That whole Santos clan, led by the she-devil herself, they can come swoopin' down on this town and push it right into the river. I'm surprised it hasn't happened yet. Now, I put Blas in jail, that's likely to get me killed. We shoot down El Gallo, the whole town's likely to get burned down and everybody in it killed." He smiled. "But it's a nice thought, boys. A real nice thought. I'm so sick of that El Gallo peacock struttin' around town. I wish we could do it."

Green and Miller studied their boots for a while. "What we need," offered Miller, "is to requisition us a few Rangers."

Rangers again. Garrison saw Charles Pownall's hand in this, though his exact motives for inciting the merchants were still unclear to him. Money, politics, land, or perhaps all of them. Perhaps Pownall himself did not know—maybe he just liked stirring up trouble for the entertainment. Or for control, to manipulate people and events. The money and the land were probably just trophies to be won along the way.

A clatter of hoof beats turned their heads toward the town. They heard men shouting, a woman screaming, though the cause of the commotion was not clear. They hurried through the alley and emerged onto Main Street, where they found two bleeding men lying in the street. Their horses shuffled beside them, lathered up and barely standing themselves. A small crowd of men had already gathered, and an onlooker offered a long-handled tin cup of water to one of the wounded cowboys. The injured man had a nose that looked a lot like a pig's, Garrison noted. Both cowboys' shirts were soaked through with blood.

The crowd parted for Garrison. He kneeled next to one of the men, the one with the pig nose, "What happened to you boys?"

"Comanche," he whispered back. The other one passed out just as his head lifted up to drink some water.

"Where you hurt?"

The pig-nosed cowboy grimaced and sucked a gulp of air. "Don't move me no more," he said. "Took two arrows in the back, Johnny there dug them out a while back. He took one, too. Had to break it off..."

Garrison glanced up at the other wounded man, the one called Johnny, but Green stared down at him, shaking his head. Gone.

"Where this happen?"

"Military road, twenty miles out."

"They follow you?"

The man nodded. "But we was better mounted."

Garrison started to rise, but the pig-nosed cowboy grabbed his wrist. "Saw fires along the way," he said, then moaned and fell back. "Ranches burning."

Garrison stood up and gestured at the barber. "Jacob, run on over to Matamoros and fetch a doctor for this boy. Reckon we'll need to plant the other one." As the barber hurried off, Garrison stepped up on the barbershop porch so that he stood a little higher than the crowd and addressed the group of thirty or so men gathered in the street.

"Looks like Comanch' is hittin' us again, men. We ought to ride out and check on settlements upriver. I'm deputizing all you men. It'll be dark soon, but we can plan what we're gonna do. Y'all get your horses and gear ready, meet me at the saloon tonight. I figure we'll ride out at first light tomorrow."

The merchants stood looking at each other for a minute, but Garrison did not wait for them. He turned and tromped back toward the river to retrieve his horse. When he returned, the crowd had dispersed, and the cowboys had been moved off the street. He took his horse over to the livery stable and ordered feed and water for it, then walked over to his office and cleaned his guns. He sent word over to Cantu in Matamoros, so the Mexican commander would be aware that the Comanche were raiding along the river.

An hour later he sat in the saloon with most of the deputized men, drinking whiskey and talking about the Comanche, telling each other stories about what they did to prisoners, what they did to women. There was passing mention of Lidia de Leon's unfortunate experience, and what the Rangers had done. When darkness came, they kept drinking, although someone mentioned somewhere along the way that they should get some sleep. They drank late into the evening, and they got the piano player drunk, too. One man rode his horse into the saloon and then fell off of it, spooking the horse. The horse kicked a few tables across the room, crapped on the floor and then backed out the door.

Garrison got so drunk that when sunrise came and went he was still in the saloon, slumped over one of the tables. Scattered throughout the room were all the other deputies who had not gone home to their beds during the night. When late morning sunlight slanted in through the big front window, bright, yellow and already hot as blazes, Garrison peeled one eye open and muttered, "Shit."

BEFORE SUNRISE, JUAN split his men into three groups. They crouched low and prepared to attack the sleeping Comanche camp. The Indians had struck the Santa Alicia ranch at dawn the day before and stolen dozens of horses, but they had left the ranch house itself alone. Throughout the day, Juan's men had found mutilated corpses of *vaqueros* out in the *brasada* alone, surprised and killed as they had gone about their business. The Comanche moved fast, but Juan organized his *vaqueros* and set up a spy network. Sitting in the Santa Alicia ranch house, he received reports of the Comanche activity. Using this information, he estimated their general direction, hazarded a guess as to where they might be found this morning, and rode out with his *vaqueros* to search through the night.

He found them camped on the Mexican side of the river. He and his men crossed into Mexico both above and below the Comanche, thus forming a semi-circle around them. If the Comanche got wind of them, their only escape would be northward across the river into Texas.

The Comanche had no campfire, but Juan knew they were there. As the night slowly turned from black to gray, a breeze came up from the northwest, and he caught the heavy scent of the river commingled with the Comanche stench.

Mingo nudged Juan in the shoulder as he sniffed the air. "Not hard to find Comanche," he muttered.

Juan grunted, looked up at the sky and across the landscape. When he could distinguish man from bush, he rose from his crouch and hurried with Mingo to his waiting *vaqueros*, whispering for them to gather around.

"Do not fire until I fire," he ordered. "It's still a little dark. We want to get in close before we start shooting. We will attack first. When the other groups hear our guns they will attack, too. Be careful you don't shoot our men." He pointed to his sombrero. "Look for the shape of a sombrero on his head if you can't make him out."

He paused, looking around at the eager men about him. Most of them were young men, accustomed to long hours in the saddle and backbreaking work, scorching sunlight and heat. They ate sparingly during the day, and at night they loved their mescal and their music. They laughed readily, but their tempers were unpredictable—sometimes easily provoked, whereas other times they laughed off conflict. They were invaluable to the ranch, and he trusted them. But they were not an army. He feared the Comanche would kill many of them on this gray and breezy morning.

Juan mounted Prieto, and his men followed his lead. They put their horses forward, slowly at first, covering the mile to the river cautiously, listening as the gurgling sounds of the river grew louder. Juan knew he had no hope of going undetected, but he wanted to get in as close as possible. He heard a shout, then a whoop. A Comanche sentry arrow came singing out of the gray morning, buzzing past his head and out into the *brasada*.

Juan cried, *"A la carga!"* They charged. The attack immediately degenerated into chaos as the Comanche unleashed a barrage of arrows that cut down five of Juan's men and some of their horses. The *vaqueros* had been bunched up behind these riders, and horses stumbled over horses, which brought down more riders. Juan regrouped his men and charged again. In the meantime, the Comanche ran for their horses, and now moved forward to meet the charge. Juan saw the dark shapes of the Comanche warriors looming out of the brush, whooping and shouting. He pulled his pistol and fired, and the ball swept one of the Comanche off his horse as if by a giant hand. At the sound of his gun, the other *vaqueros* also fired, and several of the Comanche crashed to the brush as the volley ripped through them, spraying the air with bloody chunks of flesh. The remaining Comanche fell back toward the river, but Juan's men were attacking from three sides and creating a vicious crossfire. Surprised by the sudden appearance of so many men at their flanks, the Comanche crashed their horses into the river, shooting arrows as they fled. The *vaqueros* lined the river bank and fired their ancient muskets, which were notorious for missing their marks. But the Comanche were so close and so bunched together that Juan's men could not miss. The Indians fell one by one into the river, streaking the dark, swift water red. Men and horses churned the water into foam, horses drowned as their riders dropped the reins in order to shoot their arrows and the reins became caught on their forelegs. These horses thrashed viciously in the water, pulling their riders down and drowning them and spooking the horses that struggled beside them.

Of the twenty Comanche, only a handful made it to the other side. The rest floated away with their horses until the mounted *vaqueros* looped ropes around them and pulled them out, like calves out of the brush. Sporadic pistol fire echoed across the now quieter morning as the wounded Comanche were dispatched.

Juan swung off Prieto and stood next to him, holding the reins in one hand and his pistol in the other, watching his own *vaquero* dead and wounded being dragged out of the brush. The sun spilled over the horizon in full now, bathing the camp in raw, yellow light that made the lifeless bodies seem even more starkly dead and casting long, gloomy shadows as his men moved about. All up and down the river, *vaqueros* splashed in the current or searched through the brush, gathering loose horses and dragging out bodies. In the end, fourteen Comanche and five *vaquero* bodies lined the river bank. Four of Juan's men were wounded. He holstered his pistol and tied Prieto to a bush.

"Mingo," he growled in a thick voice, "track down those *hijos de la chingada* that escaped. I don't care if you have to ride all day and all night. Kill them." Mingo nodded and pointed at a few men. They splashed across the river and disappeared into the brush on the other side.

They heard hoof beats coming fast from the east, and from the brush emerged one of Juan's spies.

"*Patrón,*" he called, sliding his horse to a halt and dismounting at the same time. Juan nodded, eager to hear the man's report. He had sent him to scout toward Brownsville.

"Many ranches burning," the panting scout reported. "Many more Comanche."

"And the *gringos* in town? Are they coming?"

"*Patrón*, El Marshal Garrison and his men are drunk and sleeping. They do not come."

Juan cursed the town, and among the *vaqueros* a general grumble arose.

"*Hombres,*" counseled Tomas, "those men in town are merchants. They don't know the brush. They come out here, they might wipe their asses with a cactus. The Comanche would kill them easy."

Juan turned and stared across the river, feeling as he always did after a battle—angry and empty.

Tomas walked up and put a hand on his shoulder. "What about our dead, Juan? Bury them here?"

Juan turned to the neat little line of dead *vaqueros*, men who minutes before had waited with him in the dim, cool dawn, their chaps wet with dew, their eyes showing fear and excitement.

"Lay them over their horses and take them home," he ordered. He turned toward the pile of dead Comanche and ordered them tied to their horses, too.

Tomas seemed surprised. "What for?"

Juan did not answer. He remounted and sat bolt upright in his saddle, watching his dead young men being lifted and tied to their horses. Tomas put his horse forward beside his and watched with him.

"Most of them were just boys," Juan said.

Tomas nodded, then took out some tobacco and rolled a corn shuck cigarette.

"You sorry you brought them out here?" Tomas asked.

Juan shook his head, then nodded toward the dead Comanche. "No. Those dogs had to be stopped."

Tomas lit his cigarette and took a long drag. Juan saw the morning breeze swirl the blue smoke, the sun slanting through it between the shadows of their bodies.

"That was a good plan you made for the attack," Tomas said. "You should have been a general."

"I don't like armies," Juan replied. "They are run by idiots, and I never could take orders."

"That's why I said you should be a general. You could *give* the orders."

Juan twisted in his saddle and squinted at the old *vaquero*, his head a dark shape surrounded by a brilliant sun halo. "Are you trying to cheer me up?"

"I'm trying to figure out what's in your head."

"Why?"

"Because I know your moods, but I never know what you're thinking."

"So?"

Tomas spat at the ground. "So," he said, "because people die around you, I like to have some idea, just in case."

"In case what?"

"In case some of those people maybe shouldn't get dead."

Juan did not smile, but he did pull back a little from the awful black precipice that had been fueling a growing hunger for more violence. "What you mean," he said, "is people my mother might not want dead."

Tomas shrugged.

"You always look out for her, Tomas."

They sat in silence and watched the *vaqueros* tie the Comanche to their horses. When they were done, Juan split his men into two groups. The larger group went home to the Santa Alicia, taking with them the bodies of the slain *vaqueros*. Juan, Tomas and eight other men turned east with the dead Comanche. After crossing the river farther downstream, they worked their way through the thick dry brush to the military road, then rode all morning, the sun shining directly in their faces. They spoke very little. On occasion, they passed a ranch hidden in the brush, and sometimes they heard a lonely rooster crowing in the distance.

They arrived in Brownsville in the late afternoon, when the heat of the day had forced nearly everyone indoors. The day hung still and silent, as if the heat had dried up every sound except the constant hush of the flowing river. Juan turned toward the center of town, toward the square, where he ordered the Comanche cut down from the horses and piled on the ground. When they were done, Juan and the *vaqueros* gathered up the Comanche ponies and rode back out in the same direction they had come, never once looking around to see if the townspeople were watching.

Afterwards, the residents of Brownsville emerged from their shops and houses, *gringos* and Mexicans alike, to gawk at the Comanche bodies. Garrison stood there, trying to focus his bloodshot eyes, his head bursting from a hangover. Around him gathered the remainder of the posse, in no better shape.

Green walked up to one of the Comanche bodies and kicked him with the toe of his expensive boot, then turned to Garrison. "He was just here," he said. "You just let him ride in here and ride out. Why the hell didn't you arrest the bastard?"

Garrison shook his head, looking down at the stack of bodies already bloating in the hot, dusty street. "Take Rangers to handle Comanche like that," he muttered. "Take Rangers to arrest him, I reckon."

He looked up to see the other men staring at him, but they looked away when he tried to meet their eyes, except for Green, who scowled at him. Garrison turned back toward his office, feeling the shadow of the building immediately cool his skin. His mouth felt dry, his fuzzy tongue seemed swollen, his stomach churned, he felt dizzy. Green followed him into his cluttered office and watched him pick up a bottle of whiskey on his desk and pour them each a glass. They drank it down eagerly, and Garrison poured them another with trembling hands.

"This town is going down bad," Green said after a while..

"Oh damn, don't you start on me, Green."

But Green just shook his head and poured himself another shot. "That won't be the last of the Comanche. You know there's little bands of them raiding for horses all up and down the river. Bandits, too. Going after the cattle. Bodies float down the river past town, seems like every day, headed for the Gulf. Ever since the army left."

"Army never did shit, anyway."

Green shot a gob of spit at the spittoon. "No, but they was here. Shit, here comes our good mayor."

Daniel Miller paused at the door, then shuffled in, heading straight for the whiskey. "I don't believe it's any accident," he said, "that El Gallo brought in them Indians."

Garrison tilted his head sideways and tried to focus one eye on Miller. "What the hell you talking about?" He watched Miller throw his head back and swallow the whiskey in one gulp, then pour another.

"It's them damn big merchants," said Miller before he took a drink. "All the rustling, the Comanche, that warehouse blowing up, the fire—"

"Damn, why don't you blame them for the weather while you're at it?"

But Green nodded in sympathy. "I think he's right," he said. "And the Mexican families are in cahoots with them. They're all trying to run us out."

Garrison collapsed into his chair and leaned back. After two attempts to focus on his visitors, he gave up and squinted at the ceiling. "Hold on," he said, "hold on. You think the large merchants and the families paid the Comanche to come raiding? Then sent El Gallo to kill them, sort of to throw us off? Keep us from getting on to them?"

The men nodded, sitting down glumly in their chairs. Outside, a general noise arose as the crowd dispersed.

Garrison shook his head and snickered. "Don't seem too likely, boys. You got no idea what it takes to kill that many Comanche. Nobody in his right mind would even try it if he didn't have to."

"Then why'd he do it?"

Rising from his chair, Garrison strode to the window to watch the bodies being dragged to the river. "Probably to protect his ranch." But then he thought about it, and he was not sure that was all there was to it. "Or maybe he just likes killing"

Two more men came into the office and poured themselves some whiskey.

"This ain't no damn saloon," Garrison complained.

One of the new men spoke up. "What the hell we gonna do here, Garrison? We need some protection."

"As mayor," said Miller, "I think I should write a letter to the governor and demand that he send a troop of Rangers down here. Between rustling Meskin bandits, them Comanche savages, and the likes of El Gallo, it ain't safe to get up in the morning. Who's going to want to come do business here with all this killing? Hell, the bodies in the river are so damn thick you could walk across 'em. Don't even need the damn ferry."

"So write the damn letter," Garrison groused. "I don't give a damn."

"Well, I am."

IT WAS ONE OF THOSE strange days along the border. The sun shone as hot as always, and not a cloud marred the sky. But there was a wind. It blew from the northwest and brought with it a fog of fine red dust that seeped though the cracks in the doors and windows, so that soon it caked in layers on every surface, indoors and out. *Vaqueros* working in the *brasada* covered their noses and mouths with their bandannas. Inside the ranch house Lidia closed the windows, despite the heat. The wind blew in gusts all day, whining around the corners of the house and under the door, keeping Ramona busy all day sweeping the floor and dusting the furniture. But it was a losing battle. Even their afternoon meal tasted gritty as the dust crunched between their teeth.

Lidia lay in bed at siesta time, listening to the moaning and the rustle of the mesquite trees as the wind whipped them. She heard horses whinnying their complaints and the cattle lowing theirs. Something in the sound of the wind depressed her, caused echoes of melancholy to respond within her. Alone except for her disabled and embittered father and the servant Ramona, she lay and listened to the sounds of the creaking house. She missed her long dead mother. Martina de Leon would take a day like today and fill it with chatter, nothing of any consequence, rushing in all directions. Her chatter and activity would be a distraction from the wind, from its melancholy wail for who knew what.

Legend had it that when the wind moaned like this, it was the sound of the dead lamenting some unbearable loss they had suffered in their lives. Martina was gone. Lidia was alone. The wind moaned, and a tear rolled down Lidia's cheek, mixing with the beads of perspiration and rolling down to her neck and into the mass of her long brown hair. She had heard that women living on the plains farther north often felt like this about the wind, and that sometimes it drove them insane or to suicide. Now as she lay staring up at the ceiling, she thought she understood why.

She closed her eyes and drifted uneasily into sleep, awakening often as the wind came up in violent gusts that buffeted the house. It was during one of these gusts that she rose and walked sleepily toward the window, peering out to assure herself that the ranch was not being blown away. She tried to focus, but a fog of red dust enveloped the ranch, and she could barely make out even the main gate. Looking up, she could see the sun still shining faintly, but it did not look like the normal August border sun. She could actually stare at it and see its shape without being blinded. A big orange ball suspended high in the sky and obscured by the reddish fog, it gave a dreamlike aspect to the afternoon. Lidia leaned her head against the window and closed her eyes. The wind moaned on.

When she looked again, she saw a shape moving through the dust. She snapped her head up and tried to focus better, but it was not her eyes that blurred the shape. It was the dust. *A man on a horse*, she thought, squinting and looking more closely, *a man riding through the gate*. Perhaps one of the *vaqueros*. But then she looked harder. The hat. That was not a vaquero's sombrero. The man riding through her gate and approaching the house was a *gringo*.

She caught her breath and drew back from the window, for in a flash she knew who it was. She staggered back to her bed and sat on the edge, asking herself, *What am I going to do? What am I going to do?* She heard the firm knock on the front door, and then she heard Ramona call out from her bed. The *gringo* did not knock again, and it took some time for Ramona to dress and open the door. Lidia heard mumblings—then, more clearly, deep voice of a man and the unmistakable anglicized pronunciation of

Spanish. She put her hand on her breast, willing her pounding heart to be calm, and asked herself again, *What am I going to do?*

In a minute a soft knock sounded on her bedroom door. Lidia took a deep breath. "Yes?"

"Señorita Lidia, *es el Señor Starr.*"

It was true. He was here. Her hands trembled a little as she rose and walked to the door, turning the knob and opening it just a crack. There stood Ramona, her face thick from sleep, but smiling.

"You don't have to look so happy about it," said Lidia. "What does he want?"

Ramona's smile turned into what appeared to Lidia to be a lecherous grin. "He didn't tell me what he wants, except to talk to you. Should I tell him you are coming?"

"No," Lidia snapped. Then, "Yes." She shook her head and ran her hand through her hair. "He didn't say what he wanted?"

"Señorita," Ramona said, her grin dropping away and her face taking on a softer look, "he has come to visit. I will make him some coffee. You get dressed. I will tell him you will see him within the hour." Ramona nodded her head as she spoke, and Lidia found herself nodding with her.

As Ramona smiled again and turned to leave, Lidia called her back. "Ask him if he would like to wash the dust off. Let him use the room across from Father."

"*Sí, señorita.*"

Lidia closed the door and then leaned back against it. She thought about Starr's letters, how he often insisted on coming to see her, how she had always refused. Now he was here, uninvited, inserting himself back into her life. She put her hands to her face and found them to be still trembling. *Stop it,* she scolded herself. Why should she be so afraid of him? The palms of her hands were moist with perspiration, her body tingled all over, she could feel her nipples under her chemise, erect and sensitive, almost hurting. A good, kind man was coming to claim her, she told herself. A good, kind man, and though her heart would always be with Juan, after more than a decade of loneliness, her body seemed to be making its own needs known. She walked away from the door to wash and to dress.

An hour later, she sat across from him in the parlor. Starr had washed, shaved, and changed into a fresh shirt. He sipped his coffee. Lidia sat demurely, her hands folded on her lap. A cup of coffee rested on the table next to her, but she had not touched it. Her stomach was in turmoil, and she knew pouring coffee into it would be a disaster.

He put the coffee down and looked at her with his pale blue eyes. "You wish I hadn't come?"

"Not at all," she replied, looking away.

"You kept refusing me in your letters."

She did not answer.

They sat in silence for a few minutes. Outside, the wind still buffeted the house and moaned around the corners. The mesquite trees hissed and creaked, the animals complained.

"What a strange wind," she finally said.

He nodded. "That red dust is from up yonder, out in the west part of Texas near El Paso, maybe even farther west. Seen it before. In Apache country."

"How strange that it blows so far, even out to here in the *brasada*. Was it difficult for you to travel in it?"

He took another sip of his coffee, then set the cup down. "Spooked my horse a bit."

They fell silent again.

"Tom, why have you come?"

He smiled. "I plumb forgot how very beautiful you are, Lidia. How full of sass you are."

"You came to look at me?"

He shook his head, put his hands on his thighs, and leaned back in the chair. Lidia could see his eyes roaming over her body, from her hair to her face to her hands, her breasts, her feet. They roamed and then fixed themselves on some part of her, like her hands, and he stared as he spoke.

"I guess you could say I came to look at you. I came to see if you were all right."

"Why shouldn't I be all right?"

"Troubles along the border, I hear."

"What troubles?"

"Bandits. Comanche. Killin's."

"Someone has sent you here?"

He shook his head and leaned forward again. "Governor sent Bill Dauterive out of San Antone. He rounded up a company of Rangers and headed down to Brownsville. I heard about it up in Austin and rode along to check on you."

"I'm all right, Tom. Nobody ever bothers us out here. We've lost some cattle, some horses, but the Comanche don't bother the big ranches. They seem to travel in small groups. They like to attack the smaller places, the ones without all the *vaqueros*." She looked up to find him staring again, this time at her face. "What is it?"

"What's happened to you, Lidia? I can't figure why you're still out here. All by yourself."

"You know why."

"But that was twelve years ago."

"Nothing has changed."

"You could have married by now," he said. "If you didn't want me, I know there are others...."

"I don't want to talk about that!" She rose suddenly and walked toward the window, and he rose to follow her.

He stood behind her, and they both looked out the window.

"I'm sorry," he said. "It's a hard thing to live with."

"How do you know anything about it?"

He sighed and put a hand on her shoulder, but she cringed and he removed it. "Comanche steal a lot of women and children. Make most of 'em slaves, adopt the little ones. Seen 'em when we steal 'em back. They ain't the same. Ain't never the same."

"Well, I'm no slave." She turned and faced him, the reddish light from the window illuminating his face as he towered over her. "But I know I'm not the same. Tom, I don't feel fit to live anywhere else but here. This is the only place I feel comfortable."

He nodded, and she felt those pale blue eyes roving over her, warming each part of her they touched. She looked at him, his thin and rugged frame full of clean lines and angles, and she felt a pang of yearning for his touch, for the warmth and comfort that she remembered he had given her so long ago.

"Tom," she whispered, "please hold me."

He stepped forward and swept her into his arms, and she relaxed into his strength, his firmness, his warmth. She put her head against his chest and drank in his musky smell, then she could feel him lower his head, rub his face in her hair, and kiss the top of her head. She lifted her face to his and he kissed her, long and gentle, as if he were kissing a dream that he was afraid he would awaken from. He cupped her face with his hands and looked upon her, and she could see the love in his eyes. He ran his hand through her hair, touched her ear gently, treating each part of her as if it were a marvel, some treasure he had long dreamed to touch. She wanted his kiss, wanted those lips to touch hers so that their warmth could reach down into that part of her that had gone cold. She reached up and drew his face back, offering her lips. He kissed her again, moving his hands to the small of her back and drawing her near. She wrapped her arms around his neck and pulled him to her.

When she drew her face away, she pushed herself back just a little, but she let those comforting arms continue to hold her. "I don't know why I did that," she whispered.

He smiled. "Well if you don't know, I sure as hell ain't ever goin' to figure it out. But I think we should do it again."

They embraced again. He kissed her face, the tip of her nose, her closed eyes. He rubbed his rough cheeks against hers. She felt her arms and legs going liquid, as if she were melting and he was holding her together.

"Lidia," he whispered, "my darling. I want you to marry me."

Her face rose up slowly, her eyes wide. She tried weakly to push herself away from him, but he would not let her go. "Please, Tom, no. Don't spoil it."

He stepped back, a frown on his face, his eyes bearing down on her in confusion. "I don't understand."

Putting her hands to the sides of her face to try to cool the flames on her cheeks, she struggled to slow her breathing down. She could see the hurt on his face. She was afraid he would go. "I'm sorry," she said, taking his hand in hers. "It's just that you surprised me. That's all."

They walked to the couch and sat side by side, holding hands and smiling, but now there was a tension of uncertainty between them.

"I've said it, Lidia, and I'm not leaving until you answer me one way or the other."

She looked down at her shoes.

"I've waited a long time for you," he continued. "I'm tired of waiting. There is nothin' that any more time will help. All these years haven't helped you. They ain't done nothin' except to waste twelve years we could've spent together."

She said, "I know that. But I wasn't ready."

"Are you ready now?"

"I don't know."

He sighed and caressed her hand. "How can I help you to decide?"

She shook her head. "I can't leave my father. He's an invalid. I am all he has left."

"Well, that's easy to solve! We'll bring him up to Austin with us. I'll help you take care of him."

She shook her head again. "I can't live in Austin. I want to live here. On the ranch. I can't stand crowds of people, all of them looking at me, as if they knew what happened."

His voice was gentle. "Well, then, I'll come live here with you, Lidia. I'll take up ranching. And we'll never go to a town unless you want to. And if anybody looks at you sideways, I'll kill him."

She looked up at him and found comfort and reassurance in his face, in the hardness of his body, in his smell, in his warmth. She felt her loneliness pushing at her from within, urging her to welcome him, to give herself to him. She knew that Starr was a violent man, that he could kill cruelly and dispassionately. But she also knew that he could be gentle and generous, and she felt that he could make her feel safe and secure. And she knew that Ophelia was right. Her youth was slipping away, wasting like a rose blooming in the desert, her loveliness unseen, her scent unsmelled. Perhaps it was Juan she had been waiting for, but that issue seemed settled now. Forever. There was nothing to hold her.

"Oh, Tom," she said finally, "I don't know. I'm not sure...."

He took her into his arms, those warm, firm, secure arms. "I'll make you happy, Lidia." He kissed her, and she let herself get lost in his embrace.

At last, however, she pushed away. "Tom, this is happening too fast. You can't just walk in here after all these years and do this to me."

He stepped back. "You want me to go?"

She shook her head and held on to his hand. "I didn't say that. I just think I need a little more time."

"Twelve years." His voice was very quiet.

"I know, I know it sounds ridiculous. But you show up here out of a dust storm and suddenly I'm kissing you and you want to marry me."

"When you put it that way—"

She smiled and squeezed his hand.

"I have business down in Brownsville," he said. "After that I'm headed back to Austin to put some things in order." He held her chin up and looked straight into her eyes. "Then I'm coming back here. I'll be gone maybe six weeks. And when I come back, Lidia, I'm coming back for you."

She felt her hand trembling in his, and the excitement she felt seemed to flow throughout her body. She felt her eyes grow bright and her smile warm. "In six weeks," she said. "Come back in six weeks, Tom. Give me that time."

"Six weeks," he repeated.

"But I'm not promising anything."

"No."

She frowned, and her smile faded away. "You're going to Brownsville?"

He nodded.

"Will you do me a favor?"

"What?"

"Will you promise me not to get mixed up with Juan? For Ophelia's sake?"

His face fell. "For Ophelia's sake?"

She brought both of his hands to her face and kissed each palm. "Yes, Tom. It's for Ophelia. She's done so much for me, and he breaks her heart. She is my dearest friend. If something were to happen between you and Juan, I couldn't bear what it would do to her."

He leaned his head forward and kissed her, then took her into his arms again. "I'll stay clear of him," he said, "long as he doesn't force my hand."

She nodded her head against his shoulder. "*Gracias.*"

ONE THING THAT BROWNSVILLE seemed to have plenty of was lawyers. With all the land claims and counterclaims and uncertainty that followed the end of the Mexican War, widespread litigation kept them all busy. Ophelia Santos had engaged the law firm of Dresser & Winkle to contest the founding of Brownsville on her land, but in the meantime dozens of suits had been brought against her, claiming title to large tracts of the Santa Alicia. These claims were brought by squatters, Texas veterans, settlers who had bought counterfeit titles from unscrupulous agents back east, and entrepreneurs hoping to carve out a piece of Texas for themselves by just taking it.

Today she sat in the Dresser & Winkle law office, glaring at Franklin Dresser, her mouth set in a firm line as she listened to his review of her case.

Her patience exhausted, she cut him off. "You've had this case for over two years, Mr. Dresser. I hired you because you said you knew real estate law. It is a simple case. The Treaty of Guadalupe Hidalgo clearly establishes, as one of the terms of peace between the United States and Mexico, that original Spanish and Mexican land titles will be honored *by law* in the United States. I have title. Brownsville was built illegally, and I am due compensation for the land! I am being more than reasonable."

Benjamin Winkle leaned back and waved his hands. "It may seem simple, Señora Santos, but in fact it is very complicated. Records show that you actually ceded the land to the city of Matamoros—"

"No, I never did that, Mr. Winkle, and you know that."

"You're absolutely right, of course," he replied. "Let me back up and review the entire situation for both of us." He rose and paced toward the window. "Stop me if you disagree. The town of Matamoros was established by thirteen wealthy landowning families in 1784. Yours was one of those families, led by your grandfather. A town square was laid out, which is now called the Plaza Hidalgo, which today has a cathedral on the west side and the town hall on the east side. They also reserved a spot for a town market. Anyone who wanted to could claim one or more lots within a league of the central plaza. The town also purchased *ejidos*, or town commons from some of the surrounding ranches for the purpose of grazing animals. One of the *ejidos* purchased, according to town records, was this strip of land on the Texas side of the river where the town of Brownsville now rests."

"Purchased," Ophelia admitted, "but never paid for!"

He nodded. "Granted. No real negotiations for payment ever took place until you inherited the land in 1824 and requested payment in 1826. The town of Matamoros agreed to pay you, but negotiations and settlement dragged on until the Mexican War. Unfortunately, squatters came in and after Texas independence some claimed pieces of the land. Completely fraudulent, of course. In 1848, the Brownsville Town Company was organized, and the company purchased the titles from these squatters. So," he took a breath, "what seems to be a simple case, Señora Santos, is actually to the courts one of conflicting claims by good citizens who all feel they are in the right."

"Mr. Winkle," she said, "it is *your job* to produce the documentation to show that it is *I* who am right. It is unfortunate that people bought and paid for land that was not rightfully for sale. But that doesn't change anything."

Franklin Dresser, who had been listening without a word, leaned forward and lit a cigar, then waved the match out. "But there is one more difficulty, Señora Santos. Possession. The town has been in place for over a decade now. The longer it sits, the weaker your claim grows."

She shook her head and let out a huge sigh. "I should have let Juan burn it down when he wanted to."

Dresser nodded. "That might have been your best course at the time, perhaps. But we all know that bloodshed is not your way."

"You know nothing of the kind, Mr. Dresser. I prefer a peaceful solution, that is true. But you are dragging your heels, and I want to know why."

The two lawyers began eager protestations, but she waved them off. "I'm giving you four weeks to produce some results. I want all of the squatter claims against my land thrown out, and I want a judgment in my favor regarding my suit against Brownsville. If you cannot accomplish that in four weeks, I'm firing both of you. Is that clear?"

Dresser nodded glumly. Winkle scratched his whiskers and nodded, too. "Señora Santos," he said, "it seems a bad time to bring it up, but there is the small matter of our bill for services rendered—"

"Bill? You haven't done anything!"

They looked away, each at a different wall, and Ophelia rose. Tomas, who was standing right outside, looked in through the window and promptly opened the door for her.

Her eye swept the two lawyers. "You get me some results, gentlemen. And then talk you can to me about your bill. Good day."

The men scrambled to their feet and bowed a little as she stormed out the door.

Outside, Tomas sensed her mood. "Ophelia? Is there—"

"It's nothing, Tomas. Don't be alarmed. Just incompetent lawyers worried about their bill."

They turned and walked across the street, heading for the Villarreal Bank. It was almost noon, and the sunlight beat down from directly overhead, stinging their necks. Tomas reached back and swung his sombrero to the top of his head, but Ophelia had left her parasol in the carriage. They walked side by side, Ophelia still fuming, her step quickening as she thought about the lawyers. She looked up and found Tomas almost loping beside her, a grin on his face.

"What are you laughing about?"

"*Nada*, Ophelia, *nada*."

She slowed down and glared at him, but he did not seem the least alarmed. "You're laughing at me, aren't you?"

"Ophelia," he replied, "you surely know that if you had listened to me or Juan, you wouldn't have any problems with lawyers. This town wouldn't be here."

"No. And maybe you and Juan would have been hanged by the Rangers."

He shrugged. "Maybe. But you wouldn't have problems with lawyers."

They both heard it at the same time, loud voices followed by the sound of running feet. Then, right in front of them, three men burst from the alley. Tomas stepped automatically forward and swept Ophelia behind him with his right arm. All three running men fell to the dusty street together in a tangled mass of arms and legs. When the dust cleared, they saw Marshal Garrison sitting on the chest of a *vaquero*, pounding him with his fists while the mayor of Brownsville held the man's arms down. The marshal slammed his fists into the *vaquero's* face with such viciousness that blood splattered up on Tomas' shirt, and a few drops fell on Ophelia's dress.

Ophelia's eyes went wide at the naked violence, but she did not look away. "Stop it!" she cried. "Stop beating that man!"

Tomas stepped forward and put his hand on the marshal's shoulder to get his attention, but Garrison whirled about and drew his pistol.

"You're under arrest, Tomas."

Ophelia stepped forward. "Arrest? Arrest for what?"

"He hit me while I was trying to arrest this drunken fool," Garrison growled, and he shook his gun at Tomas while he spoke. "Put your hands up," he demanded. Tomas crossed his arms instead.

"You weren't trying to arrest that man," replied Ophelia. "You were trying to kill him. Tomas barely touched you. He put his hand on your shoulder to get your attention."

Miller let go of the *vaquero's* arms, and Garrison rolled off of the man's chest, but he put a boot on him to hold him down.

"I saw it," said Miller. "It's like the marshal says."

Around them, people streamed out of the shops and saloons and offices, gathering around to see the grand Doña Ophelia confronting the town leaders. This included the lawyers Winkle & Dresser. Across the street came another set of lawyers, Frost & Hightower, all of them joining with the others to form a circle around the scene. The *vaquero*, meanwhile, lay on the ground and tried to rub the blood out of his eyes. He had the best view of all.

"You're under arrest, Tomas," Garrison repeated.

"He is not under arrest," Ophelia declared.

"Oh, yes, he is, ma'am. And now, you're under arrest, too."

There was a decided murmur from the crowd. Hurried whispers circulated among the Mexican onlookers.

Hearing the marshal place Ophelia under arrest, Tomas slowly uncrossed his arms. As the marshal now swung the gun toward her, she could feel the tension building in Tomas. It was like a strong, thick tree branch bent back, aching for release.

"Wait," she said, and she put a hand on Tomas' arm. "Let's talk about this...this problem, Mr. Garrison."

"The name is *Marshal* Garrison." He sneered. "And there ain't nothin' to talk about. You're both under arrest and I'm taking all three of you over to the jail and I'm gonna lock you up."

The prospect of Ophelia Santos being locked up in Garrison's dirty, stinking jail seemed so outrageous that the onlookers began to laugh, which seemed to egg Garrison on, for he laughed, too, and looked back over his shoulder at the crowd, the gun in his hand moving off toward his gaze. As the gun moved away, Ophelia was suddenly filled with dread, for her fingertips on Tomas' arm told her that the branch was about to release. Someone was about to die, and she was terrified that it would be Tomas.

"Hold it right there," a strong voice suddenly ordered. The crowd parted. At its edge, Tom Starr sat his horse, leaning on the saddle horn, his hat tipped down so that it shaded most of his face.

Garrison stepped forward. "This here is town business, Starr. These people are under arrest. This ain't your business."

Starr shifted his weight in the saddle, his horse lifting its head and snorting. "I done made it my business," he said. "Better get that gun out of my face, Marshal."

Garrison studied the gun in his hand for a moment as if he'd never seen it before, then slowly holstered it. He looked back at the crowd, but the men were all looking away. Miller was doing his best to become invisible, slinking away until he melted into the crowd.

"You're free to go, Doña Santos," said Starr. Tomas turned and took Ophelia's hand, leading her forward through the crowd to where Starr sat his horse. She stopped there and looked up at him, nodding her thanks. He lifted his hat briefly and tipped it toward her.

Tomas said, "*Capitán* Starr, we meet again."

"Tomas, how the hell are you?"

"*Muy bien,*" he replied, "but now I must escort my *patrona* home."

As they walked away, Ophelia heard Tom Starr say, in a chilling monotone, "You ever lay a hand on that lady, Garrison, I'll kill you."

Chapter 8
The Lawyers

STARR LEANED ONE ELBOW on the bar and regarded the tight bundle of Brownsville merchants crowding around him. One of them leaned forward and poured him another glass of whiskey. They were all talking at the same time until that foul-smelling marshal, Garrison, told them to shut up. Starr pulled the brim of his hat down and reached for the whiskey.

"You boys are full of shit," Starr said.

"No sir," replied Green. "It's true, Cap'n. That Santos boy kilt two Americans over to Matamoros. For no reason. Just up and stuck 'em. Then he dragged one across the river and all the way out to the brush. That rooster needs hangin' real bad, Cap'n. He's crazy mean."

Miller piped in, "Struts in here ever day with his *vaqueros* like he owns this here town."

Starr threw his head back and swallowed the whiskey. "Don't he?"

The merchants protested loudly, and after a moment Miller waved them off. "Cap'n, he's gonna come in after Garrison, after what happened with Doña Ophelia. The marshal here needs some help. You gonna do it?"

Starr laughed and turned back to the bar to pour another drink. "If I killed El Gallo," he said, "I'd be killing the only real man in these parts. Besides, you got Cap'n Dauterive over there. Why don't you go bother him?"

The men turned and regarded the snoring Captain Bill Dauterive, who was sprawled on the floor in the corner of the saloon, an empty bottle of whiskey lying by his side. Nearby, three of his Rangers had their heads on the table. They were snoring even louder than their captain.

Miller sneered. "I don't know about you boys, but I think the quality of Rangers done took a turn for the worse. Half of 'em took off for Matamoros. Whoring. We got one cap'n drunk on his ass and the other one..." he turned and looked at Starr, but the look on Starr's face convinced Miller he'd said enough.

They all heard the sound of running feet and turned to the door, where two boys came tumbling in, a huge cloud of dust sweeping in after them.

"He's here!" one of them cried. "El Gallo's here!"

The merchants turned eagerly to Starr. "Cap'n, you gonna do it?"

Starr pressed his lips into a thin line and fingered his whiskey glass. "I should have let the *cabrón* drown in the river back a while ago," he said.

The merchants backed away from the bar and took up seats at the rickety tables scattered around the tiny saloon. Garrison scooted the two boys back out the front door, but they ran back to the edge of the boardwalk and waited excitedly to see what would happen. Everyone heard, then saw Juan riding his horse up to the saloon. He stopped, dismounted, and dropped Prieto's reins over the rail. Mingo and Tomas rode up behind him, and a minute later they stood on the boardwalk beside Juan.

"Patron," Mingo nodded at the Rangers' horses at the rail, "*son rinches.*"

Juan nodded, then turned and entered the saloon. He quickly ran his eyes from one end of the smoky room to the other, observing the drunken Rangers, the eager merchants, the grinning marshal. Then his eyes rested on Starr, leaning with one boot on the bar-rail, his hat still pushed down on his forehead, looking at his whiskey glass.

As Tomas and Mingo took up stations on either side of the door, Juan strode briskly along the bar toward Starr, his big-roweled Mexican spurs clinking loudly in the quiet room. As he approached, Starr turned, his elbow still on the bar. Juan stopped about four feet away.

"Señor Starr."

"Señor Santos," Starr replied, adding an almost imperceptible nod.

They stood there a long minute, studying each other, until one of the merchants scraped a chair on the floor. Juan raised his eyebrows and shifted his eyes off Starr, keeping him in his peripheral vision, just long enough to assure himself that the merchants posed no threat.

Starr poured himself a glass of whiskey and then poured an extra one, which he lifted up and offered to Juan. "Drink?" he asked in Spanish.

Juan hesitated, then reached forward and took the glass. "*Quiero hablar.*"

Starr turned and looked at the men seated at the nearest table. "You men, move." He reached for one of the chairs, and the merchants scrambled away. Starr took up the bottle of whiskey and set it down in the center of the table. Juan walked over, and slowly they eased themselves into the creaky chairs. They sat stiffly, staring at each other.

"What's on your mind?" Starr asked in English.

"*Te debo.* I owe you twice now," Juan said. "For my life, and for your help to my mother this morning."

Starr grunted. "Not sure I'm glad I did the first one."

"It doesn't matter. Why did you help? *Quiero saber.*"

"Why?" Starr drank the glass of whiskey and poured another, but he noted that Juan had not touched his. He shrugged. "Just seemed the right thing to do."

Juan looked at him sideways, not really sure he was not making a joke. His first instinct, upon hearing of the marshal's treatment of Ophelia, had been to ride into town and shoot Garrison in the street, but Tomas had talked him out of it and calmed him down. Then it struck him that Starr had once saved his life, and now had saved Ophelia and Tomas from jail and perhaps worse. But he could not bring himself to believe that Starr was a decent man. Rangers were thugs with guns. They hated Mexicans. He shook his head. "I owe you. I don't like that."

Starr leaned back and pushed his hat up. "Don't strain yourself."

Starr took notice that Juan looked straight at a man, even a *gringo*. Many Mexicans preferred to avoid hard eye contact, but Juan seemed to enjoy boring straight in with those gray-green eyes, as if to test who would look away first. He saw Juan frown.

"Why are you Rangers back on the border?"

Starr nodded at the snoring Rangers. "Them boys are here on Texas business. I just came along for the ride."

"What business?"

Starr felt a twinge of irritation with Juan's inquisitiveness and his mode of questioning. He was not so much seeking information as demanding it. Allowing Mexicans to make demands was not Starr's style—not any Ranger's style. But the image of Lidia's beautiful face looking up at him, the sweet touch of her lips, the feel of her body flooded his mind. She had asked him to avoid trouble with Juan. For Ophelia's sake. But was it for Ophelia?

"Heard there's been Comanche raids down here," Starr finally replied. "Cattle rustling. Killings."

Juan nodded. "There have been Comanche."

"Heard you cleaned out a nest yourself, you and your *vaqueros*. Heard you stacked them out yonder in the plaza." Starr smiled. "For a bandit, you've got style."

"*Quién dice* I'm a bandit?"

Starr saw the look on Juan's face changing. There had been a spark of interest in his eyes, a frown on his forehead, lines around his mouth—now it all dissolved away. Juan stared at the back wall of the cantina, right past Starr's shoulder.

"Marshal there says he's got a warrant out for you. For cattle rustling."

Juan turned his expressionless face toward the marshal, who had stopped grinning and now threw a wistful look toward the door, where Mingo and Tomas stood with their thumbs hooked on their belts.

Juan said, "Then let him arrest me."

The marshal blinked at Juan, then turned to shoot a pleading look at Starr, but Starr simply leaned forward and fingered his whiskey glass. Garrison spread his arms out in a gesture of helplessness, then turned to the bar to pour himself some whiskey.

"I guess maybe you're not a bandit, then," Starr said.

Juan nodded, then finally reached forward and picked up his whiskey glass, but he did not drink it. He looked at it as if it were a strange brew, the likes of which he'd never tasted.

"Want some mescal?" Starr asked him.

Juan shook his head and put the drink back down.

"Now I got a question for you, Santos." Starr tried to think how to ask this next question without setting Juan off, but he finally decided that whether it did or not, he needed to know the answer. He lowered his voice just slightly

"What does Miss de Leon mean to you?"

Juan's expression changed again. His eyes flashed, his jaw clamped tighter. He sat silent for a moment, then replied, "Nothing."

Starr let out a long breath. He sensed something still there, something between Lidia and Juan. The look on his face, her pleas for Starr not to fight him. A fire still smoldered, but maybe he could put it out once and for all.

"Good," he said. "Because she's mine now."

An incredulous look spread across Juan's face, but he merely nodded and rose stiffly from the table, his chair scraping loudly on the floor. "You can have her."

Juan turned and walked across the room to the door. On his way out, he shot Garrison a look that caused the marshal to visibly pale.

Over in the corner, Dauterive rolled over on his hands and knees and stared groggily at the room. "Gimme a drink," he bellowed. "Gimme a god-damn drink!" He focused his gaze on Juan as he passed. "Jesus, it's that god-damn Gallo. Somebody shoot the sumbitch!"

But Juan sneered and strode out of the saloon before Dauterive could coordinate his body well enough to reach for his Colt. The Ranger pulled himself up on his feet and then stumbled through the tables and chairs, his dirty blonde hair covering his eyes. "Ain't nobody gonna shoot that bastard?" he cried.

As he passed Starr's table, he reached down for the whiskey glass Juan had left and sucked it down. Little rivers of whiskey ran down the sides of his mouth, through the thick bristles of his beard. He wiped his mouth with the back of his hand, looked at Starr, and winked. "Let's get him, Tom."

Starr shook his head. "Not today, Bill."

Dauterive had already launched himself, stomping through the saloon, kicking at his sleeping Rangers, then stumbling out the front door. Starr rose to follow him.

Outside, Juan had mounted Prieto. Mingo and Tomas leaned forward in their saddles as Dauterive came tumbling out the door.

"Hey, greaser!" Dauterive yelled. He crashed into the railing and almost flipped over it, but he held on and used it to stay on his feet.

Juan stared at Dauterive with interest. He slid his hand down and pulled up his bullwhip.

The sun sent golden light slanting through the dust and haze, casting long shadows on the street. Dauterive and Juan stared at each other, Dauterive in the shadow and Juan in the sunlight. Dauterive's hand dragged along the handle of his Colt, his elbow cocked at an angle. Both men were silent, expectant, but at last Dauterive drew a long, ragged whiskey breath and let his hand slip away from the gun.

"Catch any of you bastards stealing cattle," he declared, "gonna hang you."

The other patrons came streaming out of the saloon, and gathering around Starr on the boardwalk. They squinted up at Juan, and saw his chin held high, his eyes half closed.

Juan leaned forward and spat on the ground at the edge of the boardwalk. He looked down at Garrison. "Never touch my family or my men again." He let his gaze drift down to Dauterive. "That goes for you, too." He looked at Starr. "And for this whole *chingado* town."

"You just stay out of this town," Dauterive managed to reply.

Prieto snorted and pushed his ears back, and Juan pulled him away from the rail, raising a cloud of hot dust that turned bright and glittered in the low sunshine. The three horsemen turned and galloped out of town, leaving the Rangers and the merchants to stare after them.

Dauterive turned and leaned his butt on the rail, hanging on to the wooden porch post with one hand and pushing his cropped, dirty hair back with the other. His belly hung over his belt and seemed to strain the seams of his greasy shirt, which had been blue at one time. Now it was so caked with sweat and dust it had a reddish tint. He looked up at Starr. "Greaser shouldn't talk that way to Rangers. Making threats. Why didn't you kill him while you had the chance?"

Starr did not even look at him. "Dauterive," he replied, "you're a god damned fool."

"You had him," groaned Miller. "Cap'n, you had him. You coulda taken him easy, right there in the saloon. Why'd you let him off?"

Garrison stepped off the boardwalk, shaking his head. "And you, Dauterive. Why the hell didn't you shoot him?"

Dauterive put his hands to his head. "I would have, boys, but I plumb couldn't see the sumbitch. When I stepped outside, my eyes done took to spinning. All I could do to stand up."

The merchants crowded around the Rangers, murmuring angrily, looking off occasionally at the far end of town where Juan's dust still hovered in an orange fog above the dusty road.

Brown said, "What about you, Starr? Why didn't you shoot him?"

Starr turned to the rail and untied his horse's reins. "None of you jaspers is worth the bullshit on Gallo's heels," he said. "Dauterive, you get these useless dregs you call Rangers gathered up by first light tomorrow. Governor asked me to take a look around down here. I intend to ride with you boys to La Bolsa, and I'm leaving tomorrow. Any man don't show up gets shot for desertion."

Dauterive blinked, then scratched his butt. "I don't know where the hell they are. You want 'em, you find 'em."

The murmuring died down. It was well known that nobody talked back to Tom Starr. As the silence grew, Dauterive looked around uneasily. Finally it seemed to hit him that he had made a mistake. "Uhhh, I mean… well, I'll find them myself. That's what I meant, Cap'n. I'll just git these here boys over to Matamoros and round up them stragglers." He shot an arm up in the general direction of his Rangers, who straggled out onto the street to retrieve their horses. Then they all rode down to the ferry.

Late the following morning, most of them were slumped in their saddles, one of them actually snoring. Starr rode up to Dauterive and looked him over.

"Dauterive, your head still spinning?"

Dauterive shook his head, but gingerly. "I done slep' it off, Cap'n Starr. Same with my boys."

Starr nodded, but he knew they had not slept. Dauterive and his men had shot up a Matamoros cantina and left two Mexicans dead. They had also beat up a whore who'd declared she did not service *gringos*. Then they'd shot at several houses as they prowled drunkenly down the streets, looking for sport. When the Mexican army intervened, the Rangers waded their horses through the thick pall of smoke that hovered over the river to the Texas side.

Starr turned and put his horse forward, and the sleepy band followed. They rode west out of Brownsville just before noon. The mid-day breeze picked up the heavy scent of the river and spread it across the clear valley, mixing with the sweet scent of mesquite and cactus, the dew long since burned away. Overhead, hawks hovered on the updrafts, screeching fiercely at the day, their long shadows floating past the Rangers' path and across the bright blue river into Mexico.

DAUTERIVE'S RANGERS were in bad shape, but Starr pushed them hard anyway. A sultry dusk was falling when they completed the twenty-five-mile journey to La Bolsa Bend, a tiny strip of land on the Texas side of the river. It had been created by a sudden shift in the river's course and had immediately become a haven for outlaws and bandits of all kinds. A little settlement had sprung up, though it mostly consisted of tents and *jacales*, and everywhere smoky mesquite fires burned for the evening meals. When the thin line of Rangers rode in, a sudden rush began among some of the inhabitants toward the other side of the river.

The Rangers pulled up in front of William Neal's dry goods store and dismounted. Neal was standing on his porch, smoking a pipe under the lantern light. A thick cloud of flies buzzed around the light, which Neal waved away from his face. He was a big man, with curly black hair and beard and a dark complexion.

"Evening, Neal."

"Evening, Captain Starr. What brings you out here?"

Starr jerked his chin toward the Rangers, who groaned as they slid off their mounts. "Dauterive's boys here are making a sweep toward Laredo. Comanche."

Neal nodded. "They look done in."

"Too much mescal last night, I reckon."

Neal's eyes twinkled as he looked at the Rangers, who had planted themselves on the porch, some still holding their horses' reins. They all waved at the flies, some slapping their own faces.

"If you don't know mescal," Neal said, "you shouldn't overindulge. I've seen men hung over for days."

Starr almost smiled. "Well, it got to them, I reckon."

"I reckon. You men need supplies?"

Dauterive shuffled up. "I'll be needing some dry goods, Neal. Some powder, too."

Neal grinned. "Looks like you boys need whiskey more'n powder."

Later, Neal and Starr sat at a table in the back of the store and listened to Dauterive and his Rangers shooting at Mexicans' heels down by the river. Over in the corner, a cowboy lying on a cot snored loudly, his boots tucked underneath. Neal said the man was named John Stokes. He had drifted in a few days earlier and immediately started wreaking havoc on the already lawless population of La Bolsa. He had been asleep all day, the storekeeper added, and apparently intended to sleep through a second night.

A minute later, Neal brought a dinged up pot of black coffee to the table and poured Starr a cup. Between them they consumed two dozen hot and spicy tamales, which were prepared every day by the Mexican women who lived in *jacales* along the river. Starr sipped the coffee and leaned back, his pale blue eyes studying Neal.

"Neal, you don't miss too many opportunities, do you."

Neal picked his teeth with a fingernail and nodded. "Stage line business dried up with the free trade zone," he said. "This looked like as good a place as any to make a dollar." His voice sounded thick, but he ended most of his sentences softly, almost in a whisper. "And I don't much care where that dollar comes from."

"Surprised these bandits even pay you."

Neal laughed. "They pay," he said. "They pay or they float down the river."

"You the one dropping all those corpses downstream? Float by Brownsville every day." Starr sipped his coffee and watched Neal's eyes light up.

Neal's short temper was well known. Most men knew when they dealt with him that they had to be careful.

A chorus of laughter floated up from the river bank, followed by several gunshots, then more laughter. Dauterive's Rangers had taken to the whiskey, then shucked off their clothes and jumped into the river to cool off. Afterwards, they lounged on the riverbank, drinking more whiskey and taking aim at Mexicans as they darted between the *jacales*.

"Them Rangers you got ain't worth shit," Neal observed.

"I ain't got 'em. Dauterive's got 'em."

"Dauterive ain't worth shit, neither."

"Nope." Starr rose from his chair and went to the window. He saw men walking around by the riverbank but could not see what they were doing. "They'll stay here drunk a couple days, Neal. Then you need to tell them to get the hell upriver toward Laredo. Just move them the hell out of here."

"They don't quit shooting up my customers, they'll leave sooner'n that. Where you headed, Starr?"

The Ranger turned away from the window, but he did not answer right away. Lidia's face, her hands, the feel of her body swirled around his head, elusive, urgent. *There*, he thought. *Soon as I can get to Austin and back, there's where I'm headed.*

FRANKLIN DRESSER seemed unable to contain himself as he scurried across the floor of his office. He set a cup of black coffee before his client, Doña Ophelia Santos, and chortled, all the while looking up at his partner, Benjamin Winkle, who sat on the other side of the desk, grinning.

"Well," Ophelia said, "you two certainly seem to be in a happy mood. Do you have news?"

"Oh Señora Santos," Dresser bubbled, "do we have news! Yes, yes we do! Benjamin, tell her."

"Oh sit down, Franklin," Winkle said. "You're starting to annoy even me." He looked up at Ophelia and smiled. "He gets excited."

Ophelia stared at him. "I'm waiting to hear your news."

"Señora Santos, the suits filed against you have been dismissed. Thrown out. All of them. Your title is clear."

Ophelia smiled for the first time. This was very good news indeed. Finally, it was over. The squatters would have to move. And no one had been killed over it, that was critical. She wanted no trouble for her sons. "You've done well," she said. "And Brownsville?"

Dresser dropped his grin. Winkle fidgeted.

"Well," said Winkle, "that is still pending, Señora Santos. And I have to tell you, it doesn't look very good—"

"But why? I don't understand. Why? It's the same principle, the same law. For both issues, we are basing our arguments on the terms of the Treaty of Guadalupe Hidalgo."

Winkle spoke quickly, his voice confident, knowledgeable. "But the situation is different. Whereas there were really only two claims to the land with the squatters, yours and theirs, in the case of Brownsville, there are many claims. The land was sold many times, leased out, resold. It's complicated. And the same treaty that protects you seems to be protecting them." He paused and pulled out a cigar, but did not light it. "Quite frankly, Señora Santos, that one doesn't look too good."

She sighed and shook her head. "Well," she said, "I'm not giving up. I want you to keep trying. Come up with something. I'm not giving up."

The lawyers nodded soberly.

"Of course," said Winkle, "of course."

He looked up at Dresser and stared. Dresser nodded toward Ophelia and then stared back at Winkle.

"What is it?" demanded Ophelia. "What are you two hiding?"

Winkle turned to her with seeming reluctance. "Well, señora, I guess we were just trying to figure out which one of us is going to present you with our bill."

Ophelia sat back and folded her hands. "I suppose it is outrageous."

Winkle shuffled some papers nervously. "Well, ma'am, we *have* been working on this for two years, with just the retainer. It's been hard making ends meet. We've had to make frequent trips to New Orleans and Austin to the federal and Texas courts. We've had to borrow—"

"How much is your bill, Mr. Winkle?"

"Three thousand four hundred seventeen dollars."

Ophelia's mouth flew open, and the two men cringed visibly.

"Three thous—you must be out of your minds! Those plots of land you defended aren't even worth that much money. The riverfront plots, Brownsville—that's where the value is. Are you insane?"

Dresser pushed some papers toward her. "It's all here, Señora Santos. Look at the hours we've spent. Look at the detail of our expenses. Look at these receipts. We can verify everything." He turned to Winkle. "Tell her, Benjamin."

"This is a valid accounting. Surely you knew that our services would cost you money. And now, we have succeeded. We have beaten the squatters for you. We deserve to be paid for our efforts."

"But you never said anything about three thousand dollars."

"Three thousand four hundred seventeen," Dresser added, then smiled, as if the clarification had resolved everything.

Winkle sat back in his chair and stuck the cigar in his mouth with a deliberate motion, as if to emphasize a point. "You never wanted to talk about the billing, ma'am. I'm sorry if this is a shock to you," he gestured, "but there it is."

The three sat for a moment, looking at each other. Ophelia felt shocked, and actually a little foolish. It was true, she had pushed these men around and never let them explain about the billing. So if they cheated her, it was with her own help. But had they cheated her? She was not sure, but one thing she was certain of—she was not going to hand over thirty-three hundred dollars.

"I'm not about to pay you that much money," she declared.

Dresser's eyes grew wide as he tried to say something, but his words were unintelligible.

"There may be a way we can work this out," Winkle ventured.

Ophelia folded her hands again. "I'm listening."

"Why not sell us some of your land? In lieu of these fees? It is customary. Many of the other ranchers are paying their lawyers with land."

"But I just won my land back," she protested. "Why would I give it to you?" She rose to her feet. "I see now what you're up to. Do you think I fought those squatters just to lose my land to you?"

Winkle rose, too, and waved his hands at her. "No, no, Señora Santos, you misunderstand me. Not the squatters' land, no. Please, please, sit down."

Ophelia sat reluctantly, now more wary of these *gringo* lawyers.

Winkle continued. "I didn't mean the land the squatters were claiming. I meant the Brownsville strip."

Ophelia blinked. This was a surprise.

"Yes," added Dresser, "Brownsville. You haven't won the Brownsville suit."

"And quite frankly, Señora Santos," said Winkle, "I seriously doubt our chances with that one. For all the reasons we've discussed."

"Let me understand this, señores. You want me to sell you Brownsville for three thousand four hundred seventeen dollars, which you will credit against your bill for legal fees. What do you get? And what do I get?"

Winkle smiled. "You get the victory we've won for you! Your land intact, free of all claims, title clear. And our bill will be paid in full. We get a dubious title to an already bitterly disputed, small parcel of land."

Ophelia shook her head. "That land is worth much more than this, but you say we will never win. Why would you want it?"

"Because we're lawyers, Señora Santos. We have other clients, business is good, we can afford to invest our spare time in litigation for a long-term gain. Most clients can't afford to wait that long. You can see what happens—it takes time, the bills mount up. I believe, in the long run, we can win that Brownsville suit. But can you afford to pay for it? By the same token, can the town of Brownsville afford to defend itself for as long as it takes? Sooner or later, they'll want to settle, and the state will have to help pay for it. We think we can take that gamble, get back our three thousand… and maybe even a profit."

Ophelia leaned back. It sounded tempting. She had been sorely burdened by the land disputes and she was absolutely determined not to lose them. The one thing she wanted in this life was to pass on to her sons their birthright, their land—just like she had received it from her father, and he from his, all the way back to her great great grandfather, who had settled along the river region in the mid-1700s and received title to the land from the King of Spain. Her one obligation was to pass it to her sons. She would not be distracted from her goal by anyone.

But Brownsville was a different story. A small piece of land, it had always been disputed, and now a *gringo* town was thriving on it. She herself felt that her chances of winning her suit here were small. And these anxious, expensive lawyers had given her most of what she wanted—to be free of the squatters' claims. Aside from Brownsville, the land was hers again, intact. Now she could be free of all litigation for the first time in years, and she could be rid of the troublesome Brownsville problem forever. She knew the Brownsville strip was worth much more than three thousand dollars, but she doubted she would ever see a penny of it.

"All right," she said. "I'll do it."

"Wonderful," replied Winkle. "I have always known you to be a very intelligent and sensible woman, Señora Santos."

Dresser rubbed his hands together in glee and said something, but what came out of his mouth was gibberish. Ophelia glanced up at him and frowned.

"We took the liberty of preparing this simple contract," said Winkle. "In the event you agreed. As you can see, it is only four paragraphs, and it is in Spanish with an English translation. Please read it carefully, señora."

"You were so confident?"

"As I said, we knew you were sensible."

She read the document carefully, then glanced at the English version. "I cannot read the English version."

Winkle leaned over the desk and pointed to the Spanish version. "There is a clause here that refers to the English version and guarantees that they are identical. See this reference number?" He pointed to L571 written at the top of the English version. "Note how in the Spanish version it refers to L571 and this date in referring to the English version. It is perfectly legal, and we guarantee you they are identical."

Ophelia leaned forward. "May I have a pen?"

Dresser practically leaped over the desk to hand her a pen, but Winkle took it back from her and dipped it in the inkwell at the side of his desk. "There are two originals, Señora Santos. Please sign both."

Ophelia took the pen, looked up at the two men, then leaned over to sign the papers. When she finished, she handed the pen back to Dresser and the contracts to Winkle, watched them sign, then rose to her feet. "Gentlemen, you don't know how relieved I feel. I want to thank you. Despite the delays and foot-dragging, you have done a good job."

The lawyers nodded, grinning widely, and Winkle reached forward to take her hand. "It has been a pleasure to serve such an astute and demanding client as yourself, Señora Santos. Please come see us again if you have any further needs."

They walked her to the door and escorted her outside, where Tomas leaned against the wall, smoking.

AFTER HER DEPARTURE, Winkle and Dresser walked back into their office and closed the door. Winkle picked up the contract she had signed and waved it at his partner. "Three thousand dollars," he said, "and all we got was this worthless piece of paper."

Dresser slumped into a chair. "I'm glad she didn't look too closely at those billings. And I'm sure as hell glad her English is so poor. A little vagueness can be a wonderful thing, in contracts."

Winkle put the papers down and turned to look out the window as Ophelia's carriage rattled out of town. A minute later he saw what he was looking for. "Here he comes," he said.

Charles Pownall strolled into the law office, his pale face shiny from sweat and his thin lips clamped around a big dark cigar. "Well?"

Winkle waved the contract at Pownall, then handed it to him. "Exactly as planned," he said.

Pownall glanced at Ophelia's signature and smiled. "And the other one?"

Winkle pulled out another document from his desk drawer and pushed it across. Pownall put the papers down on the desk, reached for the pen and signed his own name to the new document. He reached into his pocket, took out a dollar and laid it on the table. In the meantime, Winkle brought over a bottle of brandy and three glasses, which he filled and handed to the others.

Pownall raised his glass and the lawyers clinked theirs with his. "To the town of Brownsville," said Pownall. "Bought and paid for, for the princely sum of one dollar." He laughed, and the lawyers smiled glumly.

"Come now, gentlemen," said Pownall. "We all got what we wanted. Why so down? She got her land, or most of it. For now, anyway. I got

Brownsville for a dollar. Now all those plots we sold for such handsome profits are legal. In addition, any money the federal government pays for the Fort Brown site will be mine. And you—" he paused and took a sip of his brandy "—like me, and our colleagues, you get to keep your profits. And I let you stay in business here. What's the problem?"

"The problem," replied Winkle, "is that we actually did some fine legal work here. We got those claims thrown out."

"Are you forgetting that I helped file most of those claims? Come now, gentlemen. Let's not get tangled up in our own web here. Let's drink."

They raised their glasses. "To the prosperity of our little town of Brownsville." They drank, then as Pownall refilled their glasses a huge grin spread across his face. "And now," he said, "now we just need to start again."

The lawyers looked at each other in puzzlement, but Pownall continued pouring and grinning, seemingly oblivious to their frowns and questioning looks.

"Constant pressure," he said, "until they break. The claims and suits will start coming again. Dozens of them. The land will be ours." He stopped and eyed his partners, who looked like they had been kicked by a mule. "Maybe I'll up the price this time. Two dollars."

JUST PAST THE EDGE of Brownsville, Prieto sidestepped a dead roadrunner, snorting nervously and rolling his eyes wide. It was early in the morning, and Juan and Mingo were cantering into town just as the sun flooded the eastern sky with a wash of yellow and orange. From all around them came the smells of the morning. The frying bacon, the mesquite smoke, the coffee, the corn being boiled for tortillas. They pulled up at the Mendoza coffee house and tied their horses, then stood on the porch and looked toward the river, where the ferry was already pulling people across the dark, misty water.

"Feels like the days are cooling off," said Mingo. "Mornings you can see some fog."

Juan shook his head. "September is still hot, Mingo. Maybe the mornings and nights are a little better. But the days?" He shook his head again. "When we crash through the brush after those steers, I don't feel any cooler."

Mingo sniffed at the air. "Nothing smells better than the morning," he said. "Hot or cold. Let's eat."

They walked into the coffee house and sat at a table by the window, where they could drink their coffee and watch the town come to life. Jose Mendoza hurried up to them with a big black pot of coffee, a towel swung over his shoulder.

"*Buenos días*, señores," he said, nodding, and a huge mass of thick black hair bounced forward past his ears, then back again. "How are things on the Santa Alicia?"

"Same as yesterday," replied Mingo, "except the cows are getting fatter and I'm getting thinner."

Mendoza laughed and poured their coffee. "Doña Vicenta cooks that well?"

Mingo picked up the cup and scowled halfheartedly. "Her cooking would be all right if it weren't for all the medicine she gives me with it. If she thinks I look tired, she gives me a tonic that she makes herself out of onions and insects. If I complain of a headache, she tries to feed me some black, foul stuff that I swear smells like shit."

Juan leaned back in his chair and looked out the window. Across the street he saw the mayor and one of the small merchants standing in the shade of the boardwalk, pointing toward the cafe. Standing with them, Juan saw a new man, a rough-looking character with a huge beard and a large round nose. Juan reached for his coffee and took a sip, his eyes on the street.

"I think she rubbed that on my leg last year when I had that scorpion bite," he said. "Smelled like shit, but it stopped the swelling. Glad she didn't make me drink it."

Mendoza pulled on his huge mustache. "Tell her to send me some," he said. "I'll sell it here in the cafe. People come in here all the time with bites and pains."

Mingo rolled his eyes. "I don't think you'd want this stuff anywhere near food. It'd spoil people's appetites. I'm losing mine just talking about it."

Mendoza nodded. "So just coffee then?"

Mingo leaned back and scratched his stomach. "Well, no, I might as well eat. Give me some *huevos rancheros* and some *frijolitos*. Juan?"

Juan shook his head. "Just coffee."

Mendoza hurried away, calling out the order to his wife, who worked the stove in the back of the cafe. In a few minutes, they heard the clang of a skillet on the wood burning stove, smelled the mesquite smoke, listened to the sizzling of the eggs frying in lard.

Juan looked out the window again. Across the way, the merchants and the stranger were coming toward the cafe.

When Miller and Brown stepped inside, Juan sensed something different about them. It was the look on their faces. They strolled into the room with frowns on their foreheads and smiles on their lips, as if they were trying to look serious but were unable to manage it. The new man with them grinned. They passed the table where Juan and Mingo sat and tipped their hats, an unusual act.

Juan eyed them coldly.

"Mendoza," Miller yelled. "Coffee!" Despite the fact that the cafe was practically empty, they took a table just across from Juan's. Mendoza hurried over with the big black pot, and the merchants leaned back and looked over at Juan and Mingo.

Then Miller turned back to Brown and the new man and said loud enough to heard at the next table, "Did you all hear about Pownall's good fortune?"

"Why, no, Daniel!" Brown replied, "What happened? Tell me. Tell Stokes, here, too." The two men spoke in booming voices. They were still grinning.

"Well, it seems Winkle and Dresser came into possession of the town of Brownsville as payment for legal bills from Doña Santos. But then they turned around and sold it to Pownall. For one dollar! One dollar! Can you imagine?" All three men burst out laughing. They turned to look at Juan through taunting eyes.

"Sounds to me," said Miller, "like somebody got swindled. Wonder who that could be? The whole town is laughing about it!"

The laughter died away and stopped altogether when Miller and Brown saw the look on Juan's face. Stokes let his laughter trail off uncertainly. When Juan pushed his chair back and rose to his feet, the merchants' eyes went wide and the men cringed visibly. Stokes merely leaned back in his chair, his hand dropping casually to his side. Across the café, Mendoza stood frozen with Mingo's *huevos rancheros* on a big platter, watching. Nothing happened. Then Juan turned and walked out of the café, Mingo hurrying after him. Juan ripped Prieto's reins off the rail and jerked the horse out toward the street, where he mounted and then jammed his spurs into the animal's flanks. Prieto screamed in pain, then rose up on his hind legs, came down and spun around in the street, kicking up a cloud of dust. Juan jerked the reins hard, and the stallion thundered out of town toward the ranch, with Mingo gamely quirting his horse in the trail of dust, trying to keep up.

Juan pushed Prieto along the trail to the Santa Alicia ranch until the animal slid to a halt, snorting and wheezing, in a tremendous cloud of dust at Ophelia's front door. The sound of Mingo's horse, far behind, echoed out of sight in the brush, but a cloud out on the road gave a clear indication that he was coming. Inside the house, a commotion arose as Ophelia, Blas, and Conchita rushed to the windows to see what was happening.

"*Dios mío,*" cried Conchita. "What's wrong?"

Juan walked out of the fog of dust and stomped into the house, slamming the door behind him. He barreled past Blas and Conchita and went directly to Ophelia's room, where he banged on the door with his fist.

"Mother! Open the door!"

When Ophelia threw open the door, Juan looked down at her face and became angrier still. She glared up at him, her eyes wide with questions, her mouth set in disapproval, her cheeks pale. One hand rested on the doorknob and another balled into a fist against her chest. He felt a surge of rage, and stomped into the room past her, slamming the door behind him.

"Juan," she demanded, "what is the meaning of this?"

He stopped in the middle of the room and whirled to face her. "You gave it away! You gave it away, and they're laughing at us. The whole damned town is laughing at us, Mother—" His voice tightened up and he choked on the last word. His neck bulged in its collar and his cheeks burned.

Ophelia looked him up and down and gave a quick nod. "I see," she said, as she stepped over to the water jug and poured him a drink. "I want you to calm down and have a drink of water. Then we can talk about this."

"I don't want to calm down! Why did you do it?"

She put the glass down and looked up at him, the bright light from the window blinding her. "I did what I thought was best for the family."

"Best? Do you know that those lawyers of yours sold Brownsville to Pownall for one dollar? The whole town is laughing!"

She turned and tilted her head, her face suddenly contorted. "No, I did not know. But what they did with it is their business, I sold it to them for three thousand dollars."

She stepped toward him. "That's what's really bothering you, isn't it? You don't care about the land! You've never cared about the land. Do you accompany me anywhere? Do you take the time to understand these complex matters? To find workable solutions? No! You'd rather stomp around wallowing in your temper. Do you listen? No! Do you know how many years I wanted to include you, my son, *you*, in the family business? But, no, your stupid pride, God forbid, your stupid pride be offended! All you care about it is that the merchants are making you look bad. Your precious reputation has been soiled. That they're laughing at *you!*"

"Nobody laughs at us and gets away with it!"

"If you were so interested in the good of the family, why haven't you been helping me with the affairs of the ranch? All you do is ride around and rope a few cows, then you spend days drinking and whoring and fighting. Who do you think does all the buying and selling of cattle? Who handles the legal affairs? Who keeps up the social contacts with the other families?"

Juan's anger came down from the irrational heights it had soared to, down to where he could hear her words and comprehend them. He was not sure what he had said or heard when he first came into the room. In fact, he remembered little since he had risen to his feet in the Mendoza cafe and stormed out.

"You shouldn't have given away the land," he said stubbornly.

"The land?" she cried. "You don't care about the land, that's clear! You don't care about the ranch, about your family, about anybody who loves you. You fight with your own brother! You reject the love of an innocent girl who's too good for you!"

"You don't know what I care about," he shot back. "You never have."

"I know you don't care about anything worthwhile. Tell me, Juan. Tell me what you care about. Tell me one thing, besides whores, horses, and mescal. Come on, I really want to know what passes for caring in that pathetic mind of yours."

"You?" he snarled, "you can ask me that? My own mother who couldn't stand the sight of me, you ask me about caring?"

Ophelia sucked in her breath, and she saw the look of rage and pain in his face, and her heart broke. Her eyes filled with tears.

"Oh, son," she whispered, and stood looking at him.

He blinked, reached up, and pushed his sombrero off his head, letting it hang around his neck by its leather thong. He sensed he had wounded her deeply.

"Juan, my son," she began, then the tears rolled uncontrollably down her pale cheeks, and she paused, willing herself not to break down. After a moment, she continued, "Juan, you need to learn to forgive those who love you."

He scratched his scalp where the sweat stung it and looked at her. "I don't want to talk about that."

"No," she sniffled, regaining her composure. "I can imagine you don't!" She shifted the subject to something less painful. "Do you know that Lidia is still sitting over in her ranch? That lovely, sweet girl is still there. Do you know what she's waiting for? You big, wooden-headed brute, she's waiting for you. After all these years, she still loves you—"

He shoved his sombrero back on his head and stepped toward the door. "I said I don't want to talk about this. And I don't want to talk about her."

"Wait," she said, stepping toward him and grabbing his arm. "What are you going to do?"

"I don't know."

"Juan, I don't want any more trouble. I want you to promise me.

Promise me you won't start any trouble with the *gringos*. I'm done with troubles with them. I want us to live in peace and tend to our land." She slid her hand into his, looking almost fearful. "Can you promise me that?"

He stood there a long moment, looking down at her, his mind working quickly through her words, taking in her face, the touch of her hand. But as always, it worked its way back to the same thing, to that same raw memory that lay at the back of his mind, red and angry, shoving everything else out of the way.

"Why should I promise you anything, Mother?" He pushed her hand away. He drew himself up, turned his face slightly, looking at her slantwise. "Don't ask me for promises. You never gave me any when I needed them."

He stared down at her, at the look of pain that swept across her face, at the pain that seemed to leap from him to her and back again. They both remembered, they both hurt.

"You shouldn't have given away the land," he finally muttered, and then he stomped past her, out into the hot morning to tend to his horse.

ARRIVING AT MINGO'S *JACAL*, Juan found Mingo and Tomas cleaning their guns and drinking coffee.

"Vicenta," Mingo called as Juan walked into the cool, dark room, "bring some coffee for the *patrón*."

Outside, Vicenta muttered something and banged a pot or two. Then she walked into the *jacal* with a clay cup of steaming black coffee and handed it to Juan. "I heard the evil bird, the *lechuza*, singing again last night," she said.

"Don't start with your superstitions, woman," said Mingo. He nodded at the door. "Go back outside and bring us some breakfast."

"Breakfast time is over. It's time for work. All the other *vaqueros* are out in the brush where they belong. Look at you three, sitting around in the shade drinking coffee. If I was running this ranch—"

"*Por el amor de Dios*," cried Mingo. "Vicenta, will you do one thing I ask of you without arguing my ears off? Bring us some *chingado* breakfast!"

She stopped in mid-sentence. "Bueno," she said, "but I did hear the *lechuza* again last night. Three nights now, every night. Something very bad is going to happen. I don't know what, but tonight I'm going to make a special medicine that everybody has to wear to ward off the evil."

"It isn't that shit-smelling stuff, is it?" asked Tomas.

Vicenta jerked her chin up. "My medicine does not smell like shit, unless I put shit in it."

The three men made faces, and Mingo waved her off. "Just go," he said. "And take your time. It will take a while to get our appetites back."

Muttering to herself, she whirled and stomped outside as Juan pulled a rickety chair away from the table and sat down, holding the hot cup of coffee in both hands.

"Mingo told me what happened in town," said Tomas.

"They cheated her," Juan replied.

Mingo sipped his coffee and twirled his mustache. "Lawyers," he said, disgust filling his voice. "My cousin married a lawyer over in Monterrey. The stories she tells about how he cheats people—"

"It was Pownall," Juan cut in. "He's behind all this. Maybe the small merchants are right. Maybe Pownall and the big merchants are behind all the troubles along the border."

"Or maybe it's just Pownall by himself," said Tomas.

Juan nodded, pressing his lips into a thin line. He felt suddenly like striking out, hurting something, but there was nobody here he wanted to hurt. He felt his anger sink back into itself.

"The *patrona* wants a hundred head rounded up and sent to Matamoros," said Tomas. "I've got the *vaqueros* out, starting the roundup. She says they need the cattle quick."

Mingo scratched his stomach. "Let's eat first," he said. "It's going to be a long night in the saddle."

They were eating eggs with cactus when Blas walked to the door of the *jacal* and called for Juan. Juan stepped outside and found his brother wearing fine clothes and a superb black sombrero with silver trimmings.

Blas stood stiffly, his nose in the air, and looked at Juan with half-closed eyes. "Mother sent me to ask you when the cattle will be ready." His voice was cold.

"Two days," Juan snapped. He turned to step back into the *jacal*.

"Wait a minute."

Juan turned back toward his brother. "What?"

"Mother has favored you as long as I can remember," Blas' voice started off strong, but soon it quivered a little, and he stopped to compose himself. "I don't know why," he continued, "but I do know that all you've ever given her is heartache. And I'm not going to allow you to do that anymore. I know you made her cry today."

Juan felt the steam roil up within, bubbling and splashing forward, but he still held it back. His eyes flashed, his cheeks burned, his head pounded. He balled up his hands into tight fists. His body was so taut that it began to shake, but he backed away from his brother. He stepped back into the *jacal* and slumped back down in his chair. When he heard Blas stomp away, he took a deep breath and lowered his head until his chin was resting on his chest. He could feel and hear his heart pounding in his ears. In his stomach, a dull twitch grew increasingly painful until he had to hold both hands on it.

Mingo reached behind him and pulled out a bottle of mescal. He dumped Juan's coffee out onto the dirt floor, poured a half cup of the liquor, and pushed it over to Juan, who reached out, grabbed it, and gulped it down.

The men sat in silence for a few minutes. Outside, even Vicenta seemed to know better than to stick her head inside the *jacal*.

Finally, Juan seemed to relax. He leaned back in his chair, looking up at the ceiling, feeling the mescal roll its way down his gullet, into his stomach, warming him every inch of the way. He felt the knots in his belly start to unravel, he felt the pounding pain begin to diminish. His heartbeat receded from his ears. He pushed his cup forward and Mingo poured him some more mescal.

Tomas broke the silence. "I remember when that boy thought the world revolved around you."

Mingo nodded, pouring himself a cup of mescal. "We all remember that."

This time, Juan just sipped at his second cup of mescal. He looked up at the two tough *vaqueros* sitting at the table with him. These were men who had known him his whole life.

"Nobody thinks that anymore," he said.

Chapter 9
A Storm Gathers

"CROSS DOWN THERE," Juan called to Mingo as they neared the river, driving the longhorns before them in a billowing cloud of dust. He pointed to a low part of the river where it swerved in an arc and the banks flattened out. In the hazy morning light, the riverbanks seemed gentle on both sides where the brush had been trampled by many such crossings. Juan twisted in his saddle and watched his *vaqueros* as they turned the cattle. They had been working for two days and nights and were bruised, bleeding, tired, and sore. But they had done the job. During the roundup, Juan used up five working horses. Now he opted to ride back to the ranch to pick up Prieto for the relatively easy job of herding the cattle across the river. Although Prieto could crash through the brush as well as any other horse, he was much too fine an animal to waste like that.

As Tomas rode by, Juan waved him over. Tomas flashed a half-smile at him. Juan felt good, too. Two days of intense physical effort had burned off his anger and his frustration about Ophelia's selling the town. But even now, as he thought about it again, he felt embers glow within him and revive his rage. He let out a long breath. The cattle roundup had been backbreaking work, but the results were good. The job was done, it was a beautiful morning, and here at last was the river.

"Tomas," he called, "coffee?"

Tomas dropped his smile and shrugged his shoulders. "Only get in trouble in town," he replied.

Juan turned in his saddle and spit out the dust that had been building up in the back of his throat. "Mingo said the Rangers are gone. Without Rangers, those sheep in town won't bother me. *Vamos!*"

He jerked the reins, and Prieto leaped onto the road, heading east toward the sunrise and the little town of Brownsville, just ahead. In a few minutes he reached the edge of town. When he slowed Prieto, Tomas pulled up beside him and they cantered into town and headed for the Mendoza cafe. The sun was shining full on their faces, and the early morning breeze carried the river smell inland.

Turning the corner, they found a small crowd of people gathered in the street in front of the Mendoza café. In the center of the crowd stood Marshal Tom Garrison, waving his pistol high above his head. In his other hand, he held the lapel of Alphonso Varga, one of the Santa Alicia's elderly *vaqueros*. Ophelia allowed *vaqueros* who were too old to work the brush to live on the ranch, provided they did at least some work if they were able. Alphonso had never adjusted well to the sedentary life and spent most of the day drunk on mescal, singing little songs to himself and whoever would listen.

The pistol came down, and Juan heard Alphonso cry out at the blow that scraped his skull. As he approached, he also heard the laughter of the crowd of *gringos*. Mexicans were standing around the edges of the crowd with pained looks on their faces. When they saw Juan, one of them rushed up to him and put a hand on Prieto's neck.

"*Patrón*," he cried, "look what they are doing to Alphonso!"

Juan put his horse forward through the crowd, which parted quickly. As soon as Garrison saw him, he dropped the bleeding man to the ground.

"Stay out of this, Santos."

Juan sat his horse and surveyed the scene. The crowd of merchants moved in close to Garrison. They looked surly. Behind them, the local Mexicans looked on, stone faced and silent.

"Why are you beating one of my men?" he asked in a quiet voice.

Garrison's only reply was to turn and kick Alphonso in the ribs. A loud rush of air pushed out of the old *vaquero's* lungs and he rolled on the ground, hugging his chest and moaning.

Juan felt a rush of anger, but he held it until it slowly dissipated. In its place, a cool dispassion flooded in, as if he were merely an observer in the crowd. His senses sharpened even as he felt his body relax. He saw everything clearly. He seemed to smell every trace floating on the breeze.

The slightest movement registered in his mind. Every nerve in his body seemed alert and ready.

"Drunk. Drunk and disorderly," said Garrison, slurring his words. He seemed to be drunk himself.

Juan looked up at the sun, just barely over the horizon. "So early, marshal? Alphonso never gets drunk until noon."

"Well, he's drunk now."

"All right. He's drunk, I'll take him now."

"No."

Juan started to dismount, but when he heard Garrison's "no," he stopped and leaned back in his saddle. Out of the corner of his eye, he saw Tomas moving off a little. "Marshal," he said, "I'm taking Alphonso back to the ranch. Don't get in the way."

Garrison looked up at Juan and seemed to falter. His eyes seemed to soften, his mouth drooped a little, his posture lost that hard set of determination. But the merchants in the crowd began shouting. The marshal recovered. Juan saw that in his eyes, too.

"You go to hell, Gallo," Garrison spat. "I don't take orders from no stinking greaser. You were told to stay out of town. Best get out while you can." He turned and whacked Alphonso with his pistol again, but the old *vaquero* covered his head with his arms and the blow fell on his shoulder.

Juan felt the eyes of the crowd on him. Along the far edges of the knot of people he recognized the Mexicans who followed him to the ballot box on election days, people who looked up to him. Closer in were the small merchants of Brownsville, men who hated him. On the boardwalk at the far end of the crowd stood Pownall and his lawyer friends. They were leaning against the wooden posts and smoking their cigars. Everyone was watching the drunken marshal beat an old *vaquero*. They were waiting to see what Juan would do about it.

"Garrison," he said, "this old man is harmless. I'll take him back to the ranch. He won't bother you anymore."

The crowd murmured its refusal. Garrison's eyes brightened. "Get the hell out of town, Gallo. Go back to your ranch and play with that grand whore mother of yours!"

A collective gasp escaped the crowd, Mexicans and *gringos* alike, then suddenly it fell silent. At first Garrison stood still, grinning up at Juan, his pistol dangling from one hand. He knew the crowd was with him, but then he half turned to the merchants. When he looked back at Juan his face showed dismay.

Juan pulled out his pistol and shot Garrison, who went sprawling to the ground over on top of Alphonso. Spurring his horse forward, Juan bent down toward the old *vaquero*, grabbed his arm, and pulled him up behind him on the back of his horse. Prieto danced and snorted, turning gracefully and scattering the crowd, which was staring spellbound at their fallen marshal. Juan touched his spurs to Prieto's flanks and instantly they were galloping out of town. As he passed, he heard the cheers of the Mexicans, who jammed out onto the street to run beside him, throwing their hats in the air.

When they had passed the edge of town, Tomas pulled up beside Juan and they transferred Alphonso to Tomas' horse. Juan noted the look on Tomas' face.

"What?"

Tomas shook his head, and Juan could see anger in his eyes.

"You don't like what I did?"

Prieto danced on the road, kicking up dust that swirled in soft eddies down toward the river.

Tomas touched his own horse's neck, whispering a soothing word to calm him. "There will be trouble for your mother," he said.

Juan nodded. He had not promised Ophelia anything, but he knew he had disappointed her again. A *gringo* lay shot, probably dead. The *gringos* of the town were enraged. Yes, he thought, there certainly would be trouble for Ophelia. But he had been provoked beyond all reason. He had only done what any man would have done. It was their own damned fault.

Tomas leaned back in his saddle and pulled up a small leather sack from his saddlebags. "You better ride to La Bolsa. I'll pass the word that you've gone there, so they won't try to come to the ranch. We can't have them come there. Here's some *pozole*. I'll finish with the cattle and send Mingo to catch up with you."

Juan jerked Prieto's reins a little and reached over to take the bag. "*Gracias*, Tomas."

The big horse seemed nervous, eager to run. Juan stuffed the bag in his shirt and then turned his horse west, not bothering to spur him. Prieto was ready, needing only to feel Juan relax on the reins and settle in on the saddle. In an instant, he thundered down the road, and Juan felt the dewy morning air, fresh and cool, wash into his lungs. He heard it singing past his ears. It felt good to ride, and he knew that Prieto felt good, too, able at last to stretch out on an open road and gallop away his nervousness.

As he rode, the realization came to Juan that back in Brownsville, angry men were on fire to lash back at him. Perhaps, he thought, the *gringos* would take their anger out on those cheering Mexicans who had run beside him as he rode out of town with Alphonso. Perhaps the *gringos* would ride against his own *vaqueros* as they crossed back from Matamoros. He thought about turning back, but decided against it. Going back would surely make things worse—he'd likely kill somebody else. *Let them cool off,* he said to himself. *They are sheep, they'll get over it.*

He reached up and pushed the sombrero off his head, so that the morning sun could shine on him.

WHEN THE SUN HUNG straight overhead, Juan sought out a mesquite and dismounted under the cool shade to wait for Mingo. The landscape seemed washed in a flat light, a little weaker now in September, but still blazing. He hobbled Prieto and spread a blanket under the tree. A horned toad scrambled out, so Juan pulled the blanket up and laid it down again. In the soft earth beside the tree trunk, he saw dozens of little ant lion funnels in the earth, and once in a while a tiny spray of earth came flying out of the center of one. He leaned against the trunk and looked out at the brush, wondering what he had started back in Brownsville. Things would be different now, he knew. After all these years of feuding back and forth with the *gringos*, something had changed when he shot the marshal. If the sheep let it go, the townsmen would realize that despite their one dollar title, the town still belonged to him. If they tried to retaliate, to hurt his family in any way, then they would all die, even if it cost Juan his own life. Maybe it was time. Time to push them all out, all the *gringos*. Time to take Texas back, too.

He pulled his sombrero down to his nose and closed his eyes and let his mind drift. He thought about the cattle they had rounded up, the nights in the saddle, the stubborn cows. Then an image of his father flooded into his mind, leather strap in his hand, beating him as he curled up in a ball beneath a mesquite tree like this one. Juan had declared his innocence, *I didn't do it, I didn't do it*, but his father had never believed him. Someone had cut the hamstring on Don Alvino Santos' beautiful white horse, the one he prized more than anything else on earth, and the trail of blood led to Juan. The strap came down, down, over and over, but it was the words that had hurt him the most. *I hate you*, his father had said. *I hate you.*

Hours later, a jingling sound woke him, and as he opened his eyes he saw Mingo turning off the road a half mile away and riding toward him. Juan rubbed his eyes and pushed himself to his feet. Then Prieto came ambling over, neighing nervously and pushing at Juan with his muzzle. Rolling up the blanket, Juan noticed at least one ant struggling to escape an ant lion funnel, the dirt flying out of the center of the funnel as fast as the ant tried to scramble up the slippery side. He watched the ant struggle mightily, working harder and faster, but the faster it worked, the more it slid down. Juan spat at the ant but missed.

Mingo rode up and sat his horse in the shade.

"*Que pasa*, Mingo?"

"*Patrón*," Mingo replied, pushing the sombrero off his head. "The marshal is not dead." Mingo stared down at Juan, a tired look on his face.

"What are the sheep doing?"

"Nothing. They're angry, afraid. When I left, I heard they were drinking whiskey in the saloon."

Juan tied his bedroll behind Prieto's saddle and mounted, feeling a quick ache in his stiff back from leaning on the tree trunk. A dust devil danced around the brush by the road and then took off toward the river.

"Did you send word to Mother?"

"*Sí*."

Juan nodded, then gently pushed Prieto with his knees, guiding him out from beneath the mesquite, out into the sunlight among the dusty cacti mounds. He mounted, then they navigated back to the road and turned west. It was late afternoon, and they watched the sun traverse the blue sky until it hovered straight in front of them on the horizon, reddened and softened, sending great splashes of crimson out to the land and up to the gathering clouds. The air cooled quickly.

They rode into La Bolsa that evening and tied up at Neal's store. Pulling on his pipe and nodding in the flickering lantern light, Neal looked at them as they walked in.

"Don't want no trouble, Gallo."

Ignoring him, Juan grabbed a bottle of mescal and threw some coins on the counter. He handed the bottle to Mingo and walked back out of the store. Out along the river bank a collection of *jacales* and tents sprawled, the fires lighting up the thick mesquite smoke as it drifted through La Bolsa and up to the indigo sky. They led their horses down toward the river and walked among the fires, acknowledging the quiet greetings of the Mexicans. Eventually, they found an empty spot where they could spread their bedrolls. They unsaddled and hobbled the horses, then gathered mesquite for a fire. When they returned to their camp, they found two young girls waiting for them, one holding a clay pot and the other a stack of tortillas.

"My mother sent this chicken *mole*," one of them said, and she shyly pushed the clay pot into Mingo's hands, forcing him to drop the mesquite. The other girl offered Juan the tortillas, which were wrapped in cloth and still warm.

Juan nodded, and the girls giggled, then scrambled off through the thick smoke toward one of the *jacales*. Mingo put the pot aside and got the fire going, and then they leaned back on their elbows and stared into the flames.

"Give me the bottle," said Juan.

Mingo pulled the bottle out of his saddlebag and handed it to Juan, who pulled the cork off with his teeth. Then he put his head back and took a long drink. He wiped his mouth on his sleeve and passed the bottle to Mingo, who took a short drink and handed it back, pushing the *mole* pot a little closer to the flames with his boot.

"You want to eat?" Mingo asked.

Juan shook his head and took another drink.

A few minutes later, they watched a rider come splashing across the river from the Mexican side. He tied up at one of the *jacales,* and within minutes a crowd was gathered around him. Juan could see him gesturing and talking excitedly, though he could not hear the words he said. The fact that people in the crowd kept pointing and looking over in his direction, though, told him that the rider was spreading news of the shooting. The crowd erupted—shouting, laughing, and soon a man with a guitar was singing a brisk *corrida* and people were dancing and stirring up a huge cloud of dust to mix with the mesquite smoke. Throughout the evening little presents of food and liquor made their way over to Juan's camp, where they lay spread out on his blanket. As he drank his mescal, he nodded to each person who came up to him, smiling humbly, head bent, offering him another gift.

After a while, the music died down and the man with the guitar came over and greeted him softly. *"Buenas noches,* Señor Gallo."

Juan nodded, looking up at him, trying to focus, for mescal on an empty stomach had made him woozy. *"Buenas noches,"* he replied.

The man strummed his guitar softly, then began to sing a song of love, of grief, of a man forever parted from the woman he loved more than he loved his own life. The man's voice was strong, melodious, and the song had a haunting note of sadness woven through it, and when the musician sang about wanting to die his voice turned into a cry, a grown man's wail of unspeakable grief. The hushed crowed stood several feet back and listened. Juan let his head fall as he listened and remembered the black despair he had felt for so many years over the way Lidia had betrayed him, how he had forced it out of his mind, pushed it out of his memory. But songs like this made it all come flooding back. He tried to shake it off, but the mescal made him sentimental, and he also remembered all those years they had loved each other. She had made him happy, then. When the song ended, El Gallo sat in silence looking up at the musician. Finally he said, *"Cantas muy bonito, señor. Gracias."*

The man nodded, accepting the compliment humbly, then he turned and walked back to the crowd, where for the rest of the evening and into the morning, men sat around fires and drank, asking the singer over and over to sing his sad song again.

Mingo pulled up the pot and rolled a few tacos, but Juan still would not eat.

"Look at me," said Juan. "Hiding in La Bolsa. I can't even go back to the ranch. I did exactly what my mother asked me not to. Does heaven plan these things? I know I don't."

Mingo nodded, setting the tacos down on the blanket and passing his *patrón* the bottle instead.

"The *gringos* swindled her, Mingo. They took her land for one dollar. I told her not to trust them. I warned her." He took a long drink of the mescal and then took a shorter one, leaning back to feel the burning down his throat and into his stomach. "They cheat everyone, even themselves. They have no honor. They treat *Mexicanos* like dirt. They spit on us. They kill us when they please."

He stared off at the river, listening to the man with the guitar sing his song again. He thought about Lidia and remembered the one dance at the wedding in Matamoros, how lovely she looked, how soft she felt. How her eyes reflected the light in the room. He tried to shut her out, but the song that worked its way into his mind could have been written just for the two of them. *No*, he said to himself, *no, no, no. She betrayed me. I will never forgive her.* And he pushed her back, back, farther back. But still, she lingered around the edges of his thoughts, flooding in again whenever the song turned sorrowful, whenever he looked up at the sky sprinkled with a thousand stars that made him feel lonely. He pushed her out, kept her out—until, when he finally lay back on his blanket and closed his eyes to sleep, she was there, again, waiting for him.

THE FOLLOWING MORNING, Tomas was sitting in front of Mingo's *jacal* enjoying his breakfast, when a *vaquero* named Simon Vasquez galloped through the Santa Alicia gate, and slid to a halt in a great cloud of dust.

"Tomas," Simon called from the saddle, "Tomas, *tengo nuevas!*"

The man had news. From the look on his face, it was not good news. Tomas stood up, walked over to Simon's horse, and grabbed the bridle to calm it. "What is your news?"

"In Brownsville," Simon replied, "they put Blas in the jail! They arrested him when he crossed the ferry from Matamoros. The marshal beat him with a pistol!"

Tomas felt a cold chill run down his spine, a deep foreboding of disaster. But something about this excited young man's story did not ring true. "The marshal? He's not dying?"

Simon shook his head. "No, no. I forgot to say, they have a new marshal, a man called Stokes."

Tomas nodded slowly. *"Que mas?"*

Simon had nothing more to report, so Tomas sent him back into town to observe. He watched as the young *vaquero* rode to the corral to pick out a fresh horse. Tomas reached up and rubbed his face, then looked up to the sky. Blas was in jail. He had worried that something like this would happen, that Juan's brash acts would someday set his mother or his brother in the path of the *gringos'* revenge. And now, he must go and tell Ophelia, who was already wracked with worry over Juan's safety, that her younger son was in the Brownsville jail.

"How *dare* he!" she had roared when he told her about Juan shooting the marshal. "Bring up my coach. I am going La Bolsa *now!*"

It took all of Tomas' tact and skill to convince her that doing that would put Juan in more danger. Then she had wanted to send Juan twenty or so *vaqueros* to keep around him as a bodyguard. Again, Tomas had objected strenuously. First, he argued, they needed every man here at the Santa Alicia, in case the *gringos* tried to attack the ranch. If Juan saw that many Santa Alicia *vaqueros* showing up at La Bolsa, he would immediately ride for home, he told her, because he would be worried that it was not adequately defended. Second, Juan was El Gallo. Wherever he went on the border, he could easily rouse twenty to thirty armed men to his side. He was at La Bolsa. He was secure.

Ophelia had been swayed. She trusted Tomas' counsel, though she still felt uneasy. She began pacing like a caged lioness, and then she sent word to Blas at Matamoros for him to cut his visit short and come home, to leave the cattle unsold if necessary. She had explicitly ordered him to cross the border upstream of Brownsville, to bypass the Brownsville ferry. But Blas, too proud to avoid the town, had ignored her.

Now, as Tomas crossed the courtyard to the house, he could already see Ophelia standing at the door, wondering what the commotion was about. Tomas shook his head. Proud, headstrong, and foolish, that was Blas. Violent, troubled, passionate, that was Juan. These boys would be the death of their mother.

Ophelia stepped out onto the porch as he approached. He could tell she was steeling herself for bad news.

"What is it?" she asked, putting her hand on a post.

"*Patrona*," he replied, "it's Blas. He is in the Brownsville jail."

She gasped and held on to the post with both hands, her eyes went wide with fear and worry. But she quickly regained her customary proud posture. "Tell me," she demanded.

"Blas disobeyed you. He crossed on the ferry. There is a new marshal, a man called Stokes. Simon said he beat Blas with a pistol and put him in jail."

"I want him out of that jail!"

Tomas nodded. He had to think fast. If they stormed the town, Blas would surely be killed. Tomas preferred to wait for night and send in a smaller group of men under cover of darkness. At the same time, he could send word to Juan. Once they had rescued Blas, there would be no reason for Juan to avoid the ranch, for the *gringos* would target it in any case. Juan had to come home to defend it.

Ophelia refused to wait until dark. "Bring up my carriage," she ordered. "I want to go see about my son."

When they arrived in Brownsville, they found a large, noisy crowd gathered in front of the marshal's office and jail. Standing on the porch, Mayor Daniel Miller was addressing the merchants and residents, but his voice faded away as Ophelia's carriage clattered down the street and stopped. As usual, the Mexicans were standing on the edges of the crowd. Some of them were residents of the town, others, visitors from the ranches or from Matamoros. Few of them knew any English, but somehow or other they always figured out what was being said at these gatherings. The merchants were milling around, shaking their fists, and shouting.

"...time we took our town back!"

"...tired of this talkin', let's hang 'em all!"

"...shoot our marshal and get away with it?"

As Miller put his hands up and waved them up and down, motioning for calm, Tomas dismounted and opened the carriage door for Ophelia. He glanced down the street, where he had ordered the ten armed *vaqueros* to wait at the edge of the town in the event of trouble. He had convinced Ophelia that they should ride in alone to avoid a fight until they could talk to this new marshal. Ophelia seemed exasperated by his cautious approach, but he knew that this family's reputation for its quick temper could be its own worst enemy when it came to *gringos*.

Ophelia stepped out of the carriage and headed straight for the marshal's office. As the Mexicans on the edge of the crowd murmured greetings and parted quickly to let her pass, the merchants in the center of the crowd involuntarily followed suit, though Tomas could hear them muttering under their breath. He accompanied Ophelia to the porch.

Ophelia faced the mayor. "Mr. Miller, who is in charge?"

Miller grinned, beaming as if that was the very question he was hoping she would ask. "Well now, I suppose I am, Señora Santos, since I am the mayor."

Ophelia took two steps forward and put her face as close as she could to him. He retreated in alarm.

"Where is my son, you grinning buffoon?"

Miller backed away a step, but Ophelia pursued him. "Answer me, if you're in charge! Why have you arrested my son?"

Miller backed up again and fell off the porch, landing on his ass in the middle of the crowd, which parted to give him room. A puff of dust rose up where he landed, and the Mexicans burst out in laughter.

Still standing on the porch, Ophelia snapped, "I want him out of this jail and I want him out *now*. Where is the key?"

Tomas saw a man moving toward her from the shadows along the wall of the marshal's office, a fat-nosed *gringo* with a heavy beard. It must be Stokes.

The man crossed his arms. "Doña Santos," he called from the center of the walk. "Over here."

Ophelia spun around to regard him with disdain. "Who are you?"

Stokes turned and spit a long stream of brown tobacco juice into the street, scattering some of the merchants. "I'm the new marshal. I'm the one that arrested your boy. I'm the one that's really in charge."

Tomas did not like the fact that Stokes stood between him and Ophelia. As he started moving closer, he saw that his mounted *vaqueros* at the edge of town were staring at the crowd.

"Tomas," Stokes drawled, "you just stay right there. And I can see those *muchachos* out there, too. You best keep them where they are." His voice filled with confidence, the marshal turned and looked at him. "'Cause if there's any shooting, *la patrona* here gets shot first. Understand?"

Tomas nodded and shot a glance at Ophelia. Her contempt was obvious. His only concern now was to extricate her from this situation, to get her out of town. Once he did that, he knew he would have to create some sort of diversion that might keep Blas alive until morning. He was glad he'd sent a rider to La Bolsa to notify Juan. The rider should arrive there before dark, so Juan could be here sometime before morning. They could strike in the hour before dawn, when the town would be asleep. It was a good plan. All he needed to do now was get Ophelia out of here first.

"Señor," he said to Stokes, "may I ask you a question? Inside the office?"

Stokes shook his head. "Got anything to say, you can say it out here."

"It is private, Señor Marshal. It will only take a minute." Tomas gave Stokes a look, trying to impart to him some hint of what he had in mind, something that would be of great benefit to this seedy looking marshal.

Stokes hesitated and then turned to Ophelia. "Come inside for a minute, Señora Santos. I'll let you talk to your boy." He turned to the crowd and raised his voice. "No harm in that, I say."

Ophelia and Tomas followed him inside the cramped and cluttered office, where a big black pot of old, smelly coffee sat simmering on a stove in the corner. Ophelia immediately walked to the back, where Blas stood in the cell, both hands on the bars.

"*Mi hijo*," she said, her voice strong, with only a hint of a quiver, "are you all right?"

There was a bruise on his cheek, and a big knot on his forehead, but he nodded. "Have you come to get me out?"

"You wouldn't be here if you had done as you were told!"

Blas looked at Stokes and sneered. "I am not going to go sneaking around because of what Juan did. That is his business. I had nothing to do with it."

Ophelia turned to the marshal. "He is right," she said. "You have no reason to arrest my son. Blas has done no harm."

"No," replied Stokes. "But he's here, and Gallo isn't."

"You have no right—"

"I got every right I need," roared Stokes. "And whatever other right I come to need, I make up as I go along."

"That is unlawful."

Stokes laughed. "Different law applies to Mexicans," he said. "Besides, what Gallo did broke the law, any kind of law. Mexican, Texan, American. He's going to have to pay, Doña Santos. One way or the other. His time is over."

Tomas looked over at Blas, who avoided eye contact. "Marshal," Tomas said, "how much money would it take for you to let Blas go?"

"I ain't lettin' him go. Not unless El Gallo is sittin' in that cell instead of him."

Ophelia started to speak, but Tomas held up his hand and she fell silent. "Then we will pay you," Tomas said, "to keep Blas safe until he can be released. Until this whole thing can be settled. After all, Garrison is not dead. Perhaps he can be persuaded to drop the charges. Perhaps Doña Santos can compensate him for his pain—"

"Yes," Ophelia cut in. "That is exactly right. I will compensate the marshal." She lifted her purse and held it to her stomach. "And I can make a contribution to your expenses in this matter. Would ten *reales* be enough?"

Stokes' eyes lit up. Ten *reales* was more money than he had ever seen at one time in his life. Ten solid gold *reales*. He turned so that no one could see him through the front window, then stuck out his hand. "Give me the gold."

She counted out the ten gold pieces, then turned to Blas. "My son, do not give these men any more trouble. We'll have you out of here as soon as possible. Do you understand?"

Without a word, Blas turned away, a scowl on his face. Tomas took Ophelia's arm and tugged her toward the door. She stopped and turned to look at Stokes again.

"Do we have your promise? My son will be safe?"

Stokes pocketed the gold and smiled. "You have my promise, Doña Santos. No harm will come to young Mr. Blas in there. Soon as the marshal gets his wits back, you can settle with him. You go on home now. Don't worry."

As soon as they stepped outside, the crowd turned rowdy.

"What went on in there, Stokes?"

"We gonna have us a hangin' or not?"

"I say string 'em all up!"

When Tomas led Ophelia through the crowd, some of the merchants jostled them. For a second, Tomas began to fear for her safety. He heard dark murmurings from the Mexicans as they saw Ophelia being pushed around, almost falling.

"Let them be," Stokes said. "She ain't done nothin."

The merchants backed off and grudgingly parted to let her pass to her carriage. As they passed, Tomas caught a whiff of the *gringo* whiskey on their breaths, but it was more than that. After men drink too long, the smell of liquor is not only on their breath, it starts coming out of their skin.

Ophelia boarded the carriage and they rode to the edge of town, where the *vaqueros* turned to follow them. Once they were out of sight of the town, Ophelia called a halt and beckoned Tomas over.

"Tomas," she said, "I don't trust that marshal. Do you?"

Tomas spit into the cacti beside the road. "No. But be grateful he did not arrest you, too."

"Me?" She sat in silence for a moment, clenching and unclenching her fists and trying to think clearly. "What do you think we should do?"

"I think we should leave half the men here. To keep watch. They can protect Blas as best they can, and send for us if they see anything happening. The rest of the men will escort you home. I think the marshal is a very greedy man who owes nothing to that town. If he thinks you will give him more gold, I think he will not harm Blas."

"Good," she said, but her eyes were still wide and frightened. "I want you to stay here, too."

Tomas looked down at his saddle and let out a big breath. "No, Ophelia. I must stay at your side."

"But I am not the one in danger. Blas is in jail!"

He did not answer for a few seconds, then he looked up and nodded. "I will escort you to the ranch and set the guard, then I will ride back here to wait for Juan."

"Juan is coming?"

"I sent word for him early this morning."

She took in a long breath. "I don't want him here! He won't do us any good. We have to try to negotiate with these people. He'll just…get in the way."

Tomas leaned down and put his hand on the carriage door. "Ophelia—the only way we are going to get Blas out of that jail is to break him out. Stokes might play along with us, to get more gold, but he won't let Blas go until he has Juan. If they get Juan, they will hang him. Garrison may be dying, and I have never seen the *gringos* as worked up as they are today. They want revenge. On anybody. They might even try to hang you."

Ophelia fell back in her seat. "This is all so pointless!"

Tomas straightened up and turned to the youthful *vaqueros*, ordering five of them to keep an eye on the town until he returned. In a few minutes the carriage started rolling again, and Tomas rode beside it, wishing he had Mingo or Juan to help him. Tomas needed to be back with the men, looking over Blas' safety, but he needed to be at the ranch, too, safeguarding Ophelia. He could not be in two places at once. *Juan*, he thought, *Juan. What a mess you've created this time for your family*. It could get worse. If anything happened to Blas—Tomas shook his head, trying not to imagine what Juan would do. Or what Ophelia and Juan would do to each other.

IN THE MOONLIGHT, the vast sweep of cacti and brush surrounded them, casting silvery shadows on the road and spooking their horses. From a distance Juan and Mingo could see the ranch all lit up, and Juan's heart sank. As they came closer, they spotted bonfires blazing against the night sky. Light came from every window of the house. Juan felt a wrenching knot forming in his stomach. He tried to steel himself. Now he could hear wailing, a constant flow of sound from dozens of throats. It was somewhere near three in the morning, he thought, so why were all these fires lit? As he rode into the courtyard, the women in the *jacales* saw him and their wailing grew louder, rising to a higher pitch, no harmony in their voices.

They rode up to the house, and by then Juan knew someone must be dead. The rider had said that Blas was in jail and that Ophelia and Tomas had gone to Brownsville to free him. It could be any of the three who were dead, or even all three. But then he saw Tomas standing in the shadows of the porch, holding a cup of coffee.

Juan did not dismount. He sat his horse in silence and let Tomas tell him.

"Blas is dead." Tomas held out his hand and gripped Prieto's reins.

Juan leaned back in his saddle, blinking. Though he had expected bad news, he could not absorb it. It felt like he was hearing about the death of some distant relative he had never known.

"Mother?"

"She is safe. Inside."

Juan dismounted. Mingo walked their horses to the corral as Tomas pulled Juan away from the house, out into the courtyard so they could speak without being overheard.

Juan spoke first. "Tell me what happened."

Tomas offered Juan his cup of coffee, but Juan shook his head.

"I took Ophelia into town. We paid the new marshal, his name is Stokes, to keep Blas safe. I wanted to wait until dark and then go in and get Blas out when most of the town would be sleeping. But as soon as we left, they hung him on the mesquite tree down by the river."

Juan nodded. "Go on." He needed to hear it all, right now. Somewhere inside, he began to feel the first inkling of sorrow, of despair, of anger.

But it waited behind a barrier, the barrier he had learned to hide behind since he was a boy.

"They dumped the body in the river," Tomas said. "Ophelia sent me back to talk to Garrison, to pay him off and get him to drop any charges against you. But I don't think they waited more than an hour after we left. The men I left outside of town sent a rider to warn us. Then they rode in to intervene, and they were all killed, shot out of their saddles. Stokes and the other *gringos* were waiting for them."

Juan saw Tomas' face contorting in the moonlight.

"That Stokes," Tomas said, his voice thick, "he took Ophelia's money and promised to keep him safe. Later, he was buying drinks in the saloon with it, laughing at us, at your mother." He stopped and looked off into the dark. "I'm going to kill him," he whispered.

Juan said nothing, he just stood there and looked out toward the horizon, toward Brownsville. Then he sighed, wishing he could feel something. "The body?"

Tomas nodded. "We spread word down river, out to Bagdad and further up to coast to Point Isabel. But I don't think we'll find him."

Juan turned toward the house, but Tomas caught his arm. "Your mother is inside. She's waiting for you." He paused. "Juan, don't fight with her tonight."

The old *vaquero* still had a rock-hard grip on Juan's arm. He looked at Tomas, and felt buoyed by his strength, his loyalty. "Tomas," he said, his voice slurred by lack of sleep, "you are Mother's only true friend in this world, aren't you?"

Tomas said nothing. He released Juan's arm and then just stood there, his dark face silhouetted against the pale, moonlit sky.

Inside the house, Juan found Ophelia sitting in her bedroom, a candle on the little table, an open Bible on her lap. She looked up as he entered the room, then dropped her head and began sobbing again.

"Mother," he said as he stood before her, "don't look away from me."

He saw her struggling with her emotions, her chin quivering, tears rolling down her cheek.

"Juan," she finally cried, "they killed our beloved Blas!" She rose and put her arms around him. He felt her body shake, her hot face on his shoulder soaking his shirt with tears. It was her tears that finally liberated Juan, her tears that finally broke through that hard shell underneath which his feelings hid. Blas. Little Blas! Suddenly, he choked back tears himself, and he reached out slowly, wrapped his arms around his mother's slender shoulders, and cried with her.

After a few minutes they sat down on the bed. Later, Conchita brought them coffee, and she too looked haggard and teary.

"Conchita," said Ophelia, "go to bed."

But the old woman merely nodded and padded off, hunched over, her thick arms hanging low by her side.

Ophelia looked at Juan and let him drink his coffee for a minute. Then, "Son, what do you intend to do?"

He shrugged.

"I intend to see that marshal arrested and hanged himself," she said. "I will personally see to it—but, Juan, I do not want a wholesale slaughter of innocent people."

"There are no innocent people in that town."

"Look at me, Juan. Your brother is dead. Because of what you did. You promised me you would leave the *gringos* alone. Instead, you shot their marshal. Now you're going to repeat your mistake? Leave them alone, Juan. Let this be. Let me handle it."

He stood up and set his cup on the table next to the candle. Through the window, he saw the first hint of dawn, and across the courtyard in the *jacales* the women were already boiling their corn.

It had been said. *Your brother is dead, because of you.* She did not want to know about how the drunken marshal had been beating old Alphonso, or how he had insulted Ophelia herself—an insult so vile that no man could have let it go. Blas was dead. Juan had not hanged him. The *gringos* had done it and then dumped him in the river. But she blamed Juan for it.

He turned toward the door and stopped there. He looked back at her. Her face betrayed exasperation, her mouth slightly open, her eyes pleading.

"Blas is dead, Mother. But I didn't kill him. If this is anybody's fault, it is yours—you and your trust in those people, in their lawyers, in their marshals. Those *gringos* you've been protecting all these years did it. You want promises?"

He put a balled fist to his chest. "This I promise you. They are going to pay!"

LIDIA PACED RESTLESSLY among her roses. Their sweet, early morning scent reminded her of that moonlit night she had spent in her garden with Juan, kissing, talking, sitting quietly with their arms around each other. She shook her head and scolded herself. It was Starr she should be musing about, not Juan. But she could not will him out of her brain.

It was quiet. She heard the birds singing down by the river, and in the corral the horses whinnied. She looked up and saw the morning sun surrounded by a bright blue sky. It was a cool dawning, at least by Texas standards. An hour after sunrise, the heat could be unbearable except to those accustomed to it, like the *vaqueros*. By late September, the sun mellowed in the morning. Sometimes, like today, the dew stayed on the roses until mid-morning and the air smelled fresh and cool.

Snapping off one of the roses, she carried it to a bench nearby and sat down, twirling it in her hand. The dew flew off and cool drops splashed her cheek. She held it to her nose and sniffed. Starr. She had to think about him, she had to make up her mind what she would say to him. Six weeks, he had said. Only one week remained. He could come any day. She rose and walked aimlessly along the garden path, then stood still, staring at the miles of dusty cacti and brush beyond the garden wall.

Did she love the Ranger? Or was it just her loneliness? What about Juan? Was it really beyond all hope? She shook her head, as she had done hundreds of times in the last few weeks. Even if she reconciled with Juan, would it last? Could they be happy? If, if, if, if—she was tired of ifs. Ophelia was right, Lidia was wasting her life out here alone in the brush. She looked down at her rose and twirled it again, avoiding the thorns on the short stem. She was like this rose, blooming out here in a secret garden that no one else ever saw. What good was that? It might as well bloom out there in the *brasada*, a hundred miles out in the brush, behind a rock and surrounded by cacti, where not even a passing lizard would notice, or care that it bloomed.

So what was there to think about? She would say yes. Yes! And it did not matter if she really did not love him. He was handsome, bold, strong. And he loved her, that was so plain to see. Maybe that would be enough.

She turned and strolled slowly to the house. The sun was just beginning to sting as it filtered through the mesquite leaves in the garden and touched her cheek. The only other option, she thought, was Blas. Young, handsome, fiery Blas. But she could not see herself marrying him, even though his infatuation with her was plain to see. Juan would always be in the background, and the thought of a lifetime of Juan lurking in her life, just out of reach, was unbearable.

As she approached the house, she heard the furious clatter of hoof beats in the courtyard, then someone called out. She hurried through the house and found Ramona already opening the front door. Lidia followed her outside. There a young *vaquero* sat his tired looking horse, snorting and wheezing after a hard ride.

"*Tengo nuevas*," the *vaquero* said, out of breath himself.

Lidia nodded. The man had news. Such men always had news, and it was never good news. She recognized the brand on the horse, a cross with an S. This young man was from the Santa Alicia ranch. "Come inside," she offered.

He shook his head. "Thank you señorita, but, no. I must ride to other ranches today. It is bad."

"Tell me quickly, then."

He took his sombrero off and held it to his chest. "*El patrón*, Blas, is dead Señorita. He was hanged by the *gringos* in Brownsville yesterday."

Lidia sucked in her breath and put her arm out for Ramona, who let out a stifled cry and reached for her mistress. "No!" Lidia cried. "Blas? *Dios mío!*"

The *vaquero* dropped his eyes and nodded. "It is true. They also killed many of Doña Ophelia's *vaqueros* who were trying to rescue Blas. Doña Ophelia asked me to bring you the news, señorita. She said to tell you that she is all right and the rest of the family is all right." He paused, put his hat back on, then continued. "There will be no funeral because the *gringos* threw his body in the river and it has not been found. There will be rosaries at the Santa Alicia, but she asks you not to come, señorita. There is too much danger."

She knew immediately what that meant. Juan would want revenge, terrible revenge. The magnitude of the *gringos'* act slowly dawned on her, so huge she could scarcely take it all in. They had hanged Blas and dumped him in the river. *My God*, she thought, *the town is doomed.* The image of a burning Brownsville flooded into her mind, a vision of bodies stacked in the square, and of the consequences beyond that, on and on. Some dark, ugly deeds had been done and more would follow. People would be like beasts running blind and wild in the night, out of control and trampling everything in their path. Perhaps Juan, Ophelia, and most of the people living on the border were doomed, too.

"Ramona," she whispered, "give this man some coffee." She looked up at him with eyes that burned, eyes that felt tired already despite the early hour. "Take a fresh mount from the corral," she said, "and eat some breakfast. I won't take no for an answer."

She turned and walked back into the house, then stopped and waited for Ramona. "Get my clothes ready, Ramona. I'm going to Ophelia."

Ramona's eyes grew wide, and she put one hand over her heart, and the other on Lidia's arm. "No, señorita, you mustn't. There might be fighting. And Doña Ophelia asked you not to come."

Lidia shook her head. "Do not argue with me! She is my best friend. I will not leave her alone at a time like this. I am going. Get my things ready and have the men bring up a carriage."

As Ramona hurried off, Lidia watched the tired young *vaquero* ride away toward the corral, slouching a little in his saddle. There were thousands of young men like him up and down the border—eager, willing, quiet boys that could ride and rope like no other breed in the world, and she knew that they all loved Juan. El Gallo, they called him. The Rooster. How many, she wondered, how many of these fine young men would die for El Gallo before this was over?

GENERAL JOSÉ CANTU stood with his officers in the center of the room and offered them a toast.

"Gentlemen," he said raising his glass of wine, "on this festive celebration of the *Diez y Seis*, although as usual Matamoros forgot about it and now it is ten days late, I offer you a toast. To the Mexican nation, to its independence and prosperity, forever! *Viva México!*"

"*Viva*," the officers responded, and they all lifted their glasses and sipped their wine. Several toasts had already been offered, and more would come. The *fandango* had run all day, would run all night. There was music, food, dancing, drink—in the streets, in the dance halls, on the boardwalks. There would be lasciviousness and wild behavior, violence and sheer insanity. Someone would likely die and everyone would go home with pounding heads and thick swollen tongues to sleep for another day and recover from the celebration. *Fandangos* were a way for Mexicans to release inhibitions, to blow off steam that had built up for months, perhaps years.

General Cantu did not plan to spend the whole night drinking. He had duties. The War of Reform still raged in Mexico, although Matamoros was well out of the fighting for now. The Revolution of Aytla had finally toppled Santa Anna four years ago, in August of 1855. Benito Juarez had come to power then. Juarez, who believed in championing the middle and lower classes at the expense of the military and landed elite. Those people had the audacity to resent it, and the Conservatives were fighting back. But not here. Matamoros had declared early in favor of Juarez and run General Woll and his army out of the city in a bloody uprising. The new Mexican Congress had proudly proclaimed Matamoros an Unconquered and Heroic City. The city glowed with pride. General Cantu looked at his Juarista officers, several of them Europeans, and smiled.

Across the room stood the noisy Americans from Brownsville. They invited themselves to every Mexican fiesta. They drank and laughed, slapping each other on the back and grabbing at women who walked by. Occasionally one turned and spit tobacco juice into the corner of the room, despite the fact there was no spittoon there.

Cantu leaned over to one of his officers, Cruz, whose eyes were somewhat unfocused. "Do not overindulge, Lieutenant. You may need your wits about you in the next few days."

Cruz smiled, flashing brilliant white teeth. "I don't know," he replied, slurring his words a little. "The *gringos* have the Rangers, no?"

Cantu shook his head. "Dauterive's men are drunk in Laredo, the last I heard of them." He lifted his glass and sipped the wine again, a good Madeira. "Look at them." He sniffed, nodding at the Americans. "They look like they don't have a care in the world. They act like they've won a great victory. I think they forget that Blas was my cousin."

"You think perhaps they don't know?" the incredulous lieutenant asked. "Not even the *gringos* are so wooden-headed."

"Let's go find out."

The two men strolled up to the tight knot of Americans, which opened up to greet them. "Señores," Cantu said, nodding.

Miller held up a glass. "Can we buy you a drink, General Cantu?"

"Thank you," he replied curtly, "but I have a drink." The general looked at the red, unshaven faces around him, all of them grinning. He still was not sure if they were ignorant or simply arrogant beyond all reason. Here stood Miller, Green, Stokes, Brown, and two other Brownsville merchants also celebrating the *Diez y Seis*, only a day after they had hanged the son of one of the most prestigious and powerful families on the border. Juan Santos, El Gallo, was the brother of the man so unjustly killed by these grinning idiots. Yet they appeared completely unconcerned.

The general raised his glass. "Lieutenant Cruz and I were just discussing the war, *señores*. You know that the Juarez congress has bestowed the title 'Unconquered and Heroic City' on Matamoros. Tell me, gentlemen, do you think your congress would ever bestow such an honor upon an unconquered Brownsville?"

"Nope," Green replied. "Too many words in that title. It would tax their brains to think it."

The Americans laughed at this witticism and passed their bottle of whiskey around, refilling their glasses. General Cantu looked over at his young officer and lifted his eyebrows. These brash and loudmouthed American fools had no idea what was about to happen to Brownsville, he thought, and walked away.

Chapter 10
War

FROM HIS CAMP across the dark, gently flowing river, Juan knew the *fandango* had run its course. The constant cries of "Viva Mexico" from the Matamoros town hall and all the cheers that followed had slowly died away, though they would start again in a few hours. Though Mexican celebrations started late, they continued for days. For now, only occasional drunken shouts and the sharp report of a gun or two echoed as stragglers stumbled back across the river to huddle close together and sing on street corners. The music had faded hours ago, and Juan knew that most of the residents of Brownsville had gone to bed, tired and drunk, snoring like happy pigs in their sties.

They would not be happy much longer.

He looked past the sleeping town at the barest hint of light on the eastern horizon. The stars still sprawled brilliantly across the sky in the predawn blackness, dimmed only by a half-moon directly overhead. An hour before dawn. It was time.

He turned in his saddle. Mingo and Tomas sat their horses by his side, calming them, for the air hummed with electricity, a crisp vitality that magnified every sound, every smell. The horses pricked up their ears, snorted and stamped, rolled their eyes. Behind Juan on the military road, 200 armed men struggled with their mounts, their fear and eagerness spilling over to the horses. Juan took a deep breath. It felt as sweet and rich as any wine he had ever tasted, as any kiss stolen from Lidia. *Lidia. No!* Shaking his head, he forced her image from his mind, as he would any fleeting doubt. She belonged to Starr now.

Juan turned his horse to face the men, motioning them in, pushing himself up in the stirrups. When they were huddled together, he pushed his sombrero back and boomed out his words, the crisp night air carrying them clearly to his men and out into the brush.

"*Muchachos*, some of you work on the Santa Alicia, some of you don't. But I want you all to know this—people will die today. Not Comanche, not Karankawa, not *bandidos*. *Gringos* will die today." A general murmur of approval rose from the men. "Any man who wants to change his mind can stay behind when we move out. There will be no shame. Nobody will look back to see who did not come." He paused to let his words soak in.

"You all know that the *gringos* have stolen our land," he continued. "You know they have beaten and killed our people. You know they have thrown the bodies of our people into the river like they were animals, not even worth burial. You know they treat Mexicans like dogs, and their law protects only them, not us. Every one of you—you know this is true. You have felt a *gringo* boot on your butt, seen a friend hanged or shot, felt the way they look at you, like you are dirt under their boots."

He paused, his voice dropping, catching in his throat. "And you know they hanged my brother, who was innocent of any crimes."

Blas. Juan remembered that they had parted in anger. But all those years before, that sweet boy had loved him without judgment, without conditions, just because Juan was his brother. That was the real Blas. And they had hanged him, those cowards in the town. Juan clenched his jaw, feeling the fires of rage ignite his belly, burn his lungs, make his eyes flash. He felt his heat ignite those around him, and their heat jumped to the next man, and the next, until the fire reached those dark shapes of men on the far edges of the road.

He pushed himself up in the stirrups again, feeling his voice rise from the depths of his burning body. "For all these reasons," he thundered, "I condemn this town to death!"

As a spontaneous cheer roared from 200 throats, Prieto started prancing in a circle. Juan brought him back to face the men. The *vaqueros* packed the road, cheering eagerly, clamoring for blood, their own frightened mounts screaming and crashing against each other. It was time, yes, it was time.

Juan looked over the heads of the *vaqueros*, their sombreros dotting the night in the weak blue light of the moon. He pulled his sombrero off his head and thrust it high in the night air. "*Viva México!*"

The men screamed back, *"Viva México!"*

Prieto pranced nervously again, kicking up a dusty fog in the moonlight. Twisting his head back toward the men, Juan slammed his sombrero back on his head and cried, *"Adelante!"*

Prieto needed no spurring. The animal leaped forward, and Juan heard the roar of horses and men behind him, moving en masse as they untangled themselves to follow. On his right and left, just slightly behind him, he saw Mingo and Tomas spurring their horses to keep up with him. They hit the darkened town at a full gallop, their cries echoing into every house as they clattered through the streets.

"Viva México!"

"Viva El Gallo!"

The battle cries echoed back and forth among the men as they pounded down the streets, and other men answered back, *"Viva!"*

Juan stopped his horse and pulled over to the side of the main street with Mingo and Tomas to direct the *vaqueros.* "Guard the street corners," he called. "Don't let the *gringos* gather."

He turned to Mingo. "Where is it?"

Mingo fumbled with his saddlebag, then produced a balled-up flag.

Juan nudged Prieto forward. As they rode the short distance toward Fort Brown, he saw his men deploying themselves on the corners. So far, no reaction from Brownsville's residents. As planned. They would likely think that the men were celebrating *Diez y Seis. Well, in a way,* he thought, *we are.*

In a few minutes, the Mexican flag flew again above Texas soil. Juan turned to Tomas. "Let the prisoners out of jail. Anybody gets in the way, kill him."

Tomas' eyes brightened. Juan knew he wanted to kill Stokes. "Bring Stokes to me, Tomas. This fort will be my headquarters." He looked at Mingo. "Bring them all to me here, any of them that helped hang my brother." Tomas rode off, and Juan dismounted. He wondered if Tomas would obey his order not to kill Stokes.

A few minutes later, the men came dragging two sleepy, filthy men to him in the fort's courtyard. Juan squinted to recognize them in the dim light.

"*Patrón*," one of the *vaqueros* said, "*estos son los abogados.*"

Juan walked over to the two lawyers, trembling in their night clothes, and looked them over. "You cheated my mother."

"No!" Winkle protested.

"It was Pownall," Dresser added. "He forced us."

Winkle kicked at his partner. "Shut up, Franklin!"

Dresser fell on his knees. "Don't kill us, Mr. Santos, please don't kill us."

Juan looked down at him. *This man does not look worth killing.* Groveling men never did. "Tell me about Pownall," he barked.

"There is nothing to tell," Winkle said. "Mr. Santos, turn us loose. You have no right to hold us. The transaction with your mother was perfectly legal and would be upheld in any court in the land. I don't see—"

Juan pulled his pistol and whacked the *gringo* lawyer across the forehead with it. The lawyer crumpled to the ground, slack-mouthed. He made one feeble convulsion and then lay still, his eyes open. Turning the gun on Dresser, Juan noticed a wet stain had suddenly appeared in the lawyer's crotch and was spreading to the ground where he was kneeling.

"You killed him," Dresser sputtered.

Cocking the hammer back on the pistol, Juan did not reply. He had not meant to kill Winkle, but it was just as well. The man had a big mouth.

Now Dresser went quiet. He looked up, and Juan saw resignation on his face. "Can I stand up?"

Juan nodded and turned to one of the *vaqueros*. "Pull him up." When the lawyer stood on his pale, bare feet, Juan repeated, "Tell me about Pownall."

"It was all his idea," Dresser replied. "He wanted to agitate the Mexican peasants and ranchers so they will do what you are doing now. Fight."

"Why?"

"Why else? For money. Brownsville is drying up. The real money is across the border, in Matamoros. He wants another war with Mexico. More land to confiscate. If the southern side of the river becomes U.S. territory, he figures to get rich." Dresser paused, then corrected himself. "Richer."

"The merchants here in Brownsville, they are part of this?"

Dresser shook his head and gave a high, nervous laugh. "They've been duped, just like you, Mr. Santos. Pownall's manipulating them." He paused and nodded. "He's manipulating you, too. He pays bandits and rustlers to harass everybody on all sides."

Juan took a step closer. "And he paid you to cheat my mother. Was hanging my brother part of it, too?"

"No. We had nothing to do with what happened to your brother. Taking Brownsville from your mother was Pownall's idea, but he never paid us anything. He said if we didn't do it, he would bankrupt us. He filed most of those claims himself. Or he paid other men to do it. Then we ran up bills getting the claims dropped, so your mother would pay us with the land." He paused and licked his lips. "As for your brother, well, that was Pownall, too. He paid Stokes to do it. Pownall knew you would come and do exactly what you are doing now."

As Dresser fell silent the two men looked at each other for a few seconds. Juan saw fear in the lawyer's eyes, but no longer the desperate look. Dresser dropped his hands to his sides and set his face, then shifted his eyes away from Juan and looked off behind him toward the eastern sky.

He was ready to die. This man deserved to die. But something about the way he accepted it bothered Juan. He raised the gun and pointed it at the lawyer's chest, but he did not fire.

"If you want to stay alive," he said, "you wait here at the fort. Nobody is going to guard you. But if you aren't here when I get back, I will hunt you down and kill you."

Dresser turned his gaze away from the distant horizon and looked up at Juan, but the expression on his face did not change. Juan had seen that before, too. A man ready to die does not always understand when he is allowed to live, not right away.

"Mingo," he ordered, turning briskly, "come with me. I want to find Pownall, Stokes, Garrison, Miller, Green—all of them."

A faint gray streak lit the eastern horizon as they rode through the town. Scattered gunfire echoed all over Brownsville, and bright flames dotted some rooftops. A thin layer of smoke settled as they rode down

14th Street, peering down dark alleys and side streets. In one alley, Juan saw several of his men dragging smoking bodies into a pile. Down another street he saw town residents stumbling toward the river.

"Down there!" Juan cried, and spurred Prieto forward. A bullet whizzed by his head, but as he drew his pistol and turned, he heard Mingo's gun respond. A *gringo* crumpled in a doorway, a smoking rifle gripped to his chest.

Gunfire crackled ahead, too. Juan turned on Elizabeth Street and found a tight knot of *vaqueros* standing in the street. They parted for him, and Juan put Prieto forward. Splayed on the ground was the body of Tom Garrison.

"*Esta muerto, patrón.*," said one of his men.

Juan nodded. He looked down at the dead marshal and saw the fatal wound in the head. His shoulder, where Juan had shot him, looked fine.

"Dump him in the river," he ordered, then turned Prieto back toward the next corner. Mingo shadowed him. As they crossed 12th, they spotted *vaqueros* carrying guns and ammunition from one of the stores and stacking the loot in the middle of the street. Gunfire was still booming all over town.

Mingo drew up suddenly, and Juan pulled Prieto to a halt. Up ahead, two *gringos* had burst through an intersection. One of them was Stokes. They were looking at the killer of Juan's little brother. Juan did not say anything. He did not need to. Mingo jerked his horse around and tore back down the street, then turned the corner and rode parallel to keep Stokes from slipping away. Juan spurred Prieto forward, leaning down low in the saddle and hunching his shoulders as Prieto lurched ahead, kicking up huge clods of earth.

When he turned the corner, the street looked deserted except for some of his own men several blocks away. He pulled Prieto to a halt and whistled to his men, waving them over. He advanced to the next cross street just in time to see shadows moving against the side of a house, then disappearing into an alley. When the *vaqueros* drew near, he pointed to the house.

"You three," he ordered, "go down the alley to the back of this house. Break down the back door. Shoot anyone you see, but don't kill Stokes. The rest of you spread out here on the street. Watch the shadows."

Within minutes, Juan heard shouting in the alley, then a loud banging as his men kicked at the door. He spread his men around the front door and ordered them to be ready. If it was Stokes in there, Juan doubted he would surrender, but he hoped the man wasn't going to put up a fight. He wanted Stokes alive, alive and afraid, so he could feel the rope go over his head like Blas had felt it, listening to the jeers, looking up for a last glimpse of the sun as he went, surprised and unprepared, into death.

A shotgun blast blew out a window of the house, and one of the horses screamed in pain, stumbling backward and then crashing into the middle of Levee Street, spilling a young *vaquero* in a dusty heap. His men returned fire, but the house was dark. The banging at the back door continued, then the door cracked open, the splintering noise echoing sharply through the morning air.

"Don't shoot!" a voice called from the house in Spanish. "We're coming out!"

"Throw out your guns first."

A shotgun and two pistols came flying through the shattered front window. The front door cracked open, and Manuel Lopez stepped down into the street, barefoot. Behind him came Green. Juan knew that Lopez worked at Green's store.

"Keep your hands up," Juan ordered. "Where is Stokes?"

"He went t'other way," Green said, raising his hands. "He who you're after?"

"Right now," Juan replied, "I'm after you, Mr. Green. I'm going to kill you."

Green lowered his hands slightly and backed away a step. There on his face—the look of sudden shock Juan wanted to see, the look of utter despair and helplessness he knew Blas had felt. Green looked around, up and down the street, but no rescue seemed imminent. *No, Señor Green, no one is going to help you. Nobody came to help Blas, did they?*

"Wait," sputtered Green, "just—wait. I have money, let me go, I'll pay you."

Juan laughed. "I'll give your money to the poor after you're dead. Bring him into the street." He turned Prieto and moved out a few steps.

Behind him, Lopez called, "*Patrón*, you cannot kill a man like this, in cold blood. Not even a *gringo*."

Juan half turned his head. "Go back into your house."

Lopez backed away, shaking his head, and stopped at the door of his house. He stood there in its shadow, his hands still partly raised. "You should not do this, *patrón*. It is not your way."

Two men grabbed Green's arms and dragged him into the center of the street, where they released him. Green stood looking up at Juan, his eyes huge, his legs shaking.

"Please, please," he said, spreading his arms, "don't kill me. I had nothing to do with it. I—"

"You had everything to do with it," Juan roared. He took a deep breath. Lopez was right, Green was unarmed. Juan had never purposely killed an unarmed, helpless man. But Blas had been unarmed, too. This had to be done. It was not murder, it was justice. The *only* way to justice. Yet, he hesitated.

"Give him a pistol," he finally ordered.

Mingo stepped up to Green and shoved a pistol into his hand. Green stared down at it, still shaking his head.

Juan stared at Green, looking past him, remembering the face of his beloved little brother. He saw the wild look of primal, gut-wrenching fear in Green's eyes. He slowly drew his own pistol, then extended his arm.

"For the murder of my brother, Blas Santos," he said, "I sentence you to death."

Green swung the pistol up, but Juan fired, tearing a huge hole in the man's chest.

HE HAD ALMOST GONE with Green, but Marshal John Stokes had a premonition as they turned off 11th Street to Levee. He stopped and looked back over his shoulder, but that damned greaser Gallo was not coming. Not yet. Stokes had escaped from the bloody scene at the jail, where Tomas and his men had attacked without warning, killing the night constable and two others who came to his aid. He had run to Green's house and found him standing at the front door, a pistol in his hand. They had been pursued down the alleys and side streets, until they stumbled right into the invaders' midst.

"This way," Green had said. "I've got a man lives on this street. He can hide us."

But Stokes had held back, then turned and run the other way. "Best we split up," he called as he faded into the shadows. As he ran, he heard gunfire all over town. He knew it would be a massacre. Juan and his bandits were battling Americans and burning the town. Stokes knew why. He knew very well what they wanted.

They wanted him.

STOKES QUICKENED his step, weaving along the edges of the street among the shadows, looking for a place to hide. Another pistol shot rang out, magnified by the dense morning air. Damned greasers were everywhere.

Turning the corner, he suddenly spied one of the *vaqueros* on horseback, hunched over, looking for someone. Stokes stopped and slid into the shadow of the alley beside Frank Gilbert's store. As the *vaquero* turned his head toward the rapidly brightening eastern sky, his face caught enough light that Stokes recognized him. It was that sidekick of Gallo's, the one called Mingo. That meant Gallo was nearby, probably coming down this very street. A sudden chill ran down his spine, and he felt his mouth go dry with fear.

It was just light enough that a man standing in the alley might be visible. If he stayed there, Stokes thought frantically, Mingo would see him. And then Gallo would kill him for hanging his brother. He looked back down the alley. He could hide behind the building, but eventually they would find him. He needed to get inside one of these buildings.

Then he heard a rattle, a scrape of wood against wood on the other side of the wall, inside the store. Gilbert must be in there. He ran to the back door and tapped lightly until he heard footsteps and muffled voices. He tapped again. Out on the street, Mingo's horse was coming closer, snorting and whinnying.

"Who is it?" a voice whispered.

"Stokes. Let me in, God damn it!"

The door creaked open and he slithered in, just before Mingo rode past the alley. Stokes closed the door behind him and leaned against it, letting out a long, ragged breath.

"That was close," he muttered. He squinted at the outlines of the two men in the dim room with him. Light spilled in through the store's big front windows, but the area behind the counter was still dark.

"Who's out there?" It was Gilbert's high pitched, nasal voice.

Stokes snorted. "Nobody in particular," he said, "just El Gallo and a few of his stinking friends. Come to town for their mornin' coffee, I'd say."

"What do they want? What's all the shooting?" the second shadow asked. This was a juvenile voice, probably Gilbert's son.

Stokes' eyes adjusted to the darkness. The boy looked taller than his short, round father. "I don't rightly know, son," he said. "Seems like they're tryin' to burn the town down."

They heard Mingo's horse stop outside, then other horses rode up, three or four, from the sound of it. They heard men speaking, calling each other, answering, their melodious Spanish muffled by the store walls, but even then one voice stood out. Juan Santos—El Gallo was out there.

Stokes held his breath, then reached over and took a shotgun out of the hands of the younger Gilbert, who was shaking so bad Stokes was afraid he'd squeeze the trigger too tight and blow somebody's head off inside the store. Outside, the hoof beats increased. More men rode up. Stokes heard riders coming down the alley, their rigging clinking and their leather creaking as they passed. Someone shouted orders, and the buzz of activity increased.

"Look," the boy whispered.

At the front window a silhouette appeared, a man standing tall, his sombrero tilted askew. As he stepped forward into full view, Frank Gilbert sucked in his breath.

"Shit," whispered Stokes. "Hot damn, it's that damned Gallo."

He lifted the shotgun and took careful aim, squinting in the weak morning light.

A LOUD BANGING on his door jolted General José Cabrerra Cantu from an uneasy sleep, and the pain in his head instantly awakened, too. He rolled over and tried to focus his eyes, but the morning light was blocked by the heavy curtains across the window of the sparsely furnished room. Beside him lay a woman, her long, dark hair spread across her naked breasts. She looked familiar, but in the dark he could not swear who she was. The drinking, dancing, and debauchery had lasted all night, and he was certain he had fallen asleep no more than an hour ago. He put his hands to his head and sat up.

"*Quién chingados es?*" he bellowed. "It better be damned important!"

"My General," the adjutant replied smartly through the thick door, "there is fighting in Brownsville. The Señor Villarreal is here with a petition, sir."

Cantu frowned. Fighting? Who could be fighting? And then he remembered. Those idiotic Americans had hanged Blas Santos, and now there was fighting. Of course there was fighting. What did they expect?

"Go away," he ordered. "I don't want to see anyone."

The adjutant's footsteps faded away. Cantu rubbed his face. He could hear faint popping sounds across the river, and he knew it was gunfire. He pushed himself off the bed, stumbled to the window, and looked out past the walls of the small courtyard. Under the rising sun were huge, billowing plumes of smoke in the direction of Brownsville.

The adjutant returned. "My General, sir. The Señor Villarreal begs to speak with you regarding the matter of your cousin, el Señor Juan Santos. He has attacked Brownsville and has killed dozens of people. The town is burning, sir."

Cantu chuckled. He remembered visits his family had paid to Juan's out on the Santa Alicia ranch when they were boys. Juan was a few years younger than him. In men, that made little difference, but the difference between a twelve-year-old boy and an eight-year-old boy was significant, especially when it came to fighting. And they had fought because with Juan, fighting was unavoidable. And though the general usually won the physical part of the struggle, Juan always got revenge, which would start yet another fight. A whack on the knee with a mesquite limb. A rock chucked at his head. A sudden kick in the genitals. And now, the stupid

Americans had killed Juan's brother. Yes, there would be revenge, and it would be terrible. Of course Brownsville was burning. The general was surprised it had not burned years ago.

"My General?"

"All right, Gonzales, all right. Bring him in."

General Cantu scratched his chest and walked unsteadily to the arm chair nearby, where his uniform lay wadded up underneath the woman's dress. He flung the dress in the general direction of the bed and pulled his pants on. A moment later, an urgent rap sounded on the door.

"Yes?"

"My General, the Señor Enrique María Villarreal."

The general put on his tunic but left it unbuttoned. "*Bien.* Send him in."

Villarreal rushed into the room and immediately put his hand to his nose. "My God, José. What is that stench?"

The general shrugged and looked over at the naked woman on the bed, still sleeping. It occurred to him that she had not moved or made a sound despite all the noise and commotion. "I don't smell anything," he replied. "But you didn't wake me up to smell me. What do you want, Enrique?"

"Juan has gone mad, José. Come outside! Look at what he is doing to Brownsville."

"I don't give a good *chingada* what he does to Brownsville. That is now U.S. territory. This is Mexico. Let the Americans do something about it."

Villarreal wrung his hands. "You know the U.S. soldiers pulled out in the spring. And the Rangers are upriver, toward Laredo. We are unprotected!"

"*We?* Why do you care so much about the *gringos?*"

The woman rolled over in the bed, tangling herself in the bed sheet and exposing a long, youthful leg up to her crotch.

"The *gringos?* Who's talking about the *gringos?* My bank, José, my bank! I've lent them money, made loans. How can I collect if they're dead or burned out? It's business José, and your family has interests there, too. All the leading families do."

The general smiled and scratched his whiskers. "So the leading families want me to save the *gringos?*"

"Not the *gringos*," said Villarreal. "Save the town, save our businesses. And I know that Ophelia Santos herself would want you to stop him."

"If I were Ophelia, I'd be over there burning the town down myself, for what they did to Blas."

Villarreal walked over to the window and pulled the curtains apart. The sudden flash of bright sunlight caused both men to wince and the woman in the bed to roll over into the pillows. Now she was completely uncovered except for a narrow twist of sheet around her waist. The general rose, walked over to the bed, and threw the covers over her bare buttocks.

"They should never have done that to Blas," Villarreal said. "It was that madman, Stokes. I tried to stop him." He paused and looked back at the general. "And now they are paying for it, dying for it. Ophelia's a lot smarter than you give her credit for, José. I don't think she would risk losing the ranch over this."

"You think she's just going to forget about it? No, not Ophelia. Someone will pay."

Villarreal nodded. "Yes, someone will pay. But she would want justice. Juan only wants revenge. That's always been the difference between them."

The general snorted. "I don't know, Enrique. Maybe they are not so different. I think he sees it as justice too, except with Juan, he makes his own justice. He always has." He rubbed his eyes and squinted at Villarreal. "So what do you want from me?"

"Just ride over and talk to him, José. He is your cousin, he will listen to you. Take some of your men. Just slow him down and let him cool off before he destroys the whole town."

The general slumped into the armchair again and put his hands to his head. The sudden movement made the room spin, and he closed his eyes, leaning back into the chair to steady himself. "I need to sleep, Enrique. I don't need this right now."

When the general opened his eyes Villarreal was leaning over him. "Do it for Ophelia, José. Don't let Juan destroy her along with Brownsville."

"I think he already has, Enrique."

Villarreal straightened up, his face slowly softening, and he looked toward the bright light coming through the window. In the distance a rooster crowed, and the clatter of gunfire surged even louder. "Yes," he said. "Yes, I believe he has. But we have to try."

"WAIT," WHISPERED GILBERT, reaching out and pushing the shotgun barrel down. "If you shoot, they'll know we're in here."

They crouched behind the store's counter, trying to stay in the shadows, but the sun was inching higher, and a weak light was already coming through the windows and the cracks in the walls. They would not be able to hide much longer.

"I think they already know, Frank."

The Gilbert boy looked at him with wide eyes, his face twitching. "What are they going to do?"

"Hang us, burn us, shoot us. Maybe all three. Got any preference?"

"Leave the boy be, Stokes."

Stokes grinned and leaned against the counter. He pushed his hat up, then casually pulled out his pistol and checked the caps. "Well," he muttered, "they won't get me without a fight, I'll tell you that right now."

"They wouldn't be here at all if you hadn't hung that Santos boy," the storekeeper said.

"Way I recollect it, you was in that mob, too, Frank. Hollerin' for his hide. You forget that?"

Gilbert turned away, his round face beaded with sweat, his dark hair matted in wet strands down his blubbery neck. "We shouldn't have done it. That boy—"

"That boy—shit. It's done now, Frank. So shut the hell up before his big brother out there hears you blubberin'."

The sounds of horses galloping up the street and halting right outside the store caused them to rise above the counter and peek out the window.

Juan had moved away from the window, but they could not see the street. What they heard was men talking in Spanish.

"For Chrissake," Gilbert whined, "he's got a whole goddam army out there."

"Shit," said Stokes. "I shoulda shot the son-of-a-bitch while I had the chance. You shouldn't have stopped me. We're good as dead, Frank. Your boy, too."

WHEN A BUGLE SOUNDED at the edge of town, Juan and his men turned toward 12th Street. They saw something truly amazing—thirty mounted and armed Mexican federal troops, flying the Mexican flag, riding down the street of the American city of Brownsville. In front rode General José Cabrerra Cantu, who seemed to be concentrating on not sliding off his horse.

"*Alto*," called Mingo, raising his rifle over his head with both hands, and Cantu held up his hand.

"*Alto*," a Mexican lieutenant called, and the troop came to a dusty halt.

"I want to speak to *el Señor* Juan Santos," Cantu said.

Mingo had lined up his men to face the Mexican troops, but Juan motioned them aside.

"Cousin, what do you want?"

"Cousin, we need to talk about this."

Juan looked around. Large parts of the town were on fire, and the heavy smoke wafted through the air like fog, stinging his nose as he breathed. There were dead *gringos* stacked in alleys and in the main plaza, and still the guns boomed all over the city. Stokes and the others had eluded him so far, but they would be found. They were probably hiding in the buildings, but which ones?

"José, what about this?" he replied. "This is necessary. This will continue. Cousin, go back to Matamoros. This is no concern of yours."

The general shook his head and then slipped off the horse. He stood next to it shakily, holding the reins. "Look you hardheaded *cabrón*," he said, "I'm dying here. I need a drink. I need to sleep. I don't have time for this." He walked over to the nearby rail and tied his horse to it, then pulled a bottle out of the saddlebags. "Come here and have a drink, Little Cousin."

Juan dismounted and handed Prieto's reins to one of his *vaqueros*, then walked over and sat next to Cantu on the boardwalk in front of Gilbert's store.

Cantu took a long drink of brandy and handed the bottle to Juan, who took a sip, then took another. They looked off toward the river and watched the smoke drift toward Matamoros.

"Juan," Cantu groaned, "have you gone completely insane?"

Juan kicked at the dirt with the heel of his boot, studying the hole he made. "No more than usual, José. What are you doing here? Maybe you're insane."

"I'm not the one killing *gringos*."

"But I bet you wish you were."

Cantu grinned and took another swig, then held the bottle close to his face, perhaps to minimize the distance for the next drink. Juan noticed that his cousin stank of liquor, a smell he had exuded himself many times.

"Cousin, you had a long night celebrating?"

Cantu exhaled heavily and rolled his eyes. Then he shut them, as if moving them caused him pain. He nodded slowly.

"Then go home to bed," Juan told him. "There is nothing you can do here."

"What is it you want, Juan? What will it take to get you to stop and pull your men out?" He held the bottle out to Juan, who waved it away.

"I want the men who murdered Blas," he said conversationally. "I'm going to kill them and then burn the town. In a year, it will be back to what it was before they came. Mesquite and cactus."

Cantu scratched his whiskers and nodded. "Who specifically do you want?"

"Stokes, Miller, Pownall."

"Not Green?"

"Green and the lawyers are already in hell." Juan suddenly remembered that he had let Dresser live, back in the fort. It was not clear to him just at the moment why he had done so, and he doubted that the lawyer would be waiting, unguarded, where he'd been told to stay.

"All right. Stokes, Miller, Pownall. If those men are arrested and put in jail to await charges and trial, would that satisfy you?"

"It would satisfy me to kill them. Then I'll finish burning the town."

Cantu's face turned into a frowning mask of crags and whiskers. "If I promise to arrest them," he sounded impatient now, "will you withdraw?"

"Why should I do that, cousin? And how could you arrest them? You don't have any authority here."

"Well, yes and no," the general said. "The citizens of Brownsville have asked for assistance, and in the spirit of international cooperation, I could lend a hand. Besides, isn't that the Mexican flag you're flying up at the fort?"

Juan shrugged. "I didn't have time to make a new flag."

"So you were going to make your own flag. Are you declaring your own country here, Juan? Is this a revolution?"

Juan stood up. "You better go, José."

The general held up one hand. "Help me up, cousin."

Juan pulled him up, and the two men looked in each other's faces.

"You don't want to fight me this time, Juan."

There it is, Juan thought. Though Juan always spoke directly, sometimes among Mexicans, it took a while to come to the point. There were nuances, meanings within meanings. Politeness often demanded that unpleasant business be referred to obliquely, approached in a roundabout way. But inevitably, it had to be said. Or done.

"This is not your business, José."

The general held up the bottle again, and Juan shook his head. "Affairs of state, cousin. There are some who would like to see big trouble along the border. To give the Americans another reason to attack Mexico, slice off another third of our land." He took a drink. "I love you Juan. But I can't let you bring disaster to Mexico."

Juan looked up toward the river, now bathed in brilliant sunlight. His cousin had a point. Juan had never meant to kill so many people when he attacked the town. He only wanted to kill the men responsible for hanging Blas. And to burn the town, of course, so that the *gringos* would go away.

"You'll arrest those three and hand them over to me?"

"To you?" Cantu hesitated, then nodded. "If I can find them. They may have fled."

Juan shook his head. "No. They're hiding here in Brownsville. Nobody has left, all the roads are blocked. I think I saw Stokes run down this street. He could be in one of these buildings…or he might have slipped away already. The others, I don't know." He motioned Mingo over. "Go tell Tomas we're pulling out to the edge of town."

He turned to the general. "No, I don't want to fight you, José. And I don't want Mexicans fighting Mexicans. There's been too much of that already in Mexico. I don't want it here." He pointed at Prieto, and an eager young *vaquero* spurred his horse and brought him over. "I want those men in jail, José, waiting for me to hang them, like they did to Blas. The others can leave. Then I'm torching the town. That's the bargain, cousin. In the meantime, the town will be surrounded." He set one boot in the stirrup and mounted, then sat looking down at the general.

Cantu nodded. "You're doing the right thing. Pull out for a while. We can talk more later."

"I should have done the right thing years ago and wiped out this rat's nest," Juan responded. "We don't need any more talk, either. Tell these sheep, if they want to live, to turn those killers over. Don't try any tricks, José. I'll be right outside of town." He pulled his sombrero down on his forehead and turned Prieto toward his waiting men.

FIFTY MEN WERE RIDING behind him when Juan approached the courtyard of the Santa Alicia ranch, their dust blowing before them and obscuring his view of the *jacales* across the way. In the distance behind them the city of Brownsville was burning, sending up plumes of billowing clouds, sometimes white, sometimes black, that spread across the horizon. Ophelia had sent a rider to Juan's camp, demanding that he return to the ranch to speak to her. He knew he had defied and angered her, but he was tired of her patient handling of the *gringos*. They had crossed the line with Blas. Blood had flowed, and more would flow. No matter what Ophelia said, the town would burn.

As the men rode by, children came running out of the *jacales*, shouting and cheering, and soon women and old men followed along, too. They milled in the courtyard, laughing and shouting *"Viva México!"* until the front door of the big house opened. A silence slowly descended on the crowd as Ophelia stepped out onto the porch and walked down the steps. She looked at the crowd, then turned her gaze toward the mounted men.

Juan sat calmly on his horse and waited, watching her come forward, her stare fixed on him. He saw lines in her face that he did not remember seeing before. Her tired eyes looked red, her cheeks were puffy, her hair in disarray. He felt his anger melting away at the sight of her. She had lost a beloved son.

He dismounted, and the crowd parted for him. Walking up to his mother, he kept his eyes locked with hers. Her look was hard, sharp, unyielding, a look he had seen many times before. Her brow furrowed in a deep frown. She did not speak. But behind her frown, he could feel the immeasurable grief that tore at his own heart, too. He stopped a few feet away from her. They stood under the noonday sun, and all around them, their people stood as if spellbound, unable to turn away. They all knew Juan had defied her, that she had summoned him here. They watched the drama unfolding, the clash of wills. No one spoke.

In one hand, Juan held a leather quirt. He handed it to Ophelia, then knelt on one knee before her, bowing his head and removing his sombrero.

"Mother," he said, "I have come."

A murmur of approval rippled through the crowd. Juan was showing respect for his mother as he handed her the leather strap to punish his defiance if she desired. The breeze ruffled the tops of the mesquite trees, a dust devil wound its way across the courtyard. Ophelia silently held the strap in her hand for a moment, then dropped it on the ground.

"Come inside," she said.

He pulled himself up, suddenly conscious of how weary he felt. Inside the house, he followed her to her room, where she sat in her rocker and nodded to a chair near the window for him.

"If I sit down, I'll fall asleep," he said.

"How long has it been since you've slept? Since any of those boys have slept?"

"We can sleep when our work is done."

"Work!" She jumped to her feet and took a step toward him. "Juan, you don't know what you're doing, do you? You have no idea what you're doing to me, to our people, and to all the other families. Every one of them has sent word, notes, messages, imploring me to stop you!"

"No!" he roared back. "I will not stop until justice for Blas is done. That I can promise you, Mother. The men who killed Blas will burn in hell before I'm done."

"And what about after? What about the ranch? The other ranches? Who will protect us when the Rangers come back, or even the army? Have you thought about that?"

"I'll worry about that when it happens."

She stepped up to him and placed a hand on his arm. "Juan, you're not thinking straight. You're blinded by grief and anger. Listen to me, son. Will you listen for a minute?"

He could hear the softer tone in her voice, and it relieved some of the tension from the room. He nodded, bending his head down and turning the sombrero in his hands.

"I want you to stop what you are doing," Ophelia said. "Leave the town alone. You have already killed too many, most of them innocent citizens. Stokes is hiding, or he's probably well on his way to Laredo by now."

He shook his head vigorously, but she gripped his arm tighter. "Let me finish. Leave now, go to Mexico, maybe to Monterrey. The *gringos* will send the Rangers, Juan. There will be much more fighting, and we may lose everything the family has built for generations. Can't you see that? Can't you see anything? I can't lose it all, I can't lose this land!"

He lifted his head and looked at her. Her eyes were pleading, desperate. But it was not within his power to stop, or to run and hide. He had set his mind on avenging his brother's death, and no one, not even his mother would dissuade him.

He shook his head, watching the hope drain out of her face. "No, Mother. I'm going to finish what I've started. No."

She turned slowly and slumped back into her rocker. "Then we are destroyed. A hundred years of blood and sweat, and everything gone." She looked up at him. In her eyes was a strange, lost look.

Through the window they heard the sudden clatter of hoof beats in the courtyard. Juan bent to peer outside and saw a carriage coming through the gate, followed by a large number of *vaqueros*. He recognized it instantly, for it bore the brand of the de Leon ranch on the carriage door. The image of Lidia standing in the center of the dance floor, achingly beautiful in her pale green gown, flooded into his mind.

"What does she want?" he grumbled. "This is no place for her."

Ophelia turned and looked out, too. "*Ay, no*," she moaned. "Oh, you hardheaded children are breaking my heart. I told her not to come!"

THE MEXICAN TROOPERS and hundreds of volunteers from Matamoros worked side by side with the Brownsville residents in the hot afternoon sun, putting out fires one by one, until only a few white plumes of smoke rose here and there. Stokes bit off a chunk of tobacco and stood in the plaza, staring at the twenty-five dead Brownsville residents laid out in a long line, including Green, Garrison, and Winkle. Some had been shot, others had burned to death as their homes fell down on top of them. The acrid, smoky stench of wet charcoal hung close in the air.

"Ah, there you are, Señor Stokes!"

It was that grinning general from Matamoros who had saved his hide. Stokes untied the bandanna from his neck and wiped his face with it. "What do you want, General?"

Cantu dismounted and handed the reins to his adjutant. "Simply to discuss with you the terms of the cease fire I negotiated on your behalf."

"I don't negotiate with bandits. You should have saved your breath."

Cantu straightened, the grin instantly disappearing into the lines of his puffy face.

Mayor Daniel Miller walked along the line of dead men, then saw Stokes and came over. "I can't believe it, John. Twenty-five dead. I never thought he would do it."

Stokes spit out a stream of tobacco juice. "He did it."

"Ah, Mayor Miller," said Cantu. "I was just telling the marshal here about the terms for the withdrawal of El Gallo's men. As you can see, they are still out there, at the edge of town." He pointed to the far edge of the street, beyond which the smoke of dozens of campfires rose from the brush surrounding the town.

"I done told you," said Stokes, "there ain't no terms."

"What are you talking about, Cantu?" asked Miller. "What terms?"

"Just that yourself, Marshal Stokes here, and Mr. Charles Pownall are to accompany me to Matamoros, where you will be placed under house arrest. For your protection. Only a formality, of course. You will be quite comfortable, I can assure you. This is not exactly as Señor Santos requested, but I think it is wiser. Shall we get going, before my cousin changes his mind?"

Stokes laughed, throwing his head back and slapping Miller on the shoulder. "You hear that, Daniel? The general here is arresting us in our own town! This is getting better all the time. Oh, by the way, General, Mr. Pownall took off for parts unknown sometime last night before the shooting started. He was last seen crossing the river on a horse, headin' over to Mexico."

Miller looked confused. He glanced at Cantu and shook his head, then turned to walk out among the dead again, stopping to stare down at Charles Green's body when he finally found it.

Cantu shrugged. "All right," he said. "I cannot force you. It would start another war. But we'll let my cousin have more fun with you. Then we'll see who laughs." He held out his hand, and the adjutant promptly slapped his horse's reins into it. He turned and mounted, then put his horse forward, pulling up to Stokes, who spat tobacco at his horse's hooves.

"Get the hell back on your side of the river, Cantu. And stay there."

The general jerked his horse around and spurred him through the plaza, followed by his soldiers marching in orderly lines.

Stokes watched him go. Behind the soldiers went the Matamoros residents who had crossed to fight the fire. He motioned three Brownsville men over. "Pull that wagon up here, boys. And get everybody gathered 'round."

When the townspeople had assembled, Stokes climbed up on the wagon and looked out at them. "Folks, that Gallo bastard done a foul deed today. And he might not be done, neither. We need to get started settin' up barricades at the entrance to town, up there. We're sending riders up the Point Isabel road. They ain't blocked that one yet. From Point Isabel, they can ride to Corpus Christi, San Antonio, and Austin to let them know what happened. Ask for help. Get some Rangers down here."

The men stared up at him. Looks of disbelief still marked their faces. Stokes wondered why he was wasting his time with these people.

One of them yelled out, "Why ain't we asking for federal troops, too?"

Stokes spat again. "Well, boys, we can do that, too. We can have our mayor write a nice letter to President Buchanan. 'Course by the time he gets it, we might all be feeding the fishes down in the Gulf."

This was followed by grumbling and milling around, like on that hot afternoon when they had hanged that cocky little brother of Gallo's. Stokes had been disappointed that, at the end, Blas had not broken down and begged for his life. But stretching his Mexican neck had been enjoyable, nevertheless. "We better get started, boys. That bastard Gallo's likely to come back real soon."

"Why'd we send the Mexicans away?" someone shouted.

"Yeah, get 'em back here!"

"Bring 'em back!"

A loud chorus rose up, swelling into angry cursing by frightened and tired men until Stokes held up his hands. "I don't need no greaser Federales lookin' after my hide. I ain't goin' over there beggin'."

"Well, hell, I will," said Miller. "I ain't too proud to beg. I got a wife and a daughter in town. I don't care if Santa Anna himself rides in here with his whole army. If it'll keep El Gallo out until our own army gets here, it's fine with me."

As the crowed roared its approval, Stokes shrugged. "You go right ahead, Mister Mayor. It's your town. 'Cept I think that Mex general's got his pride up now. I don't think he'll come back here."

"Won't hurt to ask, John." Miller looked around at the townspeople, who were nodding vigorously.

Hours later, fifty armed and mounted Mexican soldiers and one lieutenant rode the ferry across the Rio Grande toward Brownsville, accompanied by two small cannons. General Cantu watched from the bank at Matamoros. In the end, he had swallowed his pride and relented.

Perhaps by helping the *gringos*, he could blunt the effect of Juan's actions and prevent a wider war. Perhaps. He threw a pebble into the water and watched the ferry, the final rays of sun growing dimmer, then blinking out as it set on the first day of Juan's revolution.

LIDIA LEANED against the porch rail and watched as Tomas brought up the carriage. Ophelia stood by her side, rigid, uncommunicative, and, Lidia knew, on the verge of tears. All through the night, she had heard Ophelia arguing with Juan, begging him, threatening him, screaming at him. Juan's words were indistinct, but Lidia knew what he was saying. No. He would not change his mind. She knew he never changed his mind once he had firmly set it on something. It was, in fact, a trait he shared with his mother. They were both hardheaded and stubborn, except that Juan carried the stubbornness to an extreme.

During the night the news had come to the ranch that Cantu had reneged and was supplying soldiers to the *gringos*. Juan had been outraged and started planning to attack the town again. He wanted Ophelia to go to Matamoros, where she would be out of danger, and he wanted Lidia to accompany her. From Matamoros, he said, they were to travel up the road to Reynosa, then, far from the troubles of Brownsville, cross to the de Leon ranch. And far from Juan, Lidia thought, so he could do what he wanted without anyone arguing with him.

When Lidia had arrived yesterday afternoon, she had been puzzled by Juan's behavior. He had merely stomped away, a scowl on his face, hardly acknowledging her existence. It was, she thought, as if his new war consumed his every thought, his every emotion. No wonder he was anxious for them to go.

The carriage door opened. Juan slid off Prieto and walked to the porch, reaching his gloved hand out for Ophelia. She looked down at it and then burst into tears, clutching at it with both hands and drawing it to her breast.

"Oh, Juan," she cried. "I'm afraid I'm never going to see you again. I couldn't bear to lose both my sons! Please don't do this!"

Lidia's eyes misted over, too, and a lump grew in her throat. She watched as Juan pursed his lips, then leaned forward. For an instant, it seemed as if he wanted to take Ophelia into his arms, to comfort her.

"Mother," he said, "don't worry about me."

"You're so bold, so reckless. Something will happen, I know it."

He swallowed hard, and Lidia felt a tiny flicker of hope. Juan seemed tempted, incredibly, to bend a little for Ophelia's sake, or for Blas' sake. She did not know which.

"If it looks lost," he muttered, "I'll slip into Mexico."

Ophelia wiped her face with both hands and looked up at him. "Juan. Do you promise, *mi hijo?*"

He pulled his sombrero down tight and nodded. "I promise."

Still sobbing, she wrapped her arms around his neck and pulled him down to kiss his cheek, but he pulled away and stood stiff again. She slowly released him, squared her shoulders, and climbed into the carriage.

Lidia stepped forward off the porch, glancing sideways at him as she passed, but he held his hand out and touched her shoulder. She stopped and looked up at him hopefully, but his face gave no clue that he felt anything at all for her.

"Lidia…," he said.

She held her breath. She could feel her knees beginning to tremble. *No,* she said to herself, *no. I love Tom Starr. I belong to Tom. Juan had his chance—we only make each other miserable.*

"Take care of mother," he finally said. "Please."

She nodded, and realized she was staring intently into his eyes. She turned her head away and looked at the carriage, but he had not released her shoulder. She waited a few seconds, but he said nothing more. Then she let his hand slide away and took a step toward the carriage.

"Lidia," he repeated. She turned, and found his face had softened. "Since you were a little girl, I—I—" he stumbled, then stopped. He stepped toward her and reached down for her hand, but she gently pulled it away.

"Oh, Juan."

He pulled his own hand back now. "You're right," he said. "I guess it's too late now." He reached up and pushed his sombrero off his head, and his light brown hair caught the morning breeze. "Good-bye, Lidia. If I never see you again, I just want you to know—" He looked past her and then stood silent.

When it became apparent that he was not going to say anything else, she blinked back her tears and nodded. "Be careful, Juan," she said. "Remember your promise to Ophelia. Don't break her heart."

"And your heart?"

The tears suddenly burst through. "That, you broke a long time ago!"

His mouth was set in a grim line. "I think we both did the breaking."

She swallowed hard and willed herself to stop crying. "I will never forget you, Juan. Good-bye." She leaned forward and put her lips up to his cheek, in a sisterly fashion, but he turned his face and brushed his own lips with hers. It was the briefest of kisses. She stepped back, a lightning charge running from her lips to her knees, and sucked in her breath. Her legs were buckling. She looked up at his face, but he turned away and went back to his horse. Her head spinning, she climbed into the carriage with Ophelia, and in another minute they were pounding down the dusty road toward the river, where they would board a small boat and cross into Mexico.

Ophelia sat stony faced, wiping her eyes with her handkerchief, staring at the passing cactus and mesquite. "I wish I knew what I did wrong," she finally said. "One son dead, another a rebel. I tried so hard, Lidia. What did I do wrong?"

"Nothing," Lidia replied, drying her own tears. She slid across to sit next to Ophelia and gripped her arm. "You haven't done anything wrong. Each man is responsible for his own life. It isn't your fault what they do with it."

Ophelia wept again, putting her head on Lidia's shoulder and letting her warm tears roll down her cheeks and seep through Lidia's dress. As she held her, Lidia thought about the disaster that her own life had evolved to, and she wondered about how much of it was her own fault. That moment back there with Juan—did it mean he still loved her? What if he did? She had already decided that she would marry Tom Starr as soon as he returned for her answer. Besides, she knew all to well what love with Juan meant. Arguments. Anger. Heartbreak. Maybe Ophelia was right, she thought. Love is completely irrational. There was no reason she could think of why she would want to live like that, even if he did want her. And she could not believe that the immovable Juan Santos would ever change his mind about anything. He might soften now and then, but he had it fixed deep in his mind that Lidia had betrayed him, and nothing on earth would ever blast that out of his idiotic brain. So, she concluded, it was pointless to even worry about it. She would marry Tom Starr. It was settled.

She closed her eyes and let her head fall back. It was settled, but as she swayed with the movement of the carriage and felt the hot sun break through the window, as she shut her eyes tight and fought back the tears, on her lips the shadow of Juan's sweet kiss still lingered.

CAPTAIN WILLIAM G. DAUTERIVE walked his horse down the plank off the ferry to the cheers of the Brownsville residents. Mayor Daniel Miller rushed forward to greet him.

"Captain Dauterive, thank God you're here." Miller looked up at the ten Rangers that followed him off the ferry. "I hope you brought more men than this."

"Nope. This's all there be." He looked around for the saloon. "You glad enough to see us to buy me a drink?"

Mifflin Kennedy stepped forward from the crowd and shook Dauterive's hand. "Drinks are on me," he said. "If you wait for the mayor here to buy, you'll die of thirst."

Dauterive scratched his cheek and looked down the street toward the edge of town, where a huge barricade of debris had been built. Then he began leading his horse toward the saloon. "What's old Gallo up to?" he asked Kennedy.

Kennedy squinted toward the barricade. "In the five days since the raid, he's hit the barricades twice. Testing us. But we held him, by God!"

Dauterive snorted. "You got what, forty men? How many *vaqueros* he got?"

"He could take us whenever he wants, I guess," Kennedy said. "I hear there's Mexicans coming in hordes to join him. We got sixty white men and eighty Mexicans, including fifty Federales soldiers from Matamoros. I'm in charge of the white men and Villarreal is in charge of the Mexicans."

"So *you're* in charge. What about Stokes?"

"Stokes seems to be real good at stirring up trouble, but I ain't seen him do much once it starts except get drunk. Here, look at this." He handed Dauterive a piece of paper with handwriting in Spanish on it. "It's a proclamation," he said. "El Gallo says his cause is the liberation of land taken from Mexicans by deceit and by force. He says Texan laws treat Mexicans unfairly. Says he's fighting for liberty."

"He's a goddam bandit," said Dauterive, "and he's fighting because Stokes hung his brother. Proclamation—I didn't know the bastard could write."

"He can't write. Can't read, neither. He captured that lawyer, Dresser, and got him writing this tripe for him. Up at his ranch. As for being a bandit, that may be so, Dauterive. But just about every dirt-poor Mexican along the border is itching to help him blast us back across the Nueces."

They reached the saloon. Dauterive wrapped the reins over the rail, then stepped up to the boardwalk. "Well, tell you what, Kennedy. You get your men ready. Tomorrow morning, we'll break out of here and go pay old Gallo a little visit."

"Yes, sir!" Kennedy beamed. "We're already formed up, Captain. Been drilling for days. We call ourselves the Brownsville Tigers, and we're spoilin' for a fight!"

Dauterive smiled and nodded. "The Brownsville Tigers. Got a nice ring to it. All right, then, let's get us a drink."

"Right." Kennedy stepped forward. "And we can plan our next move."

"Hell, hombre, ain't nothin' to plan! There ain't nobody out there but a bunch of greasy *vaquero* Meskins. We'll ride out there in the morning, shoot us a few, and drag old Gallo back here by his butt and hang him. Now quit yappin' and buy me a drink."

THE EARLY MORNING CAME and went, but Dauterive still snored thunderously in the back room of the saloon, where they had dropped him sometime past midnight. Finally, Kennedy threw a pail of cold water from the river on him. The captain sat up sputtering and choking.

"I'll kill you, you ever do that again," he croaked.

"Captain," said Kennedy, unimpressed by the threat, "the men are ready. Been ready. We going or not?"

Dauterive frowned, then some faint memory that they were supposed to do something today began to nag at him. "I need a drink—" he began.

"Later," said Kennedy. "We're waiting, Captain Dauterive. You coming?"

"Help me up."

As Kennedy reached down and pulled Dauterive up, his stench washed up with him. They walked out of the storeroom and through the bar, where the Rangers were sitting around the tables, bleary-eyed and droopy, passing bottles of whiskey.

"Gimme that," Dauterive growled, and he grabbed one of the bottles and tipped it to his mouth, taking three huge swallows. He issued a huge sigh and handed the bottle back. "God help me, I needed that." He looked outside and saw over a hundred men milling around in the plaza, some of them even marching.

"Got your Tigers ready, Kennedy?"

"They been ready."

Dauterive picked up the bottle again and took another big swallow. "Well then, let's get to it."

It took a while to take down the barricade. Dauterive sat in the cool shade of the saloon porch with his Rangers, who watched the Mexicans do most of the work, passing the mesquite limbs, broken wagon wheels, busted furniture, and rocks back down the line to Kennedy's men, who piled everything up along the side of the street. When the road was clear, Dauterive stepped out into the street and mounted his horse. His Rangers followed him.

"We're riding out," he announced. "I catch any man shirking his duty, I'll shoot him myself. And any Meskin I catch running, I'll shoot him too, and the Meskin next to him." He shot a look at Stokes, who leaned against the rail. "You comin'?"

Stokes crossed his arms and grinned. "I'm gonna sit right here and watch. It should be a right entertainin' sight."

A low wave of grumbling swept through the Tigers' ranks, but Dauterive held his hand up. "Kennedy, your men formed up?"

"Formed and ready, Captain!"

"Villarreal, you got your men formed up?"

"*Sí, señor Capitán*. Ready!"

Dauterive pushed himself up in his stirrups, raised his right hand, and waved it forward. "Ho!" he cried, and the entire column began to lurch down the street. They passed the remnants of the barricade and wound their way slowly up the road, each man peering closely into the surrounding brush. A huge column of dust rose behind them, twisting its way across the sky, and drifting out toward the river. In the center of the column, pulled by one mule each, came the two cannons loaned by the Mexican army.

"Look!" cried one of the Tigers. The entire column looked where he pointed. Ten *vaqueros* were riding out of the brush, about thirty yards away. They crossed the road and stopped in the middle. The column crashed to an unauthorized halt, and Dauterive turned to his Rangers.

"Get them!" he roared.

But then musket fire crackled from the left flank, and Dauterive whirled his horse around.

"Out there," cried one of the Tigers. "I saw 'em out there in the brush!" Thirty men lifted their guns and fired at the brush, and soon all the Tigers were shooting.

"Cease fire!" cried Dauterive. "There ain't nobody out there 'cept jackrabbits. Cease fire!"

The *vaqueros* in the road lifted their muskets, aimed, and fired, creating a tremendous amount of noise and smoke, but hitting not a single man. Dauterive knew the muskets were notoriously inaccurate. He also knew that *vaqueros* in general could not shoot straight anyway.

But the Tigers didn't know that. "We're surrounded!" one of them cried, and they all began shooting at the brush again, shooting at the *vaqueros* in the road, falling back as they fired. They passed the Mexicans behind them, who looked confused. They passed the two cannons that sat in the road still hooked to the mules.

Feeling the tide of battle turning against him, Dauterive ordered a strategic retreat, then turned his horse toward Brownsville and galloped back ahead of the Tigers. When the ragtag army came charging into town a few minutes later, he was already in the saloon washing the dust out of his throat with good clean whiskey. After the Tigers came the Mexicans, still marching in orderly lines, now looking thoroughly disgusted.

"Shit," said Dauterive. "Them damned Meskins lost the cannon."

Chapter 11
They're Coming

Austin, Texas

"Starr! Is that you, Starr?"

Tom Starr turned to regard the plump mustachioed gentleman who was trotting up Congress Avenue toward him. It was retired General Forbes Britton, his face flushed and his eyes filled with a wide, wild look.

"Starr, thank God I have found you! Have you heard?"

"Calm down, General. Have I heard what?"

"Calm down? Who can be calm? There are Mexican bandits burning and looting every ranch, town, and city south of the Nueces! I just heard this morning that accursed Juan Santos has taken and burned my hometown, Corpus Christi! It's a disaster! It's a disgrace! It's—"

Starr put his hand on Britton's shoulder and shook him. "That don't sound likely, General."

Britton swallowed hard, catching his breath, then his face turned an even deeper shade of red. Starr wondered if he was headed toward a stroke.

Britton looked around. "Governor Runnels! Oh, Governor Runnels!" He dashed across the street just as Governor H.R. Runnels turned the corner. More curious than alarmed, Starr followed. The news of Juan's raid had come two days ago, and though Starr was worried about Lidia, he took comfort in the knowledge that she was miles away from Brownsville and seldom left the ranch. He had been preparing to leave for the border and return to the de Leon ranch, where he knew she would agree to become his wife. As he thought of Lidia, her lovely face looking up at him with those clear brown eyes, he became impatient to go. There was no question she would say yes. The newspaper had been sold, his home sold, his furniture and other effects dispersed. Letters had been written and sent, good-byes said to those friends and acquaintances he cared about. A day more, and he would go.

"Governor!" Britton was shouting, "it's a disgrace! What are you going to do about it?"

The governor looked befuddled. He stepped back and looked the general up and down as if he were an apparition. "What in the hell are you talking about, Britton? Get hold of yourself, man!"

"Corpus Christi, Governor. Corpus Christi, that lovely and majestic port on the Gulf, that most heavenly city…raped and plundered by Mexican bandits! Half of it burned down. Hundreds of people shot summarily in the street. Women, babies—oh, Governor, it's tragic!"

Runnels' eyebrows shot up. "Is this true, Starr?"

Starr shook his head. "I doubt it. Don't make sense to me. Juan would stick to Brownsville."

"And Brownsville, too," Britton cut in. "There is another disgrace. Mexican troops, Governor. There are Mexican troops stationed in an American city, protecting it from bandits!" He threw out his chest. "And we have done nothing! It's a disgrace! An outrage, I tell you! And my lovely city, my jewel, Corpus Christi—"

Runnels turned to Starr. "You must go," he said. "We've got to stop this—this outrage!"

Starr said nothing, but he felt his heart sinking. A trip to Corpus Christi, he felt certain, would be useless. It would merely delay his departure for the de Leon ranch.

But the governor seemed rattled by Britton's outburst. "Starr, I authorize you," he intoned, "I authorize you to put together a Ranger company and proceed to Corpus Christi forthwith, there to relieve the city from whatever perils it might face. You are then authorized to proceed down the coast to Brownsville, and clean up that mess down there."

Starr nodded. It was his duty to go, and he would not shirk it—but he had promised Lidia not to harm Juan if he could avoid it, for Ophelia's sake. This business would put them in direct conflict. Things were getting complicated, and Starr liked things simple. "I thought you'd asked for federal troops," he said.

"They're on their way from New Orleans," the governor replied. "Should reach Point Isabel soon. But they don't know a damn thing about how to fight in the brush. We need some Rangers down there."

"What about Dauterive? Ain't he still down there?"

The governor made a face, and Britton fell silent. "He's there," the governor finally replied, "but he ain't worth spit. He can handle a common bandit or two, but not Santos."

"All right, Governor. I'll send word out tonight. There's maybe fifty good men between Austin and Corpus Christi I know I can count on, and I can pick up more as I head south. I'll leave within the hour."

TWO DAYS LATER, Starr sat his horse studying a trace that split off from the road and headed south toward Brownsville. Behind him, a troop of fifty-three hand-picked Rangers rested their horses for the hard ride ahead. These were some of the toughest and most reliable men in all of Texas, most of them in their early twenties. Starr knew two were only nineteen.

Frenchy, who had been riding ahead, came back. "Nothing," he reported. "No tracks, no fires, nobody dead, nothing."

It was just as Starr had suspected. The spies he had sent ahead as they approached Corpus Christi had returned with saddlebags full of provisions and news that the town was completely untouched.

"Oh, they're all excited," Frenchy added, "the whole town, wondering when the bandits'll show up. They even strung up a couple of Mexicans, just to keep in practice."

The Rangers burst out laughing. "Cap'n," a call came from the rear of the troop, "let's go get this Santos bandit." A roar of approval rose at the remark, and Starr nodded. These young men were eager and recklessly brave. They were spoiling for a fight—any fight—but this one promised to be particularly entertaining.

He turned to Frenchy. "I never thought he'd hit Corpus."

"Me, neither. This was a waste of time. Let's ride hard, Cap'n. It'll kill the horses, but we got to get to Brownsville."

"We *been* riding hard," Starr replied, "and these horses are damn near dead already. We'll have to pick up new ones on the way." He shook his head. "Juan won't give a damn about Corpus Christi, but hitting Brownsville? That don't figure, either, except those damn fools hung his brother. He was a fuse waiting to be lit, and they lit him all right."

Frenchy eyed him, as if sensing something in his musing. "Cap'n," he said, "you bothered about the girl, Miss Lidia?"

Starr looked into Frenchy's good blue eye. It was no secret how Starr felt about her, even though he suspected most of the men did not understand how he could still want her after what the Comanche had done. "I'm going to make her my wife, Frenchy."

Frenchy's face showed no expression, but he nodded and shifted in his saddle. "She's a fine woman, Cap'n," he said after a moment. "What happened to her was...uh...too bad, them accursed Comanche ruining her like that. But I doubt any Ranger'd hold it against you. As for others, we'll shoot any man that bad-mouths her."

Starr took a deep breath, sat up straighter, and squared his shoulders. The troop writhed with impatience, talking to each other with nervous energy, and sensing this, the horses pricked up their ears and snorted. It was time to move out, time to take his eager Rangers and bear down on Juan. Time to capture or kill him. That was simple enough. It was his duty, and he would do it. As for Lidia—his sweet Lidia—Starr would just have to make her understand.

MAJOR SAM FRIEDENTHAL turned his column and entered Fort Brown to the wild cheers of the residents of Brownsville and, across the river, General Cantu's cannons fired off volley after volley in salute. The major smiled at the irony of it. It was just over ten years since the Mexican War, when those cannons would have been directed at him. He dismounted and handed his reins to one of the men, then turned to greet the delegation from the city. They looked worn and dirty, but their faces were all smiles.

"Thank God you're finally here, Major," called a thin, eager man with a bony face. "We thought Buchanan had forgotten about us."

"Major Sam Friedenthal, U.S. Army," the major responded smartly. "And your names?"

"I'm Daniel Miller, Major. Mayor of what's left of Brownsville. This here's John Stokes, our marshal, and this is Señor Villarreal, one of our leading citizens. Mr. Miflin Kennedy is here, too, but he's manning the barricades. Just in case your arrival provokes El Gallo to attack."

The major nodded and shook hands with each man, looking them squarely in the eye and repeating each man's name as he moved briskly among them. When he finished, he pointed to another man who was leaning against the fort wall, watching them.

"And who is that?"

Stokes followed the major's gaze. "Oh, that's Bill Dauterive. Texas Rangers. Got about ten men here. Or is it seven now, Bill. How many of your boys run off so far?"

Dauterive, obviously drunk, staggered forward and belched. "They ain't run off. Scouting. Scouting the enemy."

"What is there to scout?" Stokes asked. "Any fool can see they're all around us. Just ride out past the barricade, Major. About two miles to the Ebonal ranch. You'll find all the Meskin bandits you want." He looked back at Dauterive and grinned. "Right, Bill? He's out there, ain't he?"

Stokes nudged Friedenthal. The major had taken an immediate dislike to this oily, dirty man who had more the flavor of a bandit himself than a marshal.

"They got cannon, Major," the marshal continued. "Took it from Dauterive and our brave militia, the Brownsville Tigers. We never fired it. Now El Gallo uses it to wake the town up every morning. Never hits nothing, though. I think he just likes the noise."

The major gave Dauterive a disapproving look, then turned back to Stokes. "Who can give me an appraisal of the enemy's disposition?"

"That would be General Cantu," the marshal said. "Except he's gone on back across the river as soon as he seen you boys coming. And, besides, he's El Gallo's cousin. Not too likely he'll be much help."

"But he did help defend the town?"

As Stokes, Miller, and Dauterive all nodded, the major ran his hand through his hair. Anything having to do with Mexicans was bound to be complicated, and this was no exception. He knew Rangers excelled at scouting and mobile warfare and turned to the Ranger captain again. He should be able to provide the disposition of enemy forces.

"Captain Dauterive, have you determined the number of men this El Gallo, Juan Santos, has at his disposal? Their armaments? Their location?"

Dauterive stumbled forward, putting one hand on Miller's arm to steady himself. "Up to three hundred men now, Major," he replied. "Poorly armed. *Pistolas*, muskets, *escopetas*. Probably got 'em from his cousin across the river, who got them used from the British. They ain't worth spit."

Friedenthal rubbed his chin. He had only a hundred and sixty-five troopers under his command. He didn't like to be outnumbered.

"How many militiamen can you muster, Miller?"

As the mayor snapped to attention and pushed off Dauterive's arm, the Ranger wavered and slipped forward, landing against Friedenthal.

"For God's sake, Captain Dauterive," the major snapped, pushing him off, "get a hold of yourself!" He turned his dark red-rimmed eyes back to Miller, and waited.

"Now that the Federales are gone, Major, maybe eighty men. About fifty white men and thirty local Meskins. Everybody else run off. We all got our own guns, but only a few got horses."

"They don't need horses," the major replied. "They'll be here in town. But with that many men, I won't have to leave such a large garrison while we venture out after this Gallo fellow." He turned to an officer who stood ready nearby. "Lieutenant, see that the men are fed and billeted. Officers' call in one hour. Tomorrow morning, we sally forth and pay our respects to the enemy."

"Yessir!" The lieutenant saluted smartly and hurried away.

At the same time, Dauterive stumbled toward the gate of the fort without a word. The major stared after him for a moment and then turned to the others. "Would you gentlemen care to accompany me to my office?

I see it's been set up now. I'd like more details on what's been going on here. And what this is all about."

Miller and Villarreal nodded, but Stokes stood with his arms still crossed and tilted his head sideways.

"What difference does it make what happened?"

Friedenthal shrugged. "Not a hell of a lot, Marshal. I'm going out there tomorrow and kill that fellow. Capture him if I can. But I'm curious to know what he thinks he's fighting for. And sometimes the slightest bit of information can come in handy on the battlefield." He nodded toward his office. "Shall we go?"

MINGO HANDED JUAN a cup of steaming black coffee as they squatted beside the smoky mesquite fire. Several *cabritos* had been staked out, sizzling and popping and sending forth a delicious aroma, but Juan wasn't hungry. It was all going wrong, he thought. Cantu had betrayed him. Stokes and the others still walked about freely, and the town was defying him. He took a sip of the scalding coffee and looked up at the dusty horizon.

"Less than two hundred men," Mingo repeated, "but they're trained soldiers. And they've got cannon. Real cannon, not these cactus poppers we've got."

Juan nodded. He knew he should have put more men on the Point Isabel road, but he hadn't thought the army would get here so quickly. He should have met them at the beach. Damn it! "Why didn't my spies warn me?" he growled.

Mingo shook his head. "We sent two brothers up that way. They have family on a ranch up along the road. The gringo soldiers caught them sleeping at home," he spat into the dust, "and shot them as they were trying to ride off."

A young *vaquero* came riding hard from the direction of the town, working up a huge cloud of orange dust that washed in like a fog over the camp. He rolled to a halt directly in front of Juan.

"What is it, Pedro?"

"The *gringo rinche* Dauterive, *patrón*. His Rangers ran a patrol along the edge of the town and found old Simon Carbajal at his little ranch. He went to feed his chickens, and they caught him and dragged him into town. Then they hanged him by the river."

"What!" cried Juan. "Why did they do that? He wasn't fighting anybody."

Pedro yanked off his sombrero and then pulled the reins on his mount, which snorted and pranced at the edge of the campfire. "They said he was spying for you, *patrón*."

"Here comes another one," Mingo pointed toward the northern horizon where they saw a trail of dust, indicating another rider coming hard. Juan had dozens of spies spread up and down the border and several miles to the north. Day and night, they rode in and out, delivering news and carrying instructions to the other spies.

Toward the west, a faint roll of thunder rumbled, and the scent of wet earth on the wind promised rain. The horizon looked dark and ominous, at times lit up by sheet lightning, as if a massive distant battle were being waged among the brush and cactus.

The rider from the north came in on a lathered horse, another youthful *vaquero*, his face caked dark with dirt and sweat. "*Patrón*," he cried as he jumped off the stumbling horse. "*Patrón!*"

"Here," said Juan. "*Calmate. Que pasa?*"

"*Rinches*," the boy reported. "Over a hundred *rinches*, *patrón*, coming from Corpus Christi."

Mingo choked on his coffee. "A hundred?"

"Who's leading them?" Juan demanded. This was bad news indeed, if they were real Rangers, and not the kind Dauterive led.

"*El Capitán* Tom Starr, *patrón*. They are riding hard. I think they will make the Los Indios ranch tonight."

Juan threw his coffee on the fire. *Starr*. That meant these were top men, fearless and deadly. "That's where they'll probably camp," he said. "Mingo, you stay here with the rest of the men. I have to cut Starr off. If he joins up with the army...."

"It will be like Mexico City all over again." Mingo shook his head. "The Rangers out in front, the army cleaning up from behind, the cannon blasting everything in their way."

Juan called for Prieto, then mounted and gave orders for half the men to get ready to ride. "If I can ambush him at Los Indios," he said, "we have a chance. Hold here, Mingo. I'll be back tomorrow, either way. But you've got to hold!"

Mingo took hold of Prieto's reins. "Juan," he whispered, "we're not soldiers. We're *vaqueros*. Most of these boys have never shot at a man before."

"They're here to fight," Juan replied. "They can leave if they want. If they stay, point them at the *gringos* and let them fight."

"Oh, they'll stay, they'll stay. We get more every day, too. Thirty more men came this morning from across the river. Probably more tomorrow." Mingo looked at the young men. "Rough looking men, some of them soldiers," he added, "but mostly *bandidos* and thieves. Men we ought to be hanging. Well, at least they can fight. But they won't fight for me, Juan. They're here to fight for you."

Juan leaned forward and laid a hand on Mingo's shoulder. "I'll be back tomorrow, my good friend. Then we'll drive these *cabrónes gringos* back into the gulf. *Vamos!*"

He pulled Prieto around and spurred him down the line of mounted *vaqueros*, who looked anxious, expectant. As he rode by, they cheered and fell in behind him. Buoyed by their eagerness, Juan felt good. *With such men*, he thought, *anything is possible*. He pushed Prieto, then held back a little to allow the lesser horses of his men to keep pace. They had to make Los Indios before dark. His old rival Tom Starr was coming from the north. A warm welcome for him and his hundred *rinches* must be ready.

THE THUNDERSTORMS BROKE through late in the afternoon. First came a shrieking wind that spooked the animals and made riding difficult, then dust, debris, and anything not sewed on or tied down started blowing horizontally across the vast expanse of brush and cacti. Starr gritted his teeth and clutched the reins tighter as the rain began, driving with such force that it stung his skin. Despite the poncho, he was soaked in minutes, and the trail became slippery.

Starr lifted his hand and motioned Frenchy up.

"We're not stopping," he shouted, barely able to hear himself.

Frenchy held on to his hat and shook his head. "What say?"

"We're moving on," Starr yelled louder. "That's Los Indios up ahead. We'll stop there for a short rest, then push on. Make Brownsville by morning."

Frenchy nodded. "I'll pass it on."

Just then a huge lightning bolt hurtled across the sky and slammed into the earth a hundred yards away. The air around them hummed and the brilliant flash of light blinded them. A split second later a tremendous crash almost knocked them out of their saddles. Their horses bolted, bucked, and crashed into the brush in all directions, and it took several minutes before the Rangers could control them. At the site of the lightning hit, a pulsating white light illuminated the night. Brilliant at first, it flared and widened, then grew dimmer as the rain extinguished the flames. Miles away, they saw another lightning hit and a similar glow.

Starr pulled his poncho closer around his neck and pulled his hat down tighter. What a miserable night. But he had to reach Brownsville, and he intended to ride all night to do it. He looked back at the column of men behind him. They had been joining him for days, as soon as word had spread that he was moving against Juan. A few had showed up each day, mounted and armed, some having ridden over a hundred miles to join him. At last count, there were about 150 men, many of whom had served with him before. He knew their mettle. Others were strangers to him, but they came with a hard look and an easy style that gave him confidence. He had established discipline immediately, appointed lieutenants, and made it clear he would shoot any man who did not follow orders in battle. They believed him. They knew he would do what he promised.

Now he was bone tired. But it felt good to stretch himself out again, to push himself and other men to the limit. The wind howled around them viciously, and a sudden powerful gust nearly pushed him off his horse. He heard curses and a crash behind him as two of his new Rangers slid off their spooked horses into the scratchy mesquite brush. The faint path through the brush was muddy but, thanks to the lightning, not impossible to see. Besides, the brush was so thick on either side that the horses stayed on track anyway.

The trail rose a little, and at the top he halted the column and looked down at Los Indios. With all the troubles, he felt certain it was deserted. Every white man had either moved up north of the Nueces or was huddling in Brownsville. He waited for another lightning flash, then scanned the surrounding area. Juan's men were out there somewhere. He had no doubt that one of his spies was watching him right now. Juan himself might be waiting down at the ranch.

He motioned Frenchy up again and ordered two men forward to scout the ranch. If it was clear, they would stop for an hour to rest their horses, then push on. If it wasn't, he thought, well, then the boys were itching for a fight. *We will start it right here.*

"RIDERS! RIDERS COMING down the Point Isabel road!"

The morning was gray and muddy. Mifflin Kennedy stood in the square with forty of the Brownsville Tigers, looking up at the church steeple, where James Michniak was shouting and pointing.

"What kind of riders, you damned fool?" he yelled up, but Michniak was just jumping up and down with excitement.

"Riders! Riders!"

From behind the town, out toward the Ebonal ranch, cannon fire boomed, and small arms crackled like fireworks. The army had moved against Juan's forces at first light, expecting to brush them aside. Instead, Friedenthal and his Rangers had been met with fierce resistance. Those Mexican cowmen were not running this time.

William Ford came barreling in from the Point Isabel road. "I seen 'em!" he gasped. "Them damn *vaqueros!*"

"Damn!" said Kennedy. "How'd they get out there? All right. Men, form a line right here. Becker, run over to the fort and tell the army garrison to get out here on the double!"

The Brownsville Tigers formed up a long line, some kneeling, some standing.

"Boys, we're gonna stop them right here," Kennedy shouted. "I've had my belly full of El Gallo. What say?"

His men roared their defiance, even as they felt the ground shaking. They could hear the riders, a low rolling thunder closing on them, but it wasn't thunder from the sky. Behind the Tigers, the crash of battle at Ebonal seemed louder than ever. Kennedy realized he had forgotten to ask Michniak how many men were coming down the road. From the sound of the horses, he thought, there must be hundreds of them. He looked around nervously, trying to spot a possible escape route in the event they could not hold. Where were those damned troops from the fort?

Michniak came running out of the church. "Here they come!"

The approaching riders tore into the town square at a full gallop, the men's heads bent, elbows crooked and sticking out, their horses gasping for breath and rolling their eyes as they kicked up the black mud in the streets. Kennedy swallowed and fought a compelling instinct to turn and run. He saw his line sag a little and knew each man was fighting his own fear.

"Steady men, steady. Take aim!"

"Wait," cried Ford, who had taken a position at the end of the line. "They ain't *vaqueros*."

Kennedy squinted at the riders, then felt a warm wave of relief wash over him. He held his hand up. "Hold your fire!" he shouted. "That's Starr! Those are Rangers!"

Bedlam ensued as the Tigers, shouting and cheering, jumped to their feet and scrambled out of the way of the riders. Kennedy snatched his hat off and held it high in the air. "Hip, hip—"

"Huzzah!"

"Hip, hip—"

"Huzzah!"

"Hip, hip—"

"Huzzah!"

The Rangers ripped through the square past the cheering men and rode toward the opposite end of the town, toward the sound of the big guns. As they passed, Kennedy put his hat back on his head, and turned to Michniak.

"Better get back on your perch, James. No tellin' what else might come down that road."

As STARR MOVED closer to the fire, Major Friedenthal offered him a cigar. He waved it away. A steady rain had picked up again, so they had taken shelter under a mesquite tree as they drank their coffee. All around, long, brown, shiny mesquite beans littered the ground, crunching under their feet when they moved. The eerie quiet of a battleground after a battle filled the night and was broken only by the occasional rain-muffled clatter of an army on the move, off in the distance.

"Captain, good thing you came when you did," the major said. "I had them on their ears, but when they saw you flanking them, that broke them. Now they're on the run."

Starr nodded, looking off to where the cannon were being limbered for travel. "Casualties?"

The major took a slow sip of coffee. "They left eighteen men lying in the brush, most due to grape and shrapnel. We lost six dead, twelve wounded. Those *vaqueros* can't shoot worth a damn."

"No. Never could."

"But they can ride. Damn, can those boys ride. I'm told that if you let them get in close, they'll hack you to death with their damned machetes."

Starr nodded. Yes, he knew those boys could ride. Somewhere in the thunder and lightning of Los Indios, he had felt them near. He'd had that itchy feeling in his skin, and he'd even pulled in his outriders to see if they had seen anything. They were spooked, but they'd seen nothing. The rain and the wind combined to make tracking impossible. They might have missed each other by only a few minutes or by half a mile or less.

"I seen something today I ain't never seen before," the major continued. "Out on my left flank. I had eighty men dug in out in the brush. I figured that brush was like a protective wall. Those *vaqueros* came crashing through the brush! I heard a rolling popping sound, and out of the brush came fifty mounted men, acting like they were riding through prairie grass. Spooked my boys so bad, they fell back and let the cannons break the charge." He paused for a moment, then asked, "How many men does Santos have out there?"

"I figured a hundred and fifty to two hundred," one of the other men said.

Starr pondered that a moment. "I think there's more," he said. "I think there was a bunch of them laying for me last night. Couldn't find each other in the rain, though."

"That would mean they got men on our north flank."

Starr nodded. "I think it was El Gallo out there, Major. Couldn't prove it."

"Wouldn't surprise me. This bunch today, other than that charge through the brush, they didn't seem to have the heart for an attack. How many men you bring in, Captain?"

"Hundred and fifty."

The major coughed. "Between you and Dauterive, there's more Rangers in the field than regular army. All told, between us we got about three hundred sixty men. If Gallo's got two hundred out there, and maybe another hundred to the north, that's three hundred men."

"He's got Mexicans streaming across the border, joining up," said Starr. "But like you said, they can't shoot worth a damn."

"And I've got the big guns." The major stood up and stretched. "So what do you say, Captain? Shall we join forces? I'll take command, of course."

Starr threw his coffee into the fire and stood up, too. His bones had become stiff from the long night in the saddle and the constant rain. The fire felt good. The heaviness tugging at his eyes told him it was time for sleep. Way past time for sleep.

"What about Dauterive?" he asked.

The major shrugged. "He rode back to town to celebrate our victory. He says he doesn't want to take orders from me. Wants to 'tag along' and help out where he can."

"You may want to keep him close by." Starr grinned. "But I wouldn't give him too much responsibility if I were you."

"So you'll join up with me?"

"At your command, Major. Just one thing."

"Yes?"

"My boys only take orders from me. And we take the lead into action at all times. This is Texas business, Major. I expect we can settle it ourselves, but you're here and you're welcome."

The major held out his hand, and Starr grasped it.

"Done."

"Done." The major looked out at his troops. "Our cartridges are ruined by the damned rain," he said. "We need to bring up dry powder. Then we'll hit them. Can you put out some spies? Keep them in sight?"

"Already done it."

The major nodded. "I should have expected that you would. What about that bunch up north?"

"Got men out looking for them, too. My guess is they got spies looking at us and they know the fight's lost here. Gallo'll probably rendezvous with his men farther upriver."

"I see," the major said. "So we wait a day? Bring up the powder?"

"Seems prudent. Gallo ain't goin' too far. Meantime, we should pay a visit to his ranch right up the road."

"Already did, Captain. Deserted. Torched it, of course."

Starr was shocked, and the major must have seen it, because his own face registered an uneasiness. "I don't like it, either, Captain. But I can't leave him a base of operations behind my lines. And he did burn Brownsville."

"The lady. Doña Ophelia?"

"She wasn't there, Captain."

"That's her ranch."

"It's Gallo's, too."

Starr said nothing, then turned to go, crunching mesquite beans as he walked. He stopped at the edge of the dry space around the tree where the water dripped from the overhanging limbs. "There's empty ranches between here and Reynosa," he said. "And there's one in particular you better not touch."

"Which one would that be, Captain?" The major sounded indignant now, but Starr did not care. Friedenthal had better understand what he was about to tell him.

"The de Leon ranch. The woman I'm going to marry lives there."

The major smiled broadly and nodded. "Of course, Captain Starr. Now why don't you and your men rest for a few hours?"

Starr rode back to his men. The rain had let up a little, but the day was going to be cool and gray. All he felt was tired and numb, not even altogether sure if he was awake or asleep and dreaming. He looked off toward the west, out to where Juan's army melted away upriver, perhaps to turn and make a stand. Out to where Lidia waited.

Chapter 12
The Distant Fires

The next day

STARR WATCHED the dreary rain outside with disinterest, holding his hat at his side. The floor creaked as he moved away from the window and toward the table nearby to smell Lidia's roses. As long as roses bloomed, their sweet scent filled every room and soaked into the very walls. Lidia kept the de Leon *casa grande* full of them.

Starr had arrived only minutes ago, drenched from the downpour, catching the de Leon household still in their beds.

Ramona had answered the door, cried, "*Ahí Dios mío, Señor Starr,*" then scurried in a panic to Lidia's bedroom. Now he waited for Lidia to rise and come to him. He wondered what it would be like to awaken her himself, to see those lovely eyes open, to hold her in his arms, warm from her bed. To kiss her, her hair loose and tangled on the pillow. He pulled a white rose from the vase and held it to his nose, felt its petals touching his skin.

"*Perdón, señor.*" It was Ramona carrying a cup of steaming black coffee and a plate full of *pan dulce*. She placed these on the table and hurried away, wrapping her gaily colored *rebozo* tight against the moist chill of the gathering dawn. A muffled voice sounded in another room, but then the house became silent again, except for the constant drumming of the rain against the roof. He picked up the cup and sipped the coffee, then grabbed a piece of *pan dulce*, devouring it in three huge bites.

He was tired—yes, bone tired, dog tired. He knew Mingo had taken his two hundred men across the river into Mexico, then headed west, and that Juan still had over a hundred or so men north of the river. Moving west between them was the combined army of Rangers and U.S. troops. The three groups had scrapped off and on as they moved toward each other, gripped in a violent dance, during the day and the night. Under cover of rain and darkness, the Mexicans had sent small groups of men to attack the pickets and nip at the main body. It was, he thought, like the fighting in Mexico during the war. The Mexican *vaqueros* took naturally to guerrilla tactics, their mobility and knowledge of the terrain giving them the advantage. If they were well led, they could sap an army of its strength, demoralize it, and play with it until it was ready for the kill. But that was where the Rangers came in. The Rangers had learned to play that game against the masters, the Comanche. They would be more than a match for Juan's army.

"Tom?"

Yanked out of his reverie by her soft voice, he turned. Lidia stood with one hand to her breast and the other on the back of a chair, her face still puffy from sleep, her hair hanging long and loose about her shoulders. She looked more beautiful than he had ever seen her, even with a worried look on her sleepy face. He put the coffee down and took a step toward her, wanting to wrap her in his arms and feel her soft, small body against his, to thrust his hands into that long tangle of lovely hair.

"My darling," he said without moving, "I've come back."

She frowned. "Tom, what is going on? Where is Juan? What's happened to him? Ophelia is worried sick."

"She's here?"

Lidia nodded. "She's in bed, ill. How did you get past Tomas?"

"I came alone. The army's right below, headed down the military road. Tomas let me by. He knows I wouldn't hurt Doña Ophelia."

"He's worried about Juan. We all are. Is the army coming here?"

Starr shook his head. He didn't want to talk about Juan or the army. "Lidia, I said I'd be back in six weeks for you."

Her face seemed to soften and she moved away from the chair, taking a step toward him. "Oh, Tom, this is an awful time to talk about... about this. Please, not now."

An awful time to talk about this. The words slammed into his ears.

Their love was secondary, unimportant at the moment. What mattered to her was Juan.

She stood quietly, then walked closer to him and put her arms around his shoulders. "You're so cold and wet. Can you stay a while and dry off?"

He closed his eyes and held her, smelling her clean, soft hair as she put her head against his chest. He leaned to kiss her, burying his face into her hair, then rubbed his cheek against the top of her head, flooded with relief at her intimacy with him. "No," he replied. "The army is moving on. I have to go. I just wanted—to see if you were all right."

He felt her small head nodding against his chest. "We're all right here," she whispered. "We were afraid the army would burn the ranch."

"No. Not this one."

"But they've burned other ranches?"

"They won't burn this one."

She pulled away a little. "What about the Santa Alicia?"

He hesitated, and in her eyes he saw a quick accusation. "The soldiers burned it, Lidia. I was too late to stop them."

She gasped. "Oh, poor Ophelia. She'll be heartbroken! Why? What was the purpose? All this burning, all this fighting, what is it for? What does it accomplish?"

She slipped out of his arms, and he saw again that fire that both delighted and rankled him. He squared his shoulders and put his hat on. "You'll have to ask Juan, Lidia. He started all the burning and fighting. I didn't."

"But you're going to finish it?"

"That's my duty."

She whirled, and he knew she was working herself up. "Duty? Duty to kill him?"

"Lidia," he kept his voice soft, "I didn't come here to talk about him. I came to ask you to marry me." He took two steps forward and swept her into his arms again, more roughly this time. He was tired of waiting, tired of tip-toeing around, tired of worrying about breaking something. If the thing was that fragile, then the hell with it, let it break. Let it break now if it was going to. He wrapped her tightly in his arms and felt her trying to squirm away, then bent his whiskered face down and kissed her, pushing his parched and cracked lips hard against hers, so soft and sweet. She made noises like she was trying to say something, but he refused to listen. Soon she stopped struggling. He pulled back and looked down at her face. She returned his gaze not with anger, but with bewilderment. Then she pushed her face back up to his, and he kissed her again, more gently this time, closing his eyes and letting the smell and touch of her wash over him. Overhead, the steady drumming of the rain changed as a swirl of wind swept across the roof.

"Oh, Tom," she whispered.

"I love you, Lidia. I've always loved you, since that first day when I rode up here. I said I would come for your answer, and here I am. I want it. Now."

She sighed. "But how can we talk about this now?"

"What is it we should be waiting for?"

"It's this awful war!"

He shook his head. "This is about Juan, isn't it? What happens if I kill him? You won't marry me? Or he'll kill me, and you can marry him instead? I know what I feel, what I want. Do you?"

"Tom!" She took a step back and put her hand to her mouth. Starr knew he'd gone too far, but that question had been burning in his heart, so he might as well get it out.

"Don't talk like that," she cried. "It's over with Juan, but—please, don't kill him."

He shook his head. "That time is past, Lidia. He's running amuck. I'm angry. Angry and tired. Lidia, I love you, I want you to marry me, I don't give a damn about anybody else, I only want you." He touched his hand to her bare arm. "Just say one word, my darling. Yes or no. Either way, I'm riding back down that trail in a minute, back to the army. Before I go, I want your answer."

She leaned against the chair, blinking rapidly, but she didn't back away.

"Yes or no, Lidia." The rain outside swirled again, then resumed drumming on the roof. "Dammit, yes or no!"

"Yes."

He waited for the flood of relief to wash over him, the feeling of elation, of happiness, but it did not come. He wanted to hold her, kiss her, take her back to her warm bed and make love to her, but her voice sounded strained, cool and strangely distant. He had bullied her into it. The moment for sweetness and gentle kisses had passed. He took his hat off and leaned forward to kiss her on the cheek, then rammed it back on his head and stomped out of the house.

JUAN STEPPED THROUGH the open doorway into a dark, cold house, his boots trailing huge clumps of sticky black mud on the hard-packed dirt floor. Inside, Mingo sat with some of the men, eating hot *frijoles* and *tortillas*. They all sprang to their feet.

"*Patrón!* We thought maybe you got lost."

Juan laughed, and they put their arms around each other in *abrazos* and slapped each other's backs. The others gathered around, grinning and patting him on the shoulder. "I wasn't lost! You were. What were you doing in Mexico?"

Mingo pulled back and let his smile fade. "Juan," he said quietly, "I'm no general. When those Rangers came in with Starr, I knew you hadn't stopped him. But I didn't know if you were dead, or what. So I came up the river a bit then crossed over." He spread his hands out. "I thought maybe they wouldn't follow me across, and I could move way down the river then come back to this side to see what happened to you. And here we are!"

"Yes," said Juan, "here we are in Rio Grande City. And the *gringos* have to come right up that road, eventually." He turned and pointed through the open doorway to the road leading past the house, then continuing toward the cemetery and down the hill.

Mingo poured a cup of coffee from the big black pot on the table and handed it to him. "What do we do? Move on or fight?"

Juan sipped the coffee and closed his eyes, letting the biting warmth tingle in his throat and wash down to his stomach, waking up cold and numb parts of him as it went. "I'm tired of running around these *cabrónes*," he muttered. "Let's stop right here and make a stand. We've got the high ground. It's muddy and slippery out there. They'll have to come up that hill."

Mingo fell silent.

"What?"

"We won't be on horseback? We'll be squatting down behind these tombstones?"

Juan grinned. "You have a better idea?"

"Keep moving," Mingo replied. "Hit them from the sides, from behind when they aren't looking. Wear them down."

"I don't want to wear them down. I want to wipe them out and get back to Brownsville. I want to finish that business down there." Stokes, Miller, Pownall. They had escaped his grasp, but he would find them. "And who said we'd be squatting behind tombstones?" He paused. "Maybe that's what we'll let them think."

"What are your orders, *patrón?*"

Juan turned and stomped to the doorway. A sudden breeze swept some raindrops into the room. They felt cool on his face. "They'll be in position by morning," he said. "The Rangers will come in first, trying to draw us out. We'll charge out to meet them. Give them a good fight. Then we'll pretend to lose heart and fall back. They'll charge in behind us, and when they do, we'll ride in on them and wipe them out. *Pistolas*, machetes, knives, everything. We'll ride over them and fight them *mano a mano*, where their damned revolvers won't help them." He turned back to Mingo, and suddenly the room seemed to spin a little. He needed sleep. "The Rangers always get out ahead of the army. They think they can do anything. They think we're afraid of them."

Mingo grinned. "Juan, these men will follow you into hell if you ask them to. They were afraid you were dead. But now—now they will fight like demons."

"When we're done with the Rangers," Juan continued, "then we'll lay back and wait for the army to move up. How are the ammunition supplies?"

"Some cartridges are wet, but we have enough dry to fight."

Juan stepped up to the table and wrapped a *tortilla* around two big spoonfuls of cold *frijoles*, then jammed it into his mouth. The juice from the beans dripped out the bottom end of the *tortilla* and splashed on the table. He looked out at the falling rain again. "Damn," he said, "I wish I had Tomas here."

"I've heard nothing from the de Leon ranch," Mingo said. "Have you?"

Juan nodded. "My spies tell me that the *gringos* rode past it without harm. That *rinche* Starr protected them."

Mingo sniffed, shaking his head and dropping into a nearby chair. "This is a very strange war, *patrón*."

Juan closed his eyes, and sleep took him so quickly that he stumbled forward, snapping his head back, awake again, leaning against the table. Mingo grabbed him and led him to a cot in the back of the room, and he lay there for a moment listening to the rain start up again, inhaling the damp and musky air. *A couple of hours*, he thought. *Just a couple of hours*. He had been tempted to ride down to the de Leon ranch himself as he swung north of it, but he had worried that his presence would provoke fighting there, and he would not put Ophelia and Lidia in danger. He thought about Lidia as he tried to relax, closing his eyes, remembering that lovely face, the fiery spirit that lived in such a small and perfect body. It took him a long time to remember that she had betrayed him, and by then he was drifting into sleep.

MAJOR FRIEDENTHAL traced his finger across a crumpled map spread out on the table. His officers and the Ranger captains were crowded inside his field tent, straining to see what he pointed at. Besides Starr and Dauterive, two other Ranger captains were present, Swain and Mason, plus three of Friedenthal's own regular officers. They all squinted in the darkness of the tent.

"Light a lantern," Friedenthal ordered, and Captain David McHenry hurried to the rear of the tent, then reappeared with a lamp and lit it.

"That's better," the major grunted as the yellow light flared and then dimmed into a steady glow. "Now, look here, men." He put his finger back on the map. "This is Rio Grande City, right on the river. Not two miles east is the Ringgold Barracks, and ten miles farther is our position. Here." He tapped his stubby finger on the map. "I'm informed that Santos' force has grown considerably, up to five hundred men—some of them renegade

Mexican soldiers, but still poorly equipped. Beyond Rio Grande City is the road that leads to Roma. Our spies tell us that El Gallo has turned and is positioned to make a stand at Rio Grande City. That is exactly what we want him to do. But I want to make sure that we surprise him. We don't want him to change his mind and escape."

Dauterive leaned forward and poked his finger at the map. "He can cross over to Mexico anytime he wants, Major. How the hell you gonna stop him from doing that?"

"You ever try crossing the river with three hundred men shooting at you, Captain Dauterive? If we attack aggressively, crossing the river could be suicide for them. Most of them will never make it."

"They can still fall back onto the Roma road, Major," said Starr, who was hunched over the map. "I suggest you let me move around to their rear and occupy the road. In the morning, you attack from the east and I'll hit them from the rear." He lifted his head up. "Then we can pick them off as they try to cross the river."

"Bloody deadly plan," said McHenry.

Friedenthal looked intrigued. "Can you do that?"

Starr glanced out into the rainy evening. Visibility would be poor. Only a hint remained of the thin gray hue that had passed for daylight earlier. "Depends on how he's deployed his men, Major. I need to get in close enough to the town so I can approach on the road, then move out into the flats to flank him. If he's occupied the road too far out, I'll be all night and most of tomorrow moving through those thickets. Unless I drive in the pickets."

The major followed Starr's gaze out the tent flap. "It's worth a try, gentlemen. I want to end this quickly." He straightened up, and all eyes turned to him. "These are the orders, then. Captain Starr, you will move out immediately with your Ranger companies and attempt to move around the enemy. You will assume the rank of Major. Captain McHenry here has lived in the area and will accompany you as a guide. You will occupy the Roma road and attack the enemy from the rear in the morning when you hear our firing. The main body of our troops will move by forced march immediately and position ourselves for an attack at dawn." He stopped and looked at each man in turn. "Are there any questions?"

There were no questions.

The major began rolling up his map. "You'd better get started then, Starr."

"I got a question," grumbled Dauterive. "Why's Starr in command of the Rangers?"

Captains Swain and Mason rolled their eyes heavenward.

"Captain Starr is hereby promoted to Major," Friedenthal replied. "He will command all Ranger companies."

"Why ain't I in command?"

The Major stopped rolling the map. "That question, Mr. Dauterive, is precisely why you are not in command. Now, if you are willing to take orders, you may continue to assist in this operation. Otherwise, you may fall back upon Brownsville and help garrison it."

Dauterive pulled the rim of his hat down, puffed up his cheeks and blew a whiskey-scented burst of air into the room. "You got no authority over Rangers." He looked at Swain and Mason, each in turn, but found no support there, and shook his head.

The major turned to Starr. "Be very careful, Captain—that is, Major Starr. For God's sake, don't stir Santos up tonight. Don't let him know we're coming. I want him where he is, so I can smash him."

Starr tipped his hat, and the officers filed out into the swirling rain. Outside, Starr tapped Dauterive on the shoulder and motioned him under a mesquite tree. "How many men you got now, Bill?"

Dauterive sneered and looked off past Starr's shoulder. "Been reinforced. Got near sixty. Why?"

"Tell them to stay alert and quiet when we move out. We have to try to get in close to town, or the whole plan is ruined. Let's move out."

Dauterive brought his gaze back to Starr's face. "I'm coming along, Starr. Don't you get too pushy. I don't like a lot of orders."

Starr considered leaving this pompous braggart behind, but with Juan's forces growing hourly, every gun would count. "Dauterive, you better understand this. You do what I tell you. Any man rides with me knows I'll shoot the first son-of-a-bitch that disobeys an order. That's a plain fact, Dauterive. You know I done it before. Now you get your sorry bunch ready and keep them in line. We move out in fifteen minutes."

BY THE TIME the Rangers pulled within two miles of the Ringgold Barracks, the rain had slacked off to a mild, intermittent drizzle and the clouds had thinned sufficiently for the moon to shine a weak, silvery light down on the muddy road. McHenry pulled up beside Starr and tapped him on the shoulder. Starr called a halt.

"I know a Mexican who lives right off the road here, Major," McHenry said. "Might be he can give us some intelligence on the enemy's pickets."

Starr nodded, and McHenry grinned and moved off. The Rangers dismounted and stood holding the reins to their mounts, keeping them quiet by stroking their snouts and shoulders. As they waited, a fog moved in, and the air seemed to warm a little. The musty smell of wet mesquite and cactus hung heavily in the air, and the night was eerily quiet. A horse shuffled here and there. Low, muffled voices spoke in brief patches somewhere toward the rear of the column. The sound carried remarkably well, so Starr passed the word back to silence all unnecessary talk.

There was nothing to do but wait. While they waited, Starr tried to reconstruct his meeting with Lidia. She had said yes, by God. That was something. Regardless of how he had accomplished it, he would marry her. He would have her. Let the consequences fall where they might, he would have her. He only wished he could be as happy about it as he had dreamed he would be.

An hour later McHenry returned to report. Starr noticed the grin had disappeared.

"What's the news, Captain?"

"Not good, sir. There's a creek two hundred yards up this road. Gallo's got a large picket there."

Starr looked down at his boots and thought quickly. "Can we go around it?"

"Absolutely impossible. Brush is so thick it would take you Rangers all night and all day to move behind the town. You need the road, but if you attack the picket tonight, Gallo'll hear you. He might cross the river during the night."

Dauterive walked up leading his horse. "What's the news, Starr?"

"Call Mason and Swain up here."

A few minutes later Starr gave them the news. "Our plan won't work. Gallo's got pickets right up this road. If we hit them tonight, their main body could slip away before the major's regulars show up in the morning. And we can't ride around them. Brush is too thick."

Mason sighed heavily. "The sounds of our movements might carry in this fog, seems like. Any news on how he's deployed?"

McHenry gave a quick nod. "He's right behind the town. Has a hill commanding the approach. His left rests on a cemetery, his right on the riverbank. Cannon probably behind the ridge."

Starr pushed his hat back and pondered. "Here's what we'll do," he said after a minute. "It's about three hours till dawn. Each man get whatever sleep he can right here on the ground. Holding reins in hand. We'll wait here until Friedenthal comes up, then we'll break through the picket and move against Gallo's left flank on the cemetery. We'll turn it in and move past them to the rear, until we occupy the Roma road. The major can charge straight across to the center and engage Gallo's right flank along the river. If it works, we'll drive in on them and stack Gallo up on the riverbank."

"Where they will be at our mercy," McHenry finished with a whistle.

"Who said anything about mercy?" growled Starr, fixing his cool blue eyes on McHenry.

The Ranger captains grunted. Rangers were not known to be merciful in battle, and Starr wanted this business with Juan finished for good.

JUST BEFORE DAWN, the sound of artillery carriages announced the arrival of Major Friedenthal. The Rangers rose, stiff, hungry, and ill-tempered, and Starr barked out the morning order. Then he rode back briskly to advise the major of the change in plan.

"All right," Friedenthal agreed. "You take his left flank. When will you move?"

"Now! You don't think he can hear all this god-awful noise you're making down here?"

"We should coordinate the attack."

Starr turned his horse and started up the road. Looking back over his shoulder, he said, "We're done waiting on you, Major. Catch us up if you can, but I expect you in the center of his line directly."

He galloped back to the Ranger companies, rode to the head of the column, and kept on riding. No order was given. The entire column simply surged after him up the road. Suddenly, a party of mounted men moved onto the road ahead of them and fired, the noise incredibly loud in the foggy dawn.

The Rangers didn't even slow down. Instead, Starr lifted a hand into the air and cried, "Let's give 'em hell, boys! For Texas!" Spurs dug deep into the horses, and the column exploded forward in the dim gray light, thundering up the road as a spine-chilling roar rose up from a hundred and fifty throats. "For Texas!"

The Mexican picket—both horses and men—were blown away in a horrendous crash of Ranger bullets. Across the creek, the Rangers encountered an advance patrol of Mexicans, who fired from a distance and then fell back. *Well, I guess he knows we're here,* Starr thought as they pounded through the fog. After a couple of miles, he called a halt and motioned the captains up.

"The major's coming," he said, "but it'll take him a while. Rio Grande City's just up this road." He pointed. "And just beyond is a hill where Gallo is waiting. When we move, Dauterive, you take the far position along Gallo's left, up *past* the cemetery. Swain, you're next. Mason, the center of the cemetery, I'll take the near end. Boys, we've got to sweep Gallo's left and get behind them. Move out!"

Advancing toward the town, they took fire from rooftops and shot back with their carbines. The snipers soon slowed their fire. The fog seemed thicker at the base of the hill as they spread out among the thick clumps of cacti. They heard bugles blowing ahead, and within minutes both of Juan's cannons boomed sharply, but the Rangers were hiding out of range in the fog.

Starr spread his company along a position closest to the road and moved them forward briskly. To his right, he heard the crackle of small arms fire, indicating that Mason had moved up ahead of the other companies. Within minutes, they moved out of the fog into a clear patch, and Starr saw all the Ranger companies moving except for Dauterive's, which was nowhere to be seen.

As a furious volley of shots exploded on the Rangers, Starr saw men falling everywhere. "I thought these greasers couldn't shoot." He cursed under his breath and called, "Lay into 'em, boys!" The Rangers kept up a persistent fire as they galloped up the hill. *Keep moving*, thought Starr. *Keep moving, we've got to sweep them. Where the hell is Dauterive?* He'd given the fool the least strategic position in the line, but it was still critical that he at least engage the Mexicans. Though he knew the man was incompetent, it had never occurred to Starr that Dauterive would just completely hold back.

When the Rangers were within fifty yards of the Mexican line, he gave the order to dismount and proceed on foot just as Juan's cannon lowered their fire and blew a huge hole in the Ranger line. "Damn! Pour it into 'em, boys! Don't stop now!"

Just then a bugle sounded from up the hill. Starr immediately recognized it. "They're gonna charge! Fall back into the cactus! Post yourselves before your mounts and receive the charge. Fall back!"

Where the hell was Friedenthal? There was no sound of cannon from Starr's rear, and the center of the field to his left was occupied only by the clumps of cacti beside the main road. If Juan was smart, he would sweep down the center on this side of the road and through the cemetery on his far left, where Dauterive had apparently deserted, then flank the Rangers on both sides and smash them in between. As he rode among his men crouching in the chaparral, Starr looked up the hill and saw what looked like hundreds of riders streaming from Juan's lines. Damn that Dauterive! Damn Friedenthal!

"All right, boys!" he cried, his voice cracking above the roar of gunfire. "We can whip these bastards. Let 'em keep coming!"

A resounding roar of agreement rose up from the hunkered-down Rangers. The Mexicans hit them hard, and the battle turned into a swirling melee of confusion. Behind the *vaquero* cavalry came more Mexicans on foot, pouring down the hill screaming, *"Viva Juan Santos! Viva México!"* The air reeked with acrid smoke and the metallic smell of blood.

The Rangers received the charge, cutting huge holes in the Mexican line and sending dozens of horses galloping loose and riderless. After that came the frenzied foot soldiers, smashing into the cacti clumps and firing at close range, hacking away at the Rangers with machetes. The casualties were mounting on both sides. Starr emptied his Colt and knelt to reload as a Mexican rose up in the fog twenty feet away and fired. The ball whistled past Starr's ear, and he dropped the cartridges he was trying to load into his gun. The Mexican pulled a pistol from his belt and fired again, this time hitting Starr's horse in the chest. It screamed as it keeled over, thrashing in the cacti. Starr was holding the reins so tightly that as the horse fell it jerked him backwards and he dropped his Colt. The Mexican reached into his belt and pulled out a huge machete. Starr lay sprawled on the ground.

"Muerte a los gringos!"

Just then, Uriah Lee stepped up beside Starr.

"Cap'n?"

"Uriah!" Starr cried, pointing at the charging Mexican.

Uriah lifted his Colt and fired at point blank range, tearing a huge hole in the Mexican's chest. He swung off to the side and crashed into a big clump of prickly pear cacti.

"Much obliged, Uriah."

Uriah smiled and calmly knelt down. "I just thought you'd like to know we got Mexicans shooting at our arses from the rear."

"How'd they get back there?"

"Damned if I know, Cap'n—I mean, Major. Dauterive musta let 'em through. Oh, here he comes now."

Dauterive, hatless and on foot, stumbled toward them, tripping over the dead Mexican. "For God's sake, Starr, let's get out of here!"

Without a word, Starr picked up his gun, dropped a cartridge in a chamber, and fired. Dauterive, who knew what was coming as soon as Starr picked up his Colt, had already bolted down the hill, but the shot crashed into his buttocks and sent him sprawling into the cacti, where he flipped and thrashed for a few seconds, then leaped up and disappeared into the fog.

Uriah laughed, then pointed off to the left. "Look out there—the major."

"Well, damn him," Starr said. "About time. Now's our chance, Uriah. But I don't trust that clever bastard, Gallo. I think he's waiting on me up that hill. Pass the word to Mason and Swain, we move up when the major's main body comes out of the fog. Uriah, you take twenty men and plug that hole Dauterive left up at the cemetery."

Starr turned and saw the army advancing up the hill out of the fog. He grabbed the bridle of a riderless horse trotting by and swung himself up in the saddle.

"Mount up, boys! Time to pay our respects to Señor El Gallo!"

"HERE THEY COME," cried Mingo, and then he let loose an impressive string of Mexican profanities, turning his head as he spoke, spewing curse words on everyone around him.

Mingo and Juan were at the top of the hill. Juan watched as the *gringo* army came out of the fog. His plan had almost worked, except that the Rangers had moved to the left instead of attacking the center. In fact, Starr had left the center unoccupied, so Juan had quickly shifted his men to the left, then charged forward to meet them almost as planned. For a while, it looked like the charge might succeed, and Juan thought about sending a second one. But that would have left him with nothing in reserve, and he didn't trust Starr to do anything predictable. He had been right. As the charge slowly dissolved and fell back, Starr did not advance as expected. He held back until the regular army was positioned in the center. Now they were moving forward in concert. A rolling barrage of cannon came pounding in and blew huge holes in Juan's line.

"Damn the *rinches!*" he roared.

He turned and looked at the Roma road behind them. It would be difficult to pull back safely without a rout, but his line was in disarray and most of his *cañoneros* had just been blown to bits.

"Get the cannon out first," he barked. "Then bring in the left flank toward the road. We'll fight as we fall back. Let no man be shot in the back. *Move!*"

They moved, but the Rangers crashed into his lines on the left. The unearthly roar of gunfire and screaming men and horses was deafening.

"*Patrón*," said Mingo, "they are through on the left. Here they come."

Through the smoke, Juan saw large numbers of mounted Rangers on the left, fighting their way toward his center, his own men swirling among them, some swinging their *escopetas* as clubs, too desperate to stop and load. The entire mass of men moved frantically, like an army of ants, arms and legs in constant motion.

"Take some men and hold the left until we can move the artillery out," Juan called. "Then we can pull back."

He rode to the edge of the Roma road, where the cannon were being hitched up to the mules. As he encouraged the men to move faster, a roar rose up behind him. He turned to see Major Friedenthal's army charging toward his center. The line collapsed, and Juan fell back with the cannon. From his left, he saw Mingo falling back, too. They met on the Roma road, where they pulled some of their men into a line to try to slow the rout. The entire right side of Juan's army had been cut off, and he heard the sickening noises of slaughter as the men tried to cross the river into Mexico.

"Keep firing!" Juan cried. "Fire and fall back! Fire and fall back, or they'll kill us all!"

The remnants of Juan's army crowded onto the Roma road, where they fought a hasty retreat for a mile until they crossed a ravine. Here, Juan thought, he might be able to make a stand. He wheeled his force around and set up the cannon, spreading his men along the Roma side of the ravine. They lay gasping for breath, their hands trembling with fear and fury.

The Rangers charged up the road with apparent indifference, moving quickly to the ravine and opening up a withering fire that swept through Juan's line like a massive hammer, knocking men back. Many of them slid, dead, into the ravine. The two armies crouched, firing at each other from a distance of perhaps fifty yards.

The Mexican cannon fired only twice, but the elevation was too high. They spewed gravel and buckshot and smoke up into the sky, and it all rained down into the cacti beyond in the brush.

The Ranger fire was relentless, their weapons vastly superior.

Juan felt the blood draining from his face. *Dios mío*, he thought, *it's over. It's lost, all lost.* He reached back for Prieto's reins and pulled him forward as Mingo came running up to him.

"What are you doing? Get off that horse! They're gunning for you!"

But Juan swung up into the saddle. A bullet ripped through his sombrero and knocked it back off his head, where it dangled from the string around his neck. Another bullet crashed into his saddle, and a third screamed by close enough to his boot to singe the leather near the heel.

"It's over," cried Juan. "Every man, hear me! *Sálvense!* Save yourselves!"

A mad scramble ensued as the men tried to mount their horses, but the Rangers kept firing, knocking men and horses down indiscriminately.

"Split up," yelled Juan, "and God bless you. *Adiós!*"

As the Ranger fire continued to rip through the Mexicans, the defeated men spread out into the brush in small bands. Juan headed directly for the Rio Grande with Mingo and five other men beside him. They could still hear the Rangers firing, but they were soon out of range. They swam their horses across the river and pulled up, exhausted, on the other bank, then began pushing further south.

"Look," said one of the *vaqueros*, and they all turned in their saddles to look behind them. Several mounted men were rising from the river bank.

"How many?" Juan asked.

"Looks like six," Mingo replied.

Juan pulled savagely on Prieto's reins and slid to a halt. He took his pistol out of its holster and reloaded it, then loaded his musket. This was as far as he was going to run. He had promised Ophelia he would flee into Mexico if the battle turned against him, and here he was. But he would retreat no farther. He spurred Prieto forward. He heard his men behind him. Up ahead, the Rangers stopped and dismounted, each man holding his horse's reins in one hand and his Colt in the other.

Behind them flowed the Rio Grande, and as Juan burst through the cacti and brush, his gun ready to fire, he felt glad that if he was to die, it would be with that ancient river sparkling before him in the morning sun.

THEY SAT AND ATE without a word, looking at each other, unspoken fears written on their faces. In the distance, the cannons boomed, sounding like thunder rolling across the land, but Ophelia knew it was not thunder. She put her spoon down and turned toward the window, struggling with the tears, her lips stretched taut, her stomach in turmoil. When she rose from the table, Tomas quickly pushed his chair back and rose with her.

She waved him away. "Eat, Tomas. You've been outside in the rain all night. You sit there and eat. I'm all right." She put her hand to her stomach and leaned on her chair. "It's those cannons."

Lidia came around the table and put her arms around her friend. "I knew you shouldn't have gotten up this morning. You're a mass of nerves. Go back to bed, I'll bring you some soothing tea when I bring Father's breakfast."

Ophelia shook her head. "No! I can't just lie in bed. I have to know what's happening to my son. Is he dead? Is he wounded?" She put her hands to her ears and shut her eyes tightly. "Those cannons, those cannons. What are they doing to my son?" As tears rolled down her cheeks, Tomas came out of his chair again and took her from Lidia and led her to her room.

He closed the bedroom door behind them and walked her to a chair. "I will go see," he said.

"No," she cried, clutching his arm. "They'll kill you, too."

He dropped his chin to his chest, and it suddenly dawned on her how selfish she had always been with him. Every man on the ranch would give his life to fight next to Juan, and here was Tomas, as ever by her side. "I should have let you go to him before," she whispered. "Instead of keeping you here with me. He probably needs you, doesn't he?"

Tomas kept his head bent down, and she reached out to touch his hand. "Talk to me."

"He asked me to stay with you."

Is that the only reason you stayed, she wondered—but she knew the answer to that already. "Nothing can happen to me out here," she told him. "That *rinche* Starr has given orders. You know he's going to marry Lidia, God protect her. I don't know how she can marry him, after all this." She turned her face toward the window. "I thought I knew her."

Tomas did not answer. What could he say? On the subjects of cattle, horses, roping, or any activity on the ranch, he was an expert and could talk for hours if he had to, although she knew he would not. His sentences were rarely longer than five words—fewer if he could manage it. But on the subject of love, he could say nothing, not even three words. Three words Ophelia was not sure she wanted to hear. She walked to the window and peered out at the gray morning.

"Will the fog help Juan?"

"Yes," he said, "if he has to escape."

She turned to look at him. "But not in the fighting?"

He stared at her, then shrugged. "I sent riders out last night. They should be back later today with news. Why don't you rest?"

She clenched her fists. "Stop telling me to rest! I can't rest! Just leave me alone for a while!" He did not react, but just stood there. She was immediately sorry, but she couldn't help it. Yes, she felt glad he was here, but right now he was irritating beyond belief. "Send Conchita to me, please."

She spent the day in her room, sitting in a chair by the window and looking out toward the courtyard gate. Conchita sat sewing on the other side of the bed, but the two women seldom spoke. Late in the day, when a rider came charging into the courtyard, Ophelia bounded out of the chair and down the hall in an instant. When she reached the door, Tomas turned from the rider, and she looked at his face, trying to read in his caring eyes the fate of her son. They looked hard, like steel. The day he had stood at her front door and told her that Alvino was dead came flooding back. It had been a gray, foggy day then, too. Suddenly everything seemed to slow down, her every step became incredibly slow, her words reverberating in the air, echoing deep. She stopped, her eyes fixed on his face, looking for an answer.

"What's happened to my son?"

"He lost the battle."

"I don't care about the idiotic battle," she cried. "What about my son?"

Just then Lidia came running out of the house, Conchita and Ramona trailing after her, both of them out of breath.

"No one knows," said Tomas. "He escaped from Rio Grande City with some of his men. There was another battle on the Roma road.

Some say he escaped into Mexico, but there are a hundred stories already. Nobody really knows."

"Starr would know," said Lidia, coming forward and wrapping her arms around Ophelia.

Tomas shrugged. "He was at Roma road, too. Nobody knows about him, either."

Lidia and Ophelia clung to each other in the cool breezy afternoon.

"I have another man still out," Tomas added. "He's coming back in the morning. Maybe he'll know." He stepped forward. "Do you want me to go see?"

Ophelia shook her head. "No, the fighting is over, Tomas. Stay here." She looked up at him and said it again with her eyes. *Stay with me.*

A NEW STORM moved in late in the evening, and by midnight the tremendous cracks of thunder startled Ophelia out of a troubled sleep. When she rose to look out the window, a brilliant flash of lightning blinded her. Even though the wind howled through the tiny cracks under the windows and around the corners of the house, she stood at the window for a long time, wondering if Juan was lying somewhere hurt, suffering in the rain as it pounded down on him. In all her life, Ophelia had seldom been sorry she had been born a woman, but tonight she was sorry. She felt like a prisoner here. She yearned for the strength and freedom to simply mount a horse and go find her son. Tomas could do that. He longed to do it. Between lightning flashes, she saw a shadowy figure moving in the courtyard, and she remembered that Tomas was out there somewhere, guarding the approaches to the ranch. He must be cold and miserable.

She closed the curtain and wandered back to her bed. Lighting a candle, she reached for her Bible and read for a while, until her eyes grew tired. She needed to sleep. She left the candle burning, for somehow it gave her comfort, and lay down. She felt so incredibly alone. For a while, she wondered what it would be like to close her eyes and never wake up, to slip into a sweet oblivion and never have to worry about the things of this world. But she could not escape them. She had borne two beautiful sons, and now she had lost one, maybe lost them both. Her eyes misted over, but she shut them tight and fought back the tears. After a while the thunder moved off, the wind died down, and a steady rain began to fall again. The monotony of the rain on the roof made her sleepy, and she drifted off, thinking about Alvino when he was young and bright and handsome, full of hope and dreams. She had loved him then.

It was the smell that woke her. That greasy, rancid smell of leather that pushed through her sinuses and sent alarms to her brain. Her eyes flew open, and she knew in an instant that someone was in the room with her. Outside, angry voices spilled in from the courtyard, suddenly punctuated by pistol shots, cries of pain, and more shooting. She threw off her thin covers and tried to rise, but the intruder pushed her back down with such force that it knocked the wind out of her. He immediately leapt to the bed.

"*Buenas noches*, Señora Santos," the man whispered in her ear as he lay heavily on top of her. She felt his hands moving along the side of her body, reaching under her gown for her breasts.

"Get off of me, you filthy pig!" she cried, bringing her elbow up into his face with such force that it produced a spray of blood from his nose. He rolled over a little, just enough that she slipped off the bed and onto her knees on the floor.

"Come back here," he growled, no longer playful, and he reached over the edge of the bed and grabbed her long hair, jerking it back painfully. Ophelia screamed, then she turned and pummeled the intruder with her fists. She could see him now in the light of the candle, but it was not anyone she recognized. All she knew about him was that he came out of a nightmare. Outside, the sounds of fighting were louder, even as the rain continued to fall, and now the sounds of shooting came from inside the house. Lidia! Don de Leon!

"Who are you?" she screamed, but the man had rolled off the bed on top of her, pinning her on the floor. He pushed his knee between her thighs, forcing them open, then pulled his arm back and brought it forward, smashing his fist into her face once, then again, and Ophelia saw little lights floating around her head. She felt him fumbling with her clothes. Something warm and wet and sticky flowed along the side of her face, into her ear, and down into her hair.

"Who am I?" he croaked, his reeking breath reviving her a little. "Who am I? Let me introduce myself."

She felt her underclothes coming off, and rough hands scraped her soft skin like gravel, pushing down into her most private parts, roving up and down her thighs, reaching up to her breasts and hurting her.

"My name is Timo," he said. "I said a long time ago you would spread your legs for me, Señora Santos. Such soft, pretty legs." He pulled himself up and pushed his face down, his lips seeking hers, but she turned away. "Aren't you going to fight?"

Ophelia gathered up whatever strength she had left and spit a mouthful of blood into his face. He laughed. Another fist came crashing down on her, then another.

"Now," he said, "*te voy a coher.*"

She heard the door to her room crash open, and then felt Timo leap off of her. She curled herself up and crawled to the corner. When she looked up, she saw Timo standing in front of her facing the door, a knife in his hand, and in the center of the room stood Tomas, pulling on his pistol. Timo lunged toward Tomas, aiming the knife at his chest, but Tomas stepped aside and brought his boot up into Timo's ribs. They collided, and Tomas' pistol went flying, while Timo stumbled backward and slammed his head against the wall.

"Ophelia, run!"

She heard Tomas, but his words sounded distant, like in a dream. In a blur, she saw Timo reach into his belt and pull a pistol as he threw himself sideways toward the bed. The gun exploded before he even landed.

"No!" she screamed, but it was too late. Tomas went limp and fell to the floor in the center of the room. Timo picked up his knife and held it to her chest.

"I don't want you anymore," he said.

She threw her hands up, trying to ward him off. Timo slid the knife into her chest, the point grinding past her ribs, pushing her back into the corner of the room with such force that the wind left her lungs. She felt herself coughing up blood. Timo was hunched over her, trying to pull the knife out.

She heard him grunting, grabbing the knife with both hands, and she closed her eyes. He yanked it out, and rolled away.

"You don't know who I am, do you?" He laughed, a slow tired laugh that held more malice that mirth. "I am here because your son killed my brothers. *Todo se paga*, don't you think?"

She opened her eyes. He stood above her, reloading his pistol, then pointing it at her head. She saw his eyes moving up and down her body.

"You were very beautiful," he said. "To kill you is a shame. I could have found a use for you."

He grinned, then cocked the pistol. Ophelia shut her eyes tight, but in this final moment, her mind flooded with thoughts of her sons. Blas, beautiful and sensual Blas, so innocent, so new. Gone, gone away, and she never even saw his body, never had the chance to say goodbye. Juan, her bold, troubled Juan—where was he? Was he dead, too? Would they both be waiting for her, with her beloved Tomas, as she crossed out of this life?

The sound of a gun exploded in the room. She waited for the pain, for the slide into oblivion, but nothing happened. Instead, she opened her eyes and saw Timo still standing over her, the gun pointing at her head, but in his eyes was only a glassy stare, as if he were looking beyond her to some distant place. He let his gun fall and sank to his knees, then fell over on his back.

"Ophelia," she heard Tomas whisper.

"Tomas," she cried weakly. "Oh, Tomas." Beyond Timo's still body she saw Tomas lying on the floor, a smoking pistol in his hand. He raised his head slightly and then it dropped back heavily with a thud.

"Ophelia," he repeated.

"Yes," she answered, and she put her hand down on the floor and shifted some weight to it. Waves of pain took her breath away, but she managed to roll over on her side. She pushed out with her legs, using her hands to pull herself forward, and in a minute she lay beside him. She curled her legs up and sat up a little, reaching down with her hands to cradle his head. "Tomas," she whispered, "I'm here."

He opened his eyes and looked up at her with a tortured face, the pain and yearning of so many years at last written there. "*Adiós*, Ophelia." He shuddered. "I have loved you."

She burst into tears, blinking them away quickly, wanting to see him clearly. She bent her head down and pressed her lips to his cheek, whispering, "Oh, Tomas, I have loved you, too. I always have."

When she pulled her face away, he was dead. "Did you hear me, Tomas?" She caressed his head, then wrapped her arms around him, holding him tight, washing his face with her tears. "Oh, Tomas, I love you! I love you!"

"PUT HER THERE," Lidia ordered, and the three *vaqueros* placed Ophelia on Lidia's bed. Her whole torso dripped with blood, and her face was swollen and blood-smeared, too, but she was alive, though unconscious. Tomas' men had driven off the rest of the intruders, but Tomas was dead, and here was Ophelia, barely alive. Lidia ripped open the bloody nightgown and began wiping the wound clean with a wet towel.

"The bleeding won't stop," she cried to no one in particular. The *vaqueros* looked away from Ophelia's bare chest. Lidia bent forward, carefully wiping Ophelia's face. "Ophelia, can you hear me?"

Ophelia's eyes fluttered, and Lidia felt a brief warm rush of relief. "Send them away," Ophelia croaked, opening her eyes and moving them toward the three young men huddled near the bedroom door.

They crowded out of the room almost in unison, bumping into each other and squeezing through the doorway together. They closed it behind them, but as they left, Lidia saw a faint haze of smoke in the hallway. Fire! They had to get out of the house. She started toward the door to call the men back.

Ophelia reached up for Lidia's hand. "I have to tell you something," she whispered.

"Don't talk, Ophelia. We have to get out of here! Save your strength."

Outside, the rain had picked up again, and Lidia hoped it would extinguish whatever fire was burning in the house.

Ophelia shook her head. "I'm going to die. I have to tell you something."

Lidia felt the tears building, and in a second they were rolling down her face. "You can't die," she said. "I love you. You're my friend, my mother, my sister. You can't. I won't let you!"

Ophelia squeezed her hand. "Listen to me," she said. "I don't have much time." She pulled Lidia closer to her, then motioned for her to bend down, her ear close to Ophelia's lips. "Juan," she whispered, "I have to tell you about Juan."

Lidia nodded, cupping her hands over Ophelia's and squeezing them tight. She saw the chest wound continuing to bleed, the life flowing from this remarkable woman right before her eyes. The smoke was growing thicker; and she felt a rising panic to leave, but what did Ophelia want to say? Ophelia's last words and thoughts would be precious to her. She wanted to hear them, to fix them in her memory.

"I was raped." Ophelia's voice quivered. "When I had just married, and Alvino was away, a man came to the ranch and raped me. And then Juan was born."

Lidia gasped and stared in disbelief. What could she say?

Ophelia continued, "Alvino wasn't sure if Juan was his son, neither of us was, and—I didn't want Juan when he was born, not for many years." She let out a long, soulful sob, her tears streaming down her temples. "The rape...it made me crazy. It made me sick to look at Juan. Alvino was convinced that Juan was not his. He hated him, and beat him...for years." She paused, sqeeezing her eyes shut. "Oh, my son, oh, my lovely son. He only wanted love, and I sent him away." She tightened her hold on Lidia's hand, and Lidia could see tremors of pain wracking her body. In a moment they subsided, and Ophelia opened her eyes again. "Only Alvino, and I, and your father ever knew. Don de Leon thinks Juan is a bastard, too. Look at me—he is not a bastard. He never was."

Lidia lifted her head and looked into Ophelia's eyes—eyes swimming with pain and heartbreak.

"It was all my fault. His own mother. I committed the greatest sin. I rejected my infant son. He was born innocent, he had nothing to do with how he was born. It was me who ruined his life, me who made him an outcast, a rebel." She turned her head into the pillow, then turned back to Lidia. "Your father would have never let you marry him. He would have done anything to keep you two apart. I pleaded with him to give you his blessing, but he wouldn't believe me—"

"Is that why he lied to Juan? About me tricking him?"

Ophelia nodded her head. She was suddenly rocked by convulsions, and she lay there, coughing up blood. Lidia leaned forward and raised her head slightly, then wiped her mouth with a cloth, but she, too, was crying so much she could barely see what she was doing.

"I know you love him," Ophelia finally said. "Promise me you'll go to him, take care of him, for me. Do what I did not do for him, love him. Help me atone, and maybe someday he can forgive me. Oh—" her eyes fluttered, and Lidia laid her head back on the pillow.

She wiped the tears from Ophelia's face with the back of her hand. Her eyes were open, but Lidia knew Ophelia was gone. She had died asking for a promise, a promise that was not made. Lidia closed Ophelia's eyes and pulled the sheet over her face. She sat still for a moment and then lowered her head, putting her forehead to Ophelia's. "Good-bye, my sister," she whispered.

She heard loud voices in the house, and she left the room just as the smoke began curling under the door. In the hallway, she encountered chaos as the *vaqueros* ran about with buckets of water. One of them came running up to her, swiping his sombrero off his head. Another dashed into the room and lifted Ophelia off the bed.

"Señorita Lidia," he cried, "we cannot save the house, we must get you out. And your father... ."

"Where is he? Is he all right?"

"No, señorita," he said. "We carried him to the courtyard. His room got full of smoke. He is dead."

Lidia stumbled backwards into her own room, and the young *vaquero* steadied her, steering her outside to where several of the men gathered around the body of her father. He seemed so small now, like a young boy. Years of a life confined to chairs and beds had shrunk him, and now he, too, was dead. The rain had turned into a light drizzle.

She walked up to the body and stood looking down at it. "Father," she whispered, kneeling down beside him, touching his face with her fingertips. She felt numb. She could not feel the rain soaking through her clothes, could not feel the cool night air, could not feel her father's soul taking his leave of her. She dropped her head and closed her eyes. How had all this woe come upon her? Tomas, Ophelia, her father. Everyone dead, everything destroyed. She shivered, longing to be held by strong, warm, comforting arms.

One of the *vaqueros* placed his hand on her arm and gently lifted her to her feet. "Señorita Lidia," he said kindly, "what do you want us to do?"

She straightened up and sucked in a deep breath, then used the backs of her hands to wipe the tears from her face. "Dig the graves," she said, "and bury them. And then I want you to take me to Rio Grande City. There is someone there I need to see."

SHE FOUND STARR the next afternoon, directing the burials of the Ranger dead. He sat his horse far up the hill, at the edge of the cemetery. Over to the right, along the river, she saw a huge number of bodies being piled high with mesquite brush. The Rangers buried, the *vaqueros* burned.

To the victor belongs the grave, to the loser, the ashes. What a small difference when all the wars were over—not worth the pain for all those left behind who had to live on without their beloved, fallen soldiers.

When Starr saw her party, he rode away from the graves and came down to meet her. Her *vaqueros* hung back at his approach, but she rode forward.

"Lidia, what are you doing here?"

"I came to see if I could find you."

He smiled and pushed his hat off his forehead. "I was just going to finish this business and come down to the ranch."

Lidia looked at him with a heart empty of all feeling, not even enough to feel pity for him. "There is no ranch anymore," she said. "It was burned. Everybody is dead. Father, Tomas, Ophelia—"

"Ophelia? Tomas? How? I gave orders!"

She turned her face away from him and looked down at the river. The sky was clearing, and long yellow rays of sunshine slanted down through the lingering clouds. The sun brought no warmth to her. "I don't know how, Tom."

He slumped in his saddle. "I'm sorry, Lidia. Ophelia was the finest lady I've ever known. Tomas was a friend. I didn't much know your father, but I'm sure he was an honorable man."

She squinted up at him. "Can you help me get across the river?"

He sat quiet for a moment, then sighed and pressed his lips in a long thin line. He looked off past her shoulder. "You're going to him, aren't you?"

"Is he alive?"

"I don't know. He rode off across the river, killed some of my men who followed him. They took their wounded with them, off toward Camargo." He brought his gaze back to her face. "Are you going to him?"

"He has to know about Ophelia."

"Is that the only reason?"

She did not answer.

"Lidia," he pleaded, "you said yes. I asked you to marry me, and you said yes. I forbid you to go to him."

She exploded. "You forbid it? You *forbid* it? Are you men all the same? You think you can just take and have and do whatever you want and push everybody around? I knew Juan my whole life! His mother was my dearest friend, and you *forbid* it?"

"Lidia, you gave me your hand."

"You saved my life, Tom. You rescued me from the Comanche, and you gave me your love. You gave me hope. I am grateful. But I don't love you. I'm sorry."

His eyes flashed, his chin jutted forward. "It's Juan, isn't it? You're going to him, aren't you?"

She nodded. "I have to find him." She saw the muscles in his jaw rippling as he clamped his teeth together. She knew he was hurting terribly, because somewhere in the distant past she remembered she had once felt that way, when Juan had ridden away from her. There was nothing she had been able to do about it then, and there was nothing she could do for Starr now.

"Juan is my enemy," he warned her.

"Then so am I."

BY THE TIME her *vaqueros* found Juan's camp, the sun hung low on the horizon. They rode in silence past the campfires spread along the river. The haggard, bloodied *vaqueros* sitting around the fires had the glum look of beaten men, their eyes dropping as she passed. Juan was not there, she was told. He had gone scouting down the river.

She dismounted and let the reins drop, then turned to walk along the brushy riverbank. She saw smoke from Rio Grande City, rising in the distance in a dusky cloud, then turning orange as the last rays of sun spilled across the top. She walked farther, poking her way through the brush and cacti, until she found an open spot with a large flat rock to sit upon. There she sat, watching the sun slip below the horizon, the sky turn from orange to scarlet, and then finally to purple. The stars started twinkling, popping out of the sky like candles lit one by one. She felt detached from the stars, from the sun, from the sky. Even the river flowing at her feet seemed a distant object, not part of her world, but perhaps something in a dream.

She heard a horse behind her, and when she turned she saw a dark figure dismounting. Even in silhouette, she knew it was Juan. She rose to her feet and turned toward him. He stepped forward, close enough that in the dim light they saw each other's faces.

"Juan," she cried, and her voice cracked. All the feelings that had somehow abandoned her came crashing back. The grief, the fear, the hate, the love, it all came back and swept through her, carrying her with the tide. "Oh, Juan."

He reached for her, and she ran to him, letting herself be wrapped up by his strong and comforting arms, pushing her face up to him, and he kissed her, sending wave after wave of warmth spreading through her, bringing life with each kiss—but then she pulled away and covered her face with her hands.

He pulled her back gently and sat her down on the rock. "What are you doing here?"

"Your mother is dead, Juan. And Father. And Tomas. They're all dead."

She heard him suck in his breath, and when she looked up she saw his jaw sag. She had shocked him, but there was no easy way to deliver news like this.

"Dead?" he said, and then was silent. Finally, he whispered, "How?"

"Scavengers, looters, following behind the army. They burned the ranch."

He slid down beside her on the rock, and she moved closer to him.

"I'm not sure. I think one of them stabbed Ophelia, then fought with Tomas. They killed each other." She reached over to him and put her hand on his shoulder. Juan did not ask any more questions. He just sat in silence, bolt upright, watching the river flow.

"Talk to me," she said. "Don't hold it in."

He did not answer.

Leaning against him, she put her head on his shoulder and watched the river with him. After a while she felt him relax a little, and she reached up and wrapped her arms around his wide shoulders, nuzzling against him, letting him feel her warmth. She was trying to reach him, the real Juan she knew and loved, the little boy she had once comforted by the river, the man in the rose garden.

He reached out and curled his hands around her waist, and she looked up. In the dim light she saw him looking at her with eyes full of utter despair. She sobbed for a minute, then pushed her face up again and he kissed her, reluctantly at first, gently, but then with more urgency, more power. Their warm tears mingled on their cheeks, flowing down and salting their kisses. She lifted her arms again, wrapping them tightly around his neck, pulling him down to her, and he slid his hands along her body, caressing her hungrily, releasing his grief, transforming it.

When they pulled apart, she was gasping. He bent down again and kissed her neck. She threw her head back and welcomed his lips there, warm and wet, sending shivers through her whole body. He rose suddenly and lifted her in his arms. They never stopped kissing, even as he walked a few steps to the clearing, even as their trembling hands fumbled with their clothes. They made love violently, each of them exploding with all the pain and longing and despair that had built up in their hearts, and Lidia lay back, intoxicated by his power, inflamed by his hunger, and she was utterly lost in overpowering waves of passion, incapable of complete thoughts, her mind forming half-words that floated away. Then one thought escaped the flood.

It floated up and streamed around, as though caught in an eddy—*at last*, she thought, *at last, at last, at last.*

AFTERWARD, THEY SAT huddled on the riverbank, and Juan kept looking at her, still not sure if she was really here, still not sure it had really happened—all of it, the battle, the blood and death...and this. He had wrapped her in the blanket, and she snuggled warmly against him.

"It's my fault," he finally said. "I killed them all."

After a moment, she replied, "No." She pushed her lovely face up again and lightly brushed her lips against his. They sat that way for a long time, looking at the fires from Rio Grande City as they lit up the horizon.

"It wasn't you," she finally said. "It was them—all of them. The lawyers, the lawmen, the merchants swarming onto our land—those land *thieves*. They're like weeds, like wandering gypsies, taking things that don't belong to them. They have no roots, no connection to their past." She pulled herself free a little and then stood up, wrapping the blanket closer around her. "Ophelia knew that very well. She knew that a man must know his father, and his father's father, and what connects them all is the land. That's why she fought so hard for it, Juan. Not for her, it was all for you." She turned to look at him. "It was her gift, her penance, for you."

His eyes felt misty, but he gritted his teeth and choked it back. It was all true. The one thing Ophelia always wanted was for him to love and care for the land. He knew she had tried, tried for years, to bridge the gulf between them—a gulf he never understood, one he never forgave. Now it was too late.

"It isn't finished," he declared. "I'm going to make them pay." He stood up beside her. "*Todo se paga.* On the blood of my mother, they're going to pay. And I will claim our land again."

They stood together, staring across the river at Texas, at that vast and hostile land. A place of dreams, an empire lost. He put his arm around her, and she drew closer. The river flowed before them, dark and slow, as it always had, as it always would. On its surface, reflections of the distant fires sparkled in a thousand tiny flashes, winding their way with the dust and tears and ashes of war, moving gently but relentlessly toward the ever-waiting Gulf of Mexico.

Historical Note

In 1859, a young *ranchero* named Juan "Cheno" Cortina (1824-1892) attacked the town of Brownsville, Texas, damaging the town and killing five of its citizens. The town was rescued first by Mexican troops from the town of Matamoros across the river, then by Texas Rangers and finally by the U.S. Army. A running battle ensued, culminating in a defeat for Cortina at Rio Grande City, as generally described in this novel.

Cortina certainly had a justifiable animosity toward Brownsville and toward the American settlers who had flooded the border region following the Mexican War. Through intimidation, murder, and trickery, the American settlers dispossessed many of the Mexican landowners, including Cortina's mother, who eventually ceded the Brownsville tract to her lawyers in return for clear title to the rest of her land.

These events inspired me to write this novel, borrowing some of the facts and creating a fictional set of characters and events to play out a similar story. For example, the physical abuse suffered by Juan Santos, the rape of Ophelia Santos, Lidia de Leon's abduction and rescue, the hanging of Blas Santos, and the love triangle of Juan, Lidia, and Tom Starr are entirely fictional, as are the characters themselves.

Although Texas Ranger Captain Tom Starr is fictional, he was created in the mold of such true-life legendary Ranger captains as "Rip" Ford and Jack Hays. Not all Ranger captains were so admirable. The character of Ranger Captain Bill Dauterive is based on the collective real-life misadventures of some of those unfortunates.

"Rip" Ford led over one hundred Rangers who, combined with the forces of U.S. Major Samuel P. Heintzelman's 165 regulars, pursued Cortina along the Rio Grande valley until they met in battle at Rio Grande City in late December, 1859. Much of Cortina's four hundred-plus army consisted of desperate men from across the river in Mexico, who relished the opportunity to kill *gringos* and who smelled plunder. Though defeated in Texas, Cortina rose to the rank of brigadier general in the Mexican Army and continued to be a thorn in the side of Texas lawmen and citizens for decades. He died under house arrest in 1892 in Mexico City. At one point, as a result of the ever changing political landscape in Mexico, he was to be shot by a Mexican firing squad, and was only spared by an appeal for clemency from, incredibly, his old Texas nemesis, "Rip" Ford. It turned out that Cortina had protected Ford's family during the hostilities in Texas.

The following documents and resources were especially useful in researching the people, the events, the land, and the conflict of cultures surrounding the Juan Cortina rebellion of 1859.

References

Canales, J.T. "Juan N. Cortina, Bandit or Patriot?" *An address by J.T. Canales before the Lower Rio Grande Valley Historical Society, at San Benito, Texas.* San Antonio, TX: Artes Graficas, 1951.

Carlson, Shawn Bonath, et al. "Archeological Investigations at Fort Brown (41CF96) Cameron County, Texas." *Archeological Research Laboratory Report of Investigations No. 11.* Texas A&M University, 1990.

Fehrenbach, T.R. *Lone Star.* New York: Wings Books, 1991.

Ford, John Salmon. *Rip Ford's Texas, Personal Narratives of the West.* Edited by Stephen B. Oates. Austin, TX: University of Texas Press, 1963.

Gilliland, Maude T. *Rincon, (Remote Dwelling Place).* Brownsville, TX: Springman-King Lithograph Company, 1964.

Goldfinch, Charles W. *Juan N. Cortina: Two Interpretations.* New York: Arno Press, 1974.

Kearney, Milo and Anthony Knopp. *Boom and Bust: The Historical Cycles of Matamoros and Brownsville.* Austin, TX: Eakin Press, 1991.

Nichols, James Wilson. *Now You Hear My Horn: The Journal of James Wilson Nichols, 1820-1887.* Edited by Catherine W. McDowell. Austin, TX: University of Texas Press, 1967.

Author's Note

This book consumed fifteen years of my life—doing research, writing, editing and mostly procrastinating. It was an enlightening and yet daunting experience. It certainly helped that Texas history is so very rich in amazing, true stories of love, hate, hope, war, vicory, defeat, and incredible events for inspiration. To a writer of historical fiction, Texas history is a treasure to be discovered, enjoyed, and then shared.

If you enjoyed *Reflections of the Distant Fires,* I invite you to look it up on Amazon, B&N.com and other retail sites and post reviews and comments, to let us know what you think about it.

Email me at Pedernales@pedernalespublishing.com, or go to the website listed below and navigate to the contact page. You can also snail mail to my attention at Pedernales Publishing, PO Box 1503, Johnson City, TX.

Jose Angel Ramirez

www.reflectionsofthedistantfires.com

www.ingramcontent.com/pod-product-compliance
Lightning Source LLC
Chambersburg PA
CBHW020242200626
46816CB00001BA/91